Axel's Pup

A Werewolves & Dragons Story

By Kim Dare

Axel's Pup (Werewolves & Dragons, Book 1)
ISBN # 978-1-910081-06-8

Copyright © Kim Dare 2015

Published by Kim Dare
Edited by Chris Allen-Riley and Shannon Leeper
Cover Art by Kris Norris

First Edition – March 2015.

Dedication

This book is my one hundredth commercially published title.

While most of those titles have been short stories and novellas, this is by far the longest and most ambitious story I've ever published.

Completing this book was neither a quick nor an entirely painless process, but looking back now, I don't regret a second of it.

I love this book and the characters in it. I hope you love it too.

If it were not for the support of my parents, this book could not have been written. They've always believed in me, even at those times when I haven't believed in myself. So this book, like my first and my fiftieth, is dedicated to them.

Chapter One

"You're going to cum in your leathers when you see what's just rolled up outside."

Axel Carmichael raised an eyebrow at his friend. "A boy or a bike?"

"Both." Griz hauled himself up onto a barstool. "A stunning boy, straddling the most spectacular bike you've ever seen. I'd sell my right nut to take either for a ride."

Axel put a bottle of beer in front of Griz and marked it down on the tab behind the bar. "That makes him the fourth pretty boy you've fallen for this month, right?"

Griz waved that fact away. "This one's something special."

Axel shook his head. He'd known Griz for over a decade, and the guy had yet to spot a hot little sub he wasn't willing to consider something special the moment he set eyes on him. Axel had long since stopped paying attention to—

"Told you so," Griz muttered into his beer.

Axel ignored him, his attention fixed on the boy who'd just walked into his pub. Axel's predictions had been all wrong. Forget golden blond hair, big blue eyes, flirtatious mannerisms and so little muscle it was a wonder he could control anything more powerful than a damn scooter. This particular man wasn't anything like the boys Griz usually lusted after.

The boy paused just inside the door, but he seemed more interested in taking in his surroundings than in giving anyone the opportunity to get a good look at him. He was dressed inconspicuously enough—black jeans, white vest, black leather jacket hanging from his fingertips, and a motorcycle helmet in his other hand.

The boy approached the bar a yard or two away from where Griz sat. If the new guy was aware that he'd caught the attention of a lot of the regulars, he gave no sign of it. If he was nervous about walking in there on his own, he hid it well.

The boy hadn't taken his sunglasses off when he came inside, but he looked young enough for that kind of pretention to mark him out as silly rather than pathetic.

Axel moved along the bar. "ID."

"I'm twenty-three."

"Good for you." Axel pointed to the sign hanging on the wall behind him. *If you look under twenty-five you will be asked for ID. Deal with it.*

The boy glanced toward the door as if considering leaving in a huff, but he didn't give in to a temper tantrum. He passed a motorcycle licence across the bar.

"Sunglasses," Axel said, automatically.

The boy took off his glasses and looked up. His eyes were amber and brighter than any human's could be.

Axel checked the card, and there it was in red block capital letters: WOLF. "You're a shifter—a werewolf?"

"That's right." The boy tilted his chin up. "I'm not looking for trouble."

Not looking for trouble, but he obviously wouldn't be surprised if he found it. The boy squared his shoulders as if he wanted the whole world to know he could deal with any hassle that came his way. His bravado might have been more believable if he'd been a few years older, or a few inches taller. As well as Axel could judge from his side of the bar, the boy barely scraped five seven, and he was lightly built with it.

Axel glanced at the licence again. *Bayden Wolf.* The picture matched. His date of birth confirmed he was twenty-three.

Axel handed the ID back. "What can I get you, Bayden?"

Bayden hesitated, as if it might be a trick question. "A bottle of Coke, please."

By the time Axel had pulled a bottle out of the fridge, a crumpled five pound note rested on the bar. The moment Axel picked it up, Bayden grabbed his drink and headed for the door.

"Hey, kid."

Bayden's shoulders tensed. He turned back to Axel.

"Your change." Axel held out the coins.

Bayden frowned as if confused by the concept of change, but he took the money. "Thanks." He strode out of the pub, balancing his drink and all his belongings in one hand so he could put his sunglasses on as he went.

Griz moved down the bar toward Axel. "Is he really a shifter?"

"That's what his licence said."

"Still hot as hell," Griz said. "And his bike's even better."

Axel glanced along the bar. Matt, one of his summer bartenders, was serving another customer, but there wasn't anyone else queuing. Matt could handle things by himself for a few minutes, and there were plenty of club guys who'd bail him out if they saw him drowning.

Something about Bayden hinted that he was far more in need of a babysitter than Matt would ever be.

Axel stepped outside, Griz right behind him. It was already late summer. There was no guarantee that there'd be many good riding days left before autumn blew in. It wasn't just guys from The Black Dragons Motorcycle Club who'd found their way to The Dragon's Lair that day. Damn near every gay and bi man in the county had turned up. All the wooden tables outside the pub were occupied—Bayden must have snagged the last empty one. Motorbikes stretched from one end of the pub's car park to the other.

Axel ran his gaze along the line of bikes. Halfway along, he faltered. A nineteen-fifties Triumph Bonneville. Even nestled between dozens of other bikes, it stood out like a beacon of pure, classic perfection.

"The boy's riding that?"

Griz nodded. "Do you think he stole it?"

Axel frowned, looking from Bayden to the bike and back again. "Shouldn't think so." He looked way too calm for that.

"Rich boy slumming it?"

"Maybe." He wouldn't be the first spoiled brat who thought spending a fortune on a bike he was too clueless to appreciate or ride well would impress a group of bikers. But, Bayden wasn't making any attempt to show off.

"Present from his sugar daddy?" Griz offered up as an alternative.

"Could be." Bayden wasn't exactly pretty. But he was definitely hot enough to make lots of guys want to dip into their savings. If it was his benefactor who'd bought him the bike, it would explain why he seemed so oblivious to the treasure in his possession.

"I think he's gay," Griz announced.

Axel huffed. "He's twenty-three and hot—you think he's gay and interested in older men on general principle."

Griz laughed. "A bit of optimism never hurt anyone."

Axel nodded, but he kept his attention on the two men approaching Bayden's table.

"Is it true?" the smaller man, Jarvis, demanded, loudly enough to draw everyone's attention.

Bayden looked up. "Is what true?"

"You're a shifter?"

Axel tensed, wondering how many men in the pub had overheard his conversation with Bayden. *I'm not looking for trouble.*

Axel glanced at Jarvis, then at the massive bulk of Jarvis's friend, Ford. They both rode bikes, but they were more like groupies than real bikers—guys who hung around on the fringes without any real clue what they were doing. Axel had long since marked them down as not representing a danger to anyone—but he didn't usually have customers who looked even more clueless than them.

"I'm a wolf shifter," Bayden specified.

"Rumour says wolves think they're good fighters. Don't believe it myself," Jarvis said.

"Wolves fight," Bayden confirmed. He didn't speak loudly, but as hushed as everyone else was, his words carried easily on the evening air. There was that same touch of bravado in his voice, that dare to call his bluff.

"Reckon you're better than Ford here?" Jarvis asked, with a nod to his friend.

Bayden looked Ford up and down. "Yes."

He sounded confident; Axel had to give him that. He also sounded like he was about to get himself killed. Ford had to have six inches on him and a couple of stones worth of extra muscle.

"How about a wager?" Jarvis took a deep draft of his beer and wiped his mouth with the back of his hand. "Or don't your sort have the balls for that kind of thing?"

Bayden sipped his Coke. The way his lips wrapped around the rim of the bottle probably had every man there picturing him on his knees. "How much?"

"A round hundred." Jarvis smirked. "Of course, if you can't cover it, I'm sure we could find another way for you to pay us back."

Axel studied Bayden carefully, but his shades made it damn hard to get a read on him. What was visible of his expression gave away nothing.

"When and where?"

Jarvis grinned. "Now—can't give you time to get cold feet." He looked over both his shoulders, checking that everyone was paying attention. His eyes settled on each member of The Black Dragons, as if he really thought that picking a fight with a kid would make them more likely to invite him to ride with them. Tosser.

Bayden shrugged. He put the top on his bottle of Coke.

"You don't mind if we use the yard around the back of the pub, do you Axel?" Jarvis said.

Axel stepped forward.

Bayden glanced toward him. "We can take it somewhere else if you like."

Axel looked toward Jarvis and Ford. If he refused to let the fight happen there, they'd probably just pick a new location — somewhere where there might not be anyone who'd step in if it went too far. "Here's fine."

Bayden walked over to his bike. He stowed his leather jacket, his half-finished drink and his sunglasses in one of the panniers. Taking off his vest, he put that in there too. Stripped to the waist, he showed some nice lines of muscle, but he was still a small guy. There wasn't a spare ounce of flesh on him.

Axel had no doubt that most of the doms present were wondering what Bayden would look like with leather wrapped around his limbs and whip lines on his back, and trying to work out what their chances were. There was obviously no sugar daddy in the picture. A man who got by on looking pretty wouldn't risk his face in a fight. So, silly little rich boy it was.

Apparently oblivious to his fascinated audience, Bayden turned to Jarvis and Ford. "Ready?"

Jarvis hurriedly downed what was left of his pint as Ford grabbed the gym bag that had been strapped to the back of his sports bike. When they headed around the side of the pub, everyone who'd been sitting outside followed them. Word had spread quickly and a lot of those who'd been inside swelled the crowd too.

When Jarvis took Ford to one corner of the yard, Bayden headed for the opposite one. He'd brought his helmet with him and he set it on the ground at his feet as if he was familiar with the drill.

He glanced up when Axel joined him in his corner. He was short enough to have to tip his head right back to look Axel in the eye.

"I thought you said you weren't looking for trouble," Axel said.

"You want us to take it somewhere else?"

Axel ground his teeth together. "Ford's into MMA — mixed martial arts. I haven't seen him fight, but, from what I've heard, he's good."

Bayden didn't even blink.

"In case you haven't noticed, he's also damn near twice your size," Axel added. "Do you have a death wish?"

"Wolves aren't easy to kill." There was no emotion in Bayden's voice, just that touch of a Welsh accent that marked him out as a local, just like Axel.

Axel glanced across to where Jarvis was binding Ford's knuckles with fancy orange wraps before turning back to Bayden. "Is there some sort of handbook for silly little rich boys?"

Bayden blinked at him.

"Buy a flash bike, get your arse kicked in a pub full of bikers. Is it considered some sort of rite of passage?"

Bayden stared up at Axel as if he thought he'd lost his mind.

"You didn't really think you were the first idiot to ride up here with more attitude than sense, did you?"

Bayden didn't blush, he didn't bluster. He just gawped at Axel as if he couldn't believe a mere pub landlord would talk to him that way.

Axel bit back a sigh. "Ever been in a fight before?"

"Once or twice."

Axel looked Bayden over. Ford was built like an ox. In comparison, Bayden looked like he could use a few big dinners. "You got a secret black belt or something?"

"No."

Axel mentally cursed, but if this was going to happen anywhere, here was the best place. He called Griz across. "My gym bag's by the backdoor. Grab some wraps for me."

Axel glared down at Bayden until Griz returned and tossed the rolled up wraps across to him. They weren't as fancy as Ford's. They were white, basic and well used. They were okay worn under gloves when Axel wanted to beat the hell out of a punch bag, but they wouldn't offer Bayden much protection in a real fight. Hell, if this went the way Axel expected, they wouldn't have a chance to protect Bayden's knuckles because Bayden wasn't going to land a single punch. Stupid little fool...

"Hands," Axel ordered.

Bayden held out his hands and stood in silence as Axel started to wrap them.

"Ford's not the kind of guy who'll go easy on a kid. The first time you go down, show some sense and tap out — no one will think any less of you."

Bayden made no comment as Axel wrapped his other hand.

By the time Axel was done, Ford had stripped to the waist. He was pumped up, shadow boxing, showing off his skills.

All four of them made their way into the middle of the yard.

"You fight clean — first man to forget that forfeits. Clear?" Axel met Ford's gaze and held it for several seconds, damn near daring the guy to cross him.

"Sure, Axel. No problem."

Just for form's sake, Axel turned his attention to Bayden and waited for him to nod too.

"If you're down for five, it's an automatic tap out," Axel added, as he and Jarvis stepped back, leaving Ford and Bayden in the middle of the yard.

Ford was still bouncing on the spot. Bayden stood motionless, until Ford finally began to move to his left.

As they circled each other, a hush fell over the crowd.

Axel watched through narrowed eyes. It was hardly the first time two idiots had squared off against each other within the vicinity of his pub. What grown men chose to do with each other was no more his business when they were fighting than when they were screwing. But, damn it, the men were usually far more evenly matched.

If he stayed down the first time he took a fall, all Bayden would have done is gained a few scrapes and bruises while learning to pick his battles more wisely. But as Axel studied him, he doubted the boy would take his advice. Bloody bravado.

* * * * *

Bayden ignored the crowd. If they were going to be a problem, they'd have to be a problem he dealt with later. Ford grinned at their audience, obviously relishing the prospect of showing off his moves. He took a swing. Bayden swayed easily out of range.

Ford's next attempt at a right hook was just as easy to predict. Bayden side stepped. Ford was big and strong. He was also an arrogant arsehole and making no real attempt to defend himself.

Ford lunged. Bayden dodged and caught him neatly in the solar plexus. Ford grunted and doubled over. A sympathetic groan went up from the men watching.

Bayden weighed his options. He couldn't actually let Ford win, but there was no point asking for everything to go to hell. The next time Ford swung, Bayden allowed him to land a glancing blow to his face. Blood filled Bayden's mouth. A split lip. Their audience liked that.

Ducking a jab, Bayden picked his moment and punched Ford on the nose as he straightened up. Mumbled curses filled the air as Ford spat blood across the rough concrete.

One more. He'd let Ford land one more hit. Just in case it would appease the guy's friends if they thought the fight had been a closer contest than it was.

That blow to the nose had really pissed Ford off. The scent of his anger filled the air. His punch was clumsy, but it had Ford's full weight behind it. His fist connected solidly with Bayden's shoulder and knocked him off his feet. He rolled and had himself upright in less than a second, but that was enough. Time to wind it up.

If you can't cover the bet, I'm sure we can find another way for you to pay us back. Bayden bit back a growl. It would be so easy to finish the fight. A quick shift and lupine jaws could end it as quickly as they tore a jugular from a human neck.

No. Bayden pushed down his instincts. A wolf would get in trouble for doing that. He could do without a lynch mob on his tail. The skill was always to win without killing his opponent.

Shoving every other thought out of his mind, Bayden landed several hits in quick succession. They were careful blows. Nothing that would do any real harm. Just enough to take Ford down and make him want to stay down.

A left hook to the jaw, but not hard enough to break it. Jab to the ribs, just enough force to take the wind out of him. Dodge back. Sweep with the legs. There was no satisfaction in it. Bayden simply went through the motions.

Ford collapsed onto the rough concrete with a thud. Jarvis sprang forward and shook Ford's shoulder.

"Five." Bayden glanced across to the bartender with all the tattoos. What had Ford called him—Axel? Whatever his name was, he wasn't wasting any time with the count. He didn't look disappointed that his friend had lost.

Ford pushed Jarvis impatiently away, but he didn't pull himself to his feet.

"Four."

Jarvis tugged more desperately on Ford's shoulder. "Get up."

Ford peered across at Bayden. Complete realisation dawned in his gaze. Bayden could have really hurt him if he'd wanted to—he might do that if Ford got up—and Ford had a decision to make.

"Three."

Jarvis leaned over Ford, hissing at him and ordering him onto his feet.

"Two," Axel continued.

Jarvis tried to physically drag Ford upright. It was like watching a Chihuahua try to lift a Great Dane. Ford dropped his gaze. He didn't want to find out what Bayden might do to him in the next round.

"One." Axel stepped forward. "That's it. You're done."

Jarvis straightened up, leaving Ford on the ground at his feet. "What?"

"Settle your debts," Axel ordered. "And that's the end of it."

Axel looked in his direction. Bayden nodded his willingness to do that.

"No way—he cheated!" Jarvis burst out.

Bayden bit back a growl. There went his hundred pounds.

"How?" Axel demanded.

"He's a bloody wolf." Jarvis was much smaller than both Ford and Axel, but he waved his arms around a lot, like a chicken ruffling up his feathers, trying to make himself look bigger.

Axel folded his arms across his chest and glared down at Jarvis. "You both knew that before you put your money down."

"But..." Jarvis waved his arms around some more. "He—"

"Pay the boy."

"Why should I?" Jarvis whined. "He's just a wolf. They're no better than dogs and—"

"You'd have taken his money," Axel cut in. "You'd have tried to screw it out of him if he didn't have the cash."

"That's not the—"

"You made a bet. You lost," Axel cut in.

Bayden studied Axel more carefully. Axel was a big guy, but Bayden doubted it would have made any difference if Axel was five foot two and seven stone. That kind of confidence didn't come from size, or from the brightly coloured tattoos that covered Axel's arms. It came from a man knowing he was by far the most dominant wolf in the pack.

Jarvis pulled out his wallet, grabbed five twenties and shoved them into Axel's hand before turning back to Ford. Safe, now that the fight was officially over, Ford let Jarvis pull him to his feet. It wasn't easy for anyone to make a dramatic exit while supporting a man twice his size, but Jarvis seemed to be doing his best.

The crowd followed them toward the front of the pub. The only one who didn't walk away was Axel.

"You okay?"

Bayden nodded.

Axel stepped straight into Bayden's personal space. He was at least six foot two and loomed way above Bayden. He took hold of Bayden's chin and tilted his head back—as if he had the right to touch him however he pleased. Bayden tensed, but he held his ground.

"Come on. I'll sort out that lip."

"It's fine," Bayden began, but Axel was already walking away, and he still held Bayden's winnings.

Axel stepped through the pub's backdoor.

"My bike's out front," Bayden called after him.

"It's safe." Axel's smile turned crooked. "Taking a swing at a man is one thing, going after his bike is something else, and a ride like yours is sacred."

He sounded honest, and like someone who knew the men who drank there. And a hundred pounds was a hundred pounds.

"You can bring your helmet with you, if you're worried it might be nicked," Axel offered.

One hundred pounds. The right choice was obvious. Bayden grabbed his helmet and followed Axel into a small kitchen at the back of the pub.

"Sit." Axel pointed to the chairs around a rickety kitchen table. Opening the cabinet below the sink, he took out a bowl and half filled it with warm water. While the water ran, he pushed Bayden's winnings into the front pocket of his tight black jeans.

Bayden bit back a sigh and perched on the edge of the nearest chair. He looked down at the wraps around his knuckles. There was blood on them—Ford's blood. The scent of it hung heavy in the air. His own blood tasted bitter and metallic in his mouth.

Axel set the bowl of water and a first aid box on the table. "You play off that trick often?" he asked, pulling out the chair adjacent to Bayden's.

Trick? "I don't want any trouble."

"Debatable, but that doesn't answer the question." Axel dropped a cloth into the warm water and squeezed out the excess. He wiped Bayden's mouth with the damp fabric. It came away with blood on it.

Bayden pulled back. "You don't have to—"

"Hush."

Axel dipped the cloth back into the water. He caught hold of Bayden's chin and held him still so he could continue cleaning his split lip. His touch was firm but not painful. His tattoos seemed to undulate against his skin as the muscles beneath them flexed and relaxed—it was dangerously hypnotic. No scrapes and bruises for Axel—the only marks on his skin were ones he'd chosen himself.

"Who taught you to fight like that?"

Bayden shrugged. "Wolves fight," he mumbled, as the cloth rubbed against his bottom lip once more.

"I'll take your word for it. I'm not aware of knowing any other shifters."

Bayden made the mistake of looking up. Their eyes locked. It was several seconds before he could force himself to look away from Axel's intense blue gaze.

"Do you fight every man who challenges you?"

Axel's scent filled the small room, over-powering even the smell of blood. He didn't want to fight Bayden, he wanted to fuck him. Bayden shrugged.

"It happens a lot once people realise you're a wolf?"

Bayden nodded. In a certain kind of pub it was damn near guaranteed, and he'd read what kind of pub The Dragon's Lair was perfectly.

Axel opened the first aid box and pulled out a tube of something. He squeezed some onto his fingertip and dabbed it onto Bayden's lip.

It stung worse than the original blow. Bayden pulled back. Instinct made him run his tongue over the cut. The stuff tasted foul.

Axel laughed. "You'd do a better impression of a big scary wolf if you didn't act like a little pup who doesn't like taking his medicine."

Bayden glanced up. The laughter wasn't cruel. It sounded more like Axel was teasing a human child rather than taunting a dumb animal.

Bayden risked a small smile. "Wolves heal quickly enough without human medicine."

"Quickly enough to risk a beating just to teach a couple of idiots not to mouth off to a wolf?" Axel used the damp cloth to wipe away the cream he'd just applied, before turning his attention to undoing the wraps around Bayden's knuckles.

"I knew I'd win. And if I didn't..." Bayden shrugged.

"Then what's a hundred pounds here or there?" Axel asked.

Silly little rich boy. Bayden bit back a chuckle. If that's what Axel wanted to believe, it was fine with him. "Exactly."

Axel frowned. Suddenly, he looked sceptical.

"They chose the stakes," Bayden said. "If I'd thought they could have covered their side, I'd have suggested adding another zero. But since I had no interest in screwing them for the balance…"

Axel leaned back in his chair. He didn't look impressed. "So you understood how they would have tried to get you to earn the money if you hadn't had the cash?"

"Doesn't matter, since I had the cash," Bayden lied. "Anyway, isn't there a human saying about pots calling kettles black?"

"What?"

"What are you into?" Bayden asked. "What do you hope I'll do to get that hundred you pocketed?"

Axel took the folded notes out of his pocket and handed them across the corner of the table. Anger chased any arousal out of his scent.

Bayden hesitated. All five notes were there. Axel wasn't keeping any of them? "I don't understand."

"I was holding it for you while I cleaned you up, not stealing it from you."

Bayden peered down at the notes, completely off balance. Apparently, silly little rich boys got to keep all their winnings without any argument.

He pulled himself to his feet and picked up his helmet, but his gaze went to the table — the bowl of water, the first aid kit, the wraps Axel had tied around his knuckles. Axel had been kind — maybe only because he thought Bayden was a rich idiot with money to burn, but still. Bayden offered one of the twenties to Axel.

"Why?" Axel said.

"For…" Bayden waved a hand toward the things on the table.

"I'm not your waiter." His tone changed to match the anger in his scent. "You don't need to tip me."

Bayden dropped his hand to his side. "I wasn't trying to insult you."

Axel stood up. "No problem." Except it obviously was a problem. Axel's body language made his displeasure clear.

"I should go," Bayden mumbled.

Axel didn't try to stop him. It was stupid for Bayden to feel disappointed by that. He wasn't there to take an interest in any human.

In. Pick up some fast cash. Out. Quick and clean. Everything had gone exactly to plan.

Bayden was almost outside when Axel spoke. "The opening times are listed on a board next to the front door."

Bayden glanced over his shoulder. "It's okay if I come back sometime?"

Axel dipped his head once in acknowledgement. "Yeah, it's okay."

Bayden looked down. He wasn't sure what he was supposed to say, what the man who Axel thought he was would say. It was safer to leave in silence.

Around the front of the pub, Bayden was aware of men watching him. He ignored them all as he pulled his clothes on. In a few seconds, he was on his bike and riding away from The Dragon's Lair. His thoughts raced in a dozen different directions. It was more habit than conscious thought that guided his bike onto the housing estate on the other side of the city where his mother and grandfather lived.

Pulling up outside the dilapidated row of houses that made up the farthest corner of the estate, Bayden took off his helmet. He touched his lip, checking the split hadn't reopened. He was fine.

He strode up the path and knocked on the door leading to one of the upstairs flats. Taking the money he'd won out of his pocket, he folded it into his palm, out of sight.

The door creaked open. His mother peeked around the edge of it. She smiled when she saw him and undid the chain.

"How's he today?" Bayden asked.

Her smile faded a fraction. "He's sleeping now." She looked tired. She'd tied her hair into a braid over one shoulder, but several locks had escaped, and she'd obviously lacked either the time or the energy to fix it. The strain was showing around her eyes. It hadn't been an easy night.

"Do you want me to sit with him for a while?"

She shook her head. "We're fine." Her gaze settled on his lip. "Are you?"

"It's nothing. I've had worse paper cuts." He was about to smile to prove just how fine he was when he thought better of it. It wouldn't do for his lip to start bleeding in front of her. "Is there anything you need?"

"We're fine, love, really." She stroked his cheek. "You need to stop worrying about us. We're not your responsibility."

It was nothing he hadn't heard before, nothing he intended to heed this time. "I'll go and let you get some rest while he's sleeping," Bayden said. He pressed a kiss to her cheek and slipped the folded up notes into the pocket of her cardigan. It would be enough to let her finish paying off that week's rent and stock up on some food.

He was halfway down the path leading back to the road when his mother called after him. "Keep your head down, sweetheart."

Bayden looked over his shoulder and nodded at the familiar advice.

Straddling his bike, he pulled away from the curb and turned toward his own place nearer the centre of the city. It was Friday. One set of rent paid, he could start earning the money to pay his own. Bayden bit back a sigh. Two days— that gave him plenty of time, providing he wasn't fussy about how he earned the money.

Bayden paused at a set of traffic lights and his mind wandered back to Axel and The Dragon's Lair. The more he thought about it, the more being a silly little rich boy appealed. Playing pretend like that probably didn't count as keeping his head down and staying out of trouble, but it was a damn sight more fun than reality.

Chapter Two

He was there to pick up a fight; that was all. As Bayden pulled up outside The Dragon's Lair, he was very clear about that in his own mind.

He was back barely a week after his last visit because it was getting harder for him to pick up fights in pubs where he was better known. Obviously, his return had nothing to do with Axel. That would be silly.

Bayden pulled off his helmet and looked around the car park. There weren't so many bikes there today. There might not be anyone who'd want to fight. Bayden remained on his bike. Axel had probably been setting him up for a slap down when he suggested he come back. Humans were like that, and Axel really hadn't liked Bayden offering him a cut of his winnings.

Bayden stared at the swinging sign outside the pub. It showed the same design as the backs of The Black Dragons' club jackets—a dragon just like the one on the Welsh flag, but in black and on a red background. Finally he sighed and pulled himself off his bike. He was an idiot for being there, but there was no way he could leave without at least checking.

Just outside the pub door he slipped on his sunglasses. Taking a deep breath, he squared his shoulders and stepped inside.

Axel was there. For a few seconds, Bayden remained just inside the door and simply let himself stare, comparing the reality of Axel to the memory of him that he'd carried around for the last week.

Bayden had half convinced himself that he must have embellished Axel in his mind, but the man standing behind the bar matched his recollection perfectly. From the tightly cropped blond hair and sharp blue eyes, to the intricate tattoos that covered his arms, Axel was just as Bayden remembered.

Axel was a big guy, tall and broad across the shoulders. But, that wasn't the really interesting thing about him. Axel exuded pure dominance. That hadn't been Bayden's memory playing tricks on him. If there was such a thing as an alpha human, Axel was it.

It took all of Bayden's self-control to tear his gaze away from Axel and glance around the room. There were twenty-odd guys there. Most sat at the tables, a few were at the bar talking to Axel. About a quarter of the men wore those jackets that marked them out as members of The Black Dragons Motorcycle Club. Axel's jacket hung behind the bar.

Bayden stepped forward. The movement caught Axel's attention. He didn't smile at Bayden, but he didn't tell him to piss off either.

Bayden cautiously made his way to the bar.

Axel lowered his gaze, but there was nothing submissive about the gesture. His inspection went all the way down to Bayden's boots and back up to the top of his head. There was no admiration in his gaze; it felt more like a statement of ownership over everything he saw.

Bayden stopped a foot away from an empty bit of bar. A sudden rush of nerves almost translated itself into fidgeting. He tightened his grip on his helmet, hooked the thumb of his other hand through one of the belt loops of his jeans and forced himself to fall still.

Axel didn't say anything.

"You told me it was okay to come back sometime," Bayden finally reminded him.

"Did you think I'd change my mind?"

Bayden shrugged. He'd have been far from the first human to decide he didn't want a wolf in his pub.

"What are you drinking?"

A little of Bayden's tension eased. "A bottle of Coke, please."

Axel put it on the counter and took his money. "Don't wander off while I get your change." It was an order, not an invitation.

Bayden did as he was told, but once Axel handed him the coins, he knew better than to push his luck. He turned toward the door.

"Where do you think you're going?" Axel said.

Wasn't it obvious? "To sit outside." Anyone who wanted a fight would find him easily enough.

"No."

Bayden hesitated. "No?"

"You'll sit at the bar, where I can keep an eye on you."

Bayden felt the hairs on the back of his neck go up. "I'm not here to cause trouble."

Axel raised an eyebrow at him. "Who said you were?"

Bayden stared at Axel through the darkened lenses of his sunglasses, trying to get a read on him and failing.

Axel's lips twitched into a smile. "I don't think you're going to start a riot, but until you prove you have more survival instincts than a seriously stressed out lemming, you'll stay at the bar."

What the hell? "I can look after myself."

"Of course you can." He didn't even try to sound like he meant it.

Bayden frowned. Apparently, there were disadvantages to being considered rich and stupid. He looked toward the door. "My bike's out there." He had no intention of saying the words aloud, but somehow they slipped out. Bayden tensed, knowing it was stupid to let on any detail that could be used against him.

Axel turned a monitor on the shelf behind the bar toward Bayden so he could see the screen. The entire line of bikes was clearly visible. "Your baby's perfectly safe. Any other excuses?"

Bayden climbed onto the stool furthest away from the other men at the bar.

Axel nodded his approval. "Do you coddle it in every pub you stop at, or are we special?"

"What?"

"I can't imagine you being this worried about leaving it outside some posh wine bar in the middle of the city."

"I wouldn't like leaving it there either," Bayden said, honestly. "I don't even like parking it on the street outside my place when I'm just rushing inside to get something."

"Rough neighbourhood?" Axel asked, his tongue obviously in his cheek.

"No, it's a nice area." Where would he live if he had money to burn? "By the bay, where they built the new flats, overlooking the marina," Bayden decided. That would be nice. He'd ridden through there once or twice. It was quiet, peaceful.

"Sounds like it would be a safe place to park."

Bayden shrugged. "I just feel better when it's properly garaged."

Axel laughed, but it was a warm, indulgent sound, just like when Axel had called him a little pup. "How long have you been riding it?"

"Since I turned twenty-one." *I didn't steal it.* He stopped himself short, just in time. If Axel thought he had money, he wouldn't have jumped to the same conclusions as every other human seemed to when they saw a wolf riding an expensive bike. "My granddad gave it to me."

"He's got good taste." As he spoke, Axel picked up some of the empties that had been left a little further down the bar and set them on the counter behind him. "Does he ride?"

"He used to."

"Not anymore?"

"He's not well," Bayden admitted.

Axel remained silent, as if waiting for Bayden to add something, but it was too real. Bayden had no idea how to fit how ill his grandfather was into the fantasy life he'd been creating.

Just when the silence was building up to the point when someone would have to say something to break it —

"Axel?"

Axel glanced down the bar to the guy who'd called him. He lifted a hand in acknowledgement, but he didn't rush away. "I've got no problem with you drinking here, or with you keeping an eye on the monitor so you know your baby is safe, but Bayden?"

Bayden tensed, ready for anything. "Yes?"

"Lose the sunglasses."

Bayden blinked at him from behind the safety of the tinted lenses.

Axel didn't walk away. He didn't move. He just waited, with apparent patience, for his order to be obeyed.

Bayden reluctantly took off his glasses, folded them up and set them on the bar.

Axel smiled. "Good boy." He didn't sound sarcastic, or even gently amused. It didn't seem like he was making a joke out of talking to a wolf the way humans liked to talk to dogs. The way he said it, it actually felt nice.

* * * * *

"If you wanted a puppy, you could have just said. We'd have chipped in and got you one for your birthday," Hale said.

Axel grabbed a beer and set it on the bar in front of Hale. "You've had a week to come up with something, and that's the best you can do?"

"Just warming up," Hale corrected. "You know he's not what the leather gods had in mind when they invented puppy-play?"

Axel glanced down the bar. Bayden's attention was divided equally between the monitor and his drink. He showed no sign of being able to hear what was said about him.

"He'd look good in a collar though," Drac pointed out from the stool next to Hale.

Axel didn't argue with that. Bayden in a collar and nothing else would be a walking wet dream. Or, even better, a kneeling wet dream. The boy certainly had the lips for it.

Axel looked down the bar, again, just in time to see one of the pub regulars, Joe, stop alongside Bayden's stool.

The only word Axel caught was drink.

Bayden indicated his mostly full bottle of Coke, as if he really thought Joe was worried he might be thirsty. Joe went away. Bayden went back to studying the monitor.

Out of the group of Black Dragons who'd gathered at the bar, Griz was sitting closest to Bayden. The exchange had obviously caught his attention. He turned to Bayden, obviously not about to take Bayden choosing the stool furthest away from him as a sign the boy had no interest in talking to him.

Griz whistled to get his attention. "Wolf-boy!"

Bayden continued to watch the monitor.

"I thought wolves were supposed to have good hearing," Griz complained.

Axel tossed a couple of empty bottles in the bin. "Try calling him Bayden, his hearing might improve."

Griz's turned to him again. "Bayden?"

"Yes?" Bayden glance toward them, doing a stellar impression of someone unaware that anyone had spoken to him before that moment.

"Have you twigged that most of the men who drink here are gay or not?" Griz demanded.

Bayden took a swig of his drink. "I know." That was it.

"And?" Griz prompted.

Bayden glanced at him but didn't say anything.

"Are you gay?"

Axel was quite interested in the answer to that question himself. It wasn't as if there was a sign above the door advertising the fact that The Dragon's Lair was a gay pub.

Straight bikers came in all the time, not realising The Black Dragons were a gay motorcycle club. Of course, there were some self-declared straight guys who kept coming back time and time again—generally, they were the ones who became less straight the more they drank.

Bayden thought about it for a few moments. "It's different for wolves. Preferring men or women, that's a human thing."

"Do you screw guys?" Griz pushed.

Bayden kept his attention on his drink. "Yeah, I do guys."

"What about kink—do you know that most of the guys here don't just wear leather because they ride bikes?"

Bayden failed to look the least bit shocked. "I've heard that."

"Is that another human thing?" Drac asked from the stool next to Griz.

"Wolves play too." Bayden met Axel's gaze. He looked away so quickly Axel failed to get any kind of read on him. Still, Axel found himself all kinds of interested in what that look might mean.

"Do you play as well as you fight?" Hale asked, leaning back on his stool to see past Drac and Griz.

"Yeah, I do."

"That doesn't mean much."

Axel glanced past the Dragons to the young man standing behind them. One of the hangers-on had obviously been eavesdropping. As Axel watched, the guy moved down to stand closer to Bayden. "You winning last week was a fluke. Ford's an idiot—no challenge at all."

Axel tried to place the guy. He'd been around for a while, watching the play in the backrooms while he worked up the guts to try it for himself. Peterson? Something like that.

Bayden glanced over his shoulder. Peterson wasn't as muscle-bound as Ford, but he was still bigger than Bayden.

Bayden shrugged as if he really didn't care what the guy thought.

"I'm right," Peterson said, full of self-satisfaction. "A fluke. Wolves aren't half as tough as they like people to think they are."

"Ford was sure enough to put one hundred on himself to win," Bayden pointed out.

Peterson squared his stance. "I'd put one hundred on myself too."

Bayden looked him up and down and failed to appear the least bit impressed.

Peterson's eyes narrowed. "Any time you want."

Bayden shrugged. He put the top back on his bottle of Coke, got off his stool and picked up his helmet.

"Now?" Peterson asked.

Bayden nodded.

Axel moved down the bar toward them.

"You want us to take it somewhere else?" Bayden asked.

Axel stared down at him as if he was weighing his options, but he'd already made his decision. Bayden was better off where someone could keep an eye on him. "Here is fine."

The routine was the same as last time. Bayden stowed most of his stuff away in his panniers. Axel wrapped his knuckles and, despite what he considered deep provocation, managed not to launch into a lecture worthy of his grandmother in full fire and brimstone mode.

By the time Bayden and Peterson squared off against each other, Axel felt like he'd been holding his breath for hours, waiting to see which of the two boys had been talking out of his arse.

Peterson. Within seconds, it was obvious that all of Peterson's bluster about being able to take down a wolf was complete bollocks.

Ford hadn't been a fluke. Bayden had skill — and not the kind a man developed in a gym sparring with friends. Bayden moved like he'd learned to fight the hard way. He kept his guard up, because he'd been hit too hard and too often to forget to protect himself.

Peterson landed one good punch to Bayden's eye. The next moment Peterson was face down on the ground. He pulled himself up, fair play to him for that. But he didn't manage to touch Bayden again before he was down for the count.

One of Peterson's friends, another voyeur from the pub's fringes, cautiously crept forward to check on him. Bayden watched it all without any visible expression.

Axel stepped forward.

Peterson said something to his friend, who hurried across to where Peterson had left his jacket. Peterson took the money out of his wallet without a word of protest. He was about to hand it to Bayden when the blood stained wraps made him hesitate. Apparently feeling more than a little queasy at the sight of his own blood gracing another man's knuckles, Peterson handed the money to Axel instead.

Axel watched with amusement as everyone headed back inside. Peterson's tentative standing had gone up dramatically. What Ford and Jarvis had lost by being arseholes after the last fight, Peterson had gained by proving he could take being beaten fair and square.

No longer largely ignored, Peterson suddenly had a lot of friends willing to buy him a drink to commiserate.

"Has it ever occurred to you to tell someone who challenges you to a fight to just bugger off?" Axel asked when he and Bayden were left alone in the yard.

Bayden frowned. "No."

Axel shook his head. "It's not your job to take down every idiot who insults wolves."

Bayden seemed to think about that very carefully. "What would you do if someone said all gay humans are cowards, that none of them can fight worth a damn?"

"Laugh," Axel said, honestly. "If I started hitting everyone who wound me up, I'd never have time to do anything else." He tucked a knuckle under Bayden's chin. Bayden obediently tilted his head to let him see what damage had been done this time.

"You're going to have a hellish black eye."

"Wolves heal quickly."

"That's no reason to go looking for injuries, pup."

Bayden glanced up. If he seemed surprised by the nickname, he made no protest against it. Content that no real harm had been done to the boy, Axel let him step back.

"Grab your stuff, and come inside." He kept an eye on Bayden until he was sure he would do as he was told, then went in.

A quick glance confirmed that Matt was coping well enough behind the bar. And if that changed, it wouldn't kill people to queue. Axel left him to it and took a seat on one of the barstools. The fact that he hadn't retreated to his usual side of the bar seemed to throw Bayden off his game. He hesitated a few yards away.

"Come here."

Bayden shuffled a bit nearer, only to hesitate again, two feet away. Axel caught hold of his belt loops and tugged him closer. Bayden made no complaint when Axel took his things and set them on the stool next to him. He stood in front of Axel in silence while Axel began to undo the wraps.

"This isn't a hobby, is it?"

Bayden glanced up at him.

"You've been here twice. Each time you've left a hundred pounds richer. Taking fights in pubs, it's how you make your living."

Bayden frowned. If that made his eye hurt, he didn't wince. "The money's not the point."

Axel raised an eyebrow at him.

"I'd fight anyone who spoke about wolves that way for free," Bayden said, after only the slightest hesitation.

"The money's just a bonus?"

"Something like that." His voice was off.

"But not completely like that?" Axel finished with one hand and turned to the other.

"Centuries ago it was simpler. If a human picked a fight with a wolf, it would be clear who won, because the wolf would have torn the human's throat out with his teeth." The moment the last word left his lips, Bayden looked up. He obviously regretted saying it.

Axel didn't give him the chance to backtrack. "So, the money's a way of keeping score?" he asked, calmly. "When a man hands over the money, it's obvious who won and who lost."

Bayden nodded but his expression remained wary, as if he expected Axel to freak out just because he'd mouthed off and bigged up his species.

"You said you'd heard that this pub's for guys who are into leather?" Axel said.

"Yes."

"Well, there are house limits that everyone has to abide by. Ripping out throats isn't allowed—regardless of species."

Bayden opened his mouth. Just in time, he apparently realised he was being teased. He smiled slightly. "I can follow the rules."

"Good boy." Axel ruffled Bayden's hair, pushing the scruffy brown stands back off his face. "Sit down, I'm not done with you."

Bayden obediently climbed onto a stool. He pulled the rest of his clothes on as Axel went behind the bar. Grabbing some ice, Axel wrapped a towel around it to form a make shift ice pack and handed it to Bayden.

Bayden looked at him as if he'd lost his mind.

"Put it on your eye."

"I'm fine."

Axel kept holding the ice pack out until Bayden finally took it.

"On your eye," Axel repeated.

With obvious reluctance, Bayden put the pack on his eye. Axel left him to his own devices while he went to help Matt clear the backlog of guys waiting to be served at the other end of the bar. He didn't come back until the ice had been on Bayden's eye for a solid twenty minutes.

Bayden only removed the pack when Axel stopped in front of him. "Thank you."

"You're welcome, pup."

"I should get going." Bayden pulled himself off his stool. He didn't seem to know what to do with the ice.

Axel absentmindedly took the towel off him, dumped what was left of the ice into the sink and tossed the damp towel on the bar. "How's your eye to ride?"

"It's fine."

Reaching across the bar, Axel angled Bayden's head to get the best view. The ice had done its job. His eye hadn't swollen up.

"Close your good eye." He waited until Bayden obeyed. "How many fingers am I holding up?"

"Three." Not the slightest hesitation. No squinting.

"You'll do," Axel allowed. He handed over the money Bayden had won that night.

"Thanks." Bayden picked up his things. He took a step back and paused. "What you said last time…"

"You can consider it a standing invitation."

Bayden smiled. Then the sunglasses were back on, and he was heading out of the pub.

"Tough little bugger, isn't he?" Drac said.

Axel turned toward his friends. "Seems like it." It was certainly what Bayden wanted people to think.

"Wolves are trouble," Hale observed. "Always have been, always will be."

Axel raised an eyebrow, well aware he was being baited.

Hale grunted. "It's true. You can't trust a wolf. I've arrested enough of them over the years to know. Thieves, drunks and troublemakers — every one of them."

"We're still talking about the guy who drinks regular Coke and barely talks to anyone, right?"

"Actually, we're talking about the guy who just stole your towel."

Axel turned around. The towel he'd wrapped the ice in. It had been on the bar, but it was gone. Bayden was the only man who'd been within six feet of it. He must have snatched it when he gathered up his things.

Hale smirked. "I told you. The boy's trouble."

Chapter Three

Axel smiled to himself when he looked up and saw who'd just walked into his pub. Two nights in a row. At this rate, Bayden would be turning into a true regular any day.

As Bayden approached the bar, Axel looked him up and down in a quick but thorough inspection. The boy obviously had very set ideas about appropriate attire for a bikers' pub. He wore exactly the same as he had on his last two visits — right down to those bloody stupid sunglasses.

There was that same slight tension in him too, as if he was aware that he didn't quite fit in but he was doing his damnedest not to let anyone know that.

A yard away from the bar, Bayden seemed to remember Axel's orders from the day before. He took off his glasses. Another half a step forward, and he stalled.

Axel noticed the way Bayden's shoulders tensed, but it took him a moment to realise why. Apparently, people frowning at Bayden freaked him out.

"You weren't joking when you said you heal quickly, were you?"

Bayden shrugged, but the fact was, his eye should have been a mess and it wasn't. No swelling at all. There was a smudge of purple underneath his eye, but it looked like it had been healing for a week rather than a day.

He gave no indication of being about to approach the bar of his own volition.

"You'll need longer arms if you want to drink from over there," Axel said.

Bayden came closer. Another slight hesitation, and he passed a carrier bag across the bar. "Thank you."

Axel took the bag and peered down into it — the towel Bayden had walked off with the previous day. It had obviously been laundered. It looked suspiciously like it had been ironed too.

Axel looked up, realised that Bayden was watching him warily, and bit back his amusement. "You're welcome." He set the towel on a shelf under the bar.

Bayden's lips twitched into a brief smile, obviously relieved that his gesture had been so well received. Axel gave a mental shrug. As quirks went, ironing towels was a damn sight less annoying than those dark glasses.

He didn't bother to ask Bayden what he wanted. He got his Coke and set it on the bar in front of the same stool he'd sat on during his last two visits. Bayden obediently took his seat.

"How was your ride over?" Axel asked.

"Fine."

Axel studied him carefully. An answer that short from most humans would have been a brush off, but Bayden didn't seem to talk much to anyone, and, hell, at this point nothing short of a firm—sod off, I'm not interested—was going to dent Axel's curiosity.

"You said you'd heard that a lot of the guys who drink here are into leather."

Bayden nodded.

"From who?"

Shrug.

"Do you know any of the Dragons; ever played with one of us?" Axel kept his tone light, not inclined to let on how much he already hated the idea of one of the other guys having ever laid a hand on Bayden.

Bayden shook his head.

Damn it, Axel had met chattier mimes. He fell silent, but he didn't move away from Bayden. Matt could serve anyone who wanted a drink. Customers could queue out the door for all Axel cared. He remained opposite Bayden and completely silent.

Bayden glanced up at him. It took another two minutes of unwavering silence for Bayden to realise that, if the conversation was going to continue, he'd have to be the one to speak next.

He took a sip of his Coke. "Someone said that The Black Dragons started off as a club for men who like bondage rather than bikes?"

Axel nodded his approval. He'd have done that whatever Bayden found to say, but the boy throwing bondage into the conversation was definitely a plus.

"The original four of us met on the BDSM scene. When we realised we all rode, it made sense to ride together. The rest grew from there."

Bayden glanced up at Axel again, before quickly dropping his gaze. It was the same look he'd given him last time the conversation had turned to kink — not exactly flirtatious, but definitely one that Axel considered interesting.

Axel pointed to the table where several of the other Dragons had set up an impromptu poker game. "The big guy with the beard, who looks like a bear — everyone calls him Griz. He owns a bike repair place, does custom work for damn near every biker in the city. He rides the Harley Fat Boy parked out front."

Bayden glanced in Griz's direction, before turning back to Axel.

"Next to him, pale man with a pony tail, the one who looks like a vampire on steroids, that's Drac — he runs a tattoo place and rides a clapped out old thing that's only good for spare parts, but the paint job is awesome. The other founding member of the club is Hale, he's not in tonight — but he's the sarcastic one with the shaved head. I'll point him out to you next time he's here."

Bayden nodded, but it was about time for him to speak again. Axel didn't have to wait so long for Bayden to get the idea this go around.

"Did Drac do your tattoos?" Bayden asked.

"Every one of them." Axel smiled. "Do you have—?"

"Sorry, Axe?"

He looked down the bar toward Matt.

"The barrels need to be switched over," Matt said, apologetically.

Perfect timing for the one job Matt always did his damnedest to avoid. Axel looked at the queue, then at the poker players, before reluctantly setting aside the idea of seeking out any ink Bayden might have hidden away. "I'll be back in a minute."

Bayden nodded.

Axel was only down in the cellar a few moments, but the second he stepped into the bar he knew he'd been gone for too long. Someone else was talking to Bayden—fair enough, he was hot. Guys were going to hit on him. But Bayden was actually getting off his stool and it looked like he was about to leave with the guy.

Bayden stilled, as if he could sense Axel's gaze on him. He turned around. His expression turned guarded.

"Going somewhere?" Axel asked.

"If you prefer us not to use the yard out back, we can take it somewhere else," Bayden offered.

Axel glanced at the guy Bayden had been talking to. He was chatting to a few other guys—friends of his by the look of it—the kind of friends who would happily goad someone into betting on himself in a fight against a wolf.

"Here's fine," Axel said. It wasn't quite what he'd had planned for Bayden that night, but the possibility that Bayden had intended to screw the other guy rather than hit him had put things into perspective.

Axel could force himself to wait until after a fight. He looked at Bayden's newest opponent. He doubted it would take Bayden long to be done with him.

* * * * *

"Less than five minutes." Axel murmured the words under his breath, as if he was talking to himself rather than Bayden.

Unsure what to say, Bayden remained silent.

Axel tucked a knuckle under Bayden's chin and studied the results of the fight. His touch wasn't harsh, but it wasn't a suggestion either. It was an order—one that Bayden was rapidly getting used to obeying.

"Come on, pup."

Bayden followed Axel into the kitchen at the back of the pub, just as he had the first time he'd visited The Dragon's Lair. This time, he wasn't worried that Axel might want to keep the money he won, or that he might make him get on his knees to earn it.

Axel wasn't like that. Axel was…

Bayden took a deep breath and let it out slowly. It didn't help him think more clearly about what Axel was, it just filled his lungs and his mind with Axel's scent. Axel's movements were as deft and confident as ever. In moments, he was sitting with Bayden at the table.

He wiped the blood from Bayden's split lip. Bayden's memory of his last visit to that kitchen had been accurate. His realisation that it was better to get a split lip than a black eye was just as true.

Holding ice on his own eye couldn't compare to having Axel's hands on him. Sitting on the opposite side of the bar to Axel was pleasant, but nothing like being alone with him in the kitchen.

Axel didn't seem to expect talking—another bonus. Bayden was free to study Axel without having to scramble for something he could say that a human wouldn't take offense at.

Bayden traced the line of one of Axel's tattoos with his eyes, from his wrist up to where it disappeared under the short sleeve of a tight black T-shirt. Bayden furled his hand into a fist to stop himself giving in to the temptation to try to stroke the design.

The art work obviously went up higher than Axel's bicep, but Bayden had no way of knowing just how much of him was covered in the brightly coloured designs. Was it just his arms, or was his whole body decorated that way?

Bayden's heartbeat sped up. He swallowed at the idea of finding more tattoos as Axel stripped down and —

Axel chuckled.

Bayden looked up. Axel's eyes were dancing with amusement. He'd obviously finished whatever he intended to do to Bayden's split lip. Bayden hadn't been sitting obediently still while Axel worked. He'd been sitting there blatantly gawping at Axel for who knew how long.

He waited for Axel to say something, but Axel just raised an eyebrow.

"Drac does good work," Bayden offered.

Axel smiled, clearly not believing Bayden's interest in his skin stopped at admiring his art work, but he didn't call Bayden on it. "Before we were interrupted, you were about to tell me if you had any ink."

"Wolves can't."

"Really?"

"When we shift…" Bayden trailed off.

Axel didn't pull away at the reminder of what Bayden was. He stayed in his space and ran his fingers up the unmarked skin on Bayden's arm. It was all Bayden could do not to lean into his touch.

"Were you serious when you said you play as well as you fight, or were you just talking big in front of the other guys?"

"I play," Bayden said, more softly than he intended. He cleared his throat. "I can play just as well as I fight."

"You've never been here on one of the nights when the back rooms are open."

Bayden dropped his gaze. Just because Axel let him drink there, that didn't mean he'd let him do anything else there. Asking would be—

"They'll be open next Saturday night if you want to come along and play."

It could be a trap. Axel could be setting him up for anything. He…

"With you?" Bayden checked.

"Is that what you want?"

Bayden shrugged.

"That's a pity. I don't play with men who aren't interested in me."

Bayden jerked his head up. "I didn't say I'm not interested."

"You didn't say that you are."

It would be a stupid thing to tell a human. Giving up information that could be used against him, letting a human know what he wanted, it was asking for trouble.

Axel's fingertips still rested on Bayden's skin. He traced a line up the outside of his arm again before sliding his hand behind Bayden's head and caressing the nape of his neck. His hand was warm, his touch full of dominance—as if he already knew he had the right to touch Bayden any way he pleased.

"I…" Bayden took a deep breath. The desire in Axel's scent gave him courage. "If you did want to play with me, I'd…like that?"

Axel nodded his approval. "Next Saturday."

Bayden nodded.

Axel brought his hand forward and ran his thumb back and forth across the skin beneath Bayden's bottom lip. Bayden was sure that Axel wasn't thinking about cleaning his wounds anymore. He had no doubt Axel was imagining how a werewolf's lips would feel wrapped around his cock.

Bayden hardened at the possibility. His erection strained against his jeans. It had been so long since he'd sucked someone off because he actually wanted to. His mouth watered.

Their eyes met. For a moment, Bayden thought that Axel was going to order him to his knees, or even lean forward and kiss him.

Axel pulled back. "You might not want to smile for a few days, but you'll survive."

"It's fine. Wolves—"

"Heal quickly," Axel finished for him. "You've mentioned that before."

"It's true," Bayden protested.

But the moment had passed. Whatever Axel had wanted from him, he didn't want it anymore, not while his lip was still bleeding. Bayden mentally cursed, wishing he'd let the guy he'd fought give him a black eye instead.

"Werewolves can't carry human illnesses," Bayden blurted out, in case that might help.

"That's good to know, but when you come to the club, you'll follow the same rules as the humans."

"I never said I wouldn't."

"That means, unless you're wearing a guy's collar, he's wearing a condom," Axel went on, without missing a beat.

Bayden pulled back.

Axel raised an eyebrow at him.

"Wolves aren't dogs."

Axel frowned, but the expression soon passed. "A lot of subs wear collars—it shows they belong to their dom. It's nothing to do with being a dog."

"I never said I'm a sub."

Axel smiled. He looked amused again, which was better than the frown, but Bayden didn't get the joke. And humans who made jokes he couldn't understand were dangerous.

"Which of us do you think will be calling the shots on Saturday?" Axel asked.

"You." That was obvious.

Axel ruffled Bayden's hair as he stood up. "That's close enough for now."

Bayden wasn't sure what that meant either. But Axel's hand had felt good in his hair. He understood that perfectly.

Chapter Four

There was no way in hell anyone at The Dragon's Lair was going to be interested in fighting tonight. Bayden hadn't even made it into the pub, and that much was obvious. Even the air in the car park was filled with the scent of lust and leather — and it wasn't the kind of leather a man wore on a motorcycle.

Bayden joined the queue to get in. He'd been in clubs where men played with leather in the city. There was always money to be earned in them, and points to be proved, if a wolf wasn't fussy about the kind of bets he took. But, tonight wasn't about proving things like that to humans. Bayden smiled to himself. It was about proving something very different to one particular human. *I can play just as well as I fight.* Proving that to Axel would feel good and —

"Bayden."

Stepping to the side, Bayden looked to the front of the line. Axel's friend Drac beckoned him closer.

Bayden glanced at the queue. Several other men had joined it after him. He didn't want to lose his place, but everyone was staring at him, waiting for him to answer Drac's summons. Bayden reluctantly stepped out of the line.

"I'm allowed to be here. Axel —"

"You can go straight in," Drac interrupted.

Bayden studied him warily.

"Axel invited you. You don't need to queue," Drac said. "Go on." He nodded to the door. "You don't want to keep him waiting."

Bayden was about to step in, when he realised that the man in front of him had just paid an entrance fee. He reached into his jeans pocket.

"You don't need to —"

"I can pay my own way," Bayden cut in. He held out his money and kept Drac's gaze until Drac finally gave in and took the cash.

Inside, Bayden forced himself to leave his helmet and his jacket with the guy who was collecting them off everyone else. Some guys were leaving a lot more than coats and crash helmets. Half the men had stripped down to just a few bits of leather and chain.

It was hot and crowded. Music pounded, filling the gaps between the people. Each inch of progress Bayden made involved squeezing past someone. Every man there seemed determined to get in his way or cop a feel as he passed by, but he finally got to the bar.

Axel…wasn't there. Bayden frowned as he lifted himself up on his toes, trying to see over taller men's heads. A man Axel's size should have been easy to spot, but Bayden couldn't see him anywhere.

A hand landed on Bayden's shoulder. It was better than where other hands had tried to roam as he'd fought his way through the crowd, but Bayden had had enough of strangers in his space. He twisted around only to stop short.

Axel's friend, Griz, stared down at him. His nickname really was fitting. Grizzly—a big bear of a man with a full beard and a huge barrel chest.

"Axel's in the back room." Griz dipped his head, putting his lips closer to Bayden's ear in an effort to make himself heard over the pounding rhythm, but his invasion of Bayden's space stopped at the purely practical.

"Thanks."

"He's expecting you!" Griz grinned.

The way the other men talked, it almost sounded as if Axel had been looking forward to that night as much as Bayden was.

As Bayden made his way deeper into the pub, he found there wasn't one back room, there were at least four of them. Each space seemed just as crowded as the pub's main bar room. Bayden was well into the first room before other men's shoulders parted far enough for him to see that there were areas of clear space around various pieces of kinky furniture. One man lifted a flogger and brought it down hard on another man's back, making it obvious why the crowd wasn't creeping closer.

Axel wasn't one of the men playing. He wasn't in any of these audiences, either. Bayden's ability to care about anything beyond that was limited. He headed for another room.

At the last moment, a burst of laughter caught his attention. He turned around. The amusement was all directed at a young blond man standing with three older men. The boy blushed, ducked his head and rushed off into the crowd, his tail tucked firmly between his legs. The older men laughed all the more.

"What about you, wolf-boy, do you think you could take twenty from a cat?" one of them called out when he spotted Bayden.

Bayden recognised him from his previous visits to the pub. Richards. He wasn't one of the men who sat at the bar talking to Axel. He didn't ride with Axel's club, but he was often there in the background. He'd offered to buy Bayden a drink and he hadn't liked it when Bayden had pointed out he already had one.

"Well?" Richards came closer so he didn't have to yell so loudly over the music. He lifted up a cat of nine tails as exhibit A.

"I'm not interested." Bayden turned away.

"Figures, there's no such thing as a wolf who isn't a coward at heart, is there?"

Bayden pushed down his anger as best he could and went back to his search for Axel.

"I think he's scared," one of Richards's friends chipped in.

"Looks like it." It was the smug satisfaction in Richards's voice that tipped the balance.

Bayden's hackles went up. He turned to face him. "Of you?" His tone made it clear how stupid that idea was.

Richards's eyes narrowed. "I've seen you fight. You dodge well enough, but I've never seen you take a hit like a man. Wolves are just animals when it comes down to it. They can bite and claw, but when it comes to taking their licks, no wolf has that kind of self-control." He smirked. "I'd put money on it."

"How much?" Bayden demanded, before he could check the impulse.

"One hundred."

"Not very sure of yourself, are you? That's not even enough to make it interesting." Bayden turned away, dismissively.

"I'll match it if you get to thirty," one of Richards's friends offered.

"Get to forty, and I'll match it, too," another one chipped in.

"That makes three hundred," Richards said. "*If* you can take forty — all to your back on bare skin, and win the whole bet. Bail before that, and you'd owe each of us a hundred. Is that interesting enough for you, or is the truth that a wolf just can't hack it?"

The music wasn't so loud they couldn't be overheard. Bayden looked around to see who else might be listening. Everyone else's attention seemed to be on the whipping taking place in the opposite corner of the room. But, even if those three men were the only ones who heard the challenge, even if they were the only ones who thought wolves were weak, it was still three humans too many.

Axel's expecting you. "I don't have time for this bull," Bayden bit out.

"Later tonight, then. After the pub closes, at my place," Richards said. "Unless I was right about wolves, and you're just making excuses for being a coward?"

Bayden met his gaze. He couldn't afford to let humans think he was weak. If he was willing to face facts then he couldn't afford to turn away three hundred pounds, either. Axel was waiting for him, but Axel was also bound to be finished with him way before closing time.

"Three hundred says I can take forty lashes then," he agreed.

Richards rattled off his address, and Bayden was finally able to go back to his search for Axel.

There! Bayden's heart rate settled as he finally spotted Axel near the door leading into the third back room. Then it sped up again as he took in a few more details.

Axel had dispensed with his usual black jeans in favour of tight leather trousers. Without his T-shirt, the only things covering any part of Axel's chest were his tattoos. Bayden's fingers itched with the desire to reach out and touch. He pushed his hands into his pockets. Axel turned slightly. Light glinted off a nipple piercing. It was all Bayden could do to keep back a whimper.

As if he knew he was being watched, Axel turned toward Bayden. He smiled when he saw him and beckoned him closer. Bayden moved toward him, stopping the bare minimum of distance away required to be considered respectful.

Axel caught hold of his belt loops and tugged him nearer, just like he had once before, but this time he didn't need to check Bayden for injuries after a fight. He slid his arm around Bayden and settled his hand on the small of his back, encouraging him to stay close—ordering him to stay close, because he knew he had the right to give that kind of command.

"Okay, pup?" He dipped his head and put his lips near Bayden's ear, but it was different to when Griz had done it.

Bayden hadn't wanted to step forward and rub himself against Griz, or to drop to his knees and suck his cock.

Taking a deep breath, Bayden settled for filling his lungs with Axel's scent and nodding, although okay didn't seem like a good enough word. The music was far quieter in this room. Axel didn't have to shout.

"Seen anything you like?" he asked.

Bayden blinked at him. He liked every bit of Axel. He was confident he'd like all those bits he hadn't had a chance to see yet, too.

Axel's lips twitched. "I meant the scenes." He nodded toward the one he'd been watching. One man was secured in a pillory. Another man was screwing him. From all the noise they were making, they were both enjoying themselves, but the body language was all wrong. They were acting parts which didn't really fit. The guy who was bound didn't really think the man screwing him was the more dominant man. He was just pretending.

Bayden turned his back on them. Axel standing still and doing nothing was far more fascinating than anything they could ever do. "Whatever you want."

Axel stroked his fingers up and down Bayden's spine, tempting him to arch his back and press against his touch. "Is that your way of saying you're still working out what you're into?"

Bayden frowned. "It's my way of saying we can do whatever you want." He thought he'd been quite clear.

Axel chuckled. "No preference at all?"

Someone nudged Bayden's back. Axel pulled him closer to give whoever it was room to pass. Suddenly, they were pressed together. The difference in their heights meant that Bayden's lips were within an inch of Axel's shoulder. He'd never wanted to lick someone so badly in his life.

Axel encouraged Bayden to tilt his head back, just as he had so many times before.

"No preference," Bayden whispered.

"I can do whatever I want with you?"

Bayden nodded. It was the way things were meant to be. There would be no play-acting with them. The more dominant wolf would take the lead and—

"Just leave his back clear. I like a fresh canvas to work on."

Axel jerked his head up. Bayden didn't bother to look over his shoulder. He knew Richards's voice and had no interest in listening to him.

Apparently, Axel felt differently. "What did you say?" Axel was looking over the top of Bayden's head, talking to Richards rather than him, but Bayden still hated hearing the anger in Axel's voice.

"He's already agreed to see if he can take a flogging from me."

"Is that true?" Now, Axel was talking to Bayden, and he was just as pissed off as he'd been when he'd been talking to Richards.

Unease rolled down Bayden's spine. "Yes." They were so close together, Bayden felt every one of Axel's muscles knot with tension.

"You agreed to do a scene with him?"

"I..."

"I should have known better than to trust a wolf's word," Richards sneered.

"I keep my word." Bayden tried to turn to face Richards, but Axel caught hold of his shoulder and stopped him short.

"You also said you were coming here tonight to do a scene with me," Axel said.

"I can do both."

Axel's grip on his shoulder tightened. "No." Just that one word, but filled with complete confidence.

Bayden hesitated, staring up at Axel.

"No," Axel repeated. As erotic as the dominant tone was, it did nothing to disguise Axel's anger.

Bayden looked past Axel. They'd caught a lot of attention. Just as many men were watching them as were watching the guys at the pillory. Bayden had guessed they might have an audience, but he'd assumed it would be for the scene.

Axel wasn't interested in that anymore. Axel wasn't interested in him anymore. Bayden looked down. He should have known better than to come to the pub tonight. If he'd stuck to just picking up fights, he could at least have sat in the pub and day dreamed about playing with Axel. Forgetting that it would never work out that way in reality had been stupid.

Bayden tried to step away, but Axel's hand was still on the small of his back and it prevented Bayden retreating without his permission.

"Do you want me to leave?" Bayden asked.

"Rather than see you get whipped by him, yes."

* * * * *

Bayden nodded. He stepped back. He was actually going to leave rather than simply tell Richards he'd changed his mind about the scene with him?

Axel shook his head, but he let the boy back away. Bayden was obviously out of his depth there—that's why he was flailing around, making bad decisions and following the lead of anyone more experienced than him in an effort to look like he knew what he was doing. Much better that he leave now and return when he was up to speed.

Axel coaxed Bayden into looking up at him. Confusion swirled in Bayden's gaze. Yes. Let him leave. Give him a few private scenes. Just the two of them, with no one for Bayden to try to act big in front of, that would be far better. Axel would bring him back to the club when he'd found his feet. No harm done.

"Come on." He turned Bayden toward the door.

"Running away like a scared little mongrel?" Richards goaded.

Bayden spun back to face him. "The bet's still on."

"Bet?" Axel asked.

"He bet that a wolf couldn't take forty lashes," Bayden said.

"That's why you agreed to let him flog you — to win a bet?"

Bayden nodded. He looked confused. He obviously couldn't see any other reason why anyone would get within twenty yards of Richards.

A few things clicked into place inside Axel's head. Any jealousy he'd felt evaporated. Bayden was even less experienced than he'd thought. "It's not like betting on yourself in a fight, pup."

Bayden shrugged.

"You're not getting flogged in the middle of this club to win some stupid bet." Axel allowed no room for argument in his tone.

"The bet's not being done here," Bayden said.

"What?"

"I'm taking him back to my place," Richards said.

"That's not happening." Axel didn't even glance at Richards. His words were all for Bayden.

"I already took the bet," Bayden pointed out.

"Then you can un-take it." Forget jealousy. The idea of Bayden on his own with Richards turned Axel's blood to ice.

"Do you need his permission to play with other guys?" Richards laughed. "What are you, a wolf or his bitch?"

Bayden jerked around to face Richards so suddenly, Axel's grip on him failed.

"I decide who I do anything with, no one else," Bayden bit out, anger turning each word into something like a growl.

"Doesn't sound like it."

Bayden glanced up at Axel. "I said I wanted to play with you. I didn't say I wouldn't play with anyone else. It's my choice." His tone was different when he spoke to Axel, as if he was trying to be polite but he couldn't quite control his anger.

Axel stared down at him. "Do you trust me?"

Bayden didn't move for a full minute. When he finally nodded, he seemed to do so against his best instinct.

"I'm telling you that it's not safe for you to leave with him. If you go back to his place, I can't look after you."

"I can look after myself." He stepped away.

Axel grabbed his wrist before he could take a second step. "You're not leaving with him, pup."

If he let Bayden walk out of there, he would go back to Richards's place, Axel had no doubt about that. Bayden would go there and he'd get flogged and God only knew what else. Axel's ability to control what happened ended the minute Bayden stepped out of the club.

"You can't stop me from leaving."

He could. Axel was quite willing to handcuff Bayden to the nearest bit of bondage equipment and keep him there until he saw sense. He stared down at Bayden. As loudly as his instincts screamed at him, his higher-brain argued that he couldn't actually kidnap the boy. Even if he did give into the instinct, he'd have to let him go eventually. The look in Bayden's eyes made it clear that the moment he was freed he'd head straight to Richards and that God-awful bet.

"You'll do it here," Axel announced.

Bayden blinked at him, but Axel ignored him in favour of meeting Richards's gaze over the top of Bayden's head. "You made the bet here, you'll see it through here."

"That wasn't what we agreed."

"If you just want to do your bet, what's stopping you doing it here, where everyone can see?" *Where someone's around to step in the moment Bayden says his safe word.*

"Fine. If you don't trust your pet mutt to take it like a man when he's out of your sight, fine." Richards shrugged, but his petulant expression made it clear that whatever plans he'd had for Bayden had been ruined. "Let everyone see if he has the balls to back up all his big talk, right here, right now."

"We can go back to his place," Bayden said, trying to step away again. "It's not a problem. I can handle him."

No, he couldn't. Axel kept Bayden where he was. Richards might never have broken the rules in the pub, but that had nothing to do with him being a good dom and everything to do with him knowing he'd be chucked out. In his own place, without anyone to check him, Axel didn't want to know what he was capable of, but Bayden wasn't going to find out.

"If you're determined to do it, you'll do it here," Axel corrected.

He half expected Bayden to point out that he'd never actually agreed to submit to him outside a scene, but Bayden just stood there, perfectly still.

"No one here will think any less of you for telling him where he can shove his bet," Axel pointed out just in case it might make any kind of a difference.

"I would." Bayden looked up at him. "I'd think less of me."

A bitter taste filled the back of Axel's mouth. Bayden had backed himself into a corner. The only thing that Axel could do was wait until he sent up a white flag and allowed himself to be rescued. "Fine."

A trio of men were just leaving the Saint Andrew's Cross on the other side of the room.

Axel strode across to it, pushing his way through the crowd and taking Bayden with him. Two guys were about to take their turn when Axel stepped in front of them. "You can have it when we're finished."

They took one look at him and apparently decided they didn't mind waiting. They moved back, leaving Axel and Bayden alone by the cross.

Lots of men had been cuffed there since Axel bought the pub—novices, hard-core masochists, collared submissives, and pain sluts. But those guys had known what they were doing, or at the very least had been putting themselves in the hands of a guy who knew what he was doing. And those guys hadn't been Bayden—for some reason, that alone made a huge difference.

"Give me the exact terms of the bet."

"Forty lashes—all to my back, on bare skin," Bayden said.

Axel glared at the cross as if it had personally offended him. If Richards hadn't specified bondage in this stupid bet, he wasn't going to get any. And, if Bayden found it harder to take the whipping without bondage to help him stay in place, and called it off quicker as a result, well, Axel wasn't going to be heartbroken.

"We can take it somewhere else," Bayden offered again, more softly this time, as if Axel's disapproval was having some effect on him, even if it wasn't strong enough to make him rethink the whole stupid idea.

"It's your choice and your back. If you want to be an idiot, who am I to stop you?" Axel said. He'd aimed for flippant, but hit furious dead on target.

Bayden looked down. His hair fell into his eyes. He had his hands pushed deep into his pockets and didn't reach up to push it back.

"Do you have enough to cover your side of the bet if you lose?"

"I won't lose."

"Yes, or no. Do you have that amount of cash with you?"

"Yes."

"Prove it."

Bayden reached into his pocket and calmly took out a fold of notes. He peeled off three hundred pounds and handed it to Axel. He pushed the rest back into his pocket. Silly little rich boy.

Axel looked him up and down. Bayden had ignored fetish wear in favour of the same outfit he'd worn every other time he'd visited.

"You'll have to lose the vest."

Bayden stripped to the waist without a word, setting his vest on the seat to one side of the play area. He stepped up to the cross and got into position. His confident movements could have implied that he was used to being bound to a Saint Andrew's, but Axel was more inclined to think it implied Bayden could work out the bloody obvious.

Axel stepped up behind Bayden. "When you want to stop, say stop—loud and clear. Don't turn away from the cross until I tell you that you can, or the cat might catch you as you turn."

"The deal was bare skin," Richards said, from the edge of the audience.

"The deal was his back—that's bare," Axel said, turning to face him.

Apparently, everyone wanted a good view of this particular bastardisation of a scene. The audience was several men deep, with those at the back struggling to see over the shoulders of those in front.

Hale and Griz had secured places right at the front of the crowd. Axel went across to them, checking how good a view he'd have from their position.

"What the hell's going on?" Hale asked.

"Richards goaded him into taking a bet on a flogging," Axel said, as calmly as he could.

"You're saying you can't stop him doing this in your own damn pub?" Griz demanded.

"And let it happen at Richards's place?" Axel bit out.

They stood in silence as that sank in.

"It won't do him any harm if it happens here," Hale eventually said. "The boy will take a couple of lashes, call a halt, pay his debts and it'll be done."

A couple of lashes. Axel glanced across at Bayden, not sure that Hale's read on him was as accurate as Axel wished it was.

Grinding his teeth together, Axel took the money off Richards and his friends to hold during the bet before approaching Bayden one last time.

"Ready?"

Bayden nodded.

Axel bit back a curse and stepped away. His vantage point allowed him to see Bayden's face in profile. He looked calm; Axel felt anything but calm.

Richards stepped forward. Bayden tensed as if he sensed him getting closer.

Richards didn't waste any time. He brought the cat down hard across Bayden's back. He wasn't holding back, or leading into it. Axel had no doubt that Richards hit Bayden as hard as he physically could.

Bayden closed his eyes. That was it. Not a flinch, not a murmur.

Again.

Bayden remained motionless.

Axel tightened his hand into a fist. Every instinct he possessed told him to step forward and stop the bet. A right hook to Richards's jaw would make everything very simple.

Leather snapped against Bayden's back. Bayden was timing his breaths between the lashes. That was the only sign he gave of being aware of the whipping.

Richards worked quickly, obviously trying to group the lashes so close together Bayden wouldn't have any time to recover between them.

Axel counted out the strokes. With each blow he clenched his jaw more tightly. The muscles down the side of his face throbbed. His fist began to cramp.

Twenty. Halfway there. For the first time, Richards paused. He moved away from the spot he'd taken up to the left of the cross.

Axel took half a step forward, thinking that Richards was going to approach Bayden, but no. Axel silently cursed as he realised what Richards intended.

Richards smirked as he arranged himself to Bayden's right and moved the cat into his left hand. He brought the whip down hard. Every tail crossed the lines Richards had already placed on Bayden's back.

Axel stared at Bayden, taking in every detail of his expression and posture. If he hadn't seen the mess Richards was making of Bayden's back for himself, it would have been easy to look at Bayden's face and wonder if the whip was even connecting with his skin.

The control it took for a man to stand there and act like it wasn't happening was far beyond anything Axel would have expected anyone to be capable of. A glance down Bayden's body and it was obvious that he wasn't turned on. He wasn't the kind of man who could enjoy any kind of whipping—no matter how it was delivered or who was doing the whipping. But, as Axel counted out the lashes, it seemed very possible he was a man who could completely block out what was happening for long enough to take the entire forty lashes.

Axel held his breath as the last few strokes were delivered.

"Forty." Axel stepped forward as he said it.

Richards lifted the cat to try to sneak an extra blow, but Axel caught the tails mid-way down the length. The ends whipped around and encircled his forearm. Bayden's blood stained each one. A sharp jerk had the cat out of Richards's hand.

Dragged off balance, Richards stumbled. "I'm not finished!"

"Yes, you are." Axel was halfway to Bayden and was about to tell him that he should just stay where he was for a few minutes when Bayden turned away from the cross.

"Was it the whole forty?" No stammer, no slur—each word was enunciated very clearly.

"Yes."

Bayden turned to Richards. "Did your arm get tired halfway through? You should work on your stamina."

"I switched arms because it hurts more when you cross the lines!"

Bayden shrugged. If the skin across his back made him want to scream in agony, he showed no sign of it. "If you say so." His voice remained perfectly steady.

Axel narrowed his gaze. It obviously wasn't the first time Bayden had played this game. He'd taken whippings on the same basis elsewhere. It might be a stupid game, but it was evidently one that Bayden was very good at.

Even as he stood there, anger at what he'd just witnessed pounding through him, Axel couldn't help but realise that it was something that anyone who really wanted to receive Bayden's submission would have to bear in mind. A whipping wouldn't get Bayden's attention—different techniques would have to come into play.

"I won," Bayden pointed out, his tone of voice far more respectful now that he spoke to Axel rather than Richards.

Axel handed his winnings to him.

Bayden looked at the fold of notes then at Richards. "Maybe when you get more practice, you'll find someone willing to pretend you're a dom for free."

Richards stepped forward. Axel snapped back into the here and now and tossed the cat at him. "Get out. Take the other two arseholes with you."

"What?"

"Out. Now," Axel snapped. "It's not a complicated order."

"You can't throw me out!"

Axel raised an eyebrow at him. Bayden's barbs had obviously hit home—Richards usually had more sense than to provoke someone who he knew was capable of beating him senseless. Losing the bet in front of everyone had shaken him. Axel failed to feel the least bit of pity.

"I'm not having any more of this bollocks in my pub." Axel grabbed Richards's shirt collar. If he wanted to know if Axel was capable of physically throwing him out, that was fine with him.

Richards flailed around a bit, but there was no way he was ever going to do any harm. The crowd parted, scrambling to get out of Axel's way.

In the car park, a push sent Richards stumbling in the direction of his car. Richards's friends scurried out in his wake, probably more out of fear of staying rather than out of any sense of loyalty to Richards. There wasn't a biker among them. Axel watched them all get into Richard's car and drive away.

"Axel."

Axel looked over his shoulder. Drac was at his post on the door. He nodded toward the line of parked motorcycles. Bayden was heading toward his bike.

Chapter Five

"Where do you think you're going?"

Bayden looked over his shoulder. Axel was striding toward him. A wooden rail ran along the edge of the car park, just in front of the line of bikes. Bayden stopped next to the barrier. He moved his clothes and helmet to one arm so he could steady himself with his other hand on the rail.

His head was spinning. Someone had set fire to his back. And Axel was pissed off. The third fact worried him far more than the others.

Axel stopped in front of him. "I asked you a question."

"I'm going home." It was all he could do to keep his voice level, now that the adrenaline was draining away.

"No."

Bayden blinked at him.

"You're in no condition to ride."

"I'm fine." Bayden turned toward his bike.

Axel caught hold of his shoulder and dragged him back around. A wave of nausea rolled through Bayden.

"You might convince Richards he didn't hurt you, but I'm not Richards. You can barely stand."

"You don't want me here."

Axel pushed Bayden's chin up, making Bayden look at him.

Bayden swallowed. "I'm not sticking around to be thrown out."

"I had no intention of throwing you out."

Bayden studied Axel, desperately trying to both remain on his feet, and follow the conversation well enough to understand what Axel was trying to tell him. "You're angry with me."

"Yes."

Bayden met his gaze.

Axel let out a strange laugh. "Did you think I'd lie?"

"But I'm still allowed to come back sometime?" Bayden hazarded.

"Worry about that later," Axel ordered. "Right now, the important point is that you're not leaving here—not on that bike."

Bayden automatically stepped between Axel and his bike. "I'm fine." The fact the world was spinning, and the pain in his back was almost enough to bring him to his knees, was irrelevant.

Axel reached out. Most of Bayden's attention was on keeping his balance now that he'd stepped away from the rail. He didn't realise what Axel intended to do in time to stop him from snatching the keys out of his hand.

Bayden lurched forward and made a grab for them, dropping his belongings in the process. "Give them back!"

Axel held the keys out of his reach. "I take the keys off anyone who's too drunk to ride, and I'll take them off anyone who's in too much pain to ride, too." There wasn't any hesitation in his voice. He had no doubt he had the right to take whatever he wanted.

Bayden's instincts said that Axel was acting like an alpha, but experience screamed that he was just another human who thought he could ride roughshod over a wolf, who could take whatever he wanted, whenever he wanted.

Bayden stared at the keys dangling from Axel's fingertips. He could take them back, but Axel might get hurt in the process. The idea of challenging Axel's dominance was almost as off-putting as the idea of hurting him. Bayden curled his hands into fists at his sides. He shook his head, trying to clear it so he could think past the fog of pain.

He glanced across at the pub. There were a lot of humans in there—ones who were bound to take Axel's side. Could he get the keys, get on his bike and get out of there before anyone else joined them?

He'd heal from a beating but if they went for his bike rather than him…

He glanced at his bike. His stomach turned over.

"It's my bike. I won't let you take it."

"I'm not trying to steal it, pup." Axel frowned. "But there's no way in hell you're riding tonight."

Bayden was mesmerised. He couldn't take his eyes off the keys. His heart pounded so hard, it was a wonder that Axel couldn't hear each beat.

"I'll put your bike in one of the lock-ups around the back of the pub. It'll be safe there until you're fit to ride."

Bayden shook his head. "I'm not leaving it here."

"You can either stay here tonight, or I can drive you home. Either way, my decision stands, you're not riding in this condition." He said it all very calmly, as if he had no doubt his natural dominance gave him the right to make those kinds of rules.

Bayden tore his gaze away from the keys for a moment. He looked up and met Axel's eyes. Leaving his bike behind was out of the question. Through the fog, another warning flag went up. Letting Axel see where he really lived was just as impossible. Axel liked a silly little rich boy, and Bayden liked being someone that Axel liked.

There was only one choice he could really make. "I'll stay with my bike."

"That's fine. I'll help you inside and get your bike stowed away."

Bayden shook his head. "No. I'll do it."

"Bollocks."

Bayden looked down at his fist. Even in the less than perfect car park light, his knuckles were visibly white. "I'll do it."

Axel sighed and shook his head. "Stubborn little bugger, aren't you?"

Bayden bit back an instinct to apologise. "It's my bike, not yours."

"You can tag along and keep an eye on what I'm doing, but that's it—don't argue." Axel picked up Bayden's clothes and handed them to him, but he didn't give up the keys when he stepped past Bayden. In seconds, he had control of Bayden's bike and was pushing it around the back of the pub.

Bayden walked alongside. Being out in the cold air should have cleared his head more than it had. He wasn't sure how much of the lingering dizziness was from the whipping, and how much came from it being too long since he'd eaten.

When they reached the row of garages around the back of the pub, Axel unlocked one. The metal shutters were loud and overpowered the music still playing inside the pub. Axel rolled Bayden's bike inside. Taking Bayden's helmet off him, he set that with the bike. All Bayden could do then was watch, trying not to feel too helpless, as Axel pulled down the shutters and locked his bike away.

Finally, Axel gave Bayden's keys back to him. Bayden gripped them so tightly the metal bit into his palm. Axel fiddled with the big ring of keys he carried—there had to be twenty on there. He took one off the ring and offered it to Bayden.

"That's the key for this lock-up." He nodded to the shutters. "I've got a spare somewhere, but I'm damned if I can remember where, so don't lose it."

For some reason, it sounded like Axel wanted to make him feel better about it all. "Thank you."

Axel let out another one of those pissed off huffs. "You should worry less about your bike and more about your own hide."

"Wolves heal. Bikes don't."

Axel shook his head. "You're consistent, I'll give you that. Your priorities are seriously buggered up, but you are consistent about them. Come on. Inside." He put his hand on Bayden's shoulder as they turned toward the building, as if he thought he needed steadying.

Rather than stop in the kitchen at the back of the pub the way Bayden expected, Axel unlocked a door on the far side of the kitchen and marched Bayden up a flight of stairs.

The music from the pub seeped up to them, but it was muted. The pub, and the men in it, felt very far away.

Axel's scent clung to the space upstairs. It was very clear, un-muddied by other men's scents. No one else spent much time there. This was his private space, his home. Bayden didn't get much of a chance to look at the first room they passed through. Axel brought them to a stop in another kitchen.

Axel pulled a chair away from the kitchen table and turned it around. "Sit down. Face the back of the chair. I'll get something to put on your back."

"I'm fine." Bayden shuffled his feet and ignored the pain in his back as best he could.

Axel folded his arms. "You mean you're scared that it will sting the same way the cream I put on your lip did?" It was halfway between teasing and a challenge.

Bayden hesitated, but there didn't seem to be any way to protest without contesting Axel's dominance all over again.

He straddled the chair. Resting his forearms on the back of it allowed him to take some of the strain off his back and breathe a little easier.

As Axel moved around the room getting whatever it was he wanted to put on his back, thoughts ran more clearly through Bayden's head.

"Thank you," he blurted out.

"For what — standing around watching you get whipped by that arsehole?"

"No, for counting." He looked down. "I lost count."

Axel let out a bitter laugh. "You'd have been better off if you'd stopped when I reached four rather than forty."

There was nothing Bayden could say to that.

"Was it worth it?" Axel asked after a few moments.

"Yes," Bayden whispered. To prove to humans that wolves couldn't be broken so easily — yes. Even if it had only been for the three hundred pounds — yes, that would have been worth it on its own.

Three hundred pounds. That was three fights if he could find men who wanted to bet against him, and they were harder to come by the more often he won. Fifteen back alley blowjobs if no one wanted him to prove a point. A whipping was easy money by comparison — even if it didn't feel like it at that particular moment.

"Really?" Axel asked. He moved another chair and sat down behind Bayden.

"There are worse things to have to do," Bayden whispered, more to himself than anyone else.

Axel's scent changed.

It took Bayden a second to realise why. If it was a choice between anger and pity, he'd rather have anger. "I've taken bets which are much crazier than this," he rushed out. "Lots of them."

Axel's scent didn't change. "Are you in debt, is that why you're scrabbling for money?"

Bayden straightened up. He winced as his back protested and stilled. If he tried to move again, he was pretty sure he was going to throw up. "The money's not the point."

"Are you using?"

Anger flared up inside Bayden. Gritting his teeth, he pushed himself up onto his feet, willing his body not to betray him.

Axel's hand landed on his shoulder. "Sit down," he ordered. "If you don't want to answer a question, you can just tell me to sod off. You don't need to make a dramatic exit."

Bayden subsided onto the chair. He stared down at his forearms as thoughts raced around in his head. He still couldn't think entirely clearly, couldn't pin down any one idea. Did Axel think about wolves the same way as all the other humans did? Probably. He probably wasn't any different to any other human.

It was probably a lost cause, but as he felt Axel's fingers moving gently against his back, cleaning his wounds for no other reason than he'd decided that it was right that someone should do that, Bayden couldn't help but hope. "They're wrong," he whispered.

"Who are?"

"The humans who say wolves are all drunks and junkies," Bayden told the back of the chair. "They're wrong. We don't do that."

Axel moved some sort of damp cloth across his back. "And it really narks you when someone jumps to that conclusion," he finished for him.

"We don't do that," Bayden repeated.

"Like a religious thing?"

Bayden hesitated, tempted to say yes, but no. There were enough lies between them already, and it wasn't as if he was giving up information that could be easily used against him. "Alcohol doesn't work on us. Neither do human drugs."

"They don't affect you at all?"

"Once a guy bet me I couldn't down a bottle of vodka. It made me a bit sleepy." He thought back to that night. "It didn't taste very nice. Beats the hell out of me why anyone would drink it if it wasn't a bet."

* * * * *

Axel chuckled at the obviously genuine bemusement in Bayden's voice, but his expression turned serious again as he returned his attention to Bayden's flogged back.

Richards had thrown all his strength into it. He'd raised welts. The fact he'd switched hands and purposely crossed his strokes only made it worse. The skin was broken so many times. Each wound was small. There was no question of any of them needing stitches. Masochists had received harsher treatment in the pub and thrived on it, but it wasn't the same.

"Fights and vodka are one thing, but you were a fool to take this bet."

Bayden said nothing. Axel waited, wondering if Bayden was silent because he was mad or because he was in too much pain to answer.

Axel was doing his best to be gentle, but it still must have hurt like hell. Bayden hadn't complained once; he hadn't even flinched. Axel held back a sigh. He shouldn't have baited him. Silly little fool probably thought he had a point to prove about that too.

"It was worth it," Bayden said.

Axel wasn't sure if it was the pain from the wounds, but it sounded suspiciously like Bayden was reminding himself of that as much as anything. "Why? What made it worth it?"

Bayden was quiet for a long time. Axel started to think that he wasn't going to answer, but finally he did.

"It's no different than a fight. Humans think they can break us — proving they can't is always worth it."

"What?"

"Humans have always thought that if they whip us, or screw us, or whatever, they can put us in our place and prove that they're better than us. They're wrong."

Axel frowned at the back of Bayden's head, unable to think of a single thing to say.

"He threw the best he had at me, and the worst it was, was boring."

A couple of puzzle pieces fell into place. "And just in case you didn't prove that well enough during the whipping, you had to shoot him down at the end?"

Bayden's shoulders twitched as if he started to shrug, then remembered why that was a bad idea. "Humans aren't always quick on the uptake. Just not showing them respect isn't enough."

"Richards definitely doesn't deserve anyone's respect," Axel said. "But don't make the mistake of thinking all human doms are equally clueless."

"I don't think you're clueless," Bayden said. His voice was steady. Any pain was well hidden. "I think you're a hypocrite."

Axel raised an eyebrow at the back of Bayden's head. "Oh?"

"The way you're acting, anyone would think you'd never whipped a guy."

Axel straightened up in his seat. "Not for a bet, I haven't."

"You've been thinking about doing something like this to me ever since we met," Bayden said, with easy confidence.

"Yes." Axel had no intention of lying about it. "I wanted to screw you the moment I saw you. I've wanted to turn you over my knee ever since you took that first stupid bet."

"You can if you want to."

"Let me guess, you'll bet that you can take it?" Axel asked, with forced calm.

Bayden was silent for several seconds.

Axel held his breath.

"No bet," Bayden finally whispered. "But, I—"

Axel waited, but that seemed to be all Bayden intended to offer up. "But you what?"

"But nothing," Bayden said. "You can, if you want to. Either, or both."

Axel ran his gaze over Bayden's back. The wounds were clean. None of them were bleeding. Time would be the only thing that helped them further. He moved his chair around so he could see Bayden's face. "But you what?" he repeated.

Bayden stared at the table for a long time.

"I'm a damn sight more bloody minded than you. You can stall, but you won't win a standoff with me."

Bayden ground his teeth together. He closed his eyes. Axel was reasonably sure he'd just been cursed back several generations. "You can if you want to," Bayden repeated. "But I might be able to make it better for you if you wanted to wait until tomorrow."

"You really think I'd start a scene now?" Axel asked, far from impressed.

Bayden frowned. "I wasn't insulting you."

He seemed to believe that. Axel studied him for a second. It seemed more like it hadn't occurred to Bayden that a man would have to be a bastard to want him to play in that state.

"You forgot to mention that you'd be more likely to enjoy yourself if you weren't in agony," Axel pointed out.

Bayden's frown deepened. "That's not why I said it."

"Whether or not you'd enjoy a scene isn't important?" Axel asked.

Bayden shook his head, dismissing the whole topic. "It's not about me."

"Oh?"

Bayden glanced up. He looked confused, as if he really didn't understand why Axel wasn't instantly agreeing with him.

"Have you ever played when it wasn't for a bet?" Axel asked, suspiciously.

Bayden said nothing, but his silence was quite eloquent enough.

Axel got up. "It's time you went to bed."

He showed him to the spare bedroom. Bayden seemed a fraction steadier on his feet as he walked across the flat. He made no comment on anything as he stepped into the room.

"There's an en-suite through there."

Bayden hesitated. "Can I use the shower?"

Axel shook his head. Maybe Bayden wasn't thinking so clearly after all. "You don't want water against your back."

"Okay."

Axel found himself lingering in the room, not sure Bayden should be left on his own. It was on the tip of his tongue to tell Bayden to sleep in his room with him.

Bayden would go along with it. But, hell, he'd go along with it if Axel wanted to screw him too. What Bayden would go along with wasn't a reliable indication of acceptable behaviour.

Axel pushed Bayden's hair back off his face. "My room's next door. Shout if you need anything."

Bayden dipped his head once in acknowledgement. All Axel could do then was walk away before he ended up sticking around to tuck the boy in.

On the way to his own room, Axel glanced at the door leading down to the pub, but he didn't go downstairs. He needed to be there if Bayden needed him. The other Dragons were quite capable of keeping things under control and locking up at the end of the night.

Shutting his bedroom door, Axel closed his eyes and rubbed the bridge of his nose. The image of Richards's cat landing on Bayden's back rushed to greet him. He was sure it would be stuck to the inside of his eyelids for months.

Just to prove a wolf could take it…

Axel wasn't sure if the boy needed a babysitter or a psychiatrist. He busied himself with stripping down and getting into bed, but the little voice in the back of his mind was as persistent as the image of Bayden being whipped by another man.

Forget a babysitter or a psychiatrist, what Bayden really needed was a good dom.

Chapter Six

Axel jerked from sound asleep to completely awake. It was impossible to open the roller doors on any of the lock-ups without creating one hell of a racket. They were as good as a burglar alarm. Jeans tugged hurriedly on, he raced down the backstairs, buttoning his fly as he went. His brain had barely managed to catch up with his body by the time he reached the backdoor.

Bayden...

Axel paused to catch his breath. Of course it was a good thing that no one was breaking in, but the idea of Bayden sneaking off at the crack of dawn didn't exactly fill him with the joys of spring.

As Axel watched, Bayden stepped into the lock-up, but he didn't make any attempt to jump on his bike and rush away. He moved his helmet to one side and crouched down next to the bike, inspecting it.

Axel hadn't thought about boots or a shirt before he threw himself down the stairs. He didn't bother to go back for them. He made his way slowly across the yard, the concrete rough under his bare feet, the morning air chilly against his bare chest.

Bayden had had the sense to get fully dressed before coming outside. Unaware that he had company, he ran his hands over the bike as if it was a lover who needed to be carefully inspected for any injuries after an extended absence.

Axel knew he hadn't made a sound, but Bayden looked up as if a herd of buffalo would have shown more stealth.

Bayden didn't wince at the way the skin on his back had to have protested his movements. Axel glanced at the back of Bayden's jacket, wondering how the hell he could tolerate it against his wounds, but he stopped himself asking about it, sure that a direct question about it would shut the boy down.

"Will your family be worried that you didn't come home last night?" he asked instead.

Bayden shook his head. "I don't live with them." A moment's pause. "I moved out a couple of years ago. I've got my own place."

"Out by the marina," Axel remembered.

Bayden turned his attention back to his bike. "Yeah, that's right."

A couple of years ago. He was twenty-three now. "You moved out when you were twenty-one?"

Bayden gave a curt nod, but Axel wasn't about to be put off just because Bayden's conversational skills stopped at around interrogation level.

He'd said before that he'd been given his bike for his twenty-first. Just how spoilt was he? "Was your flat another present when you turned twenty-one?"

Bayden jerked his head up. Sudden anger filled his gaze. "It's not something to joke about!" He snatched up his helmet.

Axel raised an eyebrow. "Want to fill me in on what I'm supposed to be joking about?"

Bayden glared at him, then hesitated as he seemed to realise that Axel genuinely had no idea what the hell had made Bayden so angry. "The anti-pack laws. They're not a joke."

Axel frowned as he searched through deep recesses of his memory. "Those? They're ancient. We studied them in school. They're not still in force." Except, suddenly, Axel wasn't so sure. "Are they?"

Bayden still had his helmet in hand. He studied Axel through narrowed eyes for a long time before he spoke. "They're still the law."

Axel shook his head as he tried to remember what the damn things were and failed.

"No more than two adult wolves can congregate in any one place," Bayden said, curtly.

"And adult means over twenty-one," Axel finished for him.

Another jerky nod, and Axel had the distinct impression that whatever he said next could shatter their tentative beginnings of an understanding past repairing.

"People actually enforce that law?"

Nod.

"So werewolves have no choice but to move out as soon as they turn twenty-one?"

Another sharper nod.

"Well, that's fucked up."

Bayden's gaze narrowed. "Yes, it is." He thought for a moment, then nodded again, a slower more considering gesture. The fact that Axel wasn't defending the laws seemed to have reassured him that Axel wasn't a complete arsehole. Bayden set his helmet down and went back to examining his bike.

Axel rested a shoulder against the lock-up's wall. Mother. Grandfather. There hadn't been any mention of a father, but it would be stupid to push for more info on his family at this point. And, damn it, he couldn't put off asking forever. "How's your back?"

"Wolves heal quickly," Bayden said, tracing his fingers over his bike's saddle.

From a whipping like that? "Overnight?" Axel asked.

Bayden seemed to think very carefully for several moments. When he straightened up, Axel half expected to be treated to another attempt at storming away in a huff. Instead, Bayden took off his jacket and laid it neatly on the motorbike's handlebars. He turned his back on Axel and pulled up his vest.

There were still vivid red lines painted across his skin, but it was nothing compared to the mess it had been in the previous night. Axel stepped forward.

The moment Axel touched his skin, Bayden tensed. It obviously wasn't because he was in pain.

"Problem?" Axel asked.

He was silent for so long, Axel became certain Bayden was trying to find a reasonably polite way to tell him to keep his hands to himself. But no.

Bayden shook his head. "It's fine."

Axel ran his fingers over the traces of the whipping, mentally picturing the way his back had appeared less than twelve hours ago. And now... "Wolves do heal quickly," Axel allowed, as he stepped back. It didn't make him feel any better about Bayden having been whipped for a bet.

Bayden pulled his vest down but he didn't rush to meet Axel's gaze. "Does that mean you won't try to tell me I can't ride today?"

Axel laughed. "You're allowed to ride. But you can leave your bike in the lock-up while you come back in for breakfast."

"I'm fine."

"It's not a suggestion," Axel said, mostly to see how Bayden would react.

Bayden met his gaze. He held it for several long seconds before finally looking down. "Okay."

Axel waited while Bayden carefully locked up. As they walked back inside, Axel reached out and ruffled Bayden's hair.

Bayden glanced up at him, quick and fleeting. His lips twitched into a half smile.

Upstairs, when Axel set to work in the kitchen, Bayden lingered in the doorway. Axel looked up from what he was doing just in time to see him reach into the pocket where he usually carried the money he won in his bets.

"Before I bought this place, it was a B&B," Axel said. "They charged for bed and breakfast. I don't."

Bayden moved his hand away from his pocket.

"Good boy."

Bayden glanced up at him. He smiled slightly more broadly, seeming both shy and pleased by the praise. Axel smiled back and pointed to the table. "Grab a seat. It won't be long."

"You don't want me to help?" Bayden checked.

Axel shook his head. "I've got it." He opened the fridge and looked inside. "If you're a vegetarian or whatever, now's the time to say."

"Anything's fine," Bayden said. "But you really don't need to give me breakfast."

Axel ignored that. It didn't take him long to have coffee brewing, and bacon and eggs on the go, but, by the time he looked across to Bayden again it was obvious the boy had used the time to work himself up to saying something.

"What you said last night—that I was in no condition to play…"

"Yes?"

"I'm fine today."

The words hung in the air, bright, sparkling and full of possibilities. Axel kept his attention on the frying pan, as he debated his choices. Damn, but it would be so easy to tumble Bayden straight into a scene. It was obvious the boy wouldn't say no to whatever he threw at him.

Images flashed through Axel's mind—most of them involving Bayden in various states of bondage in and around the pub. There wasn't a single piece of equipment in the back rooms that he wouldn't look fantastic on.

Axel looked over his shoulder.

His gaze met Bayden's, and other images hurried forward to push aside the pretty pictures of bondage and naked skin.

Bayden agreeing to be whipped by Richards for all the wrong reasons, or, at least, for reasons that only made sense to a wolf. The anger that made every muscle in Bayden's body tense when he thought about the way some humans treated wolves. The look in Bayden's eyes when he'd all but admitted he'd only ever played out mockeries of scenes where he'd had no intention of actually submitting to anyone.

"We're not doing a scene."

Bayden dropped his gaze. He put his hands on the table, obviously about to jerk himself to his feet and rush out.

"Not today," Axel added.

Bayden hesitated.

"Unless you're telling me it's a onetime offer?" Axel asked.

Bayden shook his head. "I'm not saying that."

"Good." Axel dished up the food, filling two plates with equal servings.

Bayden seemed about to speak several times, only to stop himself short.

"Pup?" Axel prompted as he put the plates on the table and sat down.

Bayden looked up. "I should wash my hands before breakfast."

Axel didn't chuckle, but it was a near run thing. He nodded to the sink. "Knock yourself out." He watched as Bayden scrubbed his hands with the intensity of a surgeon about to operate, blatantly playing for time before he came back to the table.

They'd both cleared their plates before Bayden finally spoke up. "The scene. You'll tell me when you want to?"

"I'll tell you," Axel promised.

Bayden didn't seem to know what to do with himself then. He looked from one plate to another. "I can clean up."

"There's no dish washer," Axel warned.

Bayden didn't even blink.

"Go ahead," Axel allowed.

A challenge, a puzzle, and a sub. Axel leaned back in his chair and smiled to himself as he watched Bayden dutifully work his way through the breakfast dishes. Yes, Axel could play the slow game for a guy who was all three of his favourite things wrapped up together in one very hot little package.

Bayden carefully unloaded the shopping bags from his panniers. He checked each one. Everything had survived the short journey intact.

His mother must have spotted him from the living room window, because she opened the door before he had a chance to knock.

"You didn't need to, love."

Bayden shrugged. "I was passing the shop on my way here. I thought I might as well save you the trip." He put the bags down on the doorstep and pushed his hands into his pockets. "Is he any better today?"

She hesitated for a moment, then stepped outside, wrapping her cardigan around her to ward off the chill autumn air. "You do know he's not going to get better, love." The words were gentle, but firm. "You understand that?"

Bayden nodded, but he couldn't meet her eye. "I know." He'd known for what felt like half a lifetime. "Sometimes it's just easier to…" Hope? Pretend? He sighed.

His mother cast a last look up the stairs and stepped away from the doorstep. A low wall ran along the edge of the garden. She brushed at the moss growing between the bricks, but that would never get it clean enough. Bayden shrugged his jacket off and put it on the wall for her, leather side down.

"Thank you."

Bayden sat next to her and waited.

"He's not going to get better. All the doctor can do is keep him as comfortable as possible." She stared down at her hands as she straightened the edge of her cardigan. "I know you don't like to think about what will happen afterwards, but we have to be practical. I've been making plans."

"You mean where you'd prefer to live?" Bayden asked.

"Yes."

Bayden glanced up at the flat. There were a lot of memories wrapped up in there. Since his grandfather had fallen ill, they weren't happy ones. "If you don't want to stay here, we can find somewhere else."

"That's not quite what I mean, love."

Bayden frowned. "You'll live with me. Not where I am at the moment, but here, or somewhere else. I don't mind where. We can…"

She put her hand over his and gently squeezed his fingers. Her expression was very serious. "I've been talking to one of the ladies who works at the Danville Project."

Bayden relaxed. Was that all? "You want to go back to work there?" As much as he hated the idea, he nodded and kept a smile pinned to his lips. "You don't need to. But, if you want to, we can find somewhere to live that's close to one of their sites and—"

"They've offered me a residential place," she cut in.

It was like being punched in the stomach. "There's no need for that."

"Bayden…"

He shook his head. "There's nothing humans can do to stop *two* wolves living under one roof. You'll live with me. Money won't be a problem. You can work at Danville, if you like, or you don't need to go back to work at all. I can—"

"It's what I want, love."

Bayden met her gaze. "You…" He shook his head again. "You don't mean that. You're just tired. It's too much, looking after granddad on your own. You should let me help more."

"Bayden—"

"You didn't say how he is today," Bayden reminded her.

She slid her fingers through her hair, pushing the long brown strands back off her face. "He's in pain. He hasn't complained, but… He'll need to see the doctor again." She hesitated and looked down. "Maybe later this week, or…" She sighed. When she smiled, there was no happiness in it. "Enough about us. How are you?"

"Fine," Bayden said. "You don't need to worry about me. Shall I go up and sit with him for a while, let you get some air?"

She shook her head and moved to stand up.

Bayden jolted to his feet and put his hand on her shoulder. "At least let me carry the shopping up before I go?"

For a long time, he thought she was going to say no. He didn't live there. He wasn't part of her pack any more. He had no right to interfere. She didn't have to accept his help. He held his breath until she finally nodded.

Picking up the bags, he made his way up, careful to avoid the creaky top stair and make as little noise as possible.

Setting the shopping bags on the kitchen table, he opened the furthest wall cabinet on the left and took the battered old tin from its hiding place at the back. There were two five pound notes and a couple of coins left.

He'd already counted out the money his mother's rent man would want. He added it to the tin, just as he had so many times since his grandfather had fallen ill.

Maybe Bayden couldn't stay under the same roof as his family without breaking the law. Maybe he wasn't technically part of their pack anymore. But there were some things that human laws couldn't stop him from doing.

He pulled the money he'd won a few nights ago at The Dragon's Lair out of his other pocket, along with what would have been his own rent. He dropped it all into the tin. It would be enough to cover the doctor's fees. It should cover whatever he'd prescribe too. If it wasn't, Bayden would get more.

Once he'd returned the tin to its usual place, Bayden made his way back outside.

His mother stood up when she saw him.

He managed a smile. "You'll let me know how it goes with the doctor, or if there's anything I can do?"

"You're already doing more than you should."

Bayden stared down at her.

Finally, she sighed. "I'll tell you." She stroked his cheek. "You're getting more like your father all the time. So stubborn. He'd be so proud if he could see you now."

Bayden hugged her, not sure if he held on a little longer than usual in an effort to comfort her or himself. Finally, he stepped back.

"You'll be careful?" she asked. "Keep your head down. No risks, okay?"

"I'll be fine," he promised, smiling over his shoulder at her as he turned down the path leading back to his bike.

Somehow, when he pulled away from the curb, he found himself turning toward The Dragon's Lair.

Chapter Seven

Bayden couldn't keep wasting time like this. He held back a sigh and sipped his Coke, but the facts remained the same. He couldn't afford to keep coming back to The Dragon's Lair so often, unless he was going to earn some money while he was there. Over a week had passed. Sitting around staring at Axel while he waited for him to decide he wanted to play with him was turning out to be a bloody expensive hobby.

Bayden stared at the screen behind the bar where the lines of bikes were clearly visible, but it was more habit than fear. A lot of the guys who drank there were serious about their bikes, they wouldn't let anyone hurt a classic Triumph, not even if it was owned by a wolf.

There was nothing to worry about at The Dragon's Lair. No one was ill. No one needed anything from him. It felt like it was a different world. It was safe and —

"Wolves have always had a reputation for being good lays." The voice belonged to Drac. The words were said so loudly Bayden knew the men talking wanted him to overhear their conversation.

He continued to study the screen, not inclined to acknowledge the existence of any human other than Axel.

"What do you think, Drac, false advertising?" That voice belonged to Hale — the guy with the shaved head, Axel's friend.

Bayden was going cross-eyed from staring at the screen so much. He turned his attention to his drink for a little while and rubbed at his temple.

Axel moved down the bar and stopped in front of him. "Okay, pup?"

No. I'm not okay. I want to know when the hell you're going to want to do that damn scene. If you've changed your mind, just bloody well tell me! Bayden bit back a sigh. "I'm fine."

Axel glanced down to where the other Black Dragons were sitting. "You know they're baiting you, trying to get a rise out of you?"

"I know." *But I really am a good lay. I'm more than happy to show you just how good — any time you're ready.*

"You know, we've only actually got his word for it that he's a shifter." That was Drac's voice, floating down from the other end of the bar again.

Bayden stared across the bar, mentally willing Axel to demand that he prove just how good at sex a wolf could be.

"I've never seen a shifter in his wolf form before," Griz chipped in.

Bayden kept all his attention on Axel. Axel didn't look away from him either.

"What do you say, Bayden? You up to proving you can back up all your big talk?" Hale demanded.

Bayden reluctantly turned in their direction. He wasn't interested in proving that particular skill set to them.

"I don't think you can shift at all," Griz went on. "In fact, I'd go so far as to bet you can't…"

It took Bayden a few moments to realise that Griz didn't want to screw him, or, at least, he wasn't suggesting Bayden should actually let him do that. Griz wanted to watch him shift.

Bayden tensed. A challenge was a challenge. A bet was a bet. A bit of extra money wouldn't go amiss. And showing the other side of himself was probably the quickest way for him to make sure he'd never be allowed to return to The Dragon's Lair.

It was one thing for Axel to want to play with someone he'd only ever seen look entirely human. But once Axel saw that side of him…

Bayden weighed up his options. It didn't take long. Backing down from a challenge from a human wasn't to be considered. Acting like he was ashamed of who he was, would never be an option. Not even if it gave him a little more time to sit in Axel's pub and imagine what it would be like to play with him.

"How much?" Luck was with Bayden; he sounded bored by the idea.

"Fifty?" Griz suggested.

There was no way he could up the price without abandoning the spoilt rich kid act that Axel liked so much. Bayden shrugged, got off his stool, and headed for the door.

"Where are you going?" Axel called after him.

Bayden paused. Wasn't that obvious? "Outside."

"You can't shift inside?"

Bayden frowned. "I can, but..."

"But?" Axel prompted.

"Most humans don't like wolves inside." Hell, most pubs wouldn't even let him inside in his human form, once they knew what he was.

"Inside is fine," Axel cut in. He looked Bayden up and down as if working out a whole host of calculations Bayden couldn't even guess at. "You can use one of the back rooms."

Bayden met his gaze for a moment. He didn't look pissed off. That was good. It probably wouldn't last, but it still felt good.

Axel called one of the younger Dragons, Tolmore, across to watch the bar before leading the way toward the back of the pub. Axel unlocked one of the doors.

It was the room with the spanking bench and the cage.

Axel paused by the door. "I'll hold the money," he said, when Griz went to step inside.

Axel turned to Drac and Hale. "Are you two coming in?"

"Yeah."

Axel held out his hand to them too. Bayden wasn't sure why, but Drac and Hale seemed to get it. They muttered under their breath, but they both paid up.

They hadn't been part of making the bet, there was no reason why they should have to pay to see it carried out, but Bayden couldn't deny that one fifty was going to be a lot more useful than just fifty. It would take the pressure off. It would mean he didn't have to find another way to earn any other money after he left the pub that night.

Axel closed the door behind them and came across to Bayden. He still had that assessing look in his eye, as if Bayden was a puzzle he needed to solve.

"What are the chances of you not being able to shift?" Axel asked.

Bayden blinked. "Last time I screwed it up I was five."

Axel smiled. "Fair enough." He stepped back to stand with the others. "It's your show."

Bayden pulled his vest over his head, folded it and put it on top of the spanking bench. Boots off, he undid his jeans and pushed them down his legs. Within a few seconds, he was completely naked.

He wouldn't usually turn his back on a group of humans in a room like that, but just this once, he made an exception. He turned, letting Axel see that there wasn't a single mark on his back from the previous week's whipping. If Axel still had any interest in screwing him after he saw him in his wolf form, it might tip the balance in Bayden's favour. Maybe a blank canvas was what Axel was waiting for.

Bayden took a deep breath. There was no reason to be anxious. It wasn't as if he hadn't been naked in front of guys before. Nothing was different this time. He could sense their interest in him. The scent of arousal filled the air.

No sign of nerves. No time for hesitation. There was no room for weakness when dealing with humans. Bayden turned to face them, but he didn't look for eye contact. He crouched down and placed his fingertips on the floor in front of him. Closing his eyes, he gave all his attention to finding that part of himself that was pure wolf.

He was aware of the human side of his mind shrinking as the wolf side grew stronger. From inside the change, that was the only thing he was really conscious of.

But, if he pushed himself to focus, he could tell his body was morphing to match the uppermost part of his psyche. The shape of his ribcage altered. His collar bones shortened, his hipbones twisted to make it easier for him to walk on four legs rather than two.

His weight came to rest on paws as his fingers shortened and his nails curved into claws. His snout lengthened. The base of his spine altered as his tail returned. There was no pain, no real sensation, but the chill in the air disappeared as his fur thickened and covered his entire body.

Bayden couldn't resist shaking in an effort to make his coat settle properly around him, but he didn't waste time stretching and really getting comfortable in this skin. There was no room for distractions in a world where either anger or fear could easily cause a human to lash out at a shifter in his wolf form. Bayden looked up.

The room was different from that angle. Everything seemed to loom over him. Through lupine eyes, the colours were more muted.

No angry shouts. No swinging fists or kicks from heavy boots. The humans were still standing exactly where they'd been when he began his shift. But now they came closer.

At least, Bayden guessed the other three stepped forward, too. It was harder than ever to remember there were people other than Axel in the room. Every line of him screamed his dominance. Yes. If there was such a thing as an alpha human, Axel really was it.

As the gap between them narrowed, Bayden forced himself to study Axel as objectively as possible, to look past the dominance and see what else Axel's body language and scent could tell him.

He didn't look angry or inclined to lash out. More importantly, he didn't smell disgusted, or appalled, or any of the other things Bayden had imagined he might be when coming face to face with the wolf side of him. He smelt…curious.

Griz stepped past Axel. He reached out to touch Bayden's head.

Forcing himself to neither pull away nor snap at his fingertips, Bayden remained motionless until he knew for sure what Griz intended to do.

"No," Axel said. "The deal was for you to see him, not touch him."

Griz looked over his shoulder, his fingers hovering in the air a few inches from Bayden's head. "What?"

"You want to lay a hand on him, ask him when he's in a position to answer you." Axel's tone allowed for no argument.

Griz stepped back. He said something to Drac and Hale, but Bayden kept his attention on Axel. Crouching down in front of him, Axel stared into Bayden's eyes.

Instinct kicked in. Bayden looked down. It took every bit of self-control he could scrape together not to acknowledge Axel's obvious dominance in any more overt way.

He didn't dip his head low to the floor; he didn't try to creep closer to Axel in the hope of being allowed to nuzzle and lick him. He didn't roll over on his back in a blatant display of respect either, but it was a near run thing.

All he did was stand as still as possible and wait for an order. His tail twitched, but he managed not to wag it too much.

"You've won your bet. You can change back whenever you want." Axel sounded completely calm.

Bayden waited for Axel to go back to the others, but he stayed crouched down in front of him.

He remained there as Bayden reached for the human side of himself and pulled it to the front of his world. His mind spun as he changed back before his body had even had time to properly settle into his wolf form, let alone build up the appropriate momentum to shift back.

The air turned cold. His bones lengthened and shortened by turn, forming an entirely different skeleton within him. The colours around him swirled until they settled into a far brighter version of themselves. Bayden gasped as his shift completed.

He wanted nothing more than to lower himself to his knees and rest there on the bare floor. But he was human shaped again, and wolves who looked human weren't supposed to be naked on the floor. He pulled himself to his feet as quickly as he could, doing his best to control each pair of muscles and appear neither clumsy nor weak in front of men who might still prove to be a threat.

He blinked open his eyes just in time to see Axel rising to his full height in front of him. Without warning, Axel blurred. The room tipped sideways.

Axel caught hold of Bayden's shoulders and steadied the world. "Easy now."

Bayden only realised that he was being nudged back to sit on something when he felt it behind him. Axel's hands stayed on his shoulders, supporting him. Bayden kept his eyes closed for a few seconds. When he opened them, Axel was right there in front of him.

Bayden stared up at him for several seconds, disorientated enough to be able to meet his gaze far more easily than he usually could. Axel's eyes looked very blue as Bayden's vision settled back into human clarity.

"Okay?" Axel asked.

Not sure his voice would come out as anything other than a growl if he tried to speak, Bayden nodded. He took a deep breath to clear his head. His sense of smell was still heightened. Axel's scent was changing again, now that Bayden was back in his human form.

Curiosity was fading away to be replaced with a different kind of interest. Bayden dropped his gaze. He was still naked. In a few moments, no one would need scent to know that Axel's interest in him was returned. Bayden swallowed, wondering if that should be considered a problem or not.

Axel was just a few inches away from him. Without either his clothes or his fur to get in the way, Bayden could feel the heat radiating from Axel's body. It took all his self-control not to lean forward and snuggle against him.

"It's safe to say you won that bet by a country mile." Axel still hadn't taken his hands off Bayden's shoulders. They felt nice there.

Bayden smiled at his teasing and remained very still, hoping that would encourage Axel to keep his hands where they were.

A movement behind Axel made Bayden look past him.

"Don't worry about them," Axel said. "They're leaving."

Now, when all Bayden's thoughts were human, but his lupine instincts were right there in the forefront of his brain, it was harder than ever to see Axel as anything other than an alpha wolf who deserved every other wolf's complete respect. In their own way, even humans seemed to understand that. Whether or not they'd intended to leave, the other Dragons filed out at Axel's command.

"You okay?"

Bayden nodded.

"Words," Axel corrected.

Bayden cleared his throat. "I'm fine." There was just a touch of wolf left in his voice.

Axel didn't strike out at the reminder of what Bayden was. He didn't pull away, either. "Do you always get dizzy when you shift back?"

"It happens sometimes." Especially when he hadn't eaten much for a few days. He straightened up, knowing it was stupid to let himself appear so vulnerable in front of a human. "I'm fine now."

Axel moved his hand from Bayden's shoulder, but only to push Bayden's hair back off his face. His other hand moved to Bayden's cheek. "How long does it take for your mind to switch from one to the other?"

Bayden frowned. "I don't know what you're asking."

Axel stroked his hair.

Bayden looked down. He glanced at what he was sitting on. A spanking bench. "Are you asking if I'm human enough to do what you want?"

Axel seemed to think about that very carefully. "I'm asking if there's a delay between you shifting back to looking human, and to you being able to make decisions the way a human can."

"You want to know if you'd be screwing a man or an animal." Bayden tried to turn away.

Axel tightened his grip on his hair and held him still. "I'm not insulting you."

Bayden froze. It was exactly what he'd said to Axel before. He'd meant it. It was possible that Axel meant it, too. Maybe Bayden was seeing insults just as easily as Axel, and where they didn't really exist.

Bayden nodded, willing to believe that was possible.

Axel stroked Bayden's hair back from his face again. Bayden managed not to lean into his touch too overtly.

"Are you mad at me again?" he blurted out.

Axel raised an eyebrow at him.

"About the bet," Bayden hinted.

Axel chuckled. "I object to seeing you get hurt, not gambling in general, pup." He stepped back. The world seemed far colder. "Steady?"

Bayden nodded. He glanced at his clothes.

"Go ahead," Axel allowed.

As Bayden got dressed, Axel got the money he'd held during the bet out of the pocket of his jeans.

Bayden barely glanced at the notes when Axel handed them over. It would all be there. Axel wasn't like other humans.

About to push the notes into his pocket, Bayden hesitated. The folded money actually felt thicker than he'd expected. He studied it more carefully. It wasn't one hundred and fifty pounds, it was two hundred.

Bayden peered down at the notes, his brain taking too long to kick into gear.

"Bayden?"

"The money's wrong. Three fifties is one hundred and fifty," he said, making sure to keep his tone extra respectful in case Axel thought he was criticising him.

"Four fifties," Axel corrected. "Four men watched you shift."

Bayden took fifty and held it out to him. "No."

"No?" Axel asked.

"No. You don't pay," Bayden clarified, his horror at the prospect making his words clipped.

"Why not?" Axel made no attempt to take the notes from him. "They did."

Bayden's pulse sped up. "It's different."

"Different how?" Axel tilted his head to the side. He was curious again.

Bayden bit back a growl. Wasn't it obvious? He looked down.

Axel tucked a knuckle under his chin, making him lift his gaze. "Different how?"

"Because if you'd said you wanted to see me shift, I'd have done it for free."

* * * * *

Those weren't words Bayden took lightly. It was no throw away phrase. As Axel stared down into his eyes, he had no doubt that they meant more to Bayden than an offer to shape shift upon request.

"It was a challenge," Bayden said, with obvious care. "They knew I could shift. They knew they'd lose. But it's like the whipping. They thought that getting me to shift in front of them would put me off balance. That it would make me see them as more dominant than me."

It was one way to define the other Dragons' own particular brand of hazing the new guy, Axel supposed. "Did it work?"

"If it had worked, I wouldn't have taken the money off them." Bayden looked down at the money he still held out to Axel.

"Because the money's all about making sure that humans know who lost a challenge, right?"

"Yes, but you didn't lose," Bayden pointed out, with what sounded like increasingly strained patience. "There was no challenge. I've never doubted that you're more dominant than me. And I don't want your money."

"It's that important to you?"

"Yes." Bayden proffered the money again.

His suspicions confirmed, Axel took the notes from him and pushed them into his back pocket without ever breaking eye contact. "Feel better?"

Bayden nodded. "Yes. Thank you."

So polite. Axel stroked his fingers down Bayden's check. There wasn't even a hint of stubble there, even though he'd had a full wolf's pelt a few moments ago. Looking at Bayden now, it was hard to imagine he could appear any other way. When he'd stared down at a wolf standing in the middle of the playroom, it had been impossible to imagine he'd ever looked human.

Axel pushed Bayden's hair back from his face again. Bayden accepted every touch without comment, but he didn't reach out to him in return. Because he was still half-sure his hands were paws? Because he wasn't that tactile a person?

Because he wouldn't touch someone he saw as more dominant than him without permission?

That was the problem with Bayden, there were so many different possible answers to every single question. And some questions were more important than where Bayden might choose to put his hands.

"You said they were challenging you—do you know why?"

"Because they're arseholes?"

"That's one reason," Axel said with a chuckle. "But do you know what a hazing is?"

Bayden shrugged.

"It's a way of testing a new guy to see what he's made of, to check how he'll react and where he'll fit into the group."

Bayden glanced up. "Humans don't just know?"

"Wolves do?"

Bayden frowned. "It's usually pretty obvious."

"Well, humans like to check. They've done the same to everyone who they think might ride with us."

Bayden blinked at him.

"Have you ever ridden with a club?"

Bayden shook his head. He looked toward the door the other Dragons had just left through. "They won't like it. They won't want me riding with them."

Axel raised an eyebrow. They might not like it, but they'd bloody well learn to accept it quickly, if they had any sense. "I want you riding with us."

Bayden glanced up at him. He nodded. There was still that slight frown, as if he couldn't understand why anyone would want him around. Axel pushed his fingers through Bayden's hair again, tugging lightly at the strands. Bayden made no comment.

"Does it bother you when they challenge you?"

Shrug. If Bayden understood that some subs might find being challenged by a group of men who were all a damn sight bigger, older and more experienced than him, intimidating, he certainly didn't seem to share the sentiment.

"What if you lose?" Axel asked.

"I don't lose." He tilted his chin up. Complete confidence.

Axel smiled. "I'll give you a choice," he offered. "I can tell them to back off and leave you be. They'll accept that." Just like he'd accept it if one of them told him to stop teasing their sub—but that part of the explanation could wait for another time.

Bayden's frown didn't ease.

"Or, you can tell me that it doesn't bother you when they throw challenges at you—that you prefer to deal with them yourself."

Bayden peered up at him as if he was speaking a different language. "They're not a problem." They were apparently all filed firmly under harmless in his mind.

Axel knew damn well that they posed no actual threat to a novice sub, but that didn't mean they weren't capable of making a guy as uncomfortable as hell until they accepted him as part of the group. "They won't hurt you. They're not interested in breaking you, but they'll do their damnedest to push your buttons and try to get a rise out of you."

"I can look after myself.

"Fair enough," Axel allowed. "If you change your mind, let me know."

Bayden nodded. Axel's fingers still lingered in his hair. The gesture meant Bayden effectively tugged at the strands. From the way his lips twitched into a smile, that wasn't a problem for him.

Axel forced himself to step back. Bayden accepted that decision just as calmly as he'd accepted every touch.

If he was going to be fighting his own battles, there were a few things to clear up. "What you said before, about tearing someone's throat out?" Axel said.

Bayden suddenly looked wary. "Yes?"

"I don't care if you lose a bet," Axel said. "But if you win, stick to cash and sarcasm? Fighting dirty during a hazing is okay; fighting to the death isn't."

"Okay." His expression cleared a little.

"Ready?"

Bayden looked at the door. When he nodded again, he seemed to have realised that he'd probably need to deal with them again that night.

Back in the main room, Axel went behind the bar while Bayden returned to his stool. He barely had time to sit down.

"Is it all wolves who can't hold their drink, or just you?" Hale asked, from further down the bar.

Bayden looked up. He met Axel's eyes. Axel managed to keep a straight face, but he couldn't have hoped for a better test.

"Is that why wolves have a reputation for being drunks, because it only takes one pint to get them steaming?" Drac asked.

Bayden's fist tightened around his bottle of Coke. The plastic crunched. The light in his eyes changed as he didn't so much check his anger as much as let it cool into something far harsher. "Wolves can drink."

"We all know that wolves can drink — the question is whether you can handle it when you do?" Hale asked.

Bayden met Axel's gaze. It took Axel a moment to realise that Bayden wasn't waiting for him to step in and tell them to stop picking on him, he fully expected Axel to pass on what Bayden had told him about wolves and alcohol — to cut any advantage he had out from under him.

Axel raised an eyebrow at the idea. Bayden tilted his head to one side. He looked confused, but he gradually seemed to realise that he didn't need to worry about his secrets being revealed.

"You buy it, I'll drink it," he told the other guys.

Laughter flowed down from the other end of the bar. "What do you say, Axel?" Griz asked.

"If you drink, you don't ride," Axel warned Bayden. "You can put your bike in the lock-up and stay here tonight." He thought for a moment. "Best put it there now." He handed Bayden the key to the lock-up—for some reason, he hadn't bothered to clip it back onto his key chain since the last time Bayden borrowed it.

As Bayden went to stow his bike away, Axel turned his attention to his friends. "Sometimes I'm not sure if I'm running a motorcycle club or babysitting toddlers."

Hale laughed. "Going to step in and warn us to play nicely with your puppy?"

It was a bloody stupid choice of words. Axel raised an eyebrow at anyone but him *playing* with Bayden.

"Ha. Like we're suicidal enough to try to get your boy into a scene," Drac said.

Hale raised an eyebrow at Axel in return. "Puppy play's never been my thing."

"Does this mean you don't have a problem with us ragging on the boy?" Griz asked.

"Bayden can stand up for himself." Especially when he had no chance of losing this particular challenge.

Everyone turned as Bayden resumed his seat. "Second thoughts, wolf-boy?"

Bayden ignored him.

"You're seriously going to go deaf every time I call you that?" Drac asked.

Bayden took a sip of his Coke.

"Bayden," Griz said, with overt politeness and very obvious amusement. "What do you drink when you are drinking?"

"I tried vodka once," Bayden offered.

Griz looked across at Axel. "A double vodka then."

Axel poured the drink, marked it down on Griz's tab and handed the glass to Bayden.

"Are you supposed to down it in one?"

"Go for it," Griz suggested.

Bayden took a deep breath and tossed it back. He didn't choke on it, but from the way he wrinkled his nose when he swallowed it down, he hadn't been lying when he'd claimed to hate the taste.

Axel laughed along with everyone else.

Bayden glanced up at him.

"Almost tastes medicinal, doesn't it?" Axel said.

Bayden ducked his head at the reminder of the first time they'd met. For the first time since they returned to the bar room, he let a smile creep through.

"Ever tried anything else?" Hale asked.

Bayden shook his head.

Hale ran his gaze over the top shelf behind the bar. "Whisky, double."

"You know you're paying for this, right?" Axel asked.

From the amusement dancing in their eyes, they all seemed to think it would be worth the investment.

He poured a whisky and set it in front of Bayden.

Bayden sniffed at it. He took a cautious sip.

"Well?" Axel asked.

"It's not as bad as the last one." He took another sip.

"I wonder how far along the top row he could get?" Hale mused.

"I wonder how far along the top row a cop's wallet can get," Axel said.

"You're a cop?" Bayden said, turning to Hale.

"What's the problem, you got a guilty conscience?" Hale asked.

Before anyone else could say anything, another guy came up to the bar to order a drink. Hale smiled and turned to him. "You want to buy Bayden one at the same time. He reckons he can out drink any human."

Axel shook his head, but the gambit worked. Everyone who came up to the bar seemed more than happy to buy Bayden a drink. The fact that Bayden had turned down all their drinks whenever they'd hit on him probably didn't make them disinclined to ante up.

Half an hour, four pints, and over a dozen shots later, Bayden lifted a glass of tequila to his nose and sniffed sceptically at it. He downed the drink in one, obviously wanting to get it over with. For the first time that night, he choked. A couple of the other guys chuckled. So did Axel.

"Damn, that's disgusting," Bayden muttered as he caught his breath. "Does anyone really drink this when they don't have a point to prove?"

Axel took the empty glass and set it on the counter behind him.

"You proved yourself eight shots ago," Axel said. "At this point, they've gone straight through impressed and it's all about morbid curiosity to see what you'll do when the alcohol finally hits you."

Bayden pushed his hair back off his face. Apparently, vodka wasn't the only drink that made him sleepy. A few moments passed. Bayden shifted his position on his stool.

Axel's lips twitched. "You know the idea is to see how much you can drink without falling over, not how much you can handle without needing to take a leak, right?"

Bayden got off his stool, and promptly headed off in the wrong direction.

"Pup?"

Bayden turned back to him.

"Gents room is that way."

Bayden blinked at him. He obviously wasn't working on all cylinders, but his balance was still there. He didn't sway as he walked past the other Dragons on the way to the toilets.

"Is this where you give us the usual lecture about not picking on the new guy?" Griz asked.

"No. If he's going to ride with us, he'll have to get used to you all sooner or later."

Silence fell over them.

"Ride as in—on the back of your bike, right?" Drac asked.

"Ride as in ride—his own bike," Axel corrected. "You've seen what he rides, haven't you?"

"He's a wolf."

"A wolf that's already proven that he can fight better than any man here, and take a whipping that would scare most novices away. He's made it clear he's not afraid of any of you. Hell, he can even drink you all under the table. What's your argument against him?"

"You're serious," Hale said.

"You're the ones testing him. Can't complain if he wins, can you?"

"There are other guys who've been waiting in the wings for a damn sight longer than him," Hale argued.

Axel met Hale's gaze and held it. "If we wanted them in the club, they wouldn't have been left kicking their heels in the wings, would they?"

"Look, you want to screw a wolf, fine," Hale said. "He's hot—hell if you hadn't seen him first I might even have done him myself, but…"

"But?"

"Wolves are trouble. You can't trust them."

"If that's true, it'll show through while he's tagging along, and he won't be invited to join," Axel shot back.

"What about any trouble he causes in the meantime?" Griz asked.

"My invite, my responsibility," Axel said, without hesitation.

Just at that moment, Axel spotted Bayden making his way back to his seat. He stopped short of getting on his stool and met Axel's gaze.

"You know that if you want to ride with the club, you'll have to work for it," Hale said. "You'll have to prove to all the existing members that you're serious about wanting to be part

of the club. That means you have to do what we say—
everything we say."

Axel still held Bayden's gaze. Whatever Bayden saw in
his expression, it made him frown. He turned to the other
Dragons. He looked them up and down, each man in turn.

"Well?" Drac asked.

Bayden shrugged. "Could be worse."

"Oh?"

"I could be one of the guys who just admitted there was
no way in hell they're dominant enough to get me to do what
they say, unless they stoop to blackmail." He frowned. "Or is
it bribery?" He blinked, as if trying to work out the correct
label was his only concern in the world.

He turned back to Axel.

"Sit down, before you fall asleep on your feet." Axel
looked back down the bar to the other guys. There were a
variety of reactions on display.

Griz had decided to be amused rather than offended
and was grinning into his drink. Drac looked like he was on
the verge of labelling him a wannabe dom rather than a bratty
sub. Hale just looked pissed off.

Bayden propped his head up with one elbow on the
bar. He really was sleepy.

"Okay, pup?" Axel asked an hour later, when the last
few stragglers had been ushered out and he'd locked the door
in their wake.

Bayden slid off his stool. "I'm fine." It might have
sounded more convincing if he hadn't had to stop halfway
through his answer and cover his mouth when he yawned.

"Come on. Upstairs." He put his hand on Bayden's
shoulder and steered him along. He didn't feel as steady as he
looked.

"How are you really feeling?" Axel asked, as he closed
the door to the flat behind them.

"I'm fine."

"The truth, pup."

Bayden blinked up at him. "Fine. Just a bit sleepy." He looked down for a moment, looking just slightly shy. "We can do whatever you want."

Axel shook his head. "Bad idea." He settled his hands on Bayden's shoulders, holding him steady.

"You don't want to?"

Axel pushed Bayden's hair back from his face. "No, I don't."

Bayden frowned. "Because of the challenge?"

"Yes."

Axel expected a sleepy nod of acceptance, or perhaps a reminder that he was fine, but Bayden tensed. He tried to pull away. Axel tightened his hold on him, still not convinced the alcohol wasn't going to kick in at some point.

"I should go," Bayden said.

"That's a bad idea too."

Bayden frowned up at him.

"The challenge," Axel reminded him, patiently.

"You meant the drinking one?"

Axel caught up. "That's the only one that makes anything a bad idea."

Bayden glanced up at him, full of so much uncertainty.

"Did you think it would make a difference once I saw you shift?"

Bayden shrugged, but the alcohol had rendered his mask imperfect. He looked very young, very unsure about everything.

"Can you control the shift and make sure you stay human when we're playing or screwing?"

Bayden nodded.

"Then it doesn't make any difference at all."

Axel stroked Bayden's cheek with his knuckles. Obviously, there'd been people who'd reacted badly to seeing the other side of him. Anger spiked inside Axel. The protective feeling he'd felt toward Bayden since that first stupid fight doubled yet again.

Axel slid his knuckles under Bayden's chin. Bayden looked up at him, wary and strangely trusting at the same time.

"You're sloshed, and there's no way in hell you'll stay awake for more than five minutes of anything. I don't want you falling asleep on me."

"I wouldn't do that!"

Axel slid an arm around Bayden, tugging him closer. He pressed a kiss to his hairline and encouraged Bayden to rest his head on his shoulder.

Bayden seemed confused for a moment, but, perhaps because of his sleepiness, he soon relaxed and snuggled against him, tucking his face into Axel's neck as snuggly as a real puppy.

"Do you have anywhere you need to be tomorrow morning?" Axel asked.

Bayden shook his head.

"No, think about it properly, pup. Is there a time you need to be anywhere?"

Bayden shook his head again. "Whatever you want," he mumbled into Axel's shoulder.

"Right now, all I want you to do is get some sleep." He led Bayden into the guest bedroom and nudged him into sitting on the edge of the bed. "Do you feel sick?"

Bayden shook his head.

Axel looked him over sceptically. He wasn't sure how any species could drink as much as Bayden had and not have to throw up, but Bayden didn't even seem to understand the question. "Get some sleep."

He had barely turned to the door when Bayden leaned over and rested his head on the pillow, still fully clothed.

Axel rolled his eyes and retraced his steps. "Get up."

Bayden blinked open his eyes and obeyed.

"Clothes off."

He began to obey that order too. "You've changed your mind?"

Axel folded back the blankets. When he looked over his shoulder, Bayden was naked. Axel didn't give himself time to admire the view. "Get in."

Bayden got into bed, looking confused again. Axel quickly tossed the blanket up over him. "Sleep."

He left then, while he could still remember why it would defeat the point of putting the boy to sleep in the bloody guest room, if he gave into the temptation to sleep in there with him.

Chapter Eight

Bayden stayed by his mother's front door, watching her walk down the front garden path and out of sight, before making his way upstairs.

Rather than head straight for his grandfather's bedroom at the back of the flat, he went into the kitchen. He unearthed the tin from its hiding place and checked how much it contained. Taking his money out of his back pocket, he added another fifty to the tin.

A quick check of the other cabinets in the kitchen, and he breathed a little easier. There was plenty of food there for the next few days, and he still had enough left over to pay his own rent when he got back to his place that night.

Finally, he made his way to his grandfather's room and nudged the door open.

"I'm awake."

Bayden opened the door wider and smiled at his grandfather. "Hi." He sat on the chair next to the bed. "How are you feeling?"

"I'm fine." The words didn't mean much, but his voice was stronger than it had been the last time Bayden spoke to him. His skin was pale, but there was a touch of colour in his cheeks. His gaze was sharp. "I heard you in the kitchen."

"There's plenty in the tin. And plenty that can go in to top it up," Bayden promised. "You don't need to worry."

"Be careful. Earn too much too quickly, and you'll draw attention, set the humans' backs up."

"It's fine." Bayden looked down at his hands. "I found a new place to pick up fights. No one knows me there. It's easy money."

His grandfather tried to sit up straighter. Bayden sprang forward and altered his grandfather's pillows to give him more support. His grandfather slumped back as Bayden straightened his blankets.

"What kind of place is it?"

"A pub," Bayden said. "The Dragon's Lair, it's on the road out of the city."

His grandfather took a shaky breath. Bayden could hear his lungs fighting for each molecule of oxygen. "Just be careful."

"It's fine," Bayden promised. "The guy who owns the pub — Axel. He'd never let anything get out of hand and —"

"Not his job."

Bayden glanced up. "Axel's..."

His grandfather met his eyes. "It's not his job to look out for you, Bayden. You look out for yourself. You know that. Humans are...humans. It's one thing to fight one, another to trust him."

He's invited me to ride with his club later today. Bayden looked down. "I know."

"You have to keep your wits about you. You know what humans are like. You can't let them start making decisions for you. You know where that leads."

Bayden was about to say that Axel had no interest in making his decisions for him, but the lie stuck in his throat. The fact that Axel wanted to boss him about because he was kinky rather than because he was a bully didn't seem to be that helpful.

He could feel his grandfather's pale blue gaze moving over him, studying him, assessing him. "Your mother worries about you. She's concerned you'll get into the same trouble she did when she was younger."

Bayden kept his eyes lowered, knowing it wasn't just his mother who was worried. In that particular moment, the fact he was the most dominant wolf in the room counted for nothing. He was back to being a kid who knew that neither his mother nor his grandfather needed anything extra to deal with. "I'm fine," he promised. He wasn't a little kid who couldn't do anything to help anymore. "I've got everything under control."

"Have you eaten today?"

Axel made sure I ate before I left his place. Bayden nodded. He shuffled forward in his seat. "Everything's fine. You don't need to stress yourself out. I know better than to trust any human. Just rest, please?"

His grandfather nodded. He closed his eyes for a moment, but quickly opened them. "It won't be for long. Another week or two, and I'll be up and about. Once I'm back in work, it'll be easier all around."

Bayden forced a smile and nodded. It wouldn't be long. As much as he tried to avoid thinking about it, every time he saw his grandfather, it was increasingly obvious that it wouldn't be long. The conversation had already been too much for him. His eyelids started to drop. Bayden remained still and silent. As he heard his grandfather's struggling breaths settle into a sleeping rhythm, Bayden closed his own eyes.

As if searching for something, anything, else to focus on, his mind rushed back to Axel. There was no way he could tell his grandfather he was going to ride with them, no way he could try to explain what Axel was, how he was different than other humans. It would only worry his grandfather.

But Axel was different. He knew Bayden was a wolf, he'd seen him as a wolf, and he was still different.

And, if the other Dragons weren't so different from all the other humans Bayden had met, that wasn't a bad thing. It made them predictable in a way Axel wasn't, and predictable was a good quality in men who were inclined to challenge him.

When Bayden heard the gentle tap on the front door, he slipped silently out of the room, leaving his grandfather to sleep.

Stepping outside, he held the front door for his mother.

"He's fine. He's been sleeping for about half an hour," he said as they swapped places, so she stood just inside the flat and he was on the step outside. "How did your meeting with the people at Danville go?"

"They've agreed that I can move in there after…"

Bayden ground his teeth together.

"It will be for the best, sweetheart. There are people there who need my help. I can be useful there, and you can be free to get on with your own things."

Bayden bit back everything he wanted to say. She didn't need anyone arguing with her. He didn't even have the right to try to change her mind yet. When the time came, it would be different. He forced a smile. "You'll let me know if there's anything you need?"

She pressed a kiss to his check. "You're a good wolf, Bayden."

"You'll let me know?" he pushed.

When she finally nodded, he turned to walk down the path.

"Keep your head down, love."

Bayden looked over his shoulder. He nodded that he'd heard, but he didn't go so far as to agree to follow her advice. He doubted either she or his grandfather would approve, but spoiled little rich boys didn't need to keep their heads down. They got to ride with human bikers. They got to have Axel smile at them.

Or course, if those rich boys happened to be wolves, they also had to be practical. Bayden made a quick stop on his way back to the pub to meet the Dragons.

* * * * *

"So, is it true? Are werewolves as good a shag as everyone says they are?"

Axel raised an eyebrow. "After he drank enough to float a small navy, what kind of man would find out?"

103

"He looked sober enough to me," Hale said.

"He was drunk enough to sleep for fourteen hours straight." Axel smiled at the memory. Bayden hadn't even blinked until lunchtime, and even then, it had taken a hell of a lot of shoulder shaking to make that happen.

"So you're chasing, you just want to make sure you catch him when he's sober?" Drac asked.

"Who said I'm chasing?" Only an idiot would chase a man who was even part wolf. Wolves weren't prey. When the time was right, the boy would come to him, no chasing necessary. It was one of the very few things Axel was sure about when it came to Bayden.

"If you're not interested..." Hale mused.

"If any of you lay a hand on him, you're looking for a new place to drink and a new club to ride with, and, at that point, I'll just be getting started."

They laughed. Axel wasn't surprised. He'd have laughed at anyone else who felt so possessive over a boy who he hadn't even screwed, let alone collared.

"You know, I'm starting to wonder who the dom is between you two," Griz said. "Is wolf-boy going to be your puppy, or are you going to be the rich boy's bit of rough?"

Axel grinned. "I'm not surprised you're confused. He hasn't given any of you guys any reason to think he wants to sub to you, has he? What was it you had to stoop to— blackmail or bribery?"

Hale made a pissed off noise in the back of his throat. "Since when are you interested in brats, anyway?"

Axel had been keeping an eye on the door. He spotted Bayden the moment he stepped in and lost all interest in talking to Hale. Bayden was wearing those damn sun glasses again, but he took them off as he walked across the room.

Even if the pub wasn't open, habit had put Axel behind the bar. "Grab a seat. We're only waiting for two more before we head out."

Bayden settled himself on the stool furthest away from the other club guys, same as he always did. He'd only been there two seconds before Axel spotted a movement out of the corner of his eye. A packet slid down the bar toward Bayden.

Bayden picked it up as Axel stepped closer to get a better view. Dog biscuits. Bayden stared at the picture of an overjoyed Labrador on the front of the packet as if deep in thought. Everyone else stared at him.

Axel checked the instinct to step in. He forced himself to wait and see if Bayden could deal with it on his own first. What would a wolf think of being treated like a dog?

Bayden opened the packet. He took out a biscuit and casually popped it in his mouth. He crunched and swallowed it as he read the information on the back of the packet. Everyone gawped as if it was the most fascinating thing they'd ever seen. Axel mentally nodded his approval.

Bayden got off his stool and approached the other guys. He offered the packet to them. "It's rude not to share, right?"

Tolmore was closest to him. He was the newest member of the club and the one who'd slid the biscuits down the bar. He looked from the packet, to Bayden and back again.

"Or aren't humans up to it?" Bayden asked.

"Humans aren't dogs. We don't eat dog treats."

"Neither do wolves," Bayden said, perfectly calmly. "But we don't back down when someone challenges us, either."

Tolmore straightened up. He'd been with them for long enough to know that, even if he was dealing with a tag along, a man had to be able to take whatever he dished out.

He took a brown bone shaped biscuit out of the packet. His disgust was obvious, but he put it to his teeth and tried to bite through it. "Damn things are made of iron." He frowned at it and tossed it in the bin behind the bar.

Bayden threw a similar biscuit up in the air, caught it in his mouth and bit through it with ease. It wasn't quite a threat to tear out anyone's throat, but it was hard not to wonder how easily Bayden could snap a human bone with his teeth.

"Anyone else?" Bayden offered the bag around, taking in every man except Axel, challenging every man except Axel. No one said anything. Bayden shrugged. "More for me, I guess." He crunched another one on his way back to his seat.

Bayden had been carrying his jacket when he came in. He'd put it on the stool next to him when he sat down. Axel saw him fidget with it. A moment later, Bayden slid something along the dark, battered surface of the bar. It collided with Tolmore's arm.

Axel realised what it was at the same time as Tolmore. A tin of cheap dog food. The way Tolmore pulled back, it might as well have contained live snakes.

"Something softer for you." Bayden ate another dog biscuit with every sign of enjoyment. "The difference between you and me isn't that I can shape shift," he added, as the silence stretched out. "It's that I'll do anything I bet another man won't do."

Tolmore looked at the tin.

Bayden smiled but there was no humour in his expression. "Ante up and do half, or let the dog food bullshit drop — either is fine by me."

Tolmore grabbed the tin and threw it in the bin behind the bar without a word.

Bayden nodded his acceptance of his decision as Axel went down the bar toward him.

"You just happened to have a tin of dog food with you?"

Bayden shrugged. "Humans get predictable after a while."

"What would you have done if he'd anted up?" Axel asked.

"I told you I've done worse things than take a whipping to prove a point. I meant it." He looked at the bag of biscuits. "At least these aren't so bad. The chicken flavoured ones are quite nice."

Axel reached across the bar and stroked his cheek. "Well done, pup."

Bayden smiled that same smile that could suddenly make him look sweet as hell and not at all like the kind of sub who could stare down a dom like Tolmore.

"Do you have a mobile with you?" Axel asked.

Bayden nodded. He got it out of his pocket. Axel had expected it to be the very latest in high tech design, but it looked like a cheaper version of something Axel had owned five years ago.

"I thought you were supposed to be loaded," Griz said, as he joined them at that end of the bar.

Bayden looked up at him.

Griz nodded to the phone. "That's got to be ten years old."

Bayden huffed. "My bike's over fifty years old. That works just fine too. Throwing stuff away for no reason is a human thing." He put Axel's number into the phone and gave up his in return.

Axel went through the route with him, checking that he knew the area and what to do if he ran into trouble. "Tag alongs always ride at the back. Just follow the guy in front of you, and you'll do fine."

Bayden nodded.

"The route's a loop, so we'll end up back here," Axel added, once all the boring bits of protocol were taken care of. "Stick around when the others leave."

Bayden met his gaze for a moment. He seemed to realise that Axel wasn't just suggesting he hang around for a first-ride debrief. He smiled.

Axel found himself smiling to himself as he went off to set everything in motion, too. The boy was sober and un-whipped. Finally, the world seemed to include possibilities that didn't involve the God-damned guest room.

* * * * *

"Well?"

Bayden took off his helmet and turned to face Axel.

"This is the point where you either say you like the idea of riding with a club, or you say thanks but it's not for you," Axel said.

It's what running with a pack must have been like, back when wolves were allowed to live in packs. Bayden couldn't actually say that, but it didn't change the facts. His heart raced, his mind spun with adrenaline, and he had no doubt that riding with a club that Axel led was as close as a wolf could get to what running with a true alpha's pack must have felt like.

He took a deep breath and pushed his hair back from his face. Telling a human anything was dangerous, but, in that moment, it was a risk he was willing to take. "It was good. I liked it."

Axel didn't try to take it away the moment he found out a wolf liked it. He got off his bike and opened the lock-up next to the one where Bayden had put his bike before.

"Go on," Axel said. "You've got your key with you?"

Bayden unlocked the roller door and put his bike safely inside. Axel was done before him but he waited with apparent patience for Bayden to catch up.

He settled his hand on Bayden's shoulder as they made their way inside and up to his flat. The contact didn't seem to serve any other purpose beyond Axel liking to touch him.

Bayden took another deep breath. Scent didn't lie. Axel was as interested in him as he had ever been. And, if the only problem before was that Bayden had been drinking, there was no reason for them not to play now.

Bayden wasn't sure where he'd expected Axel to go when they got upstairs, but it hadn't been the kitchen.

"What do you usually do on Sundays?" Axel asked. "Or on any day of the week, come to that. You've never said what you do when you're not here."

Bayden shrugged, trying to work out where the conversation was going, and why the hell there even needed to be conversation.

"That's informative." Axel smiled when he said it, but he raised an eyebrow too, not entirely impressed.

Bayden half-shrugged again. What would the rich idiot that Axel wanted to screw do with his time?

"The truth doesn't need this much thinking about." Axel opened the fridge and started to get out several meals worth of food.

"Nothing much," Bayden offered.

"Maybe you meet up with other wolves?" Axel suggested.

There was no hint of condemnation in Axel's tone, but instinct took over. Bayden quickly shook his head.

"Never?" Axel asked, temporarily forgetting about his food.

Bayden shook his head again. "We don't do that." He was still standing by the kitchen door. It took all he had not to step back and retreat from both the room and a conversation that seemed destined to cover dangerous ground.

Axel frowned. "I'm not accusing you of anything, pup."

Bayden met his gaze. "You're talking about sex," he realised. He relaxed. "You're just asking me if I have sex with other wolves."

"Yes. What did you think I was asking you about?"

Bayden hesitated. "I thought you meant meet up like a…like a pack. Wolves don't do that."

"Because of the wolf-laws," Axel said.

"There's no wolf in those laws!" Bayden bit out before he could stop himself.

Axel met his gaze.

Bayden pushed his hand through his hair as he did his best to push down the wave of anger that always came with any mention of those laws. It was stupid to let a human see when something got to him, but for the first time in his life, he didn't want to hide it—he wanted Axel to understand.

"I studied them in school too. I know what the human text books say." Even as Bayden spoke, he was back in his old school—the only wolf in a class full of human children. The teacher was standing at the front of the class, reading from one of those books. The things those books said. His hand curled into a fist. "Those laws are made by humans, they're enforced by humans. They're human-laws. There's no wolf in them."

"You called them the anti-pack laws," Axel recalled.

Bayden nodded, watching Axel warily for any sign that he'd been a fool to trust him.

"Because they were designed to make sure packs never reformed after the..." Axel trailed off, as if not sure of the right word.

"The Captivities," Bayden filled in for him. His voice was entirely calm but his fingers were starting to cramp. His heart raced. As short as his nails were, they risked drawing blood as they bit into his palm.

"That's what wolves call what happened too?" Axel checked.

Bayden nodded.

Axel looked down at Bayden's clenched fist.

Somehow, Bayden managed to unfurl his fingers. "We don't talk about it." Their eyes met as they both looked away from Bayden's hand.

"We don't need to talk about that right now," Axel allowed.

Bayden breathed a little easier.

Axel worked in silence for a few moments. By the time he decided he wanted to talk again, Bayden had himself back under control, even if he still had no idea how to get Axel to forget about food in favour of sex.

"I have a theory," Axel announced.

Bayden waited, warily, to hear it.

"I don't think you've ever hooked up with a human when it wasn't for a bet. I think the only guys you've played with because you actually wanted to, have been other shifters. Am I right?"

"I know what I'm doing with a human."

Axel began cutting up some of the vegetables he'd taken out of the fridge. "Doesn't answer the question."

"Yes," Bayden said, making a real effort to keep his tone respectful. "It's always been another wolf. But, I do know—"

"Any wolf in particular?" Axel cut in.

Bayden shook his head.

"You know, I'm less likely to cut one of my fingers off if you answer out loud," Axel said.

"No one in particular," Bayden enunciated carefully.

"Good boy." Axel was working as he spoke, the words sounded casual, almost distracted, but they still went straight to Bayden's core.

He bit back a sigh. "Look, if you've changed your mind about wanting to…"

Axel turned to face him. He didn't look like a man who'd changed his mind.

Bayden looked down. "Nothing's different just because I can shift. You can treat me exactly the same way you would a human."

"You'd act differently with a wolf than a human." Axel spoke with complete confidence.

Bayden made no reply.

"I can usually read guys pretty well. I can usually tell if they're club guys who've subbed to a dozen different men, or if the closest they've got to leather is jerking off watching internet porn. You're harder to read."

Bayden rubbed the back of his neck.

"You might have screwed your way through dozens of men. You might never have done more than grope another boy in the shadows of a club. You might be used to scenes that run completely differently because you're used to wolves. I've no intention of doing anything until I know where you're coming from."

"I know what I'm doing with humans," Bayden repeated.

Axel smiled. "Tell me about how things work with another wolf." He thought for a moment. "The laws would make a club just for wolves impossible, wouldn't it? So where would you meet another wolf?"

"In a human club." There was no harm in telling a human that, was there? It couldn't be used against him.

Axel considered that. "Not all wolves have amber eyes like you, do they?"

"Not all humans have blue eyes like you," Bayden pointed out. Wondering if there was any way at all to get Axel to reconsider the whole conversation thing and skip straight to screwing him, or whipping him, or, well, anything that didn't involve talking.

Axel chuckled. "Fair point, but I meant that not all werewolves have eyes that make the fact that they're shifters obvious."

"Some wolves can pass for human among humans," Bayden allowed.

"But another wolf would still recognise them?"

"Yes."

"You could find another wolf in a crowd of humans?"

"Scent doesn't lie," Bayden said.

Axel took that announcement in his stride. "So, you're in a human club. You sense another wolf is there and…"

Bayden looked at the chopping board. "Is there anything you want me to do?"

"Yes—answer my question." Axel smiled when their eyes met. "You can pour yourself a coffee and take a seat as well."

Bayden followed the last two parts of the order, but the bit about answering his question was harder.

"Problem?" Axel asked after a while.

Bayden studied his coffee. The hot, dark liquid offered up no solutions. "It's not something that's talked about."

"You mean with humans? Am I asking you to give up species secrets?"

Bayden shook his head. "No. It's not that. It's something you just do, not something you think about or use words about. When you're reacting to another wolf it's all instinct. It's…" He shrugged as he ran out of words entirely.

Axel frowned, but his scent didn't contain any anger. "Okay. Try this. Close your eyes and picture it in your head. You're in a club. There's another wolf on the other side of the room. You'd like to hook up with him." He paused. "Calling it a hook up works?"

Bayden nodded.

As Axel spoke, he turned his back on what he'd been doing and leaned against the edge of the counter. "Good. You want to hook up with this wolf. What do your instincts tell you to do?"

Bayden forced himself to close his eyes. Blind and vulnerable, he did his best to picture it, but it wasn't easy to do that while Axel was right there, taking up so much room in his head. He pushed humanity aside as best he could and dragged his instincts to the surface. "Is he more dominant or less dominant than me?"

"He's a dom," Axel picked.

More dominant. That made it easy. "Nothing."

"Nothing?"

"If he's more dominant, I don't do anything. It's his choice if he wants to approach me."

"There are rules about things like that?"

113

Bayden shook his head, his eyes still closed. "Just instincts."

"How do you know if he's a dom or not?"

"Body language, scent," Bayden hazarded. "It's just...I just know."

"Even from the other side of the room?"

Bayden nodded. He opened his eyes.

Axel seemed to give that some thought. Bayden tried to imagine a world where things weren't so obvious. It probably went some way to explaining why humans were so screwed up.

"So, he approaches you, what happens next?" Axel asked.

Bayden sipped his coffee. "If I'm not interested, when he gets in my space, I back off. I leave the room, maybe leave the club."

"But if you are interested?"

"When he wants to get in my space, I let him do that," Bayden said. "Then we do what he wants." He put some stress on the last few words, but he wasn't sure how to make his willingness to obey Axel any clearer than he already had.

"What about what you want?"

"Staying means I'm agreeing to do what he wants, that I'm accepting that he's more dominant than me and that he has the right to have things the way he wants them." He paused. It was stupid to pretend that they were talking about anyone who wasn't right there. Axel was the most dominant man in the room. Bayden knew that. Axel knew that. If it needed to be said out loud, Bayden could do that. He took a deep breath, grabbed whatever faith he could summon up and leapt. "I'll do whatever you want."

Axel could do whatever he wanted with him. As their eyes met, Bayden had never been more aware of just how true that fact was.

Chapter Nine

Whatever you want.

Subs had said that to him in the past, but Axel wasn't sure that any human could mean it the way Bayden seemed to — so instinctively, so unequivocally. As their eyes met across the kitchen table, Axel had never been more aware of another man's submission. All the control rested with him, all the power, all the responsibility.

Axel was king of the world. All he had to do was to make sure his one and only subject was never given a reason to want to turn it into a republic.

"A lupine dom would never ask you what you want?" Axel asked.

Bayden shook his head. "Why would he?"

Axel studied Bayden for several seconds. It seemed like an honest question, as if he really didn't get why anyone would care what a sub wanted. Bayden shifted in his seat, obviously uncomfortable with the conversation, but the simple fact that he found talking about it difficult convinced Axel that he'd been right not to jump straight into a scene with the boy.

Wolves were different. It wasn't about shape shifting, it was about a different culture. In that moment, everything seemed up for debate. No assumptions were safe. Hell, they didn't even seem to be working from the same dictionary.

First things first. "You said he'd get in your space — how?"

Bayden shrugged.

Axel stepped away from the counter. "Stand up."

Bayden obeyed.

Axel came around to his side of the table. He took Bayden's coffee cup and set it to one side. "Pretend I'm the sub wolf. How do you get into my space?"

Bayden took several paces back, his movements so quick they had to be borne of pure instinct. He was two yards away before he stopped.

Axel's lips twitched into a smile. "Not one of my best ideas?"

Bayden shook his head. The look in his eyes made him appear on the edge of panic.

"What if we pretend that you're the sub wolf?" Axel suggested, trying not to make it obvious that he was choosing his words with great care.

Bayden nodded. He seemed to relax.

"You'll need to tell me what the dom wolf would do," Axel pointed out. He looked down at his own body. "What kind of body language do I aim for?"

Bayden blinked at him.

"What should I be stressing?" Axel specified.

Bayden opened his mouth, but closed it again before he managed to come up with any words. "You..." He shook his head. He looked Axel up and down. Axel remained perfectly still. "I mean, you're..."

"Communicating loud and clear already?" Axel hazarded.

Bayden nodded very rapidly.

Axel looked down at himself more carefully. He really was just standing there. As far as he could see, there was nothing unusual about his posture. "Why do I get the feeling you're trying to find a polite way to point out that I'm shouting without even realising it?"

Their eyes met. Shouting was apparently a very good word for it.

Axel laughed. "Fair enough, pup. So, you said I get in your space?" He took a few paces forward. Bayden stayed right where he was. He made no attempt to look up and meet Axel's gaze.

Axel stepped confidently into Bayden's personal space. "Is this the point where you'd back away if you weren't interested?"

Bayden nodded.

"So, just by staying where you are and letting me get in close, you're telling me you're interested in submitting to me?"

Bayden offered up another nod. He swallowed rapidly.

Body language. Bayden's gaze was lowered, his head tipped forward slightly. His hands remained at his sides. His posture was open, accepting. In that moment, he seemed far more vulnerable than logic suggested he should. His breathing was faster and shallower than it usually was. Axel had no doubt that Bayden's heart was racing. A glance further down, and it was clear that Bayden was hard behind his fly.

Axel had been right to insist that he get a better read on him before they played. Just the idea that they were relating to each other as wolves was making a huge difference to Bayden. There was no sign of the wolf who refused to give a single inch to any man he made a bet with.

Axel settled his hand flat against Bayden's abs. Bayden's fingers twitched, but he kept his arms at his sides and just let it happen.

Bayden still wore his vest. There wasn't even any skin-to-skin contact. But every beat of his heart and every breath he took was relayed directly to Axel's hand. There were no secrets now. Axel leaned in toward him, purposely crowding him and taking away the last vestiges of personal space.

Axel slid his other hand through Bayden's hair and down to rest on the nape of his neck. Bayden took a deep breath; he still didn't reach out to Axel in return. It didn't seem to be a choice. He was as bound by his instincts as he could ever have been by leather.

A dozen different occasions played through Axel's mind—all the times he'd casually reached out to Bayden without ever considering that there could be any special significance to his actions or Bayden's acceptance of them.

"Since you started drinking here, whenever you've let me into your personal space, was this what you were telling me?" Axel asked, quietly.

"I know human signals are different," Bayden whispered.

"I'm not asking about a human, I'm asking about you. When you let me into your space, was that an invitation or were you just being polite because I'm a human and I don't know what I'm doing?"

Bayden swallowed. He closed his eyes.

Axel didn't pull back. He didn't retract the question. He just stood there in Bayden's space and waited.

"I wouldn't have said no to you," Bayden finally whispered. "Not from the first day."

Axel moved one hand up to Bayden's chin and coaxed him into tilting his head back. He brought their lips together. The kiss was soft, sweet and chaste. Axel didn't allow himself to linger over it for too long.

The kiss had been over for several seconds before Bayden opened his eyes. He glanced up at Axel, their eyes met very briefly before he looked down.

If that first kiss had been all about testing the waters, Axel made sure their second kiss was a clear statement of intent.

He closed the last of the gap between them and slid his arm around Bayden's waist to pull him in against his torso. He tightened his hold on Bayden's hair.

Bayden arched, pressing his body against Axel's. His lips parted in welcome. He still didn't reach out to Axel in return. As Axel began to explore his mouth, Bayden was all acceptance. But there was caution there, too—a determination not to do anything that might be misconstrued as him trying to take the lead. Because he wasn't sure what Axel would allow, what a human would expect, or because that was what came naturally to a wolf?

Axel deepened the kiss. No rush at all, he let one kiss morph into another, then another.

As he licked his way into Bayden's mouth again, Bayden cautiously sucked the tip of Axel's tongue. Pressed together as tightly as they were, Axel felt Bayden tense at being so daring. Axel murmured his approval into the kiss and tightened his hold around Bayden.

Bayden relaxed against him, but his side of the kiss remained tentative, almost coy. Axel rocked his hips. Bayden was just as hard as him, just as ready as he was to fall into a scene and not surface for hours.

Axel broke the kiss. "Good boy."

Bayden dipped his head rather than look up and meet Axel's gaze.

Axel tugged gently on Bayden's hair until he tilted his head back. This time, Axel made him wait before he gave him his kiss. "Such a good boy."

He took half a pace forward, pushing against Bayden's smaller frame. Bayden stepped back. Another step, then another, until Bayden's back hit kitchen wall. Axel nudged his knee against Bayden's legs, encouraging him to shuffle his feet apart. Axel's hip rubbed against Bayden's crotch as he slid his thigh between Bayden's legs.

Bayden gasped, rocking his hips in return.

Axel wrapped one of his hands around Bayden's right wrist and pressed it against the wall alongside his head. In moments, Bayden's other wrist was similarly pinned to the paintwork. Bayden let it happen. No virgin could have looked quite so fascinated by each individual step in the process. He gasped for breath. There didn't seem to be any part of his body that didn't shudder under Axel's touch.

Anything. He could do anything with the boy, and Bayden would go along with it all. He'd do whatever Axel wanted for the rest of the night—there was no doubting that. But, if Axel played his cards just right, he knew Bayden would submit to him for a damn sight longer than a night.

Axel forced himself to pull away and take several paces back.

Bayden blinked at him. For several seconds, he remained still, holding the exact position in which Axel had pinned him to the wall. Axel had never seen anything so gorgeous.

The moments ticked by. Bayden frowned. He lowered his arms, but he didn't step away from the wall.

"If you approach a wolf who's a sub, and he lets you know he's up for it, what do you ask him to do?" Axel asked.

Bayden stared at Axel for what felt like several hours before looking down.

Axel allowed a full minute to pass. Bayden didn't make any movement that wasn't necessary to keep him breathing. The fact he didn't rush to answer wasn't surprising, how disorientated he seemed to be was.

"Come here."

The command flipped a switch, Bayden pushed himself away from the wall. He stopped two feet away from Axel, presumably just outside his personal space.

Axel stepped forward and closed the last of the gap. "Everything's fine," he promised. "I'm not walking away. And I'm sure as hell not saying I'm not interested. But I want you to finish telling me how things work between wolves. Okay?"

Bayden looked up at him. "It's that important?"

"Yes. Go back to your seat."

Axel gave him a few moments to pull himself back together while he busied himself on the other side of the kitchen. "The last question I asked was: what do you ask a sub to do?"

Bayden's frown deepened.

"Have you ever approached a sub?"

Bayden shook his head.

"Because you haven't had the opportunity, or because you're not interested?"

Shrug. And maybe he was right not to consider that important. Bayden obviously had no interest in switching with him.

"What about the wolves who approached you — what did they want you to do?" Axel's grip on the knife he was holding turned white knuckled as jealousy bubbled up in his mind, but even the worst topic wasn't enough to dent his erection.

"Have sex with them. Get them off."

The length of time it took Bayden to formulate his answers, had given Axel plenty of time to work. Food in the oven, he joined Bayden at the table. "What about you, would they get you off too?"

"Sometimes."

"So the sub isn't always allowed to come?" He was just about to put a tick in the mental box that said wolves understood orgasm control, when Bayden shook his head.

"There's no rule against it. It's just not important." Bayden leaned forward in his chair. "I meant it when I said we can just do what you want."

"Yeah, I know you did." Axel tapped his fingers on the table as he turned the problem over in his mind. It was no use. "Why don't you care if you get to come or not?"

Bayden frowned. Axel was tempted to do the same. Whichever angle he considered the idea from, it didn't look promising. For a species that was apparently very hierarchical and inherently bisexual, the most obvious reason wasn't to his taste at all. All the erotic possibilities that had been scrolling through his mind faltered.

"Do you actually enjoy having sex with men, or is it just about demonstrating your submission?" Axel asked, bluntly.

"I do like it. I mean, the bets are…they're different. With wolves, I liked…" He hesitated, as if worried he was giving away dangerous information.

Axel rested one elbow on the table, sure that he was missing something obvious, but not able to quite pin down what that was.

"I like it, but it's more important that the more dominant wolf is pleased," Bayden offered, carefully. "Knowing that he is pleased is the main thing. I can always…" He made a vague gesture with his hand that looked far more like masturbation than he probably intended.

Pure sexual submission. Whatever wolves called it, whatever Bayden considered it, that was what it really was. Wanting to please his lover without expecting anything in return, making do with finishing himself off with his own hand afterwards if necessary.

In a few, simple sentences Bayden had once more made the world a bloody wonderful place, and Axel was back to wondering if he owned leathers which offered more room around the crotch.

"What if you don't have permission?" Axel asked.

Bayden tilted his head to one side.

"If you don't have permission to jack off, what then?" Axel translated.

"Why not?"

"A human sub would usually need his dom's permission to come."

"Even when the more dominant man isn't there?"

"Especially then." Axel smiled, far more willing to be tolerant of Bayden jacking off if he was there to watch the show.

Bayden frowned. The concept seemed to have caught him entirely off guard.

"If a sub agrees to follow a dom's rules, those rules exist all the time." Axel still studied Bayden carefully, trying to work out how his own expectations might differ from a lupine dom's. "Some rules might be relaxed when you're around people who don't understand the lifestyle. There's room for being discreet when that's appropriate, but there's no room for disobedience, or for jacking off without permission."

"But once a human is untied, he can do whatever he wants… Can't he?"

"If he just hooked up with someone for a one off scene, sure. But if the sub belongs to his dom, no."

"And you don't play with men who don't belong to you," Bayden guessed.

"I'm not interested in that." Forget what he'd done with other guys in the past. Whether Axel had consciously realised that or not, casualness had stopped being an option with Bayden before they'd even kissed. In Axel's mind, it hadn't been about a one off scene for weeks. He'd bet the pub that Bayden felt the same way.

"If we…" Bayden ran out of words and looked to Axel for help.

Axel couldn't lie. "This isn't going to be a one off," he said, very clearly. "Once this starts, there'll be rules that exist all the time, and I'll expect you to obey them whether I'm there or not. We'll be working toward you belonging to me permanently."

It was a stupid thing to say—more likely to scare Bayden off than anything else—but it was also the truth, and Bayden deserved that from him from the start.

Bayden didn't look scared, but his expression was wary. "What kind of rules?"

"Just a few simple ones to start with," Axel promised, he relaxed back in his chair and dialled back his desire to throw Bayden in the deep end as far as he could. "I'd expect you to stop screwing around or doing scenes with other people—human or lupine. You'd have to stop jacking off without permission." He was about to go on, when he saw

Bayden tense up. He smiled. No, Bayden really didn't like the idea of needing permission to play with his own cock.

"What if it's a bet?"

Axel raised an eyebrow. "Like the bet you took off Richards?" He straightened up in his seat, all his amusement with the situation disappearing as he realised that Bayden wasn't merely trying to negotiate more orgasms. "That wasn't a real scene—but the rules would apply to any bet that looked even vaguely like a scene too."

Bayden took a deep breath. He closed his eyes. When he opened them, he didn't look up. "I should go." He stood up.

Axel was about to do the same when he remembered what Bayden said about wolves being expected to back away from doms they didn't wish to submit to. He forced himself to remain in his seat. "You don't have to leave the club."

Bayden stopped halfway to the kitchen door and turned back.

"You don't have to leave the room, either. Or the table." Axel looked pointedly at Bayden's chair.

"I won't stop taking bets. No wolf would agree to that. It's…" He shook his head. "It's not a decision that a human should make for a wolf."

"Why?"

Bayden hesitated, as if it had never occurred to him to question the idea before. "It just isn't."

"I hate to be the one to break it to you, pup, but you're not tall enough to loom, even if I'm sitting down."

Bayden blinked.

Extending one leg under the table, Axel nudged Bayden's chair.

Bayden took the hint and cautiously sat down. "You're not mad?"

"No, I'm not." Axel took a sip of his coffee. Frustrated. Pissed off with himself for not playing his hand better. But no, angry wasn't going to get him what he wanted.

"You still want to…" Bayden asked.

"Yes." Axel took a deep breath and pitched his voice very carefully. "When you're ready to agree to the rules, we will." Calm, confident and completely in control—that was what Bayden needed to see when he looked at him, what he needed to hear in his voice. Axel had made his decision and that was that.

Bayden stared across the scrubbed pine table-top. He wanted what Axel was offering. He wanted to submit to him, and for a damn sight longer than a scene. Wolf or human, Axel could sense that longing in him. He wanted to belong to him. They would get there.

Axel just needed to wait for a less experienced man to catch up with him. He could do that. If it got him what he really wanted, he could be the most patient man on the planet. He met Bayden's gaze across the table. So much uncertainty, so much need.

"Until you're ready to submit to me, things carry on as they are," Axel said.

"And that's okay?"

Axel had never heard a man sound so lost. No room for miscommunication—that had to be the goal. "You still drink here. You still tag along and ride with us. Nothing changes."

"And if someone makes a bet with me?" Bayden asked, dropping his gaze.

"Same as before," Axel said, with slightly more forced calm. "You make the bet here, you see it through here. I'll keep an eye on things." It wouldn't be so bad. Bayden wouldn't hold out for long. Hell, Axel doubted he'd even have to watch him fight more than once or twice, let alone do anything else, before they got onto the same page.

Bayden looked up at him. "That's okay with you?"

Axel nodded. "I'll be completely clear. I don't like seeing you doing things that look like scenes with other guys. But you're not my submissive—not yet. Until that changes, you're only expected to follow the club rules—just the same as everyone else." He smiled as he turned his attention to a permission he was far less reluctant to grant, for now. "And you still jack off whenever you want to."

Bayden nodded. He sipped his coffee, but he didn't relax. He remained on the edge of his chair — obviously more out of his depth with a dom who was willing to wait to get his own way, than he had ever been with a man like Richards.

"As things stand, if I get in your space, what does it mean for you?" Axel asked, as he finished his coffee.

"I know you're not a wolf," Bayden said.

"Doesn't answer the question."

Bayden shifted uncomfortably in his seat. "Just because I have instincts, that doesn't mean I can't control them."

"You still haven't answered the question."

"It means the same as it always has — that you're more dominant than me, that I'm accepting that. It means I'm offering to do as you say — for the length of a scene."

"Is that a problem?"

Bayden shook his head.

"Be sure, pup, because unless you tell me you don't like me in your space, you'll find me there a lot, and I won't apologise for it."

He wasn't above playing dirty if it got Bayden to make the right decision more quickly. Bayden seemed to understand that. He took a breath so deep he trembled as he let it out. "It's fine. You being in my space..." His voice dropped to a whisper. "I like it."

* * * * *

"Rent's due!"

Bayden paused halfway along the gloomy hallway as the door leading into his landlord's flat swung open. Reaching into one of the pockets of his leather jacket, Bayden handed his rent to Mr Phillips.

It was the right money—just like always, carefully counted and stowed away in a separate pocket ready to be handed over on time. Phillips checked it twice, huffed and disappeared back into his rooms.

Bayden made his way up the two flights of stairs to his room at the back of the building and closed the door softly behind him.

Pushing Phillips out of his mind, he took a slow steadying breath. The moment there was the slightest space inside his head, Axel's presence expanded to fill it. Bayden stayed just inside the door, letting everything that had happened that day sink into his mind.

The visit with his grandfather. Riding with the Dragons. Going back to Axel's flat above the pub afterwards.

Bayden touched his fingers to his lips. Without thinking about it, he leaned against the wall and closed his eyes. Axel's presence was so real, he might as well have been standing there.

Bayden shook his head. Axel didn't belong in a pokey little bed-sit in the very worst part of town. Pushing himself away from the wall, Bayden walked past the door into the bathroom and into the main room.

The air was chilly. He kept his jacket on as he lay down on his bed.

Bayden closed his eyes again. That was all it took for him to be back in Axel's kitchen, the air warm and the smell of cooking food only overpowered by the scent of desire.

Bayden turned his head on the pillow. When he took a breath he could almost swear Axel was right there. Axel's lips were against his, their bodies were pressed together.

Bayden squirmed, trying to find a more comfortable position on the thin mattress. His cock was hard behind his jeans. The scent of his own desire increased, as he imagined how it might have been if Axel had been interested in doing more than kissing him.

His wrists tingled at the memory of Axel pinning him to the wall. His touch hadn't been rough, it hadn't needed to be while Bayden lacked any interest in pushing him away. It would have been different if Axel had been inclined to prove a point.

Bayden massaged his cock through his jeans.

In his mind's eye, he saw Axel step back to look him over. Frozen to the spot, unable to move without an order, all Bayden would have been able to do was wait upon the more dominant man's pleasure — only in this version of events Axel wouldn't have started another damn conversation.

What would Axel have done with him, if he'd realised there was no need for talking? Axel wanted to screw him. Bayden knew that as surely as he knew that scent didn't lie, but there were a hundred different ways a man could use another person's body for his pleasure.

After a long ride, Axel wouldn't have wanted anything complicated. Quick and rough, pushed down against the kitchen table.

Bayden whimpered as he imagined strong hands shoving him into position. Bent over the table, bracing himself against the scrubbed pine, he'd have steadied himself as best he could when Axel tugged his jeans down. Harsh. Impatient. It wasn't Axel's problem if the denim ripped.

As he watched it happen in his imagination, Bayden scrabbled for his fly in the real world. Freeing his cock as quickly as he could, he wrapped his fingers around the length.

Axel wouldn't have bothered jacking him. Bayden's cock wouldn't have been his concern. The only thing he'd have been interested in was Bayden's arse.

Bayden squirmed against the bed, pumping his cock hard and fast as he imagined Axel ploughing into him, burying his cock in his arse over and over again, without caring if Bayden liked to be screwed that way. Axel wouldn't have given a damn about anything except his own orgasm, and making it clear to Bayden exactly how things worked between them.

There wouldn't have been any money on the table. It would have been very simple. One man giving another what he wanted, for free, just because it was so bloody obvious that was the way it should be.

Bayden rocked his hips, thrusting into his hand as he imagined Axel coming deep in his arse. In his mind's eye, he saw Axel pulling away, leaving him there as he walked off, not even looking over his shoulder.

Biting down hard on his bottom lip, Bayden stifled his howl as he came. In the flat above the pub, he'd have been left hard and frustrated. In the real world, he spilled in long ropes across his stomach and up over his vest. He kept his hand moving. Even when his cock started to soften and his touch became more painful than pleasurable, he couldn't bring himself to stop.

The fantasy was too perfect. Giving it up was too hard.

Bayden gasped, rolling onto his side and curling in on himself as he finally admitted defeat and let everything he wanted slip away. His ragged breathing filled the air. He had no idea how long he lay there, unable to stop reality from reasserting itself around him.

When he opened his eyes, his breathing had steadied. His cum was drying on his skin. The air was cold against his exposed cock.

Bayden's limbs felt stiff as he forced himself to roll over and sit on the edge of the bed. Given a choice between thinking about how far-fetched the fantasy was and dealing with more mundane matters, Bayden pulled himself to his feet and stripped off his clothes.

In the bathroom, he started the shower. He let it run for a few seconds on the off chance, but his luck wasn't in that day. The water failed to heat up. Stepping under the frigid spray, Bayden quickly washed himself down.

If anything, the water seemed to get even colder. Shivers ran through him by the time he stepped out of the cubicle. Towelling himself dry coaxed a bit of warmth into his muscles. He wrapped the towel around his waist as he made his way back into the main room. Boiling the kettle got him enough hot water to wash out the vest he'd come all over.

The radiator in his room wasn't working today, but it was still a convenient place to hang his vest and towel to dry.

Switching back into his wolf form, Bayden wrapped his fur around him like a security blanket. The chilly air became far less relevant. He padded over to his bed and jumped up onto it. Poking at the blankets with his nose, he burrowed under the covers. Curling into a small ball in the darkness, Bayden waited for the space to warm up enough to let him fall asleep. In the meantime, he tried not to think too hard about Axel.

It might have been like that if Axel hadn't been so focused on talking. It might even have been like that if Bayden had been able to give Axel the answers he'd wanted during their conversation. But it wasn't actually like that.

In the real world, agreeing to let a human make those kinds of decisions for him would be a mistake. It would be abandoning all the freedom and all the progress werewolves had made since they left human captivity. Just because those things didn't seem important when he thought about Axel, that didn't mean he could ignore them.

Anyway, in the real world, agreeing to follow Axel's rules would be agreeing not to be able to pay his rent next time Mr Phillips ambushed him in the hallway. It would be agreeing to see the tin tucked away in the back of his mother's kitchen cabinet go empty. That was important. Even with his head full of Axel, it was still important.

Bayden curled himself into a tighter ball. There were only two tiny points of light in a world full of darkness. Axel had given him permission to come back to the pub, and he'd given him permission to jack off. The latter had just allowed him one of the most intense orgasms he remembered having. The former gave him just a tiny bit of hope.

Chapter Ten

Bayden's mind reeled. He scrabbled for thoughts, but they careered through his brain too fast to be understood.

He gasped, but there was no air. Hands closed around his throat. Sweat broke out across his skin. He tossed his head trying to shake off the confusion that surrounded him.

Pain sliced at him, drawing slow, purposeful lines across his skin. There were people, but they were insubstantial shadowy forms. He couldn't focus on them. They were human though, they had to be. Pain and humans were inextricably linked.

Darkness gradually closed in around him, then snapped away — quick and jarring. Calm. He knew he had to stay calm, but, in the midst of his panic, that knowledge did him little good. Outwardly calm. He could do that. He was good at that.

He wouldn't let anyone see he was afraid. He wouldn't give them the satisfaction. Axel mustn't see him afraid.

No. Not Axel. Axel was different. Axel was comfort and stubbornness, he was control and longing.

The world wavered, and Bayden was trapped in a space between asleep and awake, between wolf and human. Time had no meaning. His tumbling thoughts took on different voices. His mother telling him to be careful. His father demanding that he stand up to humans. His grandfather warning him to keep his head down. Miss Kemp standing at the front of the class, talking about laws she'd never understand let alone be able to explain to school children. Axel's voice was there too, winding through all the others.

Dizzy. When was the last time he ate? No, it didn't feel like that kind of dizziness — Bayden was used to that. This was different. It came with pain that was totally unlike the hollow ache in an empty stomach.

He closed his eyes, pushing mindlessly at the world around him, not sure if he was trying to escape from reality or a dream. It didn't feel real, but it was impossible to believe that a nightmare could hurt so much.

He wanted Axel. Asleep or awake. Human or wolf. If Bayden didn't know anything else, he knew that. He wanted Axel. He needed Axel.

* * * * *

Axel bit back a curse when the pub door swung open. It was barely ten minutes to closing. After a long evening manning the bar on his own, he wanted the stragglers to bugger off, not an extra idiot to join them. He looked up from where he'd already started cashing up the till.

Bayden.

Axel's annoyance vanished. A man couldn't be blamed for feeling tolerant toward a hot sub turning up whatever the time. But still, if Axel had needed any proof of just how obsessed he was with the boy, the fact that he found it amusing rather than ridiculous that Bayden had taken the time to put his sunglasses on, even when it was pitch black outside, probably said it all.

A yard away from the bar, Bayden hesitated.

Personal space.

"Running late?" Hale asked, from his stool.

Bayden checked the clock on the wall behind Axel. He took half a step back.

Axel pointed to the stool next to Hale before Bayden had time to retreat further. "Grab a seat."

Bayden's movements were slow, almost wary. It was the first time he'd been to the pub since their discussion the previous weekend. A certain amount of nervousness was acceptable but, really, looking like an extra from a bad mafia movie wasn't.

"Lose the glasses."

Bayden didn't seem enthusiastic, but he took the sunglasses off, folded them up and set them on the bar.

"Good boy."

Bayden's lips twitched into something vaguely like a smile, but he didn't seem to be in a rush to meet Axel's gaze. He set his elbow on the bar and propped his head up with his fist on his temple.

Axel's eyes narrowed. "Have you been drinking?"

Bayden shook his head.

"You look knackered."

Bayden shrugged. "It's late. I should go. I only called in on my way past."

The pub was on a little used road leading out of the city. It wasn't the kind of place a man passed unless he wanted to, and a lie that badly thought out didn't deserve an answer. Axel grabbed a bottle of Coke and set it on the bar.

Bayden put his money on the counter. When Axel offered him his change, Bayden turned his palm up to receive it. His jacket sleeve slid back an inch.

There was a mark around his wrist—the kind bondage left in its wake. Jealousy hit Axel like a snowplough. He caught hold of Bayden's hand and pushed the sleeve back further.

The moment he saw the bruise clearly, Axel's assumptions faltered. This wasn't the kind of mark that many subs would smile about when they saw it the next day. It looked painful as hell—the kind of injury a man got when he was desperately trying to escape his bondage rather than the memento of a guy who'd enjoyed every minute of it.

Axel pushed Bayden's sleeve back another inch. His heart lurched in his chest. There were fresh cut marks on Bayden's wrist. Axel looked up.

Bayden met his gaze for a second before turning his face away. He tried to pull his hand out of Axel's grip, but Axel wasn't in control of those particular muscles. He couldn't have let go if he'd wanted to, and he didn't want to.

"Bayden?"

Nothing. He didn't even look in Axel's direction.

Someone on the other side of the room moved his chair. It scraped across the floorboards. Bayden tensed. Axel looked past Bayden to the men still there, before leaning across the bar and speaking quietly to Bayden.

"Listen to me. You don't move off that stool. Understand?"

For a long time, Axel thought he wouldn't get any answer, but Bayden finally nodded.

Somehow, Axel managed to release Bayden's hand but the thought still screamed through his mind — someone had hurt Bayden.

Autopilot kicked in. It couldn't have taken Axel more than five minutes to get everyone out of the pub, but it felt like hours. Someone had hurt Bayden. Axel couldn't stop himself looking over his shoulder every couple of seconds, checking that Bayden was still on his stool.

Bayden didn't move a muscle, not even to open his Coke and take a sip. Doors locked, Axel sat on the stool next to Bayden.

"Am I allowed to leave?" Bayden asked, quietly.

"No."

Bayden didn't react. It didn't seem to occur to him to say that Axel didn't have the right to make that decision.

"Look at me, pup."

Bayden half-turned his body, but he kept his face averted until Axel touched his cheek and coaxed him around.

There was a mark next to his eye.

Axel got off his stool. Holding Bayden's face still, he examined the wound. A narrow cut an inch and a half long and perfectly straight — it ran right onto his eyelid.

It wasn't hard to imagine Bayden getting into a fight, but it was impossible to picture the kind of blow that would cause a cut like that without leaving any kind of bruise around it. The cut had been hidden behind Bayden's sunglasses when he came in and it had been obscured by Bayden's hand when he'd supported his head on his fist—that wasn't a coincidence.

"Bayden?"

He made no attempt to pull away, but he didn't try to answer either.

"What happened?"

Finally, Bayden cleared his throat. "It's nothing."

"Bollocks. Someone hurt you. Who was it?"

Silence stretched out between them. "It was a bet."

"A bet," Axel repeated, blankly.

Bayden nodded.

"What kind of a bet?" But Axel had a horrible suspicion he already knew the answer.

"One hour, no limits. I won."

Axel still had his hand on the side of Bayden's face, holding him in place.

A bet... Axel glanced down at Bayden's wrist. The leather had fallen back over it, completely concealing his injuries. Axel took in a few extra details about Bayden's appearance.

His jacket was zipped, his collar turned up. Suddenly, that didn't seem to be a sign that the weather was turning colder.

"Take off your jacket."

"I shouldn't have come here tonight," Bayden mumbled, rubbing at his uninjured temple.

"You're exactly where you should be." Axel's voice was the complete opposite of Bayden's—full of confidence and certainty.

Bayden remained still, his gaze lowered.

Axel's hands itched with a desire to just make everything very simple. He could take the jacket off Bayden himself. Bayden wouldn't stop him. But, one wrong move, and Bayden wouldn't ever trust him again. A move like that, when he had no idea what Bayden had already been through, and he wouldn't deserve to be trusted.

"Tell me about the bet," he ordered.

"I won." He half turned away from Axel. "Coming here was a mistake."

Before Bayden had a chance to get off the stool, Axel put his hand on his shoulder. He pushed Bayden's hair back off his face with his other hand, careful to keep his movements slow and easily predictable. "Why?"

Bayden stared down at his sunglasses. His grip on them was white knuckled. "You're angry with me."

"I didn't say that." However he'd felt when he saw Bayden's injuries, Axel had been very careful not to utter those particular words.

"Scent doesn't lie."

Shit.

"I knew you didn't want me to do scenes with other guys," Bayden blurted out. "I did one anyway. I should have—"

"Should have?" Axel prompted.

"I should have had the sense to stay away until I could have pretended I hadn't done a scene." His voice dripped with contempt at himself.

"No." Axel tightened his hold on Bayden's hair, giving him no choice but to look up at him. "You don't hide being hurt—not from me."

Bayden swallowed rapidly before he tried to speak. "I'm fine."

Axel pushed Bayden's sleeve back, just enough to expose the bruise. Bayden peered down at the injury, as if he'd never seen it before.

"You were tied up?"

Bayden nodded.

Axel ran his thumb very gently over the vivid purple marks. To get bruises that bad, either the bondage was set up to hurt in itself, or Bayden fought like hell against it. Neither option appealed, but the bruises weren't Axel's biggest concern.

He nudged the sleeve back further, exposing the cuts. Some were very light, barely worse than a paper cut. Others were deeper and had been put in place with clear intent.

None of the wounds remained open, but they must have bled like hell when they were first done. Bayden's lupine healing made it impossible to work out if they were inflicted at the same time as the bruises. The cuts could have been done before, during, or even hours after the bet.

The only time Axel had seen marks quite like them had been on TV, and they hadn't been put there by a third party. It was only too easy to imagine Bayden hurting himself when he got home and the fallout from some warped bet hit him too hard for him to know how to deal with it.

"Was this part of the bet?" Axel asked.

Bayden peered at the cuts.

"Pup, look at me."

Axel waited until Bayden did as he was told. "Did someone else do this, or did you?" He pitched his voice very carefully, no judgement at all. He pushed accepting thoughts to the forefront of his mind too, just in case that might somehow come through in his scent.

Bayden look confused. "The bet."

"The guy you did a bet with had a knife?"

"One of them did. That was his thing, his kink."

Who was he? Do you know his name? Where can I find him? Axel swallowed. All that could wait. "Are there any other cuts?" he asked, doing his damnedest to keep his voice level.

Bayden nodded.

"Show me."

Bayden hesitated. It was wrong to think of a shifter as an animal, but Bayden reminded Axel of nothing so much as a wounded animal that might bolt at any sudden noise or sharp movement.

"I've looked after you when you've been hurt before, haven't I?" Axel reminded him. Adopting roughly the same tone of voice his mother had used with him a lifetime ago, when he woke up from a bad dream but couldn't accept that there weren't really monsters hiding under his bed.

"I'm fine," Bayden murmured. "I can look after myself." It had never been more obvious that he was repeating words that had become rote for him.

"Show me where you're hurt."

"I don't like it when you're angry with me," Bayden mumbled.

He sounded half-drunk, but the situation couldn't have been more different to the previous week. It wasn't a bit of harmless hazing that had put him in this state. He hadn't been surrounded by men who'd have looked after him if something had gone wrong tonight, and it showed. Bayden's current vulnerability went deeper than mere disorientation, and it sickened Axel in a way the tipsy version of Bayden never could have.

The drunk version of Bayden had been so trusting. This version was so scared — and he was afraid of Axel as well as the men who'd hurt him. Scared because there was no way Axel could disguise his fury with the men who'd done that to him.

"What do you think will happen if I get angry with you?" Axel asked.

Bayden remained silent.

"I'm not going to hurt you, pup. That doesn't change no matter how angry I get."

Bayden blinked at him. He obviously wasn't worried that Axel would lash out. That wasn't why he didn't want Axel to be angry with him. Even tonight, Bayden had the look of a man who could take a beating, if that's what life needed him to do.

It's more important that the more dominant wolf is pleased. It was a possibility.

Axel gently pushed his fingers through Bayden's hair. "Do you want to know what to do to make me pleased with you?"

The nod was quick and determined. "Yes."

"Okay. I want you to show me where you're hurt. If you do that, I'll be very pleased with you."

Bayden closed his eyes. Eventually, he nodded.

He fumbled with the catch at the top of his jacket until Axel carefully moved his hands out of the way and undid it himself. Bayden's collar fell back.

Fresh fury flooded Axel veins, but he forced himself to keep moving, slow and steady, until the zip was completely undone.

He pushed the leather aside.

There were bruises around Bayden's neck. Unlike the ones at his wrists, these had been left by a man's hand rather than bondage. The pattern showed each fingertip very clearly. There were cuts too. One had started to bleed at some point after Bayden had cleaned himself up. It had stopped again, but the air still smelt metallic with it. Axel could only imagine how strong a wolf would find the scent, but Bayden seemed oblivious to it.

Axel stood up. Guiding Bayden onto his feet, he helped him out of his jacket.

Axel stepped behind Bayden to put his jacket on the bar. There wasn't a mark on his back. He'd probably been bound with his back to something. Face up on a bed mostly likely. Axel pushed the image away—he didn't have time to worry about how he felt.

Axel moved back to face Bayden. There were already dozens of cuts visible, and Axel had no doubt there were more hidden beneath Bayden's clothes. He looked back up to Bayden's throat just in time to see him swallow rapidly.

Axel stepped closer and settled his hand on Bayden's cheek to reassure him. It wasn't until the toe of his boot nudged against Bayden's that he realised just how much he was crowding him. He was twice the size of the boy, older than him, more dominant than him. And Bayden had been given plenty of evidence of how untrustworthy humans who called themselves doms could be.

"Bayden, look at me. Listen. This is important."

It took a long time, but eventually, Bayden managed to meet Axel's gaze.

"I'm in your space. I can't look after you properly unless I am. But I'm not starting something, or challenging you. This isn't about me trying to make you feel submissive. Do you understand that?"

Bayden nodded.

"You're sure?"

"You're not interested. I get it."

Axel tucked a knuckle under his chin. "I'm interested. But, right now, I'm interested in looking after you rather than screwing you."

Bayden tried to look away.

"That's not the same as me saying I don't want to screw you. It's not either or, but there are times and places. Right now neither of us should be thinking about getting laid."

Bayden nodded.

Axel held back a sigh, not sure how much Bayden really understood, how much he was in a position to understand right then.

Axel tugged Bayden's vest up and took it off over his head, revealing a whole array of new cuts. He nudged Bayden to rest against the edge of the stool and knelt on one knee to undo Bayden's boots.

"No." Bayden put his hand over Axel's.

Axel took his hand away, but before he could say anything, Bayden clumsily began to undo his laces himself. It wasn't clothing being removed that was the problem, it was...what? Being waited on? Axel looked at the way he was crouched down in front of Bayden, almost kneeling in front of him.

Body language. Axel sat on the stool next to Bayden's—back straight, head up. It worked. Bayden relaxed somewhat. Boots off, he set them to one side.

"Jeans too, pup."

Bayden pushed his jeans down. Stepping out of them, he folded them neatly and set them with his boots. A glance at where Axel had put his vest and jacket, and Bayden folded each before setting them with the rest of his clothes.

It was difficult to tell if Bayden was working on autopilot or if he was trying to put off facing Axel, but the result was the same. Axel had plenty of time to assess the damage.

More bruises. More cuts. No individual injury looked physically serious, but the psychological toll they could have taken was obvious. Going to the edge with a dom that a sub trusted was one thing. Without that trust...

Axel took a deep breath and pushed his temper down as best he could.

The bruises on Bayden's neck overlapped. The guy who'd had Bayden by the throat hadn't grabbed him once. He'd done the same thing over and over. *This time I might not stop, I might not let you breathe.*

The placement of the cuts were just as telling. His neck, his wrists. *Look how easy it would be for me to cut a little bit deeper and find a vein.* There were cuts elsewhere on his body, but the only other place where they were heavily concentrated was around Bayden's crotch. There was a particularly deep cut right at the top of Bayden's ball sac. Yes, the cuts represented very obvious threats.

A tiny movement caught Axel's attention. Bayden's fingers furled into a tight fist. Axel looked up. Bayden's eyes were closed.

Axel touched the back of Bayden's hand to get his attention. "This is what's going to happen." Complete confidence, nothing for Bayden to have to worry about because all the decisions were already made. "You're going to stay here tonight. I'm going to put your bike in the lock-up. You're going to go upstairs, sit on the sofa and wait for me to join you. Understand?"

Bayden stared at some point around Axel's right collar bone for a long time. "You don't mind?" he whispered.

"I'm not asking you to make a decision on this, pup. I'm telling you what's going to happen."

Bayden took a deep breath. He seemed to relax slightly. "Okay."

"Good boy." Axel helped him off his stool. "I'll need your keys to move your bike."

Bayden handed them over without a word of protest. Axel would have loved to have believed that was because he trusted him. It seemed more like another sign that his mind had completely shut down.

Bayden looked at his clothes.

"Take them with you. You'll need them in the morning. I'll put your helmet with your bike."

Bayden did as he was told. Axel unlocked the door at the bottom of the stairs and sent Bayden up before heading outside to secure Bayden's bike. It was a damn sight easier to keep the bike safe than it was to keep Bayden safe.

* * * * *

There was blood on Bayden's vest. It stood out stark and red against the white material. The scent of it hadn't been a memory. One of the cuts must have opened.

Bayden sat on the sofa, just as Axel had ordered. He lifted a hand to his neck and ran his fingers over his skin until he found the patch that was sticky with drying blood.

He licked his fingers and swiped at his neck, but his eyes never left the stain on his vest. He'd been so sure he'd stopped bleeding before he left the hotel room.

He licked his fingers clean. The taste of blood was strong, but unavoidable. His vest needed to be washed too. He'd have to ask if there was somewhere he could do that. Bayden blinked. The stain was getting blurry.

Axel came back, but Bayden didn't look up. The scent of Axel's anger was worse than the stench of blood. Whatever Axel had said earlier, he wasn't pleased with Bayden at all. Axel was more furious with him than ever.

Every instinct Bayden had screamed at him to fix that. He had to convince Axel to be pleased with him, but he had no idea how. The shiver that rushed thought him had nothing to do with temperature or nudity.

Axel sat on the sofa next to him.

Bayden didn't realise he was still trying to clean the blood off his neck until Axel caught hold of his fingers and stopped him.

"You washed the cuts before you came here," Axel observed.

"The bet. We went to a hotel. There was a shower." There'd been hot water and everything. He'd felt so clean. Bayden glanced at the stained vest. The clean feeling had lasted less time than ever.

"It's not bleeding anymore," Axel murmured.

Bayden's head was in such a mess, he didn't even know if that was a good thing or not. Would apologising help?

Axel set a first aid kit on the coffee table. He smiled at Bayden, but the expression wasn't as clear as it usually was, there was a hell of a lot going on behind that smile.

He gently dabbed a bit of the gel on the cut alongside Bayden's eye. He paused then, as if waiting for some sort of reaction.

"It's fine," Bayden offered. The sting was barely a note in a cacophony of sensations.

"How much was the bet for?"

"One thousand," Bayden whispered.

"And you needed the money because…"

Bayden looked down. "They set the numbers, not me. The money wasn't the point. I'd have done it whatever the stakes."

That last bit was true. After striking out at all the places he usually managed to pick up fights, any bet had seemed like a blessing. Bayden stared down at his hand unable to stop it forming into a fist. It had been a blessing. He'd made the right choice when he took it. Everything was fine. And, if at some points during the bet, it had seemed like it wouldn't be, that wasn't important.

Axel worked his way across the cuts on Bayden's neck. The cream stung. Having Axel patching him up again stung too. If Axel was going to see him like that, Bayden might as well have taken the damn bet right there in The Dragon's Lair.

"I'm not going to think any less of you if you're doing this for the money," Axel said.

"Doesn't mean much. You said you wouldn't be angry with me and that was bollocks." It wasn't the right way to talk to a more dominant wolf, but Bayden couldn't keep the words back. He couldn't stop another shiver running through him, either.

"I'm not angry with you." Axel thought for a moment. "Maybe scent doesn't lie, but it can't give you the full story."

He moved onto a long cut across Bayden's torso. Bayden watched him work, trying to keep what he could see at that moment right at the front of his mind so that he didn't have to remember what he'd seen the last time he looked down his body.

"There are things I'm pleased about," Axel said. "Things I'm not pleased about, and there are things I'm really furious about. Scent can't tell you which is which, can it?"

Bayden shook his head, but he didn't have it in him to ask.

"I'm not pleased with you for taking that kind of bet, especially not with men who I think you knew at the time you couldn't trust," Axel said. "Nothing is going to change that."

Bayden took a deep breath.

"But, I meant it when I said I'd be pleased with you for letting me look after you, and I am. And I'm pleased that you came here tonight. It was exactly the right thing to do."

The honesty in his voice was undeniable. Relief flooded through Bayden at the simple idea that anyone thought that he'd done something right. The fact that it was Axel who thought he'd done something right was actually enough to ease the metal ring around his chest, making it possible for him to breathe properly for the first time since he'd seen the knife.

"The anger — that's there. But it's the other men involved in the bet that I'm really furious with, not you."

"Because you don't want other men doing scenes with me." And the rules Axel wanted him to follow counted whether Axel was there or not.

"What happened tonight wasn't a scene." Axel moved on to the next cut, the one that had been made when the guy held the point of his knife against the skin over Bayden's solar plexus, so Bayden's only choice became holding his breath or bleeding. Eventually, he'd had to bleed. The slightest increase in pressure behind the knife and there wouldn't have been anyone left to help his mother with the rent.

Bayden shook his head, pushing that possibility out of his mind and trying to concentrate on Axel and what Axel wanted him to be able to talk about. "It's a scene when two humans do it," Bayden said. "I've seen them do it in clubs."

"Breath play? Knife play? Quite a few doms dabble with them. Some guys are really into them," Axel allowed. "Tolmore is seriously into knives. I've watched him do scenes here in the pub. He plays with other guys who are into it. Guys who know what they're doing—who want to play with him because they share the same kink. They sign up for that. They trust Tolmore, and they're right to do that, because he plays safe. He's a paramedic out in the real world, he knows what he's doing. And he respects whatever limits a sub sets."

Axel picked up Bayden's wrist and gently began to apply cream to the cuts there.

"The men you did a bet with—did they ask you if you were into knives?"

Unable to look at the cuts without remembering each one being inflicted, Bayden turned his attention to Axel. The only marks on him were his tattoos. Bayden let his eyes trace the line in one particular design up Axel's forearm.

It was beautiful. Axel was beautiful. Not in the way men in human magazines were beautiful. Axel was strength and certainty. He was big and strong, with hands that could be gentle when he wanted them to be. He was more dominant than Bayden had ever realised a human could be, and he was gorgeous.

"Did they tell you they were into knives before you took the bet? Did they use clean kit? Did they check in with you to find out where your head was at after it started? Did they give a damn if they did any serious damage? Did they even stick around to make sure you were okay afterwards?"

Bayden remained silent until Axel stopped putting cream on his wrist, apparently waiting for an answer.

"I said no limits," Bayden managed to whisper. "I meant it. There wasn't anything to talk about."

"That's not a scene, pup. Even if it looks similar to something you saw someone do in a club, it's not the same."

"Wolves…" Bayden sighed.

"What?" Axel demanded. "Wolves aren't easy to kill? Wolves heal quickly?"

Bayden nodded. "Yes, we do."

"Wolves still get hurt, they still feel pain. They still get scared, don't they?"

Scared. Yes, he'd been scared. But he hadn't let them see that. Bayden swallowed. He shouldn't ever let a human see that. The knowledge had been drilled into him for years.

Bayden squared his shoulders. "I'm fine."

"Of course you are, pup." Axel stroked his fingers through Bayden's hair, pushing it back off his face. He sighed and went back to applying cream to the cuts.

The last cut wasn't deep but it ran down the length of Bayden's cock. He wasn't sure what hurt more, the way the cream stung or the way his cock hardened despite the sting.

Bayden closed his eyes. Heat rushed to his cheeks, but he wasn't sure if it was the embarrassment at getting turned on by Axel's touch, even when he knew Axel wasn't interested in him, or the complete humiliation of having to get patched up by Axel yet again.

"Everything's still in working order. That's good."

Bayden looked up. Axel smiled and pushed his hand through Bayden's hair again. Bayden found himself smiling back, just slightly.

"Come on, pup. You've had more than enough excitement for one day." He led Bayden into the guest' bedroom and waited while Bayden got into the bed.

Not sure what else to do, Bayden closed his eyes and pretended to fall instantly asleep.

Axel didn't rush off. He stayed just next to the bed. He was still there when Bayden felt his pretence at sleep start to become a reality.

Chapter Eleven

There were certain advantages to not sleeping a wink all night. Axel knew that Bayden hadn't crept out of the flat and down to the lock-up. As he'd lain in bed, Axel had also had plenty of time to plan his next move.

However, there were also certain disadvantages to insomnia. He'd had hours to picture how each cut and bruise had been inflicted. The sun was barely up before Axel had to get up and get away from those images. He pulled himself out of bed, tugged on a pair of jeans and headed straight to the coffee pot.

It hadn't even brewed before Bayden appeared in the kitchen doorway. He was fully dressed. His jacket was on and zipped up to the neck. Axel wondered if he should be flattered that the boy hadn't put his sunglasses on as well.

Axel pointed to one of the chairs alongside the table. "Sit."

Bayden remained in the doorway.

"Unless you're cold, you can hang your jacket by the door first," Axel added.

Bayden touched his jacket's collar. It was high enough to cover the bruises.

"You don't need to hide anything from me," Axel said.

Bayden didn't look enthusiastic, but he went and hung up his coat. When he came back, he sat in the chair Axel had indicated.

Leaning back against the counter next to the coffee machine, Axel ran his eyes over him, doing his best not to linger obviously over his wrists or neck.

"You washed your vest," he realised.

Bayden touched the fabric that had been stained with blood the night before. "In the sink in the en-suite." He met

Axel's gaze for a moment. "Should I apologise?" There was no sarcasm in the question.

"Not for any reason I know." Finally, the coffee was ready. Axel poured two cups and joined Bayden at the table.

"It's important for a wolf to be clean, to be seen to be clean," Bayden offered, softly.

Axel nodded. The coffee scalded his tongue, but he swallowed it down anyway, hoping the caffeine would let him make sense of at least some of the conversation.

As he waited for the coffee to kick in, he found himself unable to avoid assessing Bayden's injuries. They looked like they'd had a week to heal rather than a day, but they were still enough to turn his stomach.

Bayden sipped his coffee, but when he saw Axel looking at his wrists, he put the mug down and dropped his hands onto his lap, out of sight, below the edge of the table.

Axel held out one hand, palm up. He didn't say anything, he just waited.

Bayden put his wrist in Axel's grip with obvious reluctance.

"Did they give you a safe word?"

"I didn't ask for one," Bayden protested.

"Answer the question. Did you have one?"

Bayden nodded.

"Did you say it?" Axel asked. "Did you tell them you wanted them to stop?"

Bayden shook his head. "I won the bet."

Axel narrowed his gaze. "If you'd said it, would they have stopped?"

Bayden looked down.

"If you'd said it, if you told them they'd won, would they have stopped?" Axel pushed.

Bayden shook his head. It was exactly what Axel suspected. If he came face to face with one of those men, Axel wasn't sure he'd be able to stop himself from killing them. Knowing Bayden could sense his anger didn't mean Axel could check it completely. All he could do was keep his voice calm. "Then what happened last night wasn't a scene or a bet."

Bayden glanced up at him.

"In a scene you can stop any time by saying your safe word. It's part of the definition of the term. The only acceptable reason for not giving someone a safe word is because it's been made clear that no still means no, or stop still means stop, and the dom will respect those terms."

Bayden stared at him as if he was speaking a foreign language. It was just possible that he was doing exactly that. Axel leaned forward in his seat, determined to get at least a few words agreed in a common dictionary by the end of the conversation.

"In a scene, if you're playing with the right kind of dom, you'll never get in trouble for saying your safe word. You'll never be punished for that. The dom won't think any less of you. Saying it doesn't mean you failed a challenge, it just means you want to stop. You can't lose anything by saying it, because you're not competing with your dom in a scene — you're both on the same side."

Bayden frowned. Axel had his complete attention, he was sure of that. He could damn near feel Bayden absorbing every word.

Axel gave him a few moments to think that over. "Tell me how a wolf would say what I just said. What would be the right words for a wolf?"

Bayden stared into his coffee for a while.

Axel waited. He had no problem with doing that for the rest of the day if necessary, but it only took about five minutes.

"What humans call a scene only happens when both wolves have already agreed which of them is more dominant." His voice was soft, not as if he was embarrassed, but as if he was speaking about something that deserved a hushed, reverential tone. "It's what happens when a less

151

dominant wolf doesn't just acknowledge that the other wolf is more dominant, but when he says he wants that other wolf to be dominant over him and that he'll do whatever he wants."

"If you were playing with another wolf and you wanted him to stop, would he do that?"

Bayden nodded. Not even the slightest hesitation. He obviously had faith in other wolves.

"A human should too. And the way you let him know you want to stop is by saying your safe word. If you can't stop a human dom with a word, then it's not a scene." He paused for a moment. "Do you see why it would be wrong for us to call what happened last night a scene?"

"It wasn't a scene," Bayden whispered, watching Axel gently caress the injuries that the previous night had left on him as if it was the most fascinating thing he'd ever seen.

"It wasn't a bet either," Axel said.

Bayden tensed. It was the tiniest change in posture. If Axel hadn't been paying acute attention he'd have missed it.

"In a bet, you can stop by forfeiting—you might have to pay up if you tap out, but you always have that option. It might make you uncomfortable. It might give the other guy a chance to gloat, but it's still an option."

Bayden swallowed.

"In lupine words," Axel prompted.

"A bet is about a human trying to establish dominance over a wolf who doesn't accept that he's dominant over him—to make the wolf feel less than a human, to break him." He said it so matter of factly. "Years ago, they could do that any time they liked. Now, they have to make a bet. And they have to pay up if they fail."

Axel caressed the skin on Bayden's wrist again. When he spoke like that, it was easy to believe that the money really was just about keeping score.

Bayden swallowed again. "In a bet, a wolf could choose to let a human win—to let a human think he'd won. A wolf has that choice now — even if I'd never take it." He met Axel's eyes for the last few words.

It was understanding of a sort — a starting point at least. It was the best Axel could hope for. "Good boy."

Bayden took a deep breath and let it out slowly. The conversation had been tough on him, but Axel couldn't let it end yet.

"Would you take a bet from me?" he asked.

"No!" Bayden straightened up in his chair. He curled his hand into a fist, but didn't pull away from Axel's touch.

"Because that would imply that you didn't already consider me dominant over you, it would mean you thought I had something to prove?"

"I'll do whatever you want for free," Bayden said, very seriously.

"Whatever we did would be a scene rather than a bet," Axel suggested.

Bayden nodded.

"The two things are very different."

"Yes."

"So mixing up the words for them is a bad idea."

"Yes."

Axel smiled. He'd never felt success like it. "Good. We're agreed."

"I won't call any of the bets I take scenes anymore."

"Good boy." He gave Bayden a moment to relax before he pushed forward even further. "What you did with Richards was a bet."

Bayden nodded.

"Because if you'd said you wanted to stop, he would have. And, if he hadn't, there were people around who would have stepped in and stopped him."

"I would never have —"

"You had the option," Axel cut in. "If you'd said stop, the bet would have stopped. You'd have had to pay up, and

Richards would probably have tried to make you feel like shit for it, but you could have stopped it at any time."

Bayden shifted uncomfortably in his seat but he didn't remove his wrist from Axel's loose grip. "I chose," he finally said. "It was my choice."

"The same with shifting in front of the other Dragons, or drinking enough to make six humans pass out, or dog biscuits. When you made those bets, you always had an out. Yes?"

Bayden nodded, his reluctance obvious.

"Whether you're playing a scene or playing out a bet, you have an out," Axel stressed. "But last night, you didn't have an out, did you?"

Bayden didn't deny it. "What would the human word be?" he asked, cautiously.

Axel had a lot of words in mind. Abuse. Torture. Assault with a deadly weapon. 'An almighty fuck up' would be a very good term for it, but Axel forced himself to pick the least judgemental possibility. "A mistake."

Bayden looked up.

"The risks you took last night were a mistake." Axel held up his free hand. "No. I don't care if wolves heal quickly, I don't care how difficult it is to kill a wolf. The situation you were in last night was a mistake."

Bayden obviously wasn't impressed, but he eventually nodded his acceptance of the term.

Axel rolled his shoulders, trying to work some of the tension out of them before they completely cramped up. "The men who you were with last night—did you meet them here?"

Bayden shook his head.

A little of Axel's guilt lessoned.

"The White Lion, in the city. It's—"

"I know the club."

Bayden looked up.

"Yes," Axel confirmed. "I've played there. Most of the Dragons have played at most of the local clubs at one time or another. Now, we play here." He let that sink in for a few moments. "I want you to do the same."

Bayden twitched his fingers, but he still didn't try to pull away. "You said…"

"Go ahead." Axel stroked his thumb over the inside of Bayden's wrist. That loose hold was the longest they'd ever maintained physical contact. It was also the conversation where they'd made the most progress. It didn't seem like a coincidence.

"You said you didn't want to see me do another…bet that looked a bit like a scene."

Almost every muscle in Axel's body tensed. He managed to keep the ones controlling the hand touching Bayden's wrist relaxed. Forget some vague sense of guilt that Bayden might have met one of the bastards at the pub.

Axel looked at the mark around Bayden's wrist.

Bayden had gone to The White Lion because Axel had told him to play out of his sight. He'd sent him to those bastards. He'd actually sent Bayden away from the one place where Axel could guarantee that he'd be safe because, what? He'd be jealous. Bayden had put himself at risk, he'd put himself in a situation where he could have been killed, just to make Axel more comfortable.

He felt like he'd been punched in the gut. His stomach turned over. He forced more coffee down his throat. "I should have been clearer. I meant I don't want you to do bets like that anywhere."

Bayden closed his eyes. Seconds ticked past. "I should go."

Axel closed his fingers around Bayden's wrist, not firmly enough to keep him in place if he made a serious attempt to pull away, not hard enough to hurt the bruised skin, just enough to let Bayden know he wanted him to stay where he was.

"I won't stop taking bets," Bayden said.

Axel held back both a sigh and a curse. "How much of that is down to species pride and how much is down to the money?"

"It's not about the money," Bayden bit out.

"How do you make a living?" Axel asked. "You've never mentioned having a job."

Bayden looked down.

"Does your family help you out?"

"No!" Almost as vehement as when he'd denied being willing to take a bet off Axel. "Wolves don't take charity from outside the pack," Bayden bit out.

"And since you had to move out, you're not part of their pack anymore. So it would be wrong for you to take money from them? It would be...shameful?" Axel guessed.

Bayden nodded. "Wolves don't do that." He looked down.

Watching for the tiny changes in expressions paid off. Shameful had been the right word for it. It was that big a deal to him.

"Do you have a job?" Axel asked again.

Bayden shrugged.

"Or is taking bets your job?"

Bayden shrugged again.

How would a wolf put it? Axel chose each word carefully. "Maybe while so many people are willing to bet against you, you don't need to get a regular job. The bets prove your point, but they also pay the bills—they kill both birds with one stone."

Finally, Bayden nodded. "Something like that." He studied Axel very carefully. "I won't stop taking bets." He dropped his gaze. "But I can take them somewhere else."

"No."

"You said—" Bayden began.

"And now I'm telling you that the only place I want you to take bets is here, where I can see you."

"Why?"

Because you need someone to keep an eye on you. No, a wolf wouldn't get that—something more diplomatic. "Because here you can be sure the bets will be bets and they won't turn into mistakes."

"I can look after myself," Bayden protested.

"And because this is where all the Dragons play," Axel cut in.

Against all human logic, that statement seemed to carry more weight with Bayden than the fact that playing there would stop him from getting killed.

Axel wasn't above taking advantage of any gain he could get. "I'm not treating you differently because you're a wolf. I'm expecting the same from you as I would from any human who rides with us."

"You don't like seeing…"

"I don't necessarily approve of all the things that the other Dragons do. They're members of my club, not my submissives. There's a difference. Providing they obey the house rules, I don't get involved. The same would apply to you and your bets."

Bayden hesitated.

"You'll be free to take any bets you want," Axel promised.

"Because I won't be your submissive," Bayden echoed, just a little sadly.

"Yes. When you're ready to stop playing out both scenes and bets with anyone else, we'll talk about that changing. Until then, I won't try to stop you from taking any bet that's within the house rules."

Bayden stared at Axel's hand, still wrapped gently around his wrist.

"Whether it's about money or proving a point to idiots—you can do both those things here." Axel had to keep a careful check on his tone to make sure it didn't sound like begging. "True?"

Bayden nodded.

"I want your word."

"What?"

"I want your word that you'll only take bets or scenes here, nowhere else."

Bayden shook his head. "I can't turn down a bet just because I'm somewhere else. If someone challenges me, I can't just…"

He couldn't let humans think they'd won. "If you want to accept the bet somewhere else, you can," Axel offered. "As long as you carry it out here."

Bayden looked up.

"I want your word."

"Why?"

"Because a wolf won't break his word once he gives it."

Bayden froze. He didn't even breathe. Axel found his own breath lodging in his lungs. Werewolves were apparently able to hold their breath for years at a time. Axel struggled to match him.

Finally, Bayden nodded.

Axel would have bet the pub on the fact it was only him saying a wolf's word could be trusted that convinced him to do that. Bayden wouldn't be able to resist showing him it was true.

"Words," Axel pushed.

"I won't do a bet or a scene anywhere else – until you give me leave to do that."

"Good boy."

Bayden smiled. He looked down. A moment later, he cleared his throat. "I should go."

Damn it, Axel hadn't done anything to suggest they should hook up, even by scent. Hell, he wasn't even turned on. "Because?" he asked.

Bayden hesitated for a second. "My mother's expecting me to drop by. I said I'd sit with my grandfather when she goes out."

"That's a good reason," Axel allowed.

Bayden stood up.

Axel did the same. He still held Bayden's wrist. Bayden didn't try to pull away. Axel suspected that they could stand there all day. Bayden might eventually ask for his wrist to be released, but he wouldn't remove it from Axel's grip himself.

Bayden tilted his head back and peered up at him. It looked exactly like he was offering his lips up, pleading for a kiss. It would be so easy to give in to temptation and undo all the work they'd just completed. Axel stepped forward into Bayden's space but he ignored his lips.

He pressed a kiss against Bayden's temple, then let go of his wrist. "You can go."

Bayden looked up at him, surprised, but obviously pleased by the gesture. A touch of heat coloured his cheeks before he turned away.

Axel went across to the window that overlooked the back yard of the pub and watched Bayden cross the yard and open what Axel was starting to think of as Bayden's lock-up.

Money was the obvious root of Bayden's problems. It was easy to imagine him getting into money trouble since he left home and being too proud to ask his family for financial help. But it didn't feel like the full story.

From the way Bayden spoke about packs, it was just as easy to imagine that, forced out on his own, he was simply flailing around lost. No structure. No security. No one to keep him safe and point out when he took too many risks. A man might well turn self-destructive under those circumstances — he might utter a cry for help.

Throw in a fierce sense of species pride and a whole host of people ready to take advantage of a wolf who didn't understand that humans might see his actions as straight forward prostitution, and —

Axel shook his head. Screw whatever was causing the problems. Solving mysteries was an indulgence he could do without. Answers weren't important, fixing the problem was

159

the only thing that mattered. Happily, it occurred to Axel that there might be one solution to the problem whatever the underlying cause.

* * * * *

"Have you ever worked behind a bar?"

"What?" Bayden looked over his shoulder. The sound of the roller door on the lock-up had completely concealed Axel's approach. Bayden hadn't even realised Axel had followed him down from the flat. He wasn't ready to face him again.

Axel came closer. "Matt — one of my summer bartenders — is going back to university next week. That means I'm looking for a replacement to start on Monday."

"Me?" Bayden blurted out.

"Why not?"

Bayden hesitated. "I've never done bar work."

"An inability to give clear orders has never been one of my problems. Matt hadn't worked behind a bar before. He turned out okay."

Bayden studied Axel. His body language was the same as ever — complete confidence, pure dominance. "I don't need the money," Bayden reminded him.

Axel raised an eyebrow. "Too good to work behind a bar?"

"I didn't say that."

"Said...implied — it's a thin line."

Bayden shook his head. Axel worked behind the bar all the time. There was nothing shameful about that.

"Unless there's another reason?" Axel said, moving to lean against the wall of the lock-up.

Bayden glanced toward the pub. It was easy to imagine how it would be. "They won't like it."

"Your family?"

He shook his head. "The men who drink here."

Axel huffed. "When I want their opinion on who I hire, I'll let them know."

Bayden fidgeted with his keys, knowing that Axel had no idea how much trouble employing a wolf could cause, but not knowing how to explain it.

"What would your family think if they found out you were working in a pub?"

Bayden took a deep breath and let it out slowly. Money was money. He could explain it to them that way. They couldn't stop him, but—

"That bad?" Axel asked.

Bayden glanced at him. Would a rich brat's family have a problem with their son being a bartender? "It's just not quite what they'd expect," he said, carefully.

"You seem flummoxed by the idea yourself."

Bayden didn't deny it.

"You're allowed to ask questions," Axel offered.

Why do you want to employ me rather than a human? I've already told you I'll do whatever you want for free—did you think that only meant sex? "I didn't ask you for a job. I told you wolves don't take charity."

"I'm not offering you charity. You'll work damn hard. You'll do whatever jobs I give you, no complaining, and you'll earn every penny of your wages."

Bayden looked down at his keys. *I'll do whatever jobs you want for free.*

"It works out as full time and pays two hundred and fifty a week plus tips. You can have a one month trial to start with. If it goes okay, we'll talk about a permanent position."

Bayden looked down. Two hundred and fifty a week, every week. He took a deep breath and let it out slowly. That would cover the rent on his mother's flat, every week— guaranteed. It would… Bayden swallowed. Doing whatever Axel wanted for free appealed to every instinct he possessed, but rent was rent.

"What about the bets? If I'm working here…"

Axel straightened up. "No bets when you're on the clock—when you're working, you're working. But there'll be plenty of time for you to do them when you're not working."

Bayden rubbed the back of his neck. If he was two hundred and fifty in hand to start with, he'd only need to make up the extra three hundred each week. Three fights. One or two bets that looked like scenes if he couldn't find any fights.

It shouldn't have been a priority, it shouldn't even have occurred to him, but working there full time would also mean he'd be allowed to spend hours every day with Axel, and he wouldn't even have to feel guilty about it. It was a risk, trusting a human always was, but maybe it was a risk worth taking.

"You said you wanted someone to start on Monday?"

"Is that a problem?"

Bayden shook his head. "What time do you want me here?"

* * * * *

"Why do I get the impression that you're more nervous about this than you were about getting whipped by Richards?" Axel asked.

Bayden shrugged. He was obviously doing his damnedest to look at ease, but Axel's read on him was getting better. The boy was nervous as hell.

"Getting whipped is easy. All you have to do is stand there."

Stand there and take the kind of pain that would bring almost any human to his knees. Easy. Axel smiled. "You'll do fine."

Bayden nodded, but he looked far from convinced.

"Any questions?" Axel asked. Although, from the intensity with which Bayden had listened to his instructions, he was pretty sure Bayden could have recited them back to him word for word.

Bayden shook his head.

"Seriously, pup, there's not much that can go wrong. The roof's not going to fall in if you give someone the wrong change or mix up an order. The only drink you have to get right first time, every time, is Griz's. That one's important— and it stays important even if he really pisses you off."

Bayden's attention went straight to the correct shelf in the fridge and the non-alcoholic beer. He nodded.

"He's been sober for seven years, that's not something anyone messes with," Axel stressed.

Bayden nodded again. There were probably brain surgeons who looked less determined to get everything right first time.

Right on cue, the door swung open and Griz stepped inside.

He grinned when he saw Bayden behind the bar. Axel met his gaze and knew that all the humour dancing in Griz's eyes was directed at him rather than Bayden.

"So, are you back there because you're his bartender or his boyfriend?"

"Bartender," Bayden said.

Griz shook his head. "If I ever needed any extra proof you're an idiot," he told Axel.

Axel looked across at Bayden just in time to see his expression go completely blank. "It's a compliment, pup. A cack handed one, but still."

Bayden glanced toward him.

"He means he thinks you're hot, not that you'll do a bad job behind the bar."

Bayden shrugged as if he didn't care either way. Axel turned his attention to Griz, he seemed to be fooled by the act—and he wasn't as foolish as he liked to let people think he was.

Griz took a seat at the bar. "Beer."

Bayden didn't blink. He got the non-alcoholic beer and set the bottle down in front of Griz without a word. He marked it down on Griz's tab. "And one for you," Griz added.

Bayden looked across at Axel.

The pub landlord in Axel perked up and pointed out he'd damn near double his takings if he allowed Bayden to let all the men who drank there to hit on him by buying him drinks.

No. Dom outranked landlord every time, and the possessiveness he felt toward Bayden wasn't going away any time soon. "No alcohol when you're on the clock, and soft drinks are free while you're working, so there's no need."

Bayden nodded his acceptance. Griz chuckled, obviously guessing how Axel felt about letting Bayden even accept a drink off another man. Axel ignored him.

It was as if every gay and bi man in the county had somehow guessed that there would be a new bartender working that night and decided to turn up to check him out. Bikers and leather-guys came out of the woodwork.

Axel kept half an ear on Bayden's conversations and half an eye on whether he was keeping on top of his duties, but his intentions of babysitting the boy through his first shift were obliterated within the first half an hour. There was more than enough work to keep two bartenders fully occupied right up until the end of the night.

Axel sighed with relief as he ushered the last straggler out through the door. When he went back into the main bar room, Bayden was...gone.

Axel had come out from behind the bar a couple of times, but the furthest Bayden had moved all night was from one end of the bar to the other. Axel frowned. The boy couldn't have vanished into thin air.

A noise from deeper into the pub led Axel towards the gents. Stopping in the entrance, he leaned against the door jab. He'd thought that Bayden might be a bartending first for him in a lot of ways, but it hadn't occurred to him that he'd be the first employee who didn't have to be reminded that cleaning the gents fell within their list of duties.

Axel smiled. Bayden really hadn't liked being accused of thinking himself above bar work. His determination to wipe that idea from Axel's mind was palpable. As if sensing that he was being watched, Bayden tensed. He looked over his shoulder, paused and waited for Axel to speak first.

"How do you think it went?"

"It's your pub, you should decide how it went," Bayden said.

"Then it went fine," Axel said.

Bayden studied him very carefully for several seconds before he nodded his apparent willingness to believe that, against all Bayden's obvious expectations, Axel was indeed satisfied with his work. "I'll finish up here and get going, unless there's anything else you want me to do tonight?"

There were so many things Axel wanted Bayden to do. None of them involved his duties as a bartender.

"Finish in here while I cash up. There's pizza up in the flat. It won't take long to be ready."

Bayden shook his head.

"Not a pizza fan?"

Bayden sighed. "Why do you keep feeding me?"

Because it was the only way I can be sure you're eating. "Why do you always have a problem sharing a meal with me?"

Bayden dropped his gaze. "I'm sorry. I didn't mean to sound disrespectful."

"Noted," Axel allowed.

Bayden was silent for a few seconds. "I do like pizza."

Half an hour later, as they sat down at the kitchen table Axel was willing to believe that Bayden liked pizza a lot. His manners were perfect, but there was no denying that he ate quicker than a man who was just a bit peckish. Whatever he'd spent the thousand pounds he'd won the previous week on, it hadn't been food.

"You should plan on eating here either during or after every shift," Axel said.

Bayden glanced up but made no comment.

When the last slice of pizza disappeared, Axel took Bayden's first day's wages out of his pocket and handed them across the table.

Bayden looked at the money for several seconds. "Will you be insulted if I offer you money for the food?"

"Yes — very," Axel said. "And you shouldn't insult your boss on your first day — it creates a very bad impression."

Bayden looked at the money. "Would you say the same if I was human?"

"Yes," Axel said, with complete honesty. A sub was a sub whatever his species, and any chance Axel had had of lying to himself about certain facts had died a long time ago.

I'll do whatever you want for free.

Bayden had offered him a form of submission. It wasn't what Axel was used to receiving off human subs, but it was submission. Bayden already acted like his sub in a lot of ways, and whether they were screwing or not, Axel was going to take care of his sub by whatever means necessary.

Chapter Twelve

"You look worried."

"I'm fine." Bayden glanced up. His mother was studying him carefully from just inside her front door. "Really. Everything's fine." It had been almost four weeks since he did his first shift at the pub. If it was all going to hit the fan, it would almost certainly have happened by now. It finally felt safe to share the information that had been burning a hole in his mind for almost a month. "I got a job."

A worried little frown creased his mother's forehead. Her grip on the edge of the door tightened a fraction. "What kind of job?"

"It's in a pub, working behind the bar. It pays really well."

His mother's concern didn't fade. Bayden pushed his hands into his pockets, wondering if it would have been better if he'd continued to keep everything to himself, but it was too late now. "Axel, the guy who owns the pub, he's a good man. He pays me the same as he paid the last guy who worked there—and Matt was human."

If anything, his mother's frown deepened. She stepped outside, pulled the door closed in her wake, and took a seat on the wall.

"It's regular money," Bayden pointed out, sitting down next to her.

"Just for bar work?" she asked, carefully.

Bayden looked down. "Yeah, just for that."

"He doesn't expect—"

Bayden shook his head. "No, he doesn't." The possibility that he would expect anything else from his bartender had been pure wishful thinking on Bayden's part. "Axel's not like other humans. You don't need to worry."

"I met a man who seemed different when I was about your age," she said, softly. "It's the humans who seem different that are the most dangerous."

The need to defend Axel boiled up inside Bayden, but he bit the words back. She didn't need anything extra to worry about.

"You have to keep your guard up, little one," she whispered to him. "Kind words don't always come from kind people. And, just because someone tells you they want you to serve men drinks, that doesn't mean they'll never want you to do other things for those men."

Sooner or later, every wolf ends up getting paid to either fuck or fight, the important thing is to make sure you choose who you take money off. Bayden closed his eyes. He'd heard the warning so many times, sometimes put far more gently than others, but still.

"I decide who I fight, who I do anything with — Axel has no say in any of that." It was true. And, if Bayden had managed to avoid taking bets on anything other than fights since he started working at The Dragon's Lair, then that was pure coincidence and had nothing to do with him caring what Axel would think if he saw him taking a bet that might involve anything else.

Bayden pushed his hands deeper into his pockets as he did his damnedest to avoid thinking about how soon that good opinion might come to an end. For the first time, he didn't want to ask, he wanted to pretend that not asking, that not knowing, gave him the option of not having to deal with reality.

"How is he?"

When three seconds passed without an answer, Bayden knew that she was trying to work out a response that didn't require either an outright lie or an admission that it was time to summon the doctor again.

"You should call him out." Bayden met her gaze. "There's no reason not to." If the rent money he'd slipped into her pocket when they hugged hello went on doctor's fees, there'd be plenty to replace it by the time the rent was actually due. There were still plenty of guys at The Dragon's Lair who'd be happy to fight him with even the gentlest of prompts.

Bayden pulled himself to his feet. "I'll drop in again before Friday."

His mother kissed his cheek and sent him on his way with the same warnings she always issued, but she looked even more concerned than usual.

Bayden hadn't realised that he looked anything other than entirely expressionless, until he got to the pub for his shift and Axel's eyes narrowed.

"How's your grandfather?"

Bayden hung up his jacket. Keeping his back to Axel, he washed his hands in the sink behind the bar. "He's fine."

Axel's hand came to rest on Bayden's shoulder as he was drying his hands. He tugged Bayden around to face him.

They stood close together. Bayden had to tilt his head right back to look him in the eye.

Axel didn't repeat the question, he just did that thing where he remained perfectly still and patiently waited for Bayden to give in.

"I don't think he's any worse," he offered.

Axel touched his lips to Bayden's temple in one of those almost kisses that made Bayden even more desperate to be kissed properly, and not on the damn temple. It was all he could do to keep back a whimper.

"If you need time off to spend with him, or to help out your mother, tell me, and we'll work something out."

Bayden shook his head. "It's fine. Everything's fine." He wasn't sure who he was trying to convince any more. Then, a horrible thought occurred to him. He looked up. "Is everything fine?" he blurted out. "I mean with," he gestured vaguely toward the bar.

Axel frowned, as if the question didn't make any sense to him.

Bayden looked down. He was making a fool of himself. "I should get to work."

Axel put his hand on the bar, blocking his way.

Damn! "You said before that I'm on a month's trial," Bayden reminded him, scrubbing every scrap of emotion from his voice.

"And it's been almost a month," Axel said, musingly. "How do you think it's gone?"

Bayden shrugged.

Axel stroked Bayden's cheek with his knuckle. "It's gone very well. Best bartender I've ever employed."

Bayden was in no mood to be laughed at. He tried to step back, but there was nowhere to go.

Axel caught hold of his chin. "You work a damn sight harder than anyone I've ever employed. You don't moan about any of it. You don't need me to check up on you every five minutes. It's not an insult for me to tell you that you're doing a good job." There was no doubting his honesty.

Unsure what to say, Bayden looked down, but he didn't try to turn his face away from Axel's touch.

"Go on," Axel finally allowed. He stepped to one side and let him pass.

Bayden kept his eyes down and all his attention on his work for the best part of his shift before he risked glancing in Axel's direction. Axel smiled when their eyes met. It was impossible for Bayden to know if Axel had just chanced to look his way or if Axel's attention had been on him the whole time. It felt suspiciously like it was the latter.

Bayden smiled to himself. It was even easier to remember that Axel wasn't like other humans when Axel was right there and inclined to smile at him.

It was a busy night, just like it always was when the back rooms were going to be open to the public later on. Bayden turned to the next customer.

"You're a shifter!" The guy took a step back from the bar, as if he expected Bayden to bite him.

"Wolf shifter," Bayden confirmed, for far from the first time that month. He looked the guy up and down, he wasn't someone who'd want to fight. "What do you want to drink?"

The man was still staring at him in horror. "Since when do they allow dogs in here?"

"A wolf's not a dog," Bayden pointed out, with forced politeness. *A dog is nowhere near as dangerous as a wolf, would you like me to demonstrate...* He pushed his annoyance aside. "Are you going to order a drink?"

"Not if you're serving it!"

"Is there a problem?" Axel stepped up next to Bayden.

"I'm not drinking anything *that* serves. It's unhygienic."

"What?" Axel bit out.

It wasn't anything Bayden hadn't heard before, but Axel hadn't heard it. Bayden glanced up at Axel and felt his own anger climb just as quickly as that in Axel's scent.

"I don't care if it's some sort of tame bitch, y—"

A low growl stopped the guy mid-word. It halted the conversations around him as humans recognised it as a sound that evolution had taught them meant trouble. They all froze.

The sound continued to reverberate in the back of Bayden's throat until Axel put his hand on his shoulder.

The guy on the other side of the bar remembered how to breathe. "A fucking animal serving behind the bar." He glanced in the general direction of the back rooms. "God, you don't let it play here, do you? It's little better than bestiality. You can't—"

"If you think shifters are animals, you don't know anything about them. And if you think you can tell me what I can and can't do, you don't know what kind of pub this is," Axel cut in.

"I—"

"Am leaving," Axel finished for him. He nodded toward the door.

The guy blustered. He turned to Bayden, realised that Bayden hadn't looked away from his jugular when he stopped growling, and bid a hasty retreat. Bayden watched him until he was out of the room.

"Bayden?"

Bayden stared at the door until Axel made him look up.

Axel studied him carefully. "Do you need to take a break?"

"I'm fine."

Axel glanced at the clock. "It's only half an hour until you're due to clock off anyway. Why don't you —"

Bayden tensed. "I'm fine."

Axel turned back to him. "Go back to work then." He took his knuckle away from Bayden's chin and stepped out of his way.

Bayden turned to the next customer.

It was one of the younger regulars, Evan, the blond boy who Richards had sent off blushing the same day Bayden took his bet with him. He had to have heard what the guy before him in the queue had said, and the growl, but he didn't hesitate for a moment before he placed his order.

Bayden relaxed slightly as several other customers bought drinks and none of them complained about the species serving them. It was one idiot. An idiot who'd mouthed off in front of Axel. An idiot, who would have been much more to Bayden's taste if his voice box had been torn out and he'd never be able to say certain words again, but still just an idiot.

Momentarily without someone who wanted a drink, Bayden wiped down the bar with a towelling cloth. He closed his eyes for a few seconds.

Yes, the guy was an idiot. But he was an idiot who'd said what he really felt — who'd just said out loud what a hundred different men who drank there probably thought. That was the kind of thing humans always thought. Those were the kind of words that they always used about wolves.

Humans were like that. All of them—even the ones who said polite things didn't really mean them. Bayden had known that for years. The only thing any of them could be trusted to do was kick a wolf when he was down.

He jumped when Axel's hand came to rest on his shoulder.

"Shift's over, pup."

Bayden gave the bar one last wipe down and washed his hands before making his way out into the crowd of customers.

Axel followed him. Other men took their places. Bayden barely spared them a look.

"Don't rush off."

Bayden stopped, then cursed himself for being so bloody quick to obey a human. "Are you going to fire me?"

Axel nudged him into the corridor leading toward the kitchen, where it was quieter. "Why would I?"

Because humans always take the human's side. Bayden shrugged.

"He really got to you, didn't he?"

"What you said before, about me taking bets on things that look like scenes," Bayden cut in. "I want you to change your mind."

"No."

It wasn't exactly an equivocal answer, or one that invited further discussion, but he forced himself to push forward. "I want you to let me take bets like that somewhere else."

Axel shook his head. "Not going to happen."

Axel couldn't actually stop him from doing that. Breaking his word to a human wasn't the same as breaking his word to a wolf. There was no way Axel could even know.

"I'll know," Axel said.

Bayden glanced up at him. "What would happen if I did?"

"We're never going to find out, because you won't break your word to me," Axel said, still in that same confident tone of voice. "Whatever you do, you'll do it here."

Bayden swallowed. He was right. Bayden was tempted to consider the fact that Axel was right to be the worst thing about the whole situation—there was no way in hell he'd break his word to Axel.

Maybe Axel wasn't using the same tactics as other humans, but he was just as intent on controlling Bayden. That made him just as bad. Or maybe his mother was right. A human who a wolf wanted to obey, who he wanted to please, that was the most dangerous sort of all.

Following a human's lead, thinking about him as if he was a wolf, and an alpha wolf at that, it was asking for trouble. Bayden didn't want trouble. He didn't want to worry about what Axel would think before he decided if he took a bet or not. He didn't want to let Axel down.

Bayden's heart raced faster and faster. His hand curled into a fist at his side.

"What that guy said," Axel began.

"Isn't important," Bayden cut in. That guy couldn't hurt him, not the way Axel could. Bayden turned away.

Axel caught hold of his arm.

Bayden looked down at his grip on him. "Do you want to do a scene with me?"

"Not unless you're offering to obey my rules for longer than a scene."

"I'm not interested in obeying you."

Axel raised an eyebrow.

Bayden ground his teeth together, unable to claim that it was the truth without telling another lie. "I want you to let go of my arm." That was the truth, wasn't it? Bayden wasn't sure anymore, and that just made him want to lash out at the whole world. "Or does working here mean I don't get to want that?"

Axel released his arm but he didn't retreat. "You know better than that, pup. If you don't want me in your space, you only have to say. You know that, don't you?"

Bayden looked down. He nodded. He didn't have to let Axel in his space. If he had any sense he'd say that he wanted him to back off. The words stuck in his throat. He liked Axel in his space. Sometimes it felt like Axel's casual caresses were the only things that allowed him to keep even part of his sanity.

But that was the real problem, wasn't it. He liked it too much. He liked it so much he didn't want to risk losing it by disappointing Axel—so much he'd only taken bets on fights for weeks.

Bayden shook his head. It was time he grew up and stopped indulging in silly little day dreams. Fights weren't the quickest way to make money, or to remind humans just how difficult it was to break a wolf. Axel's good opinion of him was a vague concept. There was nothing vague about cash in hand.

"If you won't let me take bets somewhere else, I'll take them here."

Axel's scent became more pissed off than ever. "You don't have leave to take bets anywhere else."

Bayden turned away and headed for one of the back rooms. He was in there for less than a minute before someone offered him the chance to prove his point and pay off the doctor's bills at the same time.

* * * * *

"What the hell's going on?"

Axel didn't even glance at Hale as Hale stepped up alongside him. All Axel's attention remained on what Bayden was doing on the other side of the room.

"Axe?" Hale demanded. "Have you lost your mind?"

Yes, Axel was half sure he'd lost any scrap of sanity the moment he'd met Bayden. For the first time in his life, Axel wanted a dom who played in The Dragon's Lair to try to break the rules. The tiniest excuse was all he needed. One wrong move on the guy's part, and Axel would have a perfectly legitimate reason to throw him out.

Axel forced himself to watch as the guy led Bayden across to a play space that had just become free. An order had Bayden taking off his clothes. He folded them neatly and set them to one side. He remained completely impassive as the guy's hands moved over his body. He wasn't turned on, he didn't seem to be particularly anything.

Axel's eyes narrowed.

Bayden had no more interest in this guy than he'd had in Richards. There was no submission there.

Minutes ticked by. Axel watched it all. Bayden obviously wasn't doing a scene. As far as Axel could see, Bayden wasn't even pretending to. It was a bet, nothing more. He was physically there, but that was his only contribution. The look around his eyes was just like when he fought a guy in the back yard of the pub—like he had a job to do, it wasn't a pleasant job, but he was going to do it anyway.

Axel forced himself to take in each detail as the complete bastardisation of a scene played out in front of him.

On the one hand, it could have been a lot worse. It was just sex. There would be no bruises, no welts. It was just sex with someone who treated Bayden like dirt—who apparently thought that the only thing a man needed to possess in order to be considered a fantastic dom was a ready line of insults.

And Bayden…

Well, he let the guy use his arse and his mouth. He seemed as unconcerned about that as he was about taking a hit in a fight. If he was aware of the crowd watching, he gave no sign of it.

Axel was aware of the crowd, and the fact that quite a few of the people there cast curious glances in his direction.

Everyone was wondering what the hell was going on, if he'd ordered Bayden to play with someone else, or why he wasn't calling Bayden to heel.

By the definitions he and Bayden had agreed to use, it was a bet not a scene. But it looked like a scene. It looked like Bayden was playing with the guy. Semantics didn't reduce Axel's anger, or his jealousy.

Years passed, although it couldn't have actually been more than an hour. Bayden got up off his knees and wiped his mouth. Axel had never been more relieved that the club didn't allow doms to play without condoms unless the sub was wearing their collar.

The guy held out money to Bayden, acknowledging that Bayden had won whatever the hell the bet was. As Bayden reached out to take it, the guy pulled it back. He said something, too low for Axel to hear.

Bayden replied in the same hushed tone. The guy turned pale. He seemed too shocked to react when Bayden took the money out of his hand. Apparently content that the guy understood that he'd lost, even though he still had his jugular intact, Bayden turned away from the would-be dom without another word.

Axel waited to see if Bayden was going to look in his direction, but he didn't.

Bayden seemed to make a point of not doing that. He seemed to have a lot of points to make that night. Points like — *if you don't want to screw me, lots of other guys do.* Points such as — *you don't get to tell me what bets to do unless I bloody well give you the right.* Whether it was intentional or not, the loudest point he'd made was — *I act out whenever some idiot insults wolves, anyone I actually submit to will have to find a way to curb that.*

Bayden disappeared into the gents' room. By the time Axel caught up, Bayden was in one of the cubicles. None of the others were occupied, no one was standing at the urinals. They had the room to themselves.

Bayden had cleaned the space near the end of his shift. It was still spotless. Leaning against the edge of one of the sinks, Axel settled down to wait. He half expected Bayden to hide himself away, regretting making his point, but he came out within a minute.

He didn't look at Axel when he went to the sink and washed his hands.

"What was the bet?" Axel asked, forcing his voice to remain calm.

"That I couldn't last an hour without safe wording out." As he dried his hands, he met Axel's gaze. "I won."

"And did it work?"

"What?"

"Did it make you feel better about what the guy at the bar said to you?" Axel asked.

Bayden's eyes narrowed. "You don't like what I do, let me take it somewhere else."

"I don't reward temper tantrums."

Bayden jerked his head up. For a moment, Axel thought that Bayden was angry enough to tell him an unedited version of the truth, but Bayden corralled his temper as quickly as he'd seemed to lose his grip on it.

"You don't usually let idiots get to you. What was different this time?" Axel asked.

Bayden shrugged.

Axel mentally scrolled through as much of the conversation as he'd overheard. "He said that shifters are animals. That you shouldn't be behind the bar. That you're a tame—"

"No!" Bayden took a step forward.

Axel was shocked enough to fall silent.

"There are some words wolves don't say—not willingly, not ever," Bayden said, his words barely above a whisper, as if he felt uttering them out loud was a huge risk.

"Okay." Axel reached out, keeping his movements slow, giving Bayden plenty of time to back away if he wanted to. Bayden remained where he was when Axel stroked his cheek. His eyes dropped closed as if he was relishing the contact.

"Tell me why," Axel ordered.

Bayden leaned into his touch. Axel doubted he was aware of doing it, but the plea for reassurance couldn't have been clearer. Axel's anger faltered.

"It's what humans called..." Bayden swallowed. "In the Captivities. The wolves the humans caught, that's what they called them." He looked up, so wary, so uncertain if he should trust Axel with such information. "The things they did to those wolves. What they made wolves do—with humans, with other wolves, with..." He took a deep breath. "Those wolves didn't have a choice. Now wolves do. We choose, and that changes everything."

Axel stroked his fingers through Bayden's hair very gently, praising him for trusting him.

"Humans can't hurt modern wolves the way they hurt those wolves because now, we choose." It sounded like he was trying to convince himself more than anyone else.

Axel's heart ached for him, but he resisted the desire to pull him close. "You think that's what taking that bet with that idiot proved?" Axel asked, gentling his words as much as possible.

"He threw what he had at me. I proved my point. Nothing he can do to me will break me." Bayden cleared his throat. When he spoke again, his voice was strong and brisk. "If you don't want me to submit to guys here, give me leave to do bets like that somewhere else, or—"

"You didn't submit to him," Axel cut in.

Bayden frowned. "Yes, I did. That's what humans call it."

"I can think of a few things to call what you just did, but it didn't involve a scrap of submission."

Bayden glanced up at him, amber eyes once more full of uncertainty.

"I've watched all your bets. I've seen you fight and get screwed. I've watched you take a whipping and obey another man's orders. I've never seen you submit to anyone." It wasn't until he said it that he realised just how true it was. He'd never seen Bayden do *anything* that could be taken as an inclination to submit to anyone else. That wasn't something that happened by accident. Whether he did it consciously or instinctively, Bayden had to have worked hard to make sure of that.

"So the thing about waiting for me to give up my bets is bull?" Bayden demanded. "When you say you're not interested in doing a scene with me, what you really mean is that you don't think I can do what you want?"

"I didn't say you couldn't submit, that it's not in you. I'd bet my bike on you being able to, if you want to. But what happened out there wasn't anything like it." He met Bayden's eyes. "You're offering me more submission right here than you've ever offered him or anyone else in this place."

Bayden tensed, but he didn't pull away. "I didn't refuse to do anything he wanted me to do. That's what humans mean when they talk about submission."

"No. That's obedience, or maybe bloody mindedness. It might satisfy men who only really want a bet, a punch bag or an easy lay. But I don't think you even know what a good dom would want to do with you."

"What do you want to do with me?"

Axel met his gaze. No man who'd played with dozens of subs and established a hellishly good reputation on the local leather scene should be that pleased that a novice was willing to label him a competent dom.

"I want to get back to where we were in the kitchen when I kissed you, find that spark of deep submission I saw in you and see where I can take it. I want to screw you, and tie you up, and make you writhe for me — you know all that. But I want so much more. I want the whole thing, not just a quick scene. I want twenty-four hours a day, seven days a week. I want you to be mine. I won't take anything less." It was true. Even as he said it, Axel realised that he couldn't have anything less than that with Bayden. He wasn't capable of half measures with him.

"Submission isn't like that." Bayden looked toward the door leading back to the pub, as if he could see straight through it and watch what all the men were doing on the other side of it. "What they're doing isn't like that."

"Everyone has their own definition of real submission, real dominance," Axel allowed. "But when we're talking about what might happen between us, submission means what we say it means. It's about what feels real to us, and the fact you let me in your space means more than anything you let him do to win a bet, right?"

Bayden didn't deny it.

"I don't know if you're ready for it, but make no mistake, Bayden, what I want with you is so different to what you just did, it's not even on the same planet."

Bayden took a deep breath and let it out very slowly. Axel looked down for a moment. Bayden hadn't been hard during his bet, but he was now. Something about what Axel was offering appealed to Bayden just as much as it did to Axel.

"Real submission isn't about going through the motions or proving that you can't be broken, pup. It's strong, it's honest, it goes right down to your core and calling anything that happens in a bet by the same name cheapens it."

Bayden nodded.

Axel stroked his cheek. "The real thing, it's not something a sub can take a break from to do a bet with another guy every time he gets pissed off with some pillock who insults his species. There's no room for that in the kind of submission I'm talking about, and I won't pretend otherwise."

Bayden looked down.

"I won't play with a man who takes bets like that. But a man who *used* to take those sorts of bets, that's a very different thing."

Bayden looked up, eyes wide with surprise, as if he actually thought what Axel had just seen could have ruined any chance he had.

"When you're ready, let me know," Axel said.

Bayden nodded.

Axel studied him carefully. "Just because I didn't like watching your bet, that doesn't mean I want you to leave," he said, just in case Bayden didn't know that. "I still expect you to stay until the end of the night and eat here before you go home."

Bayden nodded again, but to Axel it looked like an absentminded gesture, as if Bayden was already deep in thought.

* * * * *

Ten minutes later, Bayden stood at the edge of one of the play areas, watching a scene being played out around a cage. It was just like what he'd always thought humans meant when they talked about submission. The man in the cage didn't really believe that the man who'd locked him in there was more dominant than him. Bayden had no doubt that when the two men left the play area, all the respect one man appeared to show the other would disappear. It was a game. They were acting, just like most of the men there.

Axel didn't act. Maybe that was why what Axel called submission sounded more like what Bayden thought of as respecting another wolf's dominance.

A more dominant wolf was more dominant all the time. An alpha was an alpha all the time. There was no need to pretend. Respect for another wolf's dominance came naturally. Instinct didn't let a wolf forget his place in the pack, or if his mate was more dominant than him.

Bayden pushed a hand through his hair as he tried to push the knowledge away, but it was right there, right in the front of his mind. Axel wasn't offering him the chance to submit the way the man currently in that cage was. He was offering him something closer to what he'd always wanted to find with another wolf—

"Does it bother you that I call you my pup?"

Bayden looked over his shoulder. He'd been so lost in his thoughts he hadn't sensed Axel approach. He blinked at him.

Axel frowned as he repeated the question.

Bayden shook his head. "No."

"It doesn't mean anything different to a wolf?" Axel pushed.

"It sounds nice," Bayden blurted out. "I like it."

Axel's frown disappeared.

Bayden smiled, thrilled that he'd pleased him if only by liking a nickname. "You don't pretend," he rushed out. It was true—Axel didn't pretend about that either.

Axel guided Bayden closer as someone tried to move through the crowd next to them. He slid his arm around Bayden. "Pretend?"

"Most people who treat wolves well, they can only do it by pretending that we're human. You don't pretend, but you still…"

Axel didn't take his arm from around him. Bayden closed his eyes and somehow resisted the temptation to lean forward and rest against Axel's body.

"Respect," Bayden whispered.

"Pup?"

Bayden swallowed. "What you were describing a few minutes ago. Wolves don't really have a word for it, but we'd call it respecting another wolf's dominance, accepting and liking that the other wolf is dominant over him."

"Then, when either of us talks about submission from now on, we know what we both mean by it," Axel said.

"Other humans..." Bayden hazarded.

"They're not important. If they want to do things differently, if they want their words to mean different things, that's none of our business."

Bayden nodded. He peeked past Axel's shoulder. "What do I call what he's doing?"

Axel glanced at the two men behind them. "Casual. Temporary. Purely play-based or scene-based." He shrugged as if what Bayden called strangers' activities wasn't important to him. The words they used with each other were the ones that really mattered. "Some people would call what we're talking about lifestyle submission or complete submission."

Bayden nodded again, filing the words away for future reference.

Axel was still pissed with him, and the scent of the bet still clung to Bayden's skin, and a man who *used to* do bets like that was okay with Axel. If there was any chance to have something more than a kiss on the temple from Axel, even for a little while then...

"How long?"

Axel pulled back far enough for their eyes to meet.

Bayden cleared his throat. "You said you wanted to work out if I'm capable of submitting to you the way you'd like. How long would it take you to work out if I can do that?"

Axel seemed to think about it for a long time.

An hour? A day? Weeks? Bayden didn't know what to hope for. He was sure he could respect Axel's dominance over him, that he could *submit* to Axel, for a lifetime, and it still wouldn't feel like long enough, but it wasn't that simple.

"It's not a quick thing," Axel said. "But at the end of six weeks, I think we could both have all the answers we needed."

"So, if I agreed to find out if I can submit to you, I'd only be agreeing to obey your rules for six weeks?"

"We could do that," Axel allowed. "We could say that this is a trial period and at the end of six weeks everything could be up for renegotiation."

Bayden nodded slowly. Six weeks would be —

"Is that what you want?" Axel asked.

Six weeks. A month and a half. He tried to make his mind work, but all he could think about was that he was keeping Axel waiting. It was what he wanted, but… "I can't, I mean…"

"Need time to think?" Axel suggested.

Bayden nodded. "I'm sorry."

Axel hushed him, a soft gentle sound completely at odds with his body language. "Think about it. If you come up with any questions, let me know what they are."

Bayden nodded. Axel didn't step back, didn't take his arm from around him. It felt good. For the first time in so long, Bayden felt safe and as if he was right where he belonged.

Six weeks. Maybe if he got enough cash saved up. Rent. Bills. Food. Doctors. His mind swirled with numbers that climbed higher and higher.

"My job," Bayden blurted out.

It had seemed like Axel was focused on the scene, but he lost all interest in it as soon as Bayden spoke.

"Submitting to you means doing whatever you want for free, doesn't it?"

"No. Your job would be separate from that. You'd still work here. You'd still get paid the same."

Bayden looked down. "I don't mind not getting paid. I just, I'd prefer to know if…"

"You were right to ask, and my decision stands. You'd get paid for the work you do in the pub, but I won't be paying you for anything else. Paid bar service, free submission."

Bayden nodded and went back to his silent calculations. He couldn't do it now. He couldn't do it until he saved up enough to top up his wages through those six weeks. But he knew how to earn money.

He couldn't do it now, but soon. It was just possible that he might be able to submit to Axel soon.

Chapter Thirteen

"Do you know what the symptoms for rabies are?" Griz asked, taking a seat at the table with Axel.

"I know I'm going to regret asking this, but—why?"

"Tolmore thinks that's what's wrong with Bayden. He's got money on it."

Axel raised an eyebrow at him.

"He saw a documentary on TV last night. He says when the rabies reaches someone's brain, they completely lose the plot." Griz glanced over his shoulder to where Bayden was working behind the bar. "That part certainly fits."

Axel didn't need to move. He already had a perfect line of sight. At the moment, Bayden was simply working away, serving the drinks, covering the entire length of the bar while Axel took his break. Bayden didn't look as if he'd lost his mind, but that was only because he wasn't allowed to take bets while he was on the clock.

Once his shift ended, well—if things had appeared to be looking up two weeks ago, Axel had since realised that there was no direction that could be sensibly referred to as up.

It was like being trapped in a leather-clad version of ground hog day. Bayden did his job; Axel had to grant him that. The boy had no problem being one hundred percent focused on his job. He worked like a Trojan. No task was too much to ask or too menial.

He also had no problem taking any bet that was offered to him. Anything would do. His only limits were the club rules, and his standards were somewhere around the bottom of the barrel. Axel had lost count of the number of guys Bayden had screwed as part of some bet or other. If the Dragons all had more sense than to approach him, there were plenty of other guys who pounced on the idea of a willing werewolf.

For someone who had apparently lost his mind, Bayden looked remarkably calm about it all.

"Well?" Griz pushed.

Axel dragged his attention back to his friend. "Bayden doesn't have rabies."

"You're sure?"

"Yes."

"What about OCD?"

"OCD?" Axel asked.

"The obsessive compulsive thing. It fits much better, doesn't it?"

"No."

"Axe, seriously. The boy cleans stuff — all the time." Griz shook his head. "A well maintained bike — fine. A highly polished pair of boots — great. But at this rate the entire damn pub is going to sparkle and that is not a good look on a bikers' pub."

Axel chuckled. "I told him I expected him to work hard, he's just proving a point."

"What's he proving when he screws every dom in the pub except for you?" Griz asked.

Axel's smile faded. He didn't know. That was the damn problem. There would be a point behind the way Bayden had acted out over the last two weeks. Bayden would have a reason. But what the hell it was, was beyond Axel. A last blow-out before he took a shot at real submission? A panicked attempt to show Axel that he wasn't submitting to him yet? Something else — something only a wolf could understand?

Axel rubbed at the stubble across his jaw line. The muscles in his face were starting to ache from the amount of time he spent grinding his teeth together watching Bayden make a mockery of real scenes again and again. Of course, it was better that Bayden did his bets there rather than anywhere else, but it didn't mean Axel had to actually like what he saw. He dropped his head back to rest on the wall behind the bench he sat on.

"There's another betting pool," Griz said.

"God help us."

Griz chuckled. "This one's about you."

Axel sighed, but he didn't look away from Bayden. "Go on. Hit me with it."

"Hale thinks you'll eventually realise that wolves are more trouble than they're worth and get rid of him without ever actually laying a hand on him. Tolmore says you've already lost interest in him—possibly because of the rabies thing. Drac thinks you're going to throttle him if he doesn't come to heel soon."

"What's your money on?" Axel asked.

"I think you're going to collar him."

Axel turned to Griz.

"I've known you for longer than any of them," Griz pointed out. "When someone gets under your skin, you won't give up on them. You're like a dog with a bone." He chuckled. "That wasn't actually a werewolf joke."

"I don't think any of you know a damn thing about rabies, OCD or shifters." Axel sighed.

"Maybe not, but I was right when I said I know you. You got Hale to believe he could beat cancer—twice. You put me back on the wagon dozens of times before I finally got with the programme. Hell, you even convinced Drac to get out of the closet and I thought that would take a crowbar. Once you decide to consider someone family, there's no point betting against you fixing whatever the hell is wrong with them—even if it's rabies."

Axel didn't deny it, but he wasn't inclined to sit around listening to it. He stood up.

"Give it up," Griz said. "You won't stop until you've put a collar on the boy, and you know it. Hell—you haven't even looked at another sub since Bayden walked in here, not even Evan."

Axel managed to bring a face to mind with some effort. Recently recruited regular, blond, quiet, a blatant lifestyle sub and way out of his depth. Prettier than Bayden, but nowhere near as interesting. "Evan's—"

"Settling in quite nicely without your help," Griz cut in.

"I was going to say he's far more your type than mine," Axel said, with a laugh.

He went back behind the bar. Bayden seemed especially focused on his work and disinclined to meet Axel's gaze that evening. It didn't feel like a good sign.

Finally, their shift ended. Axel and Bayden were both free to get out from behind the bar. And now, Axel had the privilege of watching Bayden do God knew what with a whole string of guys, while he just stood around and watched. Hell, it wasn't even as if he could do a scene of his own. Even if he could have taken his eyes off Bayden for long enough to get laid, Axel doubted he could have got it up knowing what Bayden might be doing in one of the other rooms.

As things were, Bayden was nothing if not consistent. He never approached anyone. He never suggested a bet. Men came to him, not the other way around. It was one of the nights when the back rooms were open to some of the regulars. Bayden had barely rounded the edge of the bar before someone damn near leapfrogged another man to get at him.

Axel wasn't far away, but the only word he caught was bet.

Bayden shook his head. Axel didn't hear what Bayden said, but the guy who'd offered him the bet went away alone. Bayden had obviously said no. Sirens went off inside Axel's head.

Less than a minute passed before someone else approached Bayden. Another shake of the head. Bayden moved slowly through the crowd in the main bar room but he didn't head toward the back rooms. He turned down guy after guy.

Axel kept him in sight. It was going to be the calm before the storm. It was all going to hit the fan. He tensed, trying to work out how things could actually get worse than they'd been for the last two weeks. There hadn't actually been much hard core S&M thrown Bayden's way. Most of the guys who approached him had been novices just looking for rough sex or the thrill of knowing they were topping a shifter. If Bayden was looking for something harsher now—

Bayden glanced toward Axel. That was different too. Bayden didn't usually look in his direction—in fact he'd always made a point of pretending Axel didn't exist whenever he went on one of his gambling sprees. Axel waited, wondering if Bayden was going to approach him, but no. Bayden lurked on the other side of the bar room.

A few minutes passed. Bayden looked in his direction again. Their eyes met, Bayden lowered his gaze. A little while later, the same. Eye contact and a lowered gaze. It looked almost like flirtation.

Axel thought back to what Bayden had tried to explain to him before. A wolf didn't approach a more dominant wolf—that wasn't the way it worked for shifters. It wasn't a rule, it was instinct.

Axel pushed himself away from the wall he'd been leaning against. He stopped just outside Bayden's personal space, stared down at him and simply waited to see what the hell was going to happen next.

"You said I could ask questions about what would happen if…" Bayden pushed his hands deep into his pockets.

"Questions because you're curious, or questions because you've decided you want to submit to me?"

Bayden focused on a point around Axel's right collarbone. "I'm not just curious."

Axel's pulse doubled. "Is there anything that would stop you submitting to me from tonight?" he asked, far more calmly than he felt.

Bayden shook his head. He met Axel's gaze and, even though nothing past that had been agreed, there was something different in the atmosphere. The admission had altered things. Bayden looked ready for anything from a right hook to an order to get down on his knees for the entire club.

It wasn't their busiest night. The only crowds were in the back rooms. Axel spotted an empty table in the quietest corner of the bar room. As he led Bayden across to it, Axel caught Drac's gaze.

There were plenty of club guys in. They could keep an eye on everything while he was occupied. The way Drac grinned made it clear he'd got the message. Axel wouldn't be disturbed unless someone died or the pub caught fire.

At the table, Axel studied Bayden carefully, but it was as hard as ever to get a read on him. Bayden had taken his hands out of his pockets when he sat down. Each hand rested motionlessly on the seat to either side of Bayden's legs, as if he was trying not to fidget.

"You said you have questions."

Bayden nodded. "You don't want anyone who is submitting to you to take bets?"

"You already know the answer to that."

Bayden stared down at the table for several seconds. "What if you decided some bets and he decided other ones?"

Axel narrowed his gaze. "Which bets do you want to keep control of?"

"The fights. If you're willing to let me keep taking bets on fights, then I'll—" Bayden took a deep breath. "Then you can decide what I do about everything else."

Axel was aware that close scrutiny could go in both directions. Bayden wasn't trying to be difficult, he was doing his damnedest to bend as far as he could.

"You won't take any bet that looks even vaguely like a scene?" Axel checked.

"Not while I'm submitting to you, not unless you tell me to take it."

It would be a cold day in hell before Axel did that, but he swallowed those words, not wanting to make it sound like he was throwing the offer back in Bayden's face.

"That would work," Axel said.

Bayden gave a jerky nod.

"Why is it so important to you?" Axel asked.

It took a long time for Bayden to put his answer into words. "It's not something a human should decide for a wolf."

Axel stroked his fingers down Bayden's cheek. He was so serious. The answer seemed to explain everything in Bayden's eyes. It explained exactly nothing to Axel.

"Next question," Axel ordered.

"My mother's used to me dropping by a couple of times a week."

And Bayden obviously hadn't wasted the last fortnight. He'd been working out exactly what handing over complete control to another man could affect.

Axel hadn't wasted his time either. He had very definite plans for Bayden. "While you're submitting to me, you'll live here." It was a statement, not a suggestion. "If you want to go out, you'll ask me, and wait for permission to do that. You won't get permission to be away overnight, and I won't guarantee you'll always get permission to go wherever you want in the day, either. But if it's to do with your family then asking permission will be a formality—you'll be allowed to visit them as often as you want."

Axel waited for him to protest at effectively being grounded. He had his arguments ready and was very willing to make them. But, no. Apparently Bayden was fine with that. He nodded as if it was nothing more than what he'd expected.

Axel smiled. In some ways, wolves were wonderful. "Next question."

"What happens to my bike?"

And in some ways wolves were as unpredictable as hell. "What are you worried about happening to it?"

"If you don't want me to ride it, I won't. But no one else can ride it, and I won't ride pillion." He studied Axel carefully as he spoke.

"Because you don't like what some men call the pillion seat?" Axel guessed.

Bayden tensed. Even thinking the word bitch seat seemed to push him close to the edge. He nodded, sharply. "I won't ride pillion."

During the last two weeks Axel had plenty of time to imagine every scenario he might put Bayden in. "What about being a passenger in my car?"

"That's fine."

"Then we can agree. Although, I've no intention of banning you from riding your bike. You'll go on the club runs the same as usual, and ride most other places you get permission to go."

Bayden blinked, as if surprised, but he seemed pleased with the decision.

"What else?" Axel asked.

"That's it."

Axel smiled. Bayden really was a curious mixture of experience and naivety. "That was a cue for you to tell me the rest of your limits." He waited to find out which of his plans for Bayden might have to be modified, but Bayden just frowned.

"I don't have any limits."

You just stated three. No, it wasn't worth risking their tentative negotiations just for the pleasure of adding one more word to their joint dictionary. Axel let the fact that limits didn't only apply to overtly kinky and sexual things slide for the moment. "Everyone has limits. Doms and subs. There's no shame in them. Most people have lots when they start out, some drop away over time, but a few stick forever."

"Wolves don't have limits." Bayden seemed to genuinely believe that. He tilted his head to one side and seemed to think deeply for a moment. "If more dominant humans have limits, you have them."

"Doms usually phrase their limits as rules. And, if anything, they have far more of them than subs."

Bayden's confusion disappeared. Rules were apparently a far more positive thing in his mind. He leaned forward in the chair. "What are the rules?"

Axel shook his head. "We're discussing your limits."

"I don't have any," he repeated.

Axel studied him for a few seconds. "We'll say that you don't have enough experience to know what your limits are," he decided. "When we run into one, you'll say your safe word, and we'll work it out then."

Bayden leaned back in his chair as if Axel had slapped him. "I didn't ask for a safe word."

Axel raised an eyebrow. "You're not playing without one."

Bayden opened his mouth, then hesitated. "Is that a rule?"

"Yes. And refusing to have a safe word isn't a reasonable limit."

Bayden paused for a moment. "Will you tell me the other rules?"

Axel relented. "A few of the main ones, yes." He wasn't going to throw twenty at him in the first few minutes. "If I ask you a question, I expect you to answer it honestly. If I give you an order that's within your limits, I expect you to follow it to the best of your ability. If there's a problem, I expect you to tell me about it—that includes saying your safe word if you need to, and telling me about any new limits you discover."

Bayden looked up at the last point.

"Remember what I said about the differences between a scene and a bet—we're on the same side. There's no winner and loser. Saying a safe word doesn't mean you failed, it means you're letting me know something important."

Bayden didn't look enthusiastic, but he nodded that he'd heard.

"I expect you to commit to this," Axel warned him. "You can't go through the motions and treat it like something you need to survive. So, if I catch you trying to treat anything we do together like a bet, if I think you're trying to hold back and hide something from me, I'll call you on it." The idea of finally being able to do that—of having the right to do that, sang through Axel's veins making him lightheaded with pleasure.

Bayden nodded again. And that was it. It was finally happening. All the plans and theories Axel had been working on were actually going to see the light. He was never going to have to watch another man lay hand on Bayden. This was going to happen.

Axel stroked his fingers through Bayden's hair, pushing it back from his face. "Good boy."

Bayden met his eyes for a moment, but he seemed willing to accept both Axel's touch and his praise as good things.

Axel glanced at his watch. It was close enough to closing time. He didn't have the patience to wait any longer. He left Bayden sitting at the table when he went up to the bar and rang the bell for last orders.

Aeons passed, but eventually, the last of the paying customers were gone. After the noise everyone had made on the way out, the room felt eerily quiet.

Axel turned to Bayden. "Six weeks, starting now."

Bayden dipped his head once in acknowledgement. His whole body was knotted with tension, but with that one gesture, he'd made Axel's world a very different and much better place.

Axel relaxed for what felt like the first time in several consecutive lifetimes. For the next six weeks, Bayden was his, and it was time to put some of those plans he'd made into action. It was time to find out what sort of submissive Bayden really was.

* * * * *

Bayden took a deep breath. Other men's scents still lingered in the air, but they were fading. Axel's scent remained strong and it contained more lust than Bayden ever remembered.

Axel's attitude had changed. He was always confident. His body language was always full of authority. Now, there seemed to be an extra layer of dominance there, or perhaps it was more like there was a hidden layer being revealed, one that Axel usually kept covered up under a polite veneer, but which he was suddenly allowing to show through.

He was also more relaxed than Bayden had ever seen him.

Bayden swallowed.

This was no different to what he'd done in the past, not really. There was no need to be nervous just because it was Axel who'd be giving him the orders. Bayden had no doubt he could take whatever it was Axel was into. Silence stretched out between them, until Bayden found himself searching for something to break the hush — anything.

Inspiration arrived with the fact that Axel hadn't disappeared to lock the pub's front door the way he usually did. "Do you want me to lock up?"

"Sir."

Bayden cleared his throat. "Do you want me to lock up, sir?"

It was just a word. It was no big deal. He'd have called Axel sir just because he worked for him. Hell, he'd have called him that just because it was what humans called men they respected. The way his pulse sped up when he said it to Axel for the first time meant nothing.

Axel threw a set of keys to him.

Bayden retreated into the entryway for a few moments. Door locked and bolted, he returned to the main bar room. He paused just inside, waiting to find out which way this was going to go.

There weren't many things guys hadn't done to him at one time or another. He wasn't going to let Axel down. Nerves were stupid. It took all of Bayden's self-control to stop himself from fidgeting.

While Bayden had been gone, Axel had moved behind the bar. He had to have heard Bayden return, but he didn't rush to acknowledge his presence. Bayden shifted his weight from one foot to another. If Axel had no use for him, there was work to do. Axel had praised him for working hard before. Bayden headed for the nearest table and started to collect up the empties.

"Leave them."

Bayden glanced up. Axel wasn't looking at him, he still had all his attention on cashing up. Bayden studied the back of Axel's head, but there didn't seem to be anything for him to do but obey the order. He put the glasses back on the table.

Finally, Axel came out from behind the bar.

Bayden took a deep breath, only partially to prepare himself for whatever was about to happen next. Axel's scent called to him as strongly as ever. As he let out that breath, Bayden met Axel's gaze.

Axel stopped with a yard of empty air between them. "Tell me what you like."

Bayden frowned. Hadn't they already covered that? "The idea is that we do whatever you want." He only hesitated for a moment. "Sir."

Axel raised an eyebrow. "Is it? I thought the idea was for you to submit to me. Is answering a question outside your limits?" He didn't sound angry, just curious.

Bayden squared his shoulders. "No, sir."

"Then answer the question." Axel still didn't make any move to close the last of the gap between them.

Bayden shook his head. That wasn't the information Axel needed to have. "What I like doesn't matter. I said I'll do whatever you want. I meant it."

"Does the fact you don't like answering my question matter?" Axel asked. There was a touch of amusement in his eyes.

Bayden tensed. Respecting that Axel had the right to want things his way was the whole point, but...

Axel smiled and leaned against the edge of one of the pub tables. "I told you that this wouldn't be anything like the bets you've done with other guys. There'll be a lot of questions. I'll expect honest answers to them all."

Bayden tried to hold Axel's gaze, but it became harder and harder as the seconds ticked past.

Honesty.

Telling Axel the truth about certain things wasn't an option, but at the same time, he didn't want any more lies between them than was absolutely necessary.

"Human subs do what they're ordered to do, whether they like it or not, sir," he pointed out, carefully.

"Just because they're willing to obey orders they dislike, that doesn't mean they don't still have their own preferences. It doesn't mean they get to hide what they really want from the man they're submitting to." Axel pushed himself away from the table. "It's easy for you to push everything down and pretend that nothing gets to you. I've seen you do that in a dozen different bets." He started to circle Bayden.

Bayden automatically turned to keep Axel in his line of sight.

"No, pup. I'll tell you when I want you to move."

Bayden stilled.

"Real submission isn't about faking how you feel. It's not about hiding things. It's about offering up your every thought, your every emotion and trusting me to use them wisely. It's one thing to pretend there's nothing you want off me. Admitting everything you want and then accepting that I might not grant you any of it? That's far harder."

He stopped in front of Bayden. As Bayden stared straight ahead, he was eyelevel with Axel's collarbone. What Axel described sounded beautiful and terrifying in equal measure. Giving a human information to use against him was stupid, wasn't it? His heart raced. His palms turned slick with sweat.

"Look up."

Bayden obeyed. He looked Axel straight in the eye and held his gaze as if his sanity depended on it. He was pretty sure it did.

"I kissed you a few weeks ago." Axel said, his voice hushed and strangely intimate in the otherwise silent pub. "Do you like being kissed?"

Bayden swallowed, as a sudden rush of adrenaline sped through him. He tightened his hand into a fist at his side. "I..."

When Bayden would have looked down, Axel made him keep his head tilted back, as if he was offering his lips up to be kissed.

That wasn't what he was doing. He wouldn't do that. Just because Axel had chosen to kiss him once before, that didn't mean anything. He wasn't expecting anything. He had more sense than to think that kissing was going to be a big part of the next six weeks. And—

Axel dipped his head and brushed his lips against Bayden's. It was nothing but a tease.

"The truth, pup." His lips briefly caressed Bayden's again, feather light and impossibly delicate. "Do you like being kissed?"

"Yes, sir." The words came out far more softly than Bayden intended.

"That's better," Axel said. He didn't offer praise in the form of a kiss. It wasn't until he failed to, that Bayden realised he'd expected him to.

Axel smiled, and Bayden knew he must have somehow given away his hopes, but Axel still didn't bring their lips together. Without thinking, Bayden retreated. For the first time since he'd taken a bet on something other than a fight, he stepped back from a man he'd agreed to obey.

Axel didn't try to stop him. "It's not easy, is it?"

Bayden stared at him.

"Leaving yourself vulnerable to something other than a beating is hard."

Bayden took a shaky breath. It should be easy. He'd never let any man see him struggle with anything they threw at him, but in that moment, he wasn't in control of his own responses. Axel had been right—it was different. He'd let Axel see the truth and, if it had been a bet, he'd have just lost it.

"Your safe word is red, same as the house safe word."

Bayden shook his head. "I don't need it." He lifted a hand to push it through his hair. He didn't need it and—

Axel caught hold of his wrist. Bayden tensed, but he stopped the instinct just in time, he didn't pull away from Axel again.

Axel guided Bayden's hand down to his side and released his wrist. "Your safe word is red. I expect you to remember it and to say it if you want out. Understand?"

Bayden glanced up, but it was harder than ever for him to hold Axel's gaze. He turned his attention to Axel's shoulder. If he only agreed to say it if he wanted out, then the fact he'd never want out, kind of made everything okay. "Yes, sir."

"That's better, pup." Axel pushed Bayden's hair back off his face, just the way Bayden had wanted to, but it wasn't obvious if Axel was praising him or just making it clear that there was only one man in the room who wasn't allowed to fidget that way.

Bayden swallowed.

"Finish locking up, then come upstairs."

"Yes, sir."

Axel walked away without a backward glance. As Bayden watched him go, he was desperate to rush out of the pub, jump on his bike and ride away. He had a horrible suspicion that Axel knew that and that Axel was giving him the opportunity to give in to that temptation at the last moment. He was making him choose. The only thing stronger than Bayden's desire to leave was his need to follow wherever Axel led.

He looked around the room. He had an order. All he had to do was obey it, and obeying Axel's orders had always come easily to him. He carefully locked the back entrance to the pub and checked that every other entry point was secure—determined not to prove himself unworthy of being trusted with such an important job.

At the top of the stairs, Bayden hesitated. Axel had said *upstairs*, not *into my flat*. It might be an important distinction. Bayden knocked on the door.

"You can come in."

Bayden stepped into Axel's living room and shut the door behind him. Axel sat in the armchair by the window, facing him, long legs stretched out and casually splayed.

"Leave your clothes on the chair," Axel nodded to a wooden chair positioned next to the door.

There'd never been a chair there before. It had been placed there just for his clothes.

Naked. Okay. It was an order Bayden was familiar with. It was an easy order. Quickly pulling his vest over his head, he folded it and set it on the chair. Boots off, he nudged them under the chair. It only took him a few more seconds to have his jeans off. He folded them neatly before turning to Axel.

Axel remained in his chair for several seconds, running his eyes over Bayden's body. There wasn't any part of him that Axel hadn't seen before. He'd seen Bayden do far more interesting things than stand around naked. But, his gaze felt different this time. He'd always been able to make Bayden think that he was looking over property that already belonged to him, but this time, they both knew it was true.

Axel pulled himself to his feet. He tapped the toe of one boot against the bare floorboards in the centre of the room. Bayden moved into position, and Axel began to circle him once more.

Bayden's breaths sped up as he waited for everything to click together. His cock stiffened. If Axel noticed, he didn't seem to be either pleased or annoyed by the reaction, probably because it wasn't Bayden's cock that Axel was interested in.

Any moment, Axel was going to get started. Then the nerves would go away. Everything would be very simple. Instinct would take over. Axel would have whatever he wanted, and Bayden would know he'd pleased him. It would be just like he'd imagined every time he jacked off, only better.

Axel stopped circling him. "Tell me what else you like."

That wasn't what was supposed to happen now. "Sir?"

"You've already told me you like to be kissed, what else do you like?" Axel ran his knuckles casually up and down the centre of Bayden's chest.

"I don't know what you want me to say." What were the magic words that would make Axel abandon conversation altogether?

"The truth. Trust your instincts." Axel traced a random pattern across Bayden's chest with one knuckle.

"A wolf's instincts are different than a human's, sir."

"I'll take my chances." Axel brushed the back of his fingers across one of Bayden's nipples, making it tighten and peak. Axel circled that nipple with the pad of his thumb. "What's your instinctive answer, pup? What else do you like? Forget about the bets, think about the times you've been with other wolves."

"I like being screwed," Bayden offered, not able to keep his voice entirely steady when Axel toyed with him so gently.

As if in reward, Axel scraped his thumb nail across Bayden's nipple and pinched it, briefly but firmly enough to send a shot of adrenaline shooting through him. It was harder to ignore that than a whipping from another man.

"Only bottoming, or do you like topping, too?" Axel moved his attention to Bayden's other nipple.

Bayden swallowed and tried not to lean into the teasing touch. "Depends on the man, sir."

"You can assume any question I ask is about you and me."

Bayden shook his head.

"Problem?"

Bayden cleared his throat. "I was answering the question, sir. If it's about you and me—no, I don't want to top."

"Because?" Axel prompted.

Wasn't it obvious? "It wouldn't be right, sir."

"Because?" Axel asked again. As he continued to toy with Bayden's nipple, he reached down with his other hand and palmed Bayden's balls.

"You're...you, sir," Bayden whispered, concentrating on not rocking his hips and rubbing himself against Axel's hands. He had wonderful hands, large and strong, and Bayden had wanted to feel them on his body for so long. He tried to find a mental space similar to the one he used in bets, but it wasn't coming easily that night. Completely blocking out what he'd yearned for so badly and for so long would have been sacrilege.

"You need to get a bit more specific than that," Axel corrected.

Bayden frowned.

"It's okay. There's no rush. I'm not going to get bored waiting for an answer." He rolled Bayden's balls against his palm, pulling them away from his body as he examined them. His touch was gentle. It made it so damn hard to think, to remember human words for things.

"More dominant," Bayden said. He shook his head. That was wrong. "A dominant, sir. Humans say a dominant."

"What do wolves say?" Axel asked. Keeping a hand on Bayden's balls, he stroked the other over Bayden's chest, exploring every inch of skin, massaging the muscles beneath it.

"Wolves don't talk so much, sir."

Axel chuckled. "I've noticed."

Bayden glanced up at him. He only intended to get a better read on him, but as close as they stood, he had to tilt his head back to look him in the eye. Axel brushed their lips together, as if he'd thought Bayden was asking for a kiss. Bayden hesitated.

"I'm not laughing at you," Axel said.

Bayden shrugged. He could if he wanted to. He had that right along with everything else.

"I'm looking forward to being able to get you to talk a bit more over the next few weeks," Axel went on. "Do wolves have a different term for a dom?"

"We just say one wolf is more dominant or less dominant than another, sir."

"What about the most dominant wolf in the pack? Tell me what that wolf is called." It was halfway between an invitation and an order.

"Just being the most dominant wolf in the pack isn't enough to make someone an alpha. That's... It's different..." Bayden trailed off. "Sir." He knew he had to add that, but he couldn't make any other words pass his lips. It was bad enough to think of a human as an alpha inside his head, to admit it out loud would be so much worse.

"So, topping a more dominant wolf would be wrong?" Axel asked.

Bayden nodded. Humans thought it was wrong, even if wolves didn't. He'd been around enough clubs to know human men thought it was a big thing. And no matter how much Axel might act like a wolf at times, he was a human, and that made the way humans thought about things important.

"You topping me would be wrong?"

Bayden managed another nod.

"What about me topping you?" Axel moved around Bayden until he stood directly behind him. He lined up their bodies. "Would that be wrong?"

Bayden shook his head. It was impossible to think of anything more right. It took all his strength not to push his arse back against Axel's crotch in a blatant demand to get on with it.

Axel moved one hand upward. Pressing underneath Bayden's chin, he encouraged him to drop his head back until it rested against Axel's shoulder, rendering his neck completely exposed.

Bayden tightened his fingers into fists at his sides as Axel wrapped his other hand around Bayden's cock. He didn't squeeze, didn't stroke, he just left his hand there. In a bet, it would have been mildly annoying. Right then, the temptation to hump his palm was almost all consuming.

"What else do you like?"

Bayden swallowed. "Blow jobs, sir." That wasn't dangerous information, was it? Bayden wasn't sure anymore.

"Giving them and getting them?" Axel started moving his hand around Bayden's erection, pumping him hard and determined.

Bayden shook his head. It was impossible to keep his hips still a moment longer. As Axel went back to teasing Bayden's nipple with one hand, Bayden thrust firmly into his other hand.

"Which do you like, pup?"

With Axel? The answer was easy. His mouth literally watered at the prospect. "Giving, sir."

Without any way of facing Axel, Bayden had no way of knowing if his answer pleased him. He just knew that he wanted it to please him, he wanted everything he did to please Axel in a way he'd never wanted to please anyone before.

When Axel's hand suddenly disappeared from Bayden's world, he kept thrusting forward, pushing his cock into the empty air.

"That's enough."

Axel didn't put a hand on him to tell him to stop. Just the words. Bayden whimpered as he fought for self-control. It seemed to take him years before he was able to still himself, but he eventually managed it.

"That's good, pup," Axel murmured to him. Relief rushed through Bayden.

Axel's left hand had been toying with Bayden's nipples the whole time. Now, he abandoned that in favour of turning Bayden around to face him.

Instinct kicked it. Bayden tilted his head back. If he'd been able to meet Axel's gaze, he might have been able to explain the move away as something other than what it was. As things were, it was impossible to disguise it as anything other than a request for reassurance in the form of a kiss.

Axel dipped his head, but stopped just short of bringing their lips together. Bayden's breaths were ragged. He couldn't hide that any more than he could have concealed his erection. If he leant forward a fraction, he'd be able to kiss Axel, but he didn't. Even when he realised Axel never intended to do anything other than tease him with the prospect, he couldn't bring himself to demand what he wanted.

"Good, pup," Axel whispered again. He ran his tongue delicately along the seam between Bayden's lips, encouraging him to open his mouth in offering.

Bayden swallowed rapidly and complied. It was an almost kiss, it hovered on the edge of reality, making Bayden desperate to be kissed properly, increasing his craving rather than sating it. Eyes closed, all Bayden could do was try to savour the scraps he was offered and be grateful for them.

Axel was doing something with his hand, but Bayden was too distracted by his hopes of a real kiss to work out what, until slicked fingers slid between the cleft of his buttocks.

He shuffled his feet further apart on the bare floorboards as Axel began to prepare him. Most guys didn't bother with that if they knew they were going to be screwing a shifter. Not needing to care if you hurt someone was practically the point of having sex with a wolf, wasn't it?

Those times when he'd been with another wolf had been different, but they were always conducted in a race against instincts. There'd always been the risk of humans catching them off guard. If there was no intent to hurt, there'd always been haste.

As Axel broke the not-quite-kiss, he moved to stand at Bayden's side. That gave him better access to work his fingers deeper inside Bayden's hole. Bayden found himself unable to raise the words to explain to Axel that he didn't need to fuss over him that way.

Axel twisted his fingers inside him, pressing the tips against Bayden's prostate, making him gasp. He was used to being ridden hard and rough, he wasn't used to a guy who made him want to push back against his fingers and howl with pleasure before they even got started. It wasn't what he'd fantasised about so often, but it was its own kind of perfection. Axel was doing whatever he wanted. Bayden was accepting it. Everything else was just a minor detail.

Bayden gasped for breath as Axel's fingers worked quicker inside him, taking him right to the edge. He bit back a protest as Axel took his fingers away. It was only the thought of having them replaced by Axel's cock that allowed him to stay quiet.

Axel pushed down on Bayden's shoulder. He willingly dropped down to arrange himself on his hands and knees right there in the middle of the living room.

"No." Axel tugged on his shoulder until he knelt upright.

Bayden hesitated, no longer sure he had a firm understanding of what would please Axel.

Axel took a condom out of his back pocket.

"You don't need to, sir," Bayden blurted out.

Axel undid his fly and freed his cock. Bayden barely caught a glimpse of the long, thick shaft before Axel covered it with latex.

"I know there are rules in the club, sir. But we're not in the club." He spoke faster and faster, as he realised that Axel really intended there to be a barrier between them. "Wolves can't carry human illnesses. We—"

Axel hushed him. It wasn't a harsh sound, but it made it very clear he wasn't interested in the information Bayden was trying to provide.

Axel stepped forward and offered the tip of his condom covered cock to Bayden's mouth.

Bayden fought against the urge to squirm. Prepared and ready to be screwed hard and deep, he was impatient to get on with it, but, if Axel wanted to start with his mouth, that was fair enough. He had that right. Even if Axel wasn't willing to discard the condom, he still had all the rights.

Bayden parted his lips. Axel smiled at that, so it hadn't been a stupid move. Axel pushed forward, sliding his cock between Bayden's lips. Determined not to betray how impatient he was, Bayden leant forward, more than ready to show he was willing to please a more dominant wolf in any way he preferred. He moved his tongue against the underside of Axel's cock and dipped his head lower, doing his best to work out what Axel would love best.

"No, pup."

Bayden faltered, not sure what he'd done wrong. Sliding one hand through Bayden's hair to cradle the back of his head, Axel held him still as he thrust into his mouth.

He wasn't being rough. His movements were controlled. Bayden couldn't help but like the way Axel's cock filled his mouth over and over again. If he could have tasted

Axel, perhaps it would have been different, but all he could taste was latex. As the minutes passed and Bayden realised that Axel didn't seem to be starting off in his mouth as much as staying there for the whole show, his mind was overtaken by one fact.

He wasn't offering Axel anything. He wasn't sucking Axel off or even going down on him, not really.

Axel was just using his mouth to get off. There was no skill on Bayden's part—there wasn't even any resilience required.

While part of him loved it simply because it was Axel, and while Bayden's cock remained as hard as ever, his mind raced. What could he have done wrong to make Axel want so little from him, to make Axel refuse to let him do something more than hold his mouth at the right height and keep his teeth covered?

He kept looking up at Axel, but it was impossible to read his expression, especially when Bayden found it so difficult to meet his gaze for more than a second.

Submission meant respecting the more dominant man and letting him have his own way, but in those minutes, Bayden had never found it harder to let that happen, to offer someone so little, to just kneel there and let someone believe he was capable of so little. In a bet, it would have been a relief. But Axel was right. This was nothing like a bet.

A beating would have been easier to take than just kneeling there and being so bloody useless.

Bayden's body railed against the restrictions. He wanted to be screwed, to go down on Axel properly, to show him what he could do, to offer him the whole world and prove that a wolf could please him. But, he just knelt there, trapped and useless. It was all Bayden could do to keep back a whimper.

Axel's rhythm sped up. He pushed deeper into Bayden's mouth as he came. There was no need to swallow— no opportunity to swallow. Bayden just knelt there as Axel stepped back and took his cock away. Axel walked over to the other side of the room and dispensed with the used condom. Bayden wiped his lips.

It was supposed to have been perfect. Axel was supposed to have been so impressed he'd want to keep him there forever. The reality couldn't have been further from Bayden's fantasy if one of them had been aiming for that. More off balance than ever, Bayden remained on his knees in the middle of floor and waited for an order.

Axel didn't make him linger there very long. He even offered him a hand to help him off his knees.

It was because Bayden wasn't used to humans. That had to be it. Bayden peered up at Axel, desperately trying to work out what he'd done so wrong to make things go so badly. "I don't understand, sir," he finally admitted.

Axel didn't call him an idiot. "There's nothing to understand. You said you'd do as I ordered. And you said you'd accept whatever I wanted to do. That's what you did, right?"

Bayden nodded. It was all true, but it didn't feel right.

"You said you didn't have any preferences," Axel reminded him.

It had been a lie. Bayden hadn't known it at the time, but it had been a lie. He'd wanted so many things. He still wanted those things. He looked down, not sure what to say, how to explain a realisation he didn't really understand himself. He folded his arms across his chest. His cock was still hard, but any idea of pleasure had already disappeared from his mind.

Axel pointed Bayden toward a door. At least that was a simple order. Bayden couldn't screw that up. He opened the door. It led into what was obviously Axel's bedroom. Bayden looked around the space, but he had no idea what to do with himself. At the end of a bet, he was sent on his way, and it was all very simple. If he hooked up with a wolf, that lasted until the more dominant wolf was satisfied. It hadn't occurred to him that he had no idea what to do in a scene that would last longer than it took someone to get laid.

Axel was obviously done with him for the day.

"Should I go home and come back tomorrow, sir?" Bayden asked.

"You're staying here. I told you that earlier."

And now Bayden had made it sound like he hadn't been listening. Anxiety trembled inside him. Everything he did just seemed to make things worse.

Bayden glanced across at Axel just in time to see him start to strip himself down. Humans could be funny about being seen nude. The more dominant ones were rarely completely naked in the back rooms. Not sure if he was allowed to stare, Bayden turned his attention to the room. There was one bed, a large double. There was a rug alongside it.

Seeing that made everything click into place. Axel wasn't inviting him to stay the night. He was just keeping him convenient. Maybe he'd want something in the night, or early the next day. The situation wasn't as impossible to understand as he'd feared. Bayden nodded to himself, pleased to have it straightened out in his head.

Axel sat on the edge of the bed next to the rug. Bayden risked a glance in his direction.

"Come here."

Bayden knelt on the rug in front of Axel, just on the edge of his space. Axel didn't offer any correction. Bayden's guess about where he'd be spending the night had been accurate. Axel even stroked his hair as if pleased he hadn't had to spell it out for him.

"Any questions?"

There were so many questions in Bayden's head he didn't know what to say. He couldn't lie about it. Axel didn't like it if he lied, and there were already too many lies between them. He grabbed a question at random, one that seemed safer than most of the others. "Do you prefer me to stay human, sir?"

"You usually sleep in your wolf form?"

Bayden's mind raced as he realised it hadn't been a safe question at all. It was a stupid question. The last thing he should be doing was throwing his wolf side in Axel's face. Of course he should sleep human. Only an idiot would ever think otherwise.

"Why?" Axel asked. Bayden glanced up. Axel seemed curious rather than disgusted. "Is it more comfortable?"

Bayden shook his head. "Just habit. I can sleep human, it's not a problem."

Axel frowned. "That's not the whole truth."

Bayden hesitated.

"Remember what I said about expecting honest answers to my questions?"

Bayden managed not to flinch. "It's warmer, sir," he admitted.

Axel looked from him to the rug. "I wasn't intending to let you freeze down there, pup. You'll sleep in the bed with me."

Bayden shook his head. "I didn't ask for that, sir."

"Can you control your shift in your sleep?"

Bayden nodded.

"Do you want to sleep in my bed with me?"

That was a far harder question to answer. *Tell me what you want, and then accept that I might not grant you any of it.* Bayden closed his eyes and forced himself to nod again.

"Then what's the problem?"

Bayden looked up, very briefly. Axel still didn't seem pissed off. "There's no problem, sir."

When Axel nodded toward the other side of the bed, Bayden went around and got in. It was strange, sharing a bed with another man. As Bayden lay quietly next to Axel in the dark, his whole body felt strange, too.

Prepared but not screwed. Toyed with but not allowed to come. Allowed to help Axel get off, but not permitted to try to really please him. Bayden had had just a touch of everything he wanted—enough to increase his need, but not enough to sate it.

He'd lied when he said he didn't care what happened. He did care. He cared a lot. All his big talk about not wanting anything for himself, and it had lasted two damn minutes.

It was all he could do not to squirm in frustration—furious with himself for having screwed everything up the one time he was with a man who was important to him.

The only thing that kept Bayden still was the idea that Axel wouldn't be pleased with him if he woke him up, and pleasing Axel was important.

Bayden closed his eyes. He'd suspected as much for a long time, but now he was sure—pleasing Axel was everything.

Chapter Fourteen

Axel half-stretched. When he realised he was unable to move any further, his sleepiness faded away to make room for confusion. He lifted his head. In the early morning light, he was able to make out a head of scruffy brown hair resting on his chest.

That allowed other facts to arrange themselves more easily in his mind. The reason he could barely move was because there was a werewolf pinning him to the mattress.

One of Bayden's arms lay across Axel's body, his head rested near the middle of Axel's chest. At some point in the night, Bayden had hooked a leg over Axel's thigh, and his knee now rested on the mattress between Axel's legs. Bayden's torso was a solid weight against him. Bayden's cock pressed against Axel's hip letting him know that humans weren't the only species who could wake up with morning wood.

Axel had wrapped an arm around Bayden's shoulders in his sleep and was already holding him close. He absentmindedly stroked Bayden's back as he ran through the previous night's brief scene. He still didn't know if it had achieved the desired effect.

Patience. That requirement hadn't disappeared the moment Bayden offered him his submission—the need for it was only really beginning.

He trailed his fingertips down Bayden's spine again, glorying in the amount of bare skin at his disposal. Bayden murmured and arched his back against Axel's hand. Still mostly asleep, he stumbled on a very nice side effect of that move. Bayden rocked his hips a couple more times, rubbing his erection against Axel's hip, before snuggling back down so only the very top of his head peeked above the blankets.

He might not complain about being cold during the day, but in the night his desire for warmth had been obvious, not least in the way he'd quickly migrated toward Axel's body heat and wrapped himself around it.

Axel smiled. Leather, motorbikes, fistfights and *snuggling*. No, this really wasn't part of the image Bayden worked so conscientiously at projecting to the guys in the pub.

The moment Bayden woke up, tension flooded his body. All attempts at snuggling stopped.

"Sleep well?" Axel asked.

Bayden quickly retreated to the other side of the bed. "I'm sorry, sir. I didn't realise I was…"

He'd remembered the honorific. He was nine parts asleep, embarrassed as hell, but he'd still remembered it. Perhaps it didn't mean anything definitive, but it was certainly interesting.

"Were you warm enough in the night?" Axel asked.

Bayden looked up at him through his lashes, as if he wasn't sure if Axel was teasing or insulting him, but he eventually nodded.

"Good." Axel pushed back the blankets.

"Is there anything you want me to do, sir?"

Axel shook his head. Morning sex was not part of his plans, worst luck. He pulled himself out of bed. "You can get a few more minutes."

When Axel came out of the bathroom, still towelling his hair dry after his shower, he expected to find Bayden tucked back under the covers. Instead, the bed was neatly made. Bayden stood next to it—naked, hard and waiting for an order.

It would have been so easy to topple him back onto the bed and Axel had no doubt that whatever followed that move would be nigh on perfection. He resisted and nodded toward the bathroom. "Your turn."

"Yes, sir." Bayden was halfway through the door when he hesitated. "Do you mind if I use the shower, sir?"

He sounded ridiculously wary considering the question. Axel ruffled Bayden's sleep-mussed hair as he joined him in the doorway. "Go ahead."

There was no way he could close the door while Axel stood there. Bayden made no complaint. He got straight into the shower, not the least bit embarrassed at having an audience.

Bayden looked up to the ceiling and allowed the hot water to slick his hair back from his face. His expression was damn near blissful. It had never occurred to Axel to wonder if a species that spent half its time in a fur coat, spent the other half of its time struggling to stay warm.

Bayden never dressed as if he was trying to keep out the chill. But did that really mean anything?

Bayden glanced toward the bottles of shower gel and shampoo, but he didn't reach out to take what he wanted. He didn't ask for permission either.

"Use whatever you want," Axel offered.

Bayden glanced across at him, apparently both pleased and surprised by the offer. "Thank you, sir."

"There's plenty of hot water. Take your time, if you like," Axel said, finally turning away. "But, Bayden?"

Bayden stopped vigorously scrubbing his skin and gave Axel his full attention.

"You have permission to shower—not to jack off, and not to come. Understand?"

"Yes, sir."

Axel closed the door behind him and wandered into the kitchen. By the time Bayden joined him, breakfast was ready.

Axel handed a plate to Bayden. He took it, apparently on autopilot. The plate held a bacon sandwich, the same as Axel's did. Bayden couldn't have looked more shocked if it had supported a tarantula.

"You don't have to keep feeding me all the time, sir."

Axel pointed to one of the chairs at the table. "Well, I don't intend to starve you."

217

Bayden sat down. He was still staring at the plate as if breakfast was a strange and alien concept to him.

Axel had wondered how much Bayden ate when he wasn't at the pub. This clue wasn't to his taste. "Eat," he ordered, more gruffly than he'd intended.

Bayden did as he was told, but his mind was obviously elsewhere.

Axel swallowed his reservations. "Tell me."

Bayden glanced at him.

"There's obviously something on your mind. Tell me."

"If I offer you money for the extra food, will you be offended, sir?"

"Very," Axel said, with slightly false cheerfulness. As he joined Bayden at the table, he stroked his cheek to soften any rejection.

Bayden stared at his sandwich for a few moments. "I should have thought it through before I agreed to stay here all the time."

"Thought about what?"

"How much trouble it would put you to."

"You could have thought as much as you'd liked, but where you'd live while you're submitting to me was never up for debate," Axel said. "Stop feeling guilty about something that wasn't your decision."

Axel watched Bayden through breakfast. Part of him wanted to chuckle at the silliness of the boy's concerns, except they obviously didn't seem silly to Bayden. A comfortable bed for the night, a hot shower and a solid breakfast, they were all things that meant something to him.

Axel bit back a sigh, wondering exactly how much trouble Bayden had got himself into since he moved into his own place.

* * * * *

218

Bayden didn't mention the scene the previous night. Axel didn't really expect him to. He'd long since accepted the fact that Bayden wasn't someone who'd start any conversation that he could avoid. As they cleaned the pub and got it ready for opening that afternoon, Axel kept a careful eye on him.

Technically, Bayden wasn't on shift, but he still worked like he was afraid of getting fired if he paused for a moment. Axel didn't once catch the boy looking in his direction. By the time the pub was as clean as it could get, Axel had had enough of being ignored.

"Last night you mentioned sleeping in your wolf form," Axel said.

Halfway through lifting the chairs down off the tables and placing them back on the freshly mopped floor, Bayden turned his complete attention to Axel. "It's not a problem, sir. I can sleep human. And I can make sure I stay on the right side of the bed. I mean, if you decide you want me to sleep in your bed again. I—"

Axel held up one hand, stopping Bayden before the offer became tangled beyond all sense. "I don't do guessing games. If I have a problem with something, I'll tell you. And you're about half my weight, I'm quite capable of picking you up and moving you if you're in my way."

Bayden nodded. He lifted another chair down.

"You're used to shifting every day." Axel didn't make it a question.

"I don't need to. I can go six weeks human, sir," he promised. "I won't shift without your permission."

"No."

Bayden stopped fidgeting with the chairs. "Sir?"

"You don't need my permission to shift."

Bayden made no comment.

"Unless we're playing or screwing, you can shift whenever you want."

Bayden still didn't say anything.

Axel rounded the bar and closed the gap between them.

"I'm not ordering you to shift, but I want you to."

"Why?" Bayden blurted out.

"Why won't I make it an order, or why do I want you to?"

Bayden swallowed. "Both. If you don't mind, sir." The desire to trust was obvious, but so was the fear that Axel wouldn't prove worthy of that trust.

"I won't order you because it's not some sort of party trick that I expect you to perform on command," Axel said, stopping just a yard away from Bayden. "But when you agreed to submit to me, you agreed not to hide anything from me — that includes the lupine side of you."

Bayden's hand rested on the back of a chair. His gripped tightened and released several times in quick succession. "Now, sir?"

"Yes."

Bayden indicated his clothes. "Can I?"

"What would happen if you didn't?"

"Sometimes the jeans survive. The top usually doesn't."

It wasn't a complete run down of Bayden's entire life, but it was information that was offered up without obvious reluctance. Axel was pleased with it. "You can take off whatever you want."

Bayden stripped. He put his clothes neatly on the chair. He didn't look at Axel as he crouched down.

The process was just as seamless as the first time Axel saw him shift. It was so much less dramatic than Hollywood always made it seem. No writhing around in agony — no popping and twisting of joints. One minute there was a naked man there, the next there was a wolf in a fur coat.

"Does it hurt?" Axel asked, without thinking.

The wolf shook its head — his head. Bayden shook his head. Axel smiled. Damn, but this was going to take a bit of getting used to. He crouched down. "Come here."

Bayden padded forward, his nails clicking against the wooden floor. He dipped his head and hesitated a little way off.

"All the way, pup."

Axel stroked Bayden's ears when he came within reach, just like he was saying hello to a dog rather than a wolf. Bayden accepted the gesture, the same way he accepted a caress in human form, but it was dangerous ground. Getting the balance wrong would break any trust Bayden had in him.

"I'm going to have to be careful to remember who you are, aren't I, pup?"

Bayden made a soft sound in the back of his throat, halfway between a whine and a whimper.

"It wouldn't do to forget that you're a wolf rather than a dog."

Bayden offered no comment. It was difficult to put that down to him having a lupine voice box. In his human form, Axel probably wouldn't have got more than a shrug out of him.

"What do you usually do when you're a wolf?"

Bayden blinked big amber eyes at him.

Axel chuckled and scratched Bayden behind the ears. "I should have asked you that before."

He straightened up. Bayden watched him with apparent curiosity.

"Anything you particularly want to do?"

Bayden shook his head. He obviously still understood every word Axel said.

Axel rubbed his fingers along his jawline as he considered his options. "If I treat you like a dog rather than a wolf, I'm going to get bitten, aren't I?"

Bayden shook his head. He stepped forward. Dipping his head, he nudged at Axel's knee and whimpered.

"Hey."

Axel caught hold of his muzzle and held Bayden's head still as he looked him in the eye. "That wasn't an insult, pup."

Bayden shook his head again, but he didn't pull away from Axel's touch.

"Okay," Axel said, as he reached a decision. "I'm going to make lunch. You can rest in your wolf form until it's ready. That'll give you a little while to…stretch your paws."

Axel carried Bayden's clothes up stairs. It was still hard to think of the wolf that padded along in his wake as being Bayden. It felt more like he was pet sitting Bayden's dog while Bayden was somewhere else.

In the flat, Axel glanced around. What would a wolf need to know? "You're allowed on the furniture." Nothing else came to mind.

Axel headed into the kitchen, leaving Bayden to it. He'd barely got food out of the fridge before he realised he was being watched. Bayden stood in the doorway, all four paws on the other side of the threshold, only his nose inside the kitchen.

"Want to keep me company?" Axel guessed.

Bayden hesitated for a second, then nodded.

Axel glanced at the floor, it was tiled and, he guessed, not the most comfortable thing for a wolf to lie on. "Stay there."

There was a stock of thick cushions in one of the pubs back rooms, for subs who were allowed to be comfortable even if they weren't given permission to use the furniture. Axel retrieved one and put it in the corner of the kitchen.

Instinct took over, he whistled. "Here, pup."

Bayden did as he was told.

Axel tapped the cushion. In his wolf form, Bayden had the same build as a large Alsatian. He hopped onto the cushion. It seemed about the right size. Axel smoothed Bayden's ears again before turning his attention back to lunch.

He was aware of Bayden watching him, but he ignored him, just letting him get comfortable being a wolf around him. Axel's mind went back to when he'd enjoyed doing puppy play with humans. That was easy. He could do that without even really needing to think about it. But, it wasn't actually helpful in this situation. All the qualities that puppy play aimed to bring to the surface were already visible in Bayden. Anyway, it was one thing to have a human act like a dog, but another thing to expect a wolf to.

Suggesting they play fetch would probably be a bad idea. Going for a walk with Bayden on a lead wasn't an option—especially not when Axel was willing to be damned before he risked putting Bayden off the idea of wearing his collar by letting him link it with being treated like a dog.

The food was ready before Axel had worked out any answers. He turned to Bayden.

"If you're coming to the table, now's the time to shift back." Casual, accepting, as if he wasn't the least bit uncertain how to command a man who currently looked like he'd make a damn good guard dog. At least, that was what he hoped he sounded like.

Axel kept an eye on Bayden as he shifted. The boy had barely settled into his human shape before he pulled himself to his feet.

"Take it slow," Axel ordered.

Bayden shook his head, dismissing any concern that he might get dizzy this time. "I wouldn't bite you, sir."

Axel chuckled, turning his attention back to their food now that he was sure Bayden wasn't going to topple over.

"I wouldn't do that, sir," Bayden reiterated. There was no humour in his voice.

Axel looked over his shoulder. "If I treated you like a dog rather than a wolf, you'd have every right to be angry with me," he translated.

Bayden shook his head. "Things are supposed to be the way you want, sir. You don't need to make allowances for me—you can treat me just like you would a human or…" He only faltered for a moment. "Or the way you'd treat a dog." It was obvious how much he hated the latter.

Axel held out a plate. Bayden took it with hands that had been paws just a minute earlier. His coordination seemed to be fine. He glanced at the sink.

"You don't need permission to wash your hands before you come to the table."

Axel didn't mention his clothes, wondering if Bayden would ask for them, but Bayden washed his hands and sat at the table nude as if it was the most natural thing in the world.

The food was almost finished before either of them spoke.

"I wouldn't bite you, sir," Bayden said again. "Not for any reason."

It was obvious just how important that was to him. Axel held his gaze as he studied him, trying to work out why that should be the thing that bothered him more than anything else

"I believe you," Axel promised.

The first time Bayden nodded, it was a sharp little gesture. A minute later, he nodded again, and seemed to relax a little. For some reason, his world was a better place when he knew his dom wasn't worried about getting bitten.

* * * * *

"Since when do you call Axel sir?"

Bayden put Griz's beer on the bar in front of him. He looked from Griz, to Hale and Drac who were sitting alongside him. They all appeared more than a little bit amused.

Bayden ran through everything he'd said to Axel since the pub opened that afternoon. There had been orders — the kind Axel always gave Bayden when he was working a shift. Bayden's answer to every one of them had included the honorific.

"Well?" Hale pushed.

They were Axel's friends, telling them to piss off and that what he called Axel was none of their business probably wasn't an option. "Since last night," he said.

"Made an impression, did he?" Drac asked.

Bayden put Hale and Drac's drinks down in front of them, marked their tabs and wiped down the bar.

"Are you ignoring us?"

"Whatever Axel wants you to know, he'll tell you," Bayden said. It was far safer that way. There was nothing Bayden could say wrong if Axel did all the talking.

"If you're going to be a sub to one of the Dragons, you should call all doms who ride with us sir," Hale said.

Bayden met his gaze across the bar. Polite—he had to be polite to him, even if he was a cop—especially because he was a cop. Bayden took a deep breath. "If Axel tells me to, I will."

"Does he really have to spell it out for you?" Hale shook his head. "Poor sod. He must be regretting taking on a wolf already."

Bayden tensed, his fist tightened around the cloth he'd been using to wipe down the bar. Hale couldn't know that was true, he was just guessing.

"Axel's taking a hell of a risk on you. Whatever you do is a reflection on him and his skills as a dom." Hale looked Bayden up and down as well as anyone could from the other side of the bar. "How you address other doms, how well you obey their orders, it's all a reflection on Axel."

Bayden studied him carefully. There was a human brand of logic attached to everything he said, but his scent was off and there was something around his eyes. Not everything he said was true. He was no more honest than any other cop.

"A good sub knows what's expected of him," Hale went on. "He knows what he'll be expected to do for his dom's friends, and an honorific isn't even the start of it."

There was some truth to that. It was Axel's choice who he did those kinds of things with. Anything that looked even vaguely like a scene was Axel's decision. If Axel said Bayden would do something, whether there was cash on the table or not, it was Bayden's job to prove that what Axel said was right.

Bayden had known what that might involve when he agreed to submit to Axel, but he should have asked for more specific information before his shift started. Suddenly, that was obvious. He'd let himself get distracted by his own worries, and screwed up, again.

"Axel's a good dom, but you're making him look incompetent," Hale said.

No, Bayden was the incompetent one for not checking with Axel before anyone else turned up. Just then, Axel came back up from the cellar where he'd been switching over the barrels.

Bayden went straight across to him. No excuses. No trying to hide anything. Bayden wasn't going to make his mistakes even worse. "I screwed up, sir."

"Someone's drink?" Axel asked. "Who—?"

"No. The rules about bets and obeying other men, I—"

Axel held up a hand. "The rules are very clear—you don't take a bet on anything other than a fight."

"Not without your permission," Bayden agreed. "I should have asked—"

"Asking won't get you my permission," Axel cut in, before Bayden could say anything else. "So if you have taken a bet with anyone, you're going to untake it right now."

Bayden tensed as he sensed the anger building in Axel's scent. He forced himself not to take a step back, but when everything he said just made things worse, silence seemed by far the better choice.

"Well?" Axel pushed.

And there went silence as an option. "I said that I'd only obey someone else if you told me to, sir."

Axel frowned for a second. "That's how you think you screwed up?"

Bayden nodded.

Axel's anger disappeared as quickly as it arrived. "That's not screwing up, pup." He pushed Bayden's hair back from his face.

The whole truth, on this subject at least. "Even if the guy I said I wasn't going to obey was a Dragon?"

Axel sighed, but he smiled, as if he wasn't really worried about anything anymore. "Give me the whole story. Who said what?"

Bayden recounted the conversation.

Axel leaned against the edge of the counter on the wall opposite the bar and tugged Bayden closer by his belt loops. They were still within sight of the men at the bar, but Axel didn't seem to care. "And now you want to tell me that you've found one of your limits," Axel prompted.

Bayden shook his head. "No. I wanted to ask you if I should wait until after my shift, sir."

"What?"

"When I was taking bets—I had to wait until after my shift."

Axel raised an eyebrow at him. "So, you have no problem submitting to them?"

Bayden hesitated. "Obeying, sir. Submitting is different—you said we shouldn't confuse what the two words mean."

Axel studied him carefully, until Bayden had to say something.

"A bet's not about the money on the table, sir. I'm used to proving I can take whatever humans throw at a wolf. Proving I can be a good submissive for you isn't so different." He looked down for a moment, before forcing himself to meet Axel's gaze. "I won't embarrass you in front of them, sir. I just wanted to check if the rules about when I'm working are the same."

Axel straightened up. "The rules did change—they're the complete opposite to what they were. The only time any of them are allowed to give you orders is while you're working."

Bayden nodded. That wasn't so bad. It was a small price to pay in exchange for being able to spend the rest of his time with Axel, and—

Axel slid his hand behind Bayden's neck and pulled him closer. Pressed against him, with Axel's grip on him tight and perfect, Bayden had no doubt that whatever commands he had to obey in order to keep on submitting to Axel, it would be worth it.

"The orders they're allowed to give you are limited to *get me another beer*, or *check how much I owe on my tab*," Axel bit out. "They get to give the *bartender* orders—that's it. They don't get to lay a hand on you. They don't get to play the dom with you."

Bayden blinked up at him. Axel's instructions were very clear, but if he'd wanted perfect higher brain function, Axel probably should have left a couple of feet of empty air between them.

"You're not their submissive, pup. You're my submissive. Mine." His voice was almost a growl.

Bayden managed not to whimper with pleasure, but it was impossible for him to keep his cock soft. Axel had to have felt his erection pressing against his leg, but he didn't mention it.

"Something obviously got lost in translation before, so I'm going to be very clear and give you a complete list of the people I expect you to submit to—and this covers all the different kinds of submission, from calling someone sir to letting him collar you, understand?"

Bayden nodded.

"Me." Axel caught hold of Bayden's chin. "That's the beginning and the end of the list. You submit to me, no one else in any way. I took control of those decisions so I can *stop* you from doing things with other guys, not so I can order you to."

Bayden nodded again.

Axel studied him carefully. "Tell me what a wolf would say," he ordered.

Bayden licked his lips. "He wouldn't, sir."

Axel frowned. "A lupine dom wouldn't want to keep you for himself?"

Bayden shook his head. "He wouldn't have to say. It's… A wolf doesn't need to say that he wouldn't expect someone to pretend to obey a less dominant wolf. Humans are the ones who—"

Axel laughed.

Bayden hesitated. When all past experience of humans made him see an insult, he forced himself not to jump to any conclusions. "I wasn't making a joke, sir." He kept his tone carefully polite.

Axel pressed a kiss to his temple. "No, pup. But you have explained exactly why they're giving you such a rough ride. Have you noticed how they're all nicer to Evan than they are to you?"

"Because Evan's human, sir."

"No, because he finds them all as intimidating as hell. Giving him a hard time would be like kicking a kitten." He chuckled. "It's obvious where he'd fit into the group, but you confuse the hell out of them."

Bayden wondered if he should admit that he didn't have a clue what Axel was talking about. It would be honest, but would it be polite?

"They all assume that because they're doms in the sack they're automatically more dominant than you in the real world," Axel explained. "They don't understand why you're not acting like Evan and deferring to them all the time."

Bayden opened his mouth. He closed his mouth. Dismissing the other Dragons from mind, he focused on what was important. "Would you prefer me to be more like Evan, sir?"

"Why would I? I've never doubted who you consider to be the most dominant man between the two of us, and I don't give a damn about anyone else." He tucked a knuckle under Bayden's chin.

He kissed him, slow and lingering, obviously not caring who was watching.

Bayden blinked as Axel eventually pulled away.

"If they become a problem, tell me, and I'll get them to back off. Otherwise, deal with them however you see fit."

Axel let Bayden go, only to stop him before he'd gone more than an inch. "You understand 'as you see fit' refers to sarcasm and trash talk, right?"

"It's against the house rules to tear anyone's throat out, sir," Bayden recounted.

Axel smiled and stroked his cheek. "Good boy."

"Well that was disappointing," Griz said as Axel and Bayden both made their way to the Dragons' end of the bar.

"He's not as gullible as he looks," Drac chipped in. "I was sure we'd at least get a temper tantrum out of him."

"You're not that believable a liar," Bayden told Hale.

"Bollocks." Hale tossed back the rest of his beer. "All cops are good liars. Part of the job. So is spotting trouble. I'm good at that too."

Bayden shrugged and turned away to serve someone else a drink, but a cop even mentioning trouble was enough to make his hackles rise. He automatically ran over everything he'd said in front of Hale, just like he had so many times since he found out the guy was a cop.

His conclusion was the same as always. He'd lied about certain things when playing up to the rich and stupid idea, but he hadn't actually lied himself into admitting that he was guilty of any crime against the anti-pack laws.

Serving another man a drink on complete automatic pilot, Bayden glanced along the bar. Axel was talking to Hale.

Hale looked pissed off, but Axel looked amused. And it was Axel who was the important one.

Hale was just someone who was best avoided. If that meant not responding despite provocation, Bayden could do that. And he would do that, because Bayden would be damned before he let worrying about a cop ruin his time with a man who was as unlike any human cop as it was possible for a man to be.

* * * * *

By the time the pub closed for the night, Bayden had given up trying to anticipate what Axel intended to do with him. The last twenty-four hours hadn't been anything like he'd predicted; Bayden didn't have huge hopes for the next few hours being anything like he expected either.

He stopped just inside the door to Axel's flat, alongside the chair.

Axel nodded his approval. "Yes."

It only took Bayden a few moments to dispense with his clothes. He'd been hard ever since Axel growled in his ear, making sure Bayden knew exactly who he'd be submitting to. Bayden couldn't help but hope that growl meant that what they did that night would be closer to the way he had imagined them being when he was alone in his room on the other side of town.

Axel headed straight for the bedroom. Lacking an order to do anything else, Bayden trailed along in his wake. He half-watched Axel strip himself down, trying to be subtle but unable to resist the opportunity to admire the lines of muscle and intricate tattoos being exposed.

Completely nude, Axel sat on the bed, leaning back against the headboard and stretching his legs out in front of him. He looked across at Bayden.

The silence continued until Bayden had to break it. "Will you tell me what you want me to do, sir?"

"Whatever you want."

Bayden froze, unable to move a muscle—even to blink.

"I did wonder if you'd spent so long forcing yourself not to care what someone ordered you to do during a bet, that you'd forgotten what it's like to hope things will turn out the way you want them to." Axel's lips twitched into a crooked smile. "But last night, that wasn't what you wanted, was it?"

"It wasn't what you wanted either, sir," Bayden realised. His heart raced as possibilities rushed through his mind, fear and hope twisting around each one.

"I wanted to see if part of you still remembered what it was like to want something."

Bayden looked down.

"If you felt something, even if it was just annoyed with me for not giving you a better scene, that's a good thing," Axel promised. "And you did feel something, didn't you?"

Bayden hesitated.

"Look up. Look at me."

Bayden did as he was told. Axel's expression was very serious.

"Sometimes submission isn't about waiting for an order. It can just as easily be about taking a risk and admitting what you really want, even when you're not sure that it will please your dom, or if it would be less embarrassing for you to pretend you only want what your dom wants."

Bayden held Axel's gaze through every word.

Axel pulled one knee up and rested an elbow on it. He looked so relaxed, so at ease with the whole world and his place in it. "I've seen you do things you hated lots of times. I've never known you to ask for anything from anyone."

Bayden's breath caught in his throat at the idea of doing anything of the sort.

"Tonight, I've only got one order for you," Axel said. "Show me what you want. Ask for things to be how you'd want them to be, if you weren't embarrassed to admit anything."

"If you don't want…" Bayden asked. "If I ask for something that your rules don't…"

"I'll let you know," Axel said.

That answer didn't help. But Axel was sitting there, waiting for him. And Axel hadn't treated him any differently because he'd seen him in his wolf form, or because he annoyed the hell out of his friends. Ever since they'd met, Axel had been kind to him, even when he'd had no reason to be. And all Axel had asked for in return was his honesty and his submission.

And, when it came right down to it, Axel was Axel. He appealed to Bayden's instincts just as much as he'd ever appealed to the logical or fair minded parts of his brain.

But, being honest about the way he wanted to show his submission to Axel… It would be the biggest risk he'd ever taken.

"If you want to go straight to sleep, that's as valid a choice as any other," Axel said.

Part of Bayden genuinely wanted that. Closing his eyes and hiding from admitting his own desires would be the easiest thing in the whole world. He took a deep breath. He wanted to run and hide, but it wasn't what he wanted most of all. "Tell you what I want or show you what I want, sir?" Bayden asked.

"Show," Axel chose.

Was that more embarrassing or not? Bayden didn't have the words, least of all the right human words, but scraping up the courage to step forward and offer what he wasn't sure would be well received went against every instinct he had regarding humans.

Axel didn't say anything else. There was no order to hurry the hell up. There weren't going to be any orders. If he was going to do this, Bayden would have to do it without any help. He slowly approached the bottom of the bed. What did he want to do? After the previous night, when he hadn't been allowed to offer Axel anything, Bayden wanted to correct that — to please Axel properly.

Bayden's mouth watered at the idea of being able to take Axel's cock between his lips and work it without any kind of barrier in the way. He knelt on the edge of the mattress and, without ever making a conscious decision, began to crawl forward.

He hesitated at the edge of Axel's space.

"You're allowed as close as you like."

Honesty. Keep nothing back. Do exactly what you want. Hide nothing. Bayden closed his eyes for a moment. When he opened them, he couldn't look up at Axel.

One of Axel's legs was still extended toward the bottom of the bed. Bayden pressed a kiss against the inside of his ankle, then another a few inches higher. He lapped gently at his skin between kisses, as he worked his way up Axel's leg. There were no tattoos on the lower half of Axel's body. The only decorations were the wiry blond hairs that tickled Bayden's lips as he nuzzled Axel's skin.

Axel didn't move, didn't speak.

Bayden could smell Axel's arousal. Something about what he did was pleasing him, but Bayden didn't rush to do what had the best chance of getting Axel off. He progressed inch by inch, his kisses as soft as he could make them. There were tiny freckles on the inside of Axel's knee. Bayden lapped at them before moving higher.

Axel's other leg was still bent up. As Bayden reached his thigh, he nudged his temple against the opposite ankle, silently begging for more room. Axel complied — possibly because he was already more than half-hard and was impatient for Bayden to get on with the damn blowjob.

Instinct told Bayden that he should just give Axel what he wanted, but the one order Axel had issued had been very clear. For whatever reason, Axel wanted to know what Bayden wanted for himself, and that meant rushing wasn't an option.

Ignoring Axel's cock, Bayden dipped his head lower to nuzzle against Axel's balls. He ran his tongue over the short blond hairs that densely covered Axel's sac. Axel shifted his legs further apart. That was all the encouragement Bayden needed. He worked his mouth against every inch of Axel's balls, kissing and licking until his lips were sensitive and tingling with pleasure.

He took each testicle into his mouth in turn. Murmuring his pleasure at being allowed to taste Axel that way, he let Axel hear and feel his gratitude at the same time. Yes, gratitude. Bayden's cock was so hard he thought he might go insane from frustration. His whole body ached with pent up desire. But the emotion that overrode everything else was gratitude.

Merely being allowed to linger in Axel's presence and work alongside him in the bar was a privilege. Being there in Axel's bed, with his lips tingling from the pleasure of exploring Axel's body, was a pleasure he'd never really believed he'd experience, and there was nothing he wouldn't do to thank Axel for it.

Bayden had no idea how long he spent glorying in being allowed to worship Axel's balls. He only turned his attention to Axel's cock when the temptation became impossible to resist. The scent of Axel's arousal had increased until, to a werewolf's senses, it was so intense it was almost heady.

Bayden whimpered as he took the tip of Axel's cock into his mouth and tasted his pre-cum for the first time. His own erection throbbed in time with his pulse, but that wasn't important. As much as he would have loved to come, what he needed was Axel's orgasm.

It took all of Bayden's self-control to slow himself down. There would be no rushing. He wanted to savour every second and be able to play it back in his mind, over and over again for the rest of his life. Rushing would mean lying about that.

Axel's hand came to rest on the back of his head. Bayden glanced up. He expected Axel's grip to tighten, for him to take control of his movements and force his cock deeper into his mouth, but Axel simply rested his hand in his hair.

"That's good, pup." It was murmured so softly, it was just on the edge of Bayden's hearing.

Bayden cautiously bobbed his head, working his tongue against Axel's shaft. Axel made no attempt to stop him from doing that tonight.

"That's right," Axel whispered, his voice deep and rough with desire. "Look up, let me see you."

Bayden tried to do as Axel ordered. It wasn't easy. He was sure far too much showed in his expression. One glance into his eyes, and Axel would know exactly how much he loved servicing him that way. Bayden threw caution to the wind and met Axel's gaze anyway—unable to keep anything back from a man who deserved his complete respect. It was the exact opposite of facing a man in a bet, or facing a cop who hated wolves on principle. It was far more frightening than both put together.

Axel rocked his hips, a tiny movement, as if he was trying to keep it back, but couldn't.

Bayden began to dip his head lower and move his mouth more quickly around Axel's cock. His desperation to taste Axel's orgasm was intense. He tossed every trick he knew into the ring. Unable to take all of Axel's cock in his mouth, he tilted his head to a different angle and welcomed Axel into his throat.

Whimpering and moaning around his shaft, Bayden begged for Axel's orgasm with sounds and vibrations.

Axel's hand remained gentle on the back of Bayden's neck until the very last moment. Axel tossed his head back, gasping for breath, as if pleasure had suddenly overloaded his body. His grip on Bayden's hair turned tight and perfect. He held Bayden's head still as he came into his mouth.

His cum spilled directly onto Bayden's tongue. Bayden swallowed rapidly, joyfully taking everything Axel had refused to give him the night before. He moaned his pleasure around Axel's cock as he finally got to taste him.

All too soon, Axel's shaft began to soften. Axel released Bayden's hair, but he didn't push him away.

Cautious, not sure how sensitive Axel might be after his orgasm, Bayden delicately licked Axel clean of any trace of the blowjob before retreating. Crawling backwards, he left Axel's bed by the same route he'd entered it.

He didn't look in Axel's direction until he once more stood, hard and still desperate to come, at the foot of the bed.

Axel stood up. Bayden tensed. Wolves weren't the only species that liked to make it clear who had won and who'd lost a challenge. A lot of humans had a habit of lashing out as they came down from their orgasm. If Axel was disappointed in him, he had every right to make that clear.

Axel joined him at the bottom of the bed.

Bayden kept his gaze down until Axel tucked a knuckle under his chin.

Axel brushed his mouth against Bayden's. He hadn't used a condom when he sucked Axel off. Axel had to taste himself in Bayden's mouth, but that didn't stop him from deepening the kiss. Slow, lethargic and full of afterglow, Axel kissed as if he was in no rush at all—a real kiss that held nothing back. Bayden moaned his relief against Axel's mouth.

He didn't manage an entire thought until Axel left him alone in the bedroom when he went into the en-suite.

Bayden took a deep breath. The risk had paid off. He closed his eyes and relished that knowledge for several seconds. By the time Axel returned to the room, Bayden had pulled himself together, even if he suspected that his cheeks were still flushed with both pleasure and a touch of embarrassment.

He paused at the bathroom door when Axel indicated it was his turn. "Sir, is it okay if I...?"

"Jack off?" Axel asked, amusement lending warmth to the words.

Bayden shook his head. "My clothes. Am I allowed to wash them ready for tomorrow?"

Axel seemed surprised by the question. He shook his head. "There's no need. You can get more from your place tomorrow."

"I wasn't asking—"

"You were right to mention it," Axel cut in.

There didn't seem to be anything else to say.

When Bayden returned to the bedroom a few minutes later, Axel was already in bed. He nodded to the other side of the bed, giving permission for Bayden to sleep there again, even after he'd come close to clambering on top of Axel in his sleep the previous night.

Bayden couldn't just remain silent. "Thank you, sir." He rushed the words out and prayed that Axel wouldn't ask for an explanation to go with them. He didn't ask. He just smiled at him before he switched off the light. He looked happy. Bayden smiled into the darkness. He liked it when Axel was happy.

Chapter Fifteen

The hail pelted down against the kitchen window, hard enough to rattle the glass. But, as soon as Axel spotted a movement in the window pane's reflection, he lost all interest in watching the storm.

Bayden halted in the kitchen doorway.

Axel continued to face the window, waiting to see what Bayden might do. Nothing. A full minute passed, and Bayden didn't move a muscle.

"I know you're there," Axel said.

Bayden still didn't step forward or say anything.

Axel left his phone on the kitchen counter and turned to face Bayden.

"I texted everyone to let them know the club's not riding this morning—not in this." Axel nodded toward the window. "We'll ride later if the worst of it clears."

Bayden nodded. He still didn't speak, he just waited for an order. Entirely naked with his hair damp from his shower, he was gorgeous. He was also completely unselfconscious—not in a vain way, or even in a sexual way. It seemed like it didn't occur to him to be ashamed of his body.

If it was a lupine trait, Axel was entirely in favour of it. He smiled to himself as he ran his gaze over Bayden from top to toe. Somehow, he was pretty sure this was one wet Sunday when he wouldn't get bored.

Axel pulled his attention back up to Bayden's face. Bayden had been watching him intently, but he looked away when their eyes met.

"Come here."

Bayden stopped eighteen inches away from Axel. He didn't offer his lips up for a kiss good morning. He seemed to make a point of staring straight ahead. His hands remained at his sides.

Axel slid one arm around him and pulled him closer. Bayden still didn't look up. Axel tucked a knuckle under his chin. Once Bayden's head was tilted back, Axel took his hand away. Bayden kept his head in that position, offering his lips up to be kissed.

For a moment, he met Axel's gaze. He looked so uncertain about everything, just like the previous night. Axel's cock jerked at the memory of Bayden's lips wrapped around his shaft. He made him wait a few seconds, but when he finally kissed him, he didn't tease.

Bayden remained tense, completely controlling his every response to the kiss. It was far too close to the way he acted during his bets. Axel nipped Bayden's bottom lip. Bayden didn't react to that; Axel didn't expect him to.

Axel kissed the non-existent injury better. There was nothing subtle about the move. He made it completely obvious what he was doing. As soon as Axel offered that touch of comfort, Bayden's breathing sped up. He leaned more firmly against Axel's body. Even if Bayden wasn't ready to admit it, there was something about a dom who took care of him that snuck past all his defences.

The boy needed someone to look after him more badly than anyone Axel had ever met. Axel deepened the kiss. Bayden gently sucked the tip of Axel's tongue and let out a needy little whimper. By the time Axel lifted his head, he knew Bayden was mentally in the moment.

Bayden swallowed. He looked down, but he didn't pull away. He jumped as, right on cue, the dinger sounded on the cooker. He peered up at Axel, as if he was looking to him for both reassurance and safety.

Axel smiled at the idea — that was far more to his taste than a boy who was afraid to get within a foot of him.

Bayden remained exactly where he was until Axel handed him his breakfast.

The kiss seemed to have shaken Bayden. It had also turned him on. He was hard and ready to play, and he made no attempt to hide his erection as he sat at the table. He seemed as comfortable with that as with his nudity.

Time to get him comfortable with something else.

"I know you think I'm more dominant than you. I know you respect that. I'm not going to think you're challenging me if you come into my space," Axel said.

"Yes, sir." It was an acknowledgement that he'd heard him, nothing more.

"I want you to work on it."

Bayden glanced up at him, his eyes so serious.

"Don't ride roughshod over your instincts, don't pretend to be human. But I want you to work out a way you can get closer to me without feeling like you're challenging me."

"Yes, sir."

"Good boy." Axel kissed him, very briefly. "Once you're dressed, I'll drive you to your place so you can pick up your things."

Bayden's fork clattered against his plate. "You don't need to do that, sir."

"Oh?"

"I can ride there. It won't take me long, sir."

"Do you think I'll slow you down?" Axel asked, amused.

Bayden shook his head. "But you don't need to. I didn't ask you to, sir."

"I haven't accused you of doing anything wrong." His breakfast finished, Axel sat back in his chair and settled himself for the duration. "Any particular reason you don't want me to drive you?"

"You said yourself that it's horrible weather, sir."

"To ride, yes. We'll be taking my car. Unless the roof has sprung a leak overnight, I don't imagine either of us will get too damp."

"Maybe—" Bayden looked up and seemed to realise that, while Axel had no problem with listening to any arguments he wanted to put forward, he had no intention of altering his plans unless Bayden anteed up properly.

Bayden looked down, obviously out of his depth.

It was one of those times when rescuing him was acceptable. "Yesterday, when they told you that I expected you to let them all screw you, did it occur to you to tell me that was a limit for you?"

Bayden shook his head. "It's not a limit. I don't have any limits, sir."

And this was as good a moment as any to deal with that kind of bull. "You have three options," Axel told him.

Bayden nodded that he'd heard.

"You can suck it up and deal with the decision I've made."

Bayden tensed.

"You can tell me why you don't like the idea of me going to your place and ask me to change my mind. Depending on the explanation, I might do that, or I might stick with my original decision—in which case you end up with the first option by default."

Bayden failed to look any more enthusiastic about that prospect.

"Or, you can tell me that you're setting me visiting your place as a limit. In which case, I'll respect that, and you'll be allowed to go on your own."

Bayden stared down at his hand. It had furled into a tight fist. He frowned and relaxed his fingers with obvious effort. The idea of Axel visiting his place seemed to scare him more than being passed around an entire club full of men. Was that because he was embarrassed about where he lived since he moved into his own place? Or was that it—the law said he should have moved out, but he hadn't? That would be something he'd want to hide, something he'd never let anyone find out unless he was sure he could trust them. It made sense.

"Reasonable," Bayden blurted out. "You said I'm allowed to have reasonable limits."

Axel turned the matter over in his head. If he still lived at home, taking Axel there would mean introducing him to his family as well as showing him where he lived. It was too soon to demand that. "Until we renegotiate at the end of the trial, it's reasonable," he decided.

Bayden let out the breath he'd been holding.

"You still need to choose one of the options," Axel reminded him.

"You said…"

"I gave you the options and answered your questions about them."

Bayden ground his teeth together.

Axel waited.

His choice was obvious. It would be so easy to step in and rescue him again, but Axel remained silent and let Bayden struggle. He was going to learn how to set limits. Axel was past the point of caring what the particular limit was. Bayden was going to learn how to negotiate a scene and damn well set limits above and beyond the, *make sure no one gets killed*, limits that the club set.

Bayden glanced up at him again, his gaze full of emotion.

Axel still forced himself to wait him out.

"You going to my place. It's a limit," Bayden whispered. He told the table rather than Axel, and he looked ready to leap off his chair and retreat at a moment's notice.

"Good boy."

Bayden's jaw twitched as if he were clamping his teeth together more firmly than ever.

"I'm the one who decides what constitutes good behaviour in this household," Axel said. "Not you."

Confusion flashed across Bayden's face.

"I'm not sarcastic about important things," Axel told him. "If I say you did something good, I mean it."

Bayden didn't look down, he kept his gaze on Axel's face, trying to read him.

"Learning how to set limits is good," Axel repeated.

"Do I need to apologise, sir?"

Axel shook his head. He stood up. "You can go to your place to collect your things. If you want to call in and see your family, there's time for you to do that too. I need to pick up some things in town. When you're done, you can meet me back here for lunch."

Axel reached into one of the kitchen drawers, fished out his spare backdoor key and tossed it to Bayden.

Bayden frowned at it as if he'd never seen a key before. "Sir?"

"If you get back before me, let yourself in."

Bayden's frown deepened. He seemed to be about to say something, then he checked himself. He nodded and put the key on his key ring.

Guilty that he didn't trust Axel to know where he lived, but Axel trusted him with a key? Uncertain about how any arrangement longer than a hook up should work? Axel let the matter slip away but, two hours later, when he drove back into the yard at the rear of the pub, he realised that might have been a tactical error on his part.

* * * * *

When Bayden heard Axel's car, he straightened up from where he'd been crouched down alongside his bike. The rain had eased off. It no longer pounded on the flat roof of the lock-up.

Axel parked his car near the back entrance to the pub and got out. He didn't look pleased. "You were supposed to let yourself in."

"I haven't been back that long, sir."

Axel glanced past him. Bayden followed his line of sight. Water had dripped off both his leathers and his bike, both were now dry. Damn.

Axel shook his head at him, but he seemed bemused rather than offended. "Did you get everything you wanted from your place?"

Bayden held up his backpack.

"That's all you wanted to fetch?"

Bayden glanced at the bag, would a rich boy have brought more? "Wolves travel light." He shrugged, as if he'd had lots of options and chosen that one on purpose.

"Well, not this time." Axel opened the car boot. "Lock up. You can help me carry."

Bayden locked his bike away in record time, slung his back pack over his shoulder and hurried across to take some of the shopping bags from Axel.

It took two trips each to take everything upstairs to the flat's kitchen. Axel must have spent more on food in one trip than Bayden would have spent in the whole six weeks he'd be living there.

Bayden paused, staring down into one of the bags. He hadn't spent much on food at all since he started working at The Dragon's Lair. He hadn't needed to. Axel had been feeding him for weeks—it must have cost him a fortune already.

"Bayden?"

Bayden jerked his head up.

"You were in your own world."

"Sorry, sir." He washed his hands at the sink as Axel started to take food out of the bags. Axel had never invited him to handle food, but most of it seemed to be wrapped. "Is there anything I can do?"

Axel nodded to the closest bag. "Go ahead."

As they put the food away, a companionable silence fell over them, broken only by Axel's occasional instructions on where different things were supposed to be stored. It was nice—like working behind the bar with him, but without having to deal with any customers.

"Catch."

Bayden turned to Axel, hands out ready to receive one of the less fragile things that needed to be put away on his side of the kitchen. Something grey, fluffy and blatantly inedible flew toward him.

"Try it on."

Bayden turned the soft, knitted fabric around until it became obvious it was a sweater. He frowned at the jumper. It was grey wool with a black fleck running through it. It had a tag on it, but the price label had been removed. It was obviously far too small for Axel. "Sir?"

"Try it on," Axel repeated.

"Why?"

"Because I told you to. Isn't that a good enough reason?"

Yes, it was. Bayden took off his jacket. He carefully pulled the sweater over his head and smoothed it into place over his vest. It was soft against his bare arms. He looked back to Axel.

Axel nodded his approval. "It suits you." He went back to unpacking as if that was the end of the matter and no further explanation was needed.

Bayden studied Axel carefully, trying to work out what was going on. Had he given himself away somehow? His heart raced at the possibility. Did Axel think he expected him to—?

"If you want to know something, ask," Axel said. "Staring at me across the kitchen won't get you any answers."

"I can afford to buy my own clothes, sir."

"I don't doubt it." It sounded like he meant that.

"I don't need…" Bayden hesitated. The jumper was nice. And Axel had picked it for him. And Axel said it suited him. It was an indulgence, but maybe just this once… He reached into the back pocket of his jeans. "How much do I owe you for — ?"

"It's a present," Axel cut in. "That means I'll be very offended if you try to pay for it."

"You don't need to give me presents, sir."

"A wolf wouldn't?" Axel asked.

"I'll do whatever you want without you…"

Axel put down the tins he'd just taken out of a bag. "It's not payment, pup. It's a gift. It's different." He stroked Bayden's hair back from his face. "You've got a couple of options."

"It's not a limit, sir," Bayden rushed out.

Axel ignored that. "You can think of it as a human thing — maybe it's something that doesn't make sense to a wolf, but humans are weird, you have to make allowances."

Axel didn't seem insulted, Bayden still shook his head very quickly. "I didn't say that, sir."

"Or you could decide that the only thing I've given you is an order."

Bayden looked up. Orders were good. From the look in Axel's eye, Bayden was pretty sure Axel knew he thought that.

"I'm telling you to wear something that it pleases me to see you wear," Axel went on. "That's all. You're just doing something that will please me. There's nothing worrying about that, is there?"

Bayden looked down at the jumper. It was nice. It wrapped around him, warm and comforting, like a memory of Axel's touch that would linger even when Axel wasn't in the room.

"Tell me what the problem is." That was definitely an order.

Bayden hesitated, not sure if it was wise to tempt fate.

"The truth," Axel reminded him.

"It's not the kind of thing that humans usually want to see a wolf wear, sir," he said cautiously.

Axel ran his hand down Bayden's sleeve. "It makes you look warm and comfortable. It makes you look as if I'm taking good care of you."

Bayden shook his head very quickly. "You don't need to take care of me, sir." He could take care of himself. He'd been taking care of himself for years.

"Maybe I want to look after you even if you don't need me to." Axel encouraged Bayden to look up at him. "Me fussing over you isn't any different just because you're a wolf, pup. I'd do exactly the same if you were a human."

Complaining about that would be dangerously close to saying he wanted Axel to make allowances for his species. "Yes, sir." That was always a good thing to say.

Axel kissed him gently on the lips, confirming it was the right response, then went back to unpacking as if nothing that had happened was a big deal.

Several minutes passed before Bayden realised one part of the process had been missed out. "Thank you, sir."

Axel glanced up at him and smiled. "You're welcome, pup."

Bayden nodded, glad that no extra explanation had been necessary. He didn't look toward Axel again until the last item had been put away, and he needed a new order to follow.

"You can put your things in the bedroom. The bottom drawer in the chest by the window is empty. You can use that."

Bayden carried his bag into the bedroom. Kneeling in front of the chest, he arranged his clothes and his wash bag neatly in the drawer. Bayden looked at his leather jacket. There was plenty of room for that too.

He automatically took the money from the various pockets of his jacket before placing it alongside his clothes. He looked at the money.

Leaving cash at his bedsit would have been asking for someone to steal it. Leaving it here wasn't the same. Bayden looked at his keys. Axel trusted him. Maybe it was time he started to trust Axel too—maybe just a little bit—just with things that were replaceable.

Bayden took a deep breath and placed the money in the drawer. A second's thought and he added the stash he'd tucked in his boot to the drawer, followed by the money from his back pocket.

He hesitated, staring at the bank notes. Maybe if he just tucked the money underneath his spare pair of jeans, or… Bayden shook his head. Trust. Axel wouldn't steal from him. The money was safe.

A footstep on the squeaky floorboard outside Axel's bedroom door made Bayden look up.

Axel appeared in the doorway. "The weather's cleared. We're riding after all. We'll stop halfway and eat there."

"Yes, sir." Bayden quickly exchanged his jumper for his leather jacket, picked up enough money to deal with anything that might come his way during the ride and followed Axel down to the pub.

Within a few minutes, bikes were rolling in. There weren't so many today, although more of the Dragons had brought men with them on their pillion seats. Evan was riding behind Griz. Bayden recognised some of the others as people who sometimes played in the back rooms of The Dragon's Lair.

Scent made it obvious that most of them had been thinking about sex rather than motorcycles until Axel had sent out a text telling them the ride was on, but they didn't seem unhappy about being able to ride out as a club.

If what Axel had said about a lot the men being biker groupies was true, maybe they thought the ride was part of the foreplay. The Dragons didn't see it that way. Bayden could sense it in them. They were there to ride. Their attention was on their bikes and each other as much as on the men who'd be riding behind them.

The routine had become familiar, but that didn't dull the feeling of riding with a club—it didn't make it feel any less like running with a pack. Bayden's heart pounded as he rode out of the car park and fell in line behind Tolmore. His whole body tingled with pleasure. It was like humans talked about feeling when they were drunk. It was easy to see why they got addicted to it. Bayden knew he could ride with a pack every day for the rest of his life and it would never feel like it had been too much.

When he got off his bike at the halfway point, Bayden found himself smiling. He glanced around. It was a nice neighbourhood. It was the middle of the day. He didn't have to worry about his bike.

Helmet off, he got his sunglasses out of his pocket and slipped them on. There were more than twenty men in total—all of them wearing a fair amount of leather. They caught everyone's attention as they strode into the pub. None of the Dragons seemed to care, or even notice that people were staring, but some of the pillion riders preened under the attention, obviously enjoying it.

Strangers were staring at the group, not him in particular. Bayden still tensed up as they all made their way toward the tables at the back of the pub. He kept his head down until Axel slid his arm around his shoulders.

"Good ride, pup?"

Bayden nodded and leaned into Axel's side. All other humans forgotten, he was once more unable to keep his smile in check. It was like running with a pack—one that was led by a fantastic alpha.

Axel took a seat on a bench and tugged Bayden down to sit alongside him. When Axel reached out to him, Bayden assumed it was too push his hair back from his face, but Axel took Bayden's sunglasses instead.

"That's better."

Their eyes only met for a moment before Bayden gave in to the instinct to drop his gaze.

Axel brushed their lips together, obviously pleased with Bayden for not complaining about losing his glasses.

Already high on the feeling of being part of the pack, Bayden murmured his pleasure against Axel's lips. It wasn't just him. When Axel pulled away, he was smiling just as broadly as Bayden.

"Whose buying?" someone asked, from the other side of the group.

"It's my turn." Griz pulled out his wallet.

Evan whispered something to Griz, who nodded and handed over some money.

"He'll need help to carry the drinks back," Axel pointed out.

Bayden got up. He reached for his sunglasses but Axel put his hand over them before Bayden had a chance to pick them up.

"You can have them back when we get outside." His amusement was obvious, but his tone didn't invite any argument.

"Yes, sir."

Bayden followed Evan up to the bar and took his place beside him in the queue. He didn't have a clear line of sight to Axel from there, but there was a window that looked out over the car park. All the bikes were in view. They were all fine.

"Your bike's amazing."

Bayden tore his gaze away from the motorcycles. "Thanks."

What Axel had said before was right—it was clear what place Evan would occupy in any pack. Humans could be omegas as well as alphas.

Brushing off men who postured and swaggered, thinking they were more dominant than him was easy. Shooting down an omega would be cruel. "You like old bikes?" Bayden hazarded.

Evan hesitated for a moment. "I'm doing one up."

Bayden glanced at the queue, it didn't seem to be moving at all. "How's it going?"

"It's a nineteen-forties Royal Enfield." Another little hesitation. "I've, um…" He pulled his phone out and tapped the screen a few times before turning it toward Bayden. "Griz is helping me do it up." He swiped at the screen, moving on to another photo, then another. Each picture showed a bike that was a bit less beaten up looking. "When it's finished, Griz says he'll invite me to tag along with the Dragons riding my own bike."

He swiped again. The next picture wasn't of a bike. Embarrassment flooded Evan's scent. He quickly moved onto the next picture but his scent didn't change at all. His cheeks flushed just as brightly as his buttocks had in the picture of him being spanked by Griz.

"You'll like it."

Evan met Bayden's gaze for a moment.

"Riding with the Dragons, you'll like it," Bayden said.

Evan pushed his phone back into his pocket. "Some of the guys in the pub said they've given you a hard time since you started riding with them…"

Bayden shrugged.

Evan nibbled on his bottom lip.

"Axel says they won't hassle you so much because you're more impressed with them all than I am," Bayden offered.

Evan chuckled, but he didn't get the chance to say anything else before they reached the front of the queue. He began to recite the order. He was about six words into it when the bartender stopped him short.

"ID." The guy's scent was full of anger. Bayden half turned toward him, then thought better of it.

"Sorry." Evan's blush rushed back full force. He scrambled for his ID. "I'm almost twenty-one."

"And you?"

There was no avoiding it. Bayden met his gaze.

"Get out."

"What?" Evan looked from one of them to the other, all confusion.

"There's a sign on the door saying no dogs. It's there for a reason," the bartender bit out.

Bayden held the man's gaze. His hand furled into a fist at his side. If any of the humans understood scent, they'd have realised that Bayden was just as furious as the bartender. The difference was that Bayden's anger was all at himself.

"You're a shifter." The bartender spat the species like a curse.

Bayden didn't deny it.

"Get out, both of you."

Bayden stepped forward. "I'm a shifter, he's not. You saw his ID. There's no reason for us both to leave."

The bartender squared his stance. "Are you going, or do I have to throw you out?"

Bayden looked him up and down. It was on the tip of his tongue to tell the stupid idiot to try, but, no. He didn't want trouble and the pack came first—even if it was full of humans and called a motorcycle club.

Bayden turned to Evan. "You'll have to take two trips. Get the soft drinks first. Come and get the alcoholic ones afterwards."

"But—"

"It's fine. Tell Axel that I'm going outside and I'll keep an eye on the bikes." He turned on his heel and walked out before it could all go to hell.

He was several yards outside, head buzzing with fury, before he realised that it was raining again. He looked up. Droplets pattered down on his face, cold and heavy, like the first drops of a fresh downpour. Bloody typical.

* * * * *

"Where are the drinks?" Drac asked.

253

Axel looked over Evan's shoulder. Sod the drinks. "Where's Bayden?"

"He asked me to tell you he's going outside. He's going to keep an eye on the bikes."

"What the hell does he think's going to happen to them here?" Drac asked.

"Yeah, I thought you'd cured him of that," Hale said.

Axel sighed as he pulled himself to his feet. He'd thought he had too.

"That's what he asked me to tell you," Evan repeated. The stress he put on the words registered.

"And the truth?" Axel asked.

Evan glanced toward Griz and received an encouraging nod. "The bartender said that the no dogs sign on the door applied to wolves too."

"What? How the hell did he even know he's a wolf?"

Evan dropped his gaze, but not in submission. Axel followed his line of sight. Bayden's sunglasses lay on the table. His eyes. "Shit!" Axel grabbed the glasses and his helmet, and rushed outside.

Bayden's bike was still there. Axel didn't actually have to jump on his bike and chase him down. But Bayden wasn't standing by the bikes either. Lifting a hand to shield his eyes from the rain, Axel scanned the area until he spotted Bayden.

He was tucked under the arched porch of the building opposite, keeping out of the rain as much as possible. He was leaning against the wall, his hands shoved in his pockets. He seemed to have settled himself for the duration. His attention was on the line of bikes, rather than the pub door.

It obviously hadn't occurred to him that anyone would come out after him.

Axel was halfway across the car park when he saw Bayden tense up, only to relax when he saw who was heading in his direction. He had thought someone might come out there after him, Axel realised. Bayden had been ready for the bartender and maybe a couple of the bastard's friends.

Axel stepped under the porch and wiped the rain off his face.

A glance in his direction seemed to offer Bayden a wealth of information. "Evan told you what happened."

"Did you doubt he would?" Axel slid his hand through his wet hair. "You shouldn't have asked him to lie."

Bayden shrugged. "I'm outside. I'm keeping an eye on the bikes. I didn't ask him to say anything that isn't the truth."

"Were you planning on telling me the whole story at any point?"

"No." Bayden thought for a little while. "Sir." It was completely disconnected from his original answer, but it was there—he hadn't forgotten.

"Because?" Axel asked.

"It's no big deal. I've been thrown out of plenty of places before. It'll happen often enough in the future." He looked down. "You should go back inside, sir."

Axel ignored the last part—it didn't deserve to be acknowledged. "And it happens a lot more often if your eyes are visible," he finished for him.

Bayden glanced at his sunglasses in Axel's hand, but he didn't try to take them. He shrugged again.

"Why didn't you tell me, pup?"

Bayden turned his attention back to the bikes. "It's not your problem, sir."

"What?" Axel grabbed his shoulder and made him face him.

"You gave me an order, sir. I'm supposed to obey it, not get you to change your mind." He glanced at the shades again, then looked quickly away. He folded his arms across his chest. "I should have stopped wearing them the first time you told me you didn't like them."

"Do you think I'd have insisted you obey me if I knew it would make things more difficult for you?"

"Yes, sir."

Axel caught hold of his chin and made him look up.

"I said I'd obey any order you gave me. I meant it," Bayden bit out.

"Any order within your limits," Axel corrected.

"It's not a limit! I'm not going to set limits because some humans are arseholes. They don't get to control how well I submit to you." Fury burned in his eyes. It was the only outward sign that he wasn't entirely calm, everything else was carefully controlled. "Sir."

"I told you at the start that there's room for discretion in front of some people."

Bayden hesitated.

"You can wear them—"

Bayden shook his head. "No. I'll—"

"They aren't controlling anything. I am. It's my decision. I'm making it. You have permission to wear them when we're out. But you're not allowed to wear them in The Dragon's Lair—ever."

Bayden hesitated.

"If anyone in The Dragon's Lair has a problem with you, they'll be the ones who have to leave." Axel held out the glasses.

Bayden took them. "I'm not ashamed of who I am, sir."

"I know." Axel stroked his cheek.

Bayden looked up at him, so wary.

Axel dipped his head and brought their lips together, slow and gentle at first. When Bayden leaned up into the kiss, Axel stepped forward, trapping Bayden between his body and the wall, coaxing a whimper out of him.

Suddenly, Bayden turned his face away.

Axel lifted his head.

"Watching," Bayden whispered.

Axel looked over his shoulder. The Dragons had congregated in the pub's doorway. Evan was carrying Bayden's helmet.

They could go back in, all of them together. No bartender could throw them all out. If he tried, it would be just the kind of excuse Axel wanted.

He glanced down at Bayden. If he ordered Bayden to go back in there, he would. He'd do as his dom commanded, no matter how much he hated it.

I don't want any trouble.

Going back in might teach the bartender not to be an arsehole. It would also teach Bayden that Axel thought proving a point to an arsehole was more important to him than looking after his pup.

Axel nodded to Hale and the other Dragons all headed for their bikes.

"Sir?" Bayden looked so confused as Axel stepped away and let him see who was there. It really hadn't occurred to him that they would all walk away from a place that had a problem with any one of them.

Axel stroked his cheek again. "You still have a lot to learn about riding with a club, don't you, pup?"

Chapter Sixteen

Bayden cursed himself using almost every insult he knew, human and werewolf, as they rode back to The Dragon's Lair. None of the things he called himself sufficiently summed up his anger with himself.

Up in the flat, Axel nodded toward the chair by the door.

Naked. At least that was something Bayden couldn't screw up. As Bayden took off his clothes, Axel settled himself in the armchair by the window.

Bayden had ruined Axel's ride. Bayden tried to push the knowledge out of his head, but it was impossible. The club was the most important thing in Axel's world, and Bayden had ruined the entire club's ride. The need to fix that was an ache deep in Bayden's soul. He had to make up ground, to prove that he respected Axel and his right to give any order he wanted.

He should...

Bayden's mind went blank until one word finally bobbed up.

Close.

Axel had told him what he wanted him to do that morning before the ride.

Close.

Bayden stared at the floorboards. Close, like a human submissive. Bayden had seen them in the pub. They got close to their doms in their scenes, or sometimes even outside the scenes. If they could do it, he had to be able to do it. Being incapable wasn't an option.

Without waiting for an order, Bayden stepped forward. He was aware of Axel watching him, but he didn't lift his gaze. He kept all his attention on his own bare feet as he crossed the room.

The moment he entered Axel's personal space, he lowered himself onto his knees. He sat back on his heels so he was lower still and dipped his head, stressing every sign of respect as he tried to work out what would constitute clarity to a human.

It wasn't as formal or as symmetrical a move as he'd seen some of the human submissives perform, but he was in Axel's space.

His heart was racing so fast he wasn't sure he was going to survive kneeling there for very long unless Axel said something, but he couldn't bring himself to look up. A touch to his hair finally ordered him to tilt back his head.

"You said to, sir," Bayden reminded him, his voice barely a whisper.

"Yes."

Bayden swallowed.

"Beautiful." Axel ran his fingers through Bayden's hair.

Bayden breathed a little easier, although his pulse didn't slow down at all. He stared up at Axel, drinking in his approval. The arousal in Axel's scent had gone up several notches. Nobody that turned on could be pissed off with him.

He was on his knees. Axel was turned on. The next order should have been obvious, but Axel tugged at Bayden's hair, encouraging him up onto the chair.

There wasn't room for two men there. Bayden frowned, trying to work out how the hell he was supposed to fit without crushing Axel.

"You're not heavy, and I'm not as fragile as you think I am," Axel whispered into his ear. He tugged Bayden firmly onto his lap and wrapped one arm around him holding him securely in place. Axel was still wearing his leather trousers. Bayden squirmed against them until Axel settled his free hand on Bayden's chest in a silent order to fall still. There was no way Bayden could hide how fast his heart raced.

Axel pressed a kiss to his temple. "You did good, pup."

Bayden cautiously relaxed against Axel's chest.

"Was coming into my space as hard as you thought it would be?" Axel asked, so softly Bayden had to concentrate to make out the words.

Bayden thought about it. Axel didn't like lies. He nodded.

"Do you think it will be easier in the future, now that you know how much I approve?"

Bayden nodded again. His cheek rubbed against Axel's shoulder with the motion. Axel seemed to completely surround him. He'd wanted Axel to be pleased with him so badly, and now he was. It was almost enough to make Bayden dizzy with pleasure

"Good pup." Axel stroked his hands over Bayden's bare skin. "So good."

Bayden leaned more firmly into Axel's embrace.

"If there's something you're worried about, you should tell me."

Bayden shrugged.

"Or something you don't understand, something you have questions about," Axel suggested.

It was the tone of voice that meant there was going to be a conversation whether Bayden thought that one was necessary or not. The quickest way to get to the part of the evening that might involve sex would be to give in and go with the whole human-talking thing.

"You said I have a lot to learn about riding with a club, sir."

"Yes, you do."

"Am I allowed to know what I'm doing wrong, sir?"

Axel idly ran his hands over Bayden's skin. "You ride fine. You might want to work on being a bit more sociable with the other guys, but what I meant was—you're expectations are skewed. Like today, when you were sent out of the pub."

"I didn't expect you all to leave, sir." He thought he'd been clear about that.

Axel chuckled. "That's my point, pup."

Bayden studied him, trying to get a better read on him. Axel let him move, encouraging him to turn and straddle his legs so they sat face to face.

"They didn't have a problem with any of you, sir."

"If they have a problem with one of us, they have a problem with all of us. It's part of what riding with a club is all about."

Bayden looked down until Axel made him look up.

"I'm not really part of the club, neither were a lot of the other guys there."

"You might not be a full member of the club, but you're riding with us — that means you'll be treated as if you're a Dragon in every way there is. If any of their hook ups had suggested leaving you hanging, they'd be walking home."

Bayden looked down and watched Axel's hands slide up his legs. Whether Axel intended it to or not, his touch went straight to Bayden's cock.

"You don't pick a hook up over a man you ride with. A submissive might be different, and a collared submissive — well, that's a different thing altogether."

It was far from the first time Axel had mentioned collars, or made it clear that a collared submissive was the best kind. Bayden met Axel's gaze, but he didn't seem to be inclined to offer up anything else on that topic. Axel stroked his hands up and down Bayden's back.

"The club is like a..." Axel began. Bayden held his breath, half sure Axel was going to say pack. "Family."

Their eyes met. Whatever Axel had actually said, he'd been thinking the word pack. Bayden would have bet his soul on it.

"And family is important, isn't it?"

Bayden nodded.

"If it had been Evan who'd been sent out of the pub, would you have been happy staying in there while he stood outside?"

"It's not the same. Humans…"

Axel stroked his knuckles along the length of Bayden's erection. "Not all humans are the same," Axel said. "Good humans and good wolves might be more similar than you think."

Bayden tried to work out what Axel would be pleased with him for saying, but he couldn't come up with anything suitable, not while Axel toyed with him that way.

"But that doesn't mean that there aren't differences, or that I don't want to know what they are." As he spoke, Axel continued to tease Bayden's shaft.

It was all Bayden could do not to wriggle on Axel's lap and try to push his cock against his hand. It already felt like months since he'd been allowed to come.

"And yes," Axel added. "Just so we're both clear—we're not talking about the club any more, we're talking about us and about sex."

Bayden swallowed and tried to make his brain keep working. He shook his head. "You can treat me the same as a human sub, sir."

"Can and will are too different things. When was the last time you came?"

"Friday, before we—" Bayden broke off into a gasp. Closing his eyes, he looked for that calm space inside himself, where nothing could get to him and every touch was irrelevant.

"No!"

Bayden jerked and opened his eyes at the sudden snap in Axel's voice.

"This isn't a bet, you don't block me out."

"I…" Bayden blinked at him.

"Yes, I can tell when you're doing that," Axel said, slipping back into his usual tone of voice. "No, it's not acceptable — not with me, not ever."

Bayden stared straight into Axel's eyes for several seconds, trying to get a read on him. He'd never seen him so serious.

"I don't like being ignored, and I don't like it when you hide your reactions to me. So, unless you can look me in the eye and tell me that it's an intrinsic part of you being a shifter, you don't do it with me. Understand?"

Bayden swallowed. "Yes, sir."

Axel still had his hand wrapped around Bayden's cock. He tightened his grip and stroked him several times.

Bayden managed to hold Axel's gaze through it.

"How often are you used to getting off?"

"You said I was allowed to, sir," Bayden reminded him, doing his best not to rock his hips and push forward into Axel's hand, but unable to remain perfectly motionless.

"No, I said you're *not* allowed." Axel stilled his hand. "I was quite clear about that."

Bayden frowned. "Before, sir. You said until I agreed to obey your rules, I was allowed to. You gave me permission."

Axel smiled and began to move his hand again. "Then, yes. You were allowed to then. How often did you take advantage of that permission?"

Bayden hesitated, not entirely sure what was normal for a human.

"Every day?" Axel asked.

Bayden nodded. Axel didn't seem to think that was strange.

"More than once a day?"

He cautiously nodded again.

"So, the last couple of days must have felt like a long time," Axel mused. He seemed pleased by the idea. He kept his hand moving, tempting Bayden to thrust in counterpoint.

"I don't mind, sir. It's not important." Axel being pleased was important.

"You'll have permission to come later," Axel promised.

Bayden nodded.

"First, tell me something that would have been different if you'd been with a wolf the last few days."

Bayden stared down at his cock as Axel continued to stroke him. He was leaking pre-cum and it smeared over Axel's palm each time he caressed the head.

"There's no rush," Axel said. "We've got all the time in the world."

Bayden looked up. It was easy for Axel to say that. Axel had come last night, and the night before.

Axel chuckled, as if he could read the thoughts straight out of his head, but it was that gentle kind of laughter that never made it sound like Axel was laughing at his expense, not really. "One difference," he prompted.

"It's not... Wolves don't... There's not so much talking about what people like... It's more instinctive, more...physical, sir?" he hazarded, keeping his tone extra respectful just in case Axel thought he was criticising him.

"So, a wolf wouldn't ask what you like—he'd just do what he wanted and find out how you'd react."

Bayden nodded.

"Your honest reactions?"

"I..."

"Maybe the reason wolves treat you differently is because you don't hide things from wolves?"

Bayden swallowed rapidly.

"Would you hide your reactions from a wolf?" Axel asked.

Bayden looked down. "I..."

Axel wrapped the fingers of his free hand around one of Bayden's wrists. He didn't try to move his hand, he just held the joint in his grip. "You like being held, don't you?"

Bayden only hesitated for a second. He couldn't tear his gaze away from the way Axel's fingers encircled his wrist, but he managed to nod.

Axel released Bayden's cock and took his other wrist in a similar grip. It wasn't painful. It wasn't something a werewolf would have any trouble escaping if he needed to, but it was very clear, very simple and so bloody perfect Bayden wouldn't have been able to speak even if he had been inclined to.

"If you stop hiding your reactions from me, I'll do whatever I want with you," Axel said. "No words, just actions."

Bayden frowned. Completely naked, there was no way that he could hide how turned on he was. Axel was turned on too. Bayden could sense it in his scent. He could feel how hard Axel was behind his fly. Actions rather than words appealed to both of them. And Axel was willing to offer actions to a wolf that didn't hold back.

He could have everything he wanted, if he just trusted Axel. Bayden closed his eyes. He could do it. Trusting Axel with that particular information was an acceptable risk.

"Yes, sir."

"Bed," Axel said. "Not just in the bedroom. I want you on the bed waiting for me by the time I get in there. Now. Go." He released Bayden's wrists.

Bayden hurried to obey. Technically, all he'd received were more words, but these ones promised actions were soon to follow, and they were beautiful.

In the bedroom, Bayden climbed onto the bottom of the bed and knelt there. Axel strode into the room. He didn't even glance in Bayden's direction. All his focus was on taking off his clothes and tossing them on the chair in the corner of the room.

Completely ignored, it was all Bayden could do to keep back a whimper and not plead for Axel's attention. Finally naked, Axel came closer. He didn't say anything—not with words, but his body language was loud and clear. He caught hold of Bayden's wrists as he joined him on the bed.

In seconds, Bayden was on his back with his wrists pinned to the mattress on either side of his head. Axel loomed over him, partly supporting himself with his hands, but using the rest of his weight to pin Bayden in place. And he didn't say a word.

Axel put his knee against Bayden's legs, pushing his thigh between them. Bayden squirmed in the small space between Axel and the bed, moving his legs further apart.

Axel rocked his hips. Bayden's cock rubbed against Axel's abs. Bayden whimpered. This he understood. This made sense. After so many months of trying to work Axel out and trying to find the right words, it was bliss.

For a moment, old habits tried to force their way to the surface. Acting like he didn't care what a human did to him, was easy and safe.

No. Bayden made himself ignore the siren call of the benign and familiar. He pulled lupine instincts to the fore, using them to block out everything life had taught him about humans.

He arched under Axel, pressing up against his body. Bare skin and strength filled Bayden's world. He moaned his approval, letting Axel know how much he loved it all.

Axel's mouth covered his. The kiss wasn't sweet. There was no tenderness, no restraint. For the first time, it felt like Axel held nothing back. It was fierce and demanding. It made no allowances for Bayden's inability to keep up.

It wasn't Bayden's job to prove a point. It wasn't even his job to return the kiss. All he had to do was to accept the kiss, accept Axel's dominance over him. Nothing could be easier.

A nip to Bayden's bottom lip made him gasp. He rocked his hips in time with Axel's thrusts, pleasure racing through his body.

Suddenly, Axel broke the kiss, he stared down at Bayden. Tightening his grip on Bayden's wrists, he dipped his head again, putting his mouth to his ear.

"Mine."

Bayden nodded. In that moment, when there were no thoughts and just his most basic instincts, it was true. He was as much Axel's as any man, any wolf, could ever be.

"Make no mistake about that, pup. You are mine, every inch of you. I own you body and soul, and by the time I'm done with you you're never going to want to look at another man or another wolf ever again. You are mine."

The tone of voice went straight past any part of Bayden that had ever understood concepts and syllables. It was everything he'd wanted for so long, everything he'd been afraid of getting.

Every note was pure dominance, pure alpha. Bayden writhed on the bed, tilting back his head, exposing his neck in an instinctive display of submission.

Axel dipped his head and nipped at Bayden's throat.

Bayden didn't think. He didn't need to. His body took over. Ecstasy burst through him. He jerked beneath Axel, pushing up against his body and tugging at the grip Axel had around his wrists as his orgasm tore through him.

* * * * *

Axel pulled away just in time to see the look on Bayden's face as he came, damn-near untouched. His eyes were closed, his lips parted. He'd tipped back his head and arched his spine. His arms were tensed, pulling at Axel's restraining hold as he abandoned himself to his orgasm. It was only luck that Axel didn't come too—just from the sight of Bayden finally losing himself in the moment.

Bayden's cum spilled between them, smearing against their torsos. As suddenly as it seemed to have overtaken him, Bayden's orgasm ended. He collapsed back on the bed.

Axel grinned. He'd wanted to know what Bayden liked. That was a pretty clear answer.

There was nothing but satisfaction and peace in Bayden's expression for several seconds. Then, Bayden tensed. He closed his eyes more tightly. When he opened them a moment later, Axel saw the horror in his gaze.

"I don't want to hear an apology," Axel said, before Bayden had a chance to utter a word.

Bayden looked down. He took a shaky breath. He tugged at Axel's grip around his wrists. It seemed more about testing Axel's interest in maintaining a hold on him than anything else. When Axel showed no inclination to release him, Bayden subsided.

"Look at me," Axel ordered.

It seemed to take Bayden several life times, but finally he managed it. His uncertainty was just as obvious as his embarrassment. He was way out of his usual experience.

"You're not in trouble," Axel promised.

Bayden turned his face aside.

Axel released one of his wrists. Bayden instantly tried to squirm out from underneath him. Axel let more of his weight rest on him, keeping him pinned down. He moved Bayden's wrists together and put one hand over them, just to let Bayden know he wanted them to stay there.

With his hand free, Axel turned Bayden back to face him.

"What's the punishment, sir?"

Axel frowned. Bayden didn't sound afraid of the prospect, but there was something very definitely off in his tone of voice—something more than embarrassment at having a hair trigger. "There isn't one."

"I didn't have permission, sir."

"You showed as much control as anyone could expect you to."

Bayden pulled back as if he'd been slapped.

Axel automatically tightened his grip on him in case he was about to make a bid for freedom. "That statement has nothing to do with you being a shifter. I don't expect instant expertise from anyone—human or wolf."

That seemed to convince Bayden that he wasn't specifically insulting a wolf's control. It didn't completely solve the problem. When Bayden glanced up at Axel he looked as angry with himself as ever. Even worse than that, right in the back of his expression, he looked heartbroken at his failure.

"I'm not going to punish you for doing something I like," Axel said, his tone inviting no argument.

Bayden shook his head. "You like it when I do what you say and—"

"I like it when you submit to me," Axel cut in. "That's more important than obedience."

Bayden squirmed against the bed sheet.

"Did you choose to come?" Axel asked. "Were you thinking about coming?"

Bayden hesitated before shaking his head.

"Did you do anything to make yourself come?"

He shook his head again.

"You came because…" Axel prompted.

"You…" Bayden peered up at him.

It was a short answer, but it was also complete. Axel had no doubt that Bayden's orgasm had one cause. "And you think that means you failed to give up control to me, that you failed to submit to me?"

Bayden looked down. "I…"

"You were so focused on me and on your submission, there was only one person in this bed capable of controlling whether or not you got off. And that's exactly the way I like it."

"A human sub—"

"Wouldn't be able to hand over control the way you just did without months of training."

Bayden hesitated.

"Maybe humans are better at denying their instincts, at controlling responses themselves."

Bayden quickly shook his head. Axel ignored the gesture.

"But wolves are better at following their instincts and handing over control to other people," Axel went on. "I'm not going to punish you for showing me I have options I wasn't aware of." He smiled down at Bayden. "Because if there's only one thing hotter than orgasm denial it's orgasm control—not just what you can get through obedience, but the real thing, from pure submission." Even as Axel said it, ideas raced through his mind of the fun he could have with that.

Bayden frowned. "I...I don't understand, sir." His breaths were shaky by the time he reached the end of the sentence. It was obvious just how much it had cost him to admit that, how much he had hated saying it.

"That's fine," Axel murmured, stroking his cheek with his free hand. "I don't expect you to understand yet. You'll see what I mean quickly enough."

Bayden squirmed. "I can't obey rules I don't know about, sir."

"The rules about not getting yourself off still apply. You'll be punished if you sneak away and jack off—and it will be a real punishment—one that will teach you never to do it again."

Bayden nodded.

"But, from now on, whenever we're together, you don't need permission to come; you just need to wait for me to give you the opportunity. I don't want you to think about coming, or not coming, at all."

Bayden nodded once, a sharp, jerky little motion. It seemed to indicate that he'd heard rather than that he agreed that the new rules were a good idea. He twitched his wrists, as if checking whether Axel still wanted to keep him where he was.

"You're not allowed off the bed," Axel ordered, but he released him and let him sit up.

Bayden pulled away, but he didn't even approach the edge of the bed. He brought one knee up in front of him.

Axel wasn't sure if he was aware that he was creating a barrier between them, but wolf or human, as body language went, it seemed pretty clear to Axel.

"Instincts," Axel prompted.

Bayden didn't even glance in his direction. "A human sub would—"

Axel sat up. "I'm not interested in a human sub."

Bayden rubbed the back of his neck, obviously struggling to get his mental balance back. "My instincts just tell me to do what you want, to do what will please you, sir."

"I want you to offer me whatever your instincts tell you would be best received," Axel said. He was aware that he was pushing Bayden well out of his comfort zone at a time when he might not be able to handle it, but he was also sure that, if Bayden's trust could be extended just a little further, it was what would get Bayden back on balance faster than anything else.

Bayden took a deep breath. His Adam's apple bobbed. "Show, sir?"

"Yes."

Bayden kept his gaze down as he turned and, dipping his body as close to the mattress as possible, crawled toward Axel. He headed straight for Axel's crotch.

A blow job wasn't a bad thing under the vast majority of circumstances. There was logic in wanting to get him off, since Bayden had already come. Axel was hardly heartbroken by the idea, especially after experiencing Bayden's skill with his mouth the previous night. But Bayden bypassed Axel's cock entirely. Instead, he lapped delicately at the smears of cum he'd left on Axel's skin when he came.

Axel watched, completely fascinated, as Bayden cleaned his orgasm from his skin without any kind of prompt to do that. There was something very natural about his movements. For once, he seemed to have successfully forced himself out of the habit of second guessing himself at every turn.

Axel stroked his fingers through Bayden's hair. Bayden paused at the first caress, as if uncertain whether or not he was about to be pushed away.

"Good boy," Axel murmured.

Bayden went back to what he was doing with what might have been a little extra confidence.

Apology. Service. Submission. It was hard to tell exactly what Bayden's actions represented. Axel smiled down at the top of Bayden's head. As spotless as he liked everything to be, it could be a simple desire to clean up the mess he'd made.

Some of Bayden's cum had smeared against Axel's cock. Bayden cleaned that up too. His tongue worked against him in short, firm, strokes. It wasn't necessarily intended to be sexual, but Bayden was licking his cock. Axel's ability to set aside what something meant to a human in favour of seeing it from a wolf's perspective wasn't bullet proof.

He forced himself not to guide Bayden's actions in any particular direction but to let him have free rein while he merely stroked his fingers through Bayden's hair.

Once every drop was gone, Bayden paused and looked up at him.

"Feel better?" Axel asked.

Bayden nodded. Another glance up. Bayden seemed to realise that an explanation could be required.

"Even if you'd given me permission, it still wouldn't have been appropriate, sir."

Axel slid his hand behind Bayden's head and stroked his neck. "Inappropriate because a sub shouldn't..." What would be the right term? "Mark his territory?"

A touch of colour rose to Bayden's cheeks making him look young and unexpectedly innocent. He nodded.

"What about a dom?"

Bayden shrugged, but his facade was imperfect. There was certainly something about the idea that appealed. It was worth noting for future reference.

"You don't have to rush away just because there's nothing left to clean up."

Bayden glanced at Axel's erection. "That wasn't what you wanted when we came in here, sir."

"Plans change," Axel said, easily.

Bayden stared at the blanket for a second, apparently deep in thought. "Is it a human thing, sir? Not wanting to screw someone if he's already…"

Axel thought about it. "Not necessarily. But wanting a blow job after someone's started licking your cock—I guess that might be a human thing. You have a beautiful mouth, and an amazing tongue."

Axel stroked his thumb across Bayden's lips. Bayden's tongue darted out and caressed the tip of the digit. Axel smiled, mostly because the move was all about instinct rather than a conscious decision to do what Bayden thought would please him.

Bayden in complete control of his every action might be impressive, but Bayden so focused on his instincts and his submission that he was unable to control himself, was the hottest thing Axel had ever seen.

* * * * *

Bayden wasn't sure why Axel should be inclined to smile at him when he'd just screwed everything up, but it still wasn't in him not to return the gesture. Axel being happy was the aim. Complaining about getting exactly what he wanted would be silly.

Axel had asked him so many times, maybe that made it okay for him to ask Axel. "Tell me what you like, sir?" he said, more softly than he'd intended.

"Different things in different moods."

Bayden kept his gaze on Axel's face, hoping that some more helpful information might be forthcoming.

"I loved what you did last night. But just keep it simple this time. Nothing complicated. No fancy techniques. Don't try to impress me. Just get me off, quick and simple, and swallow every drop."

Bayden nodded. He could do that.

Without wasting any more time, he took Axel's cock between his lips and dipped his head, allowing more of the length to slide into his mouth. He set up a far quicker rhythm than he had the previous night. Axel had been hard for longer, it made sense that he didn't want to be teased—that was information worth filing away for the future.

The fact Axel had said he'd liked what they did the previous night, combined with concrete information on what he wanted to be different, settled some of Bayden's nerves.

Working his tongue against the head every time he pulled back, Bayden did his best to keep it simple, but he couldn't help but try to do his best and maybe use a little bit of extra technique. This wasn't about earning twenty quid in a back alley. It wasn't about paying his rent or winning a bet. Bayden closed his eyes. This was as different from that as anything could ever be. Maybe knowing how to do that wasn't any use here.

Maybe that was why things kept going wrong. Maybe the alleyway was what he was really cut out for.

Axel's hand came to rest on the back of his head. Bayden froze, abandoning his attempts to please Axel. He relaxed every muscle under his conscious control and waited for Axel to move his head whatever way he chose. Nothing. He looked up.

"Yes," Axel said, as their eyes met. "I like that sometimes, too." He thought about it for a few seconds, as if debating within himself whether he wanted it that particular night. "Yes," he repeated.

274

He applied pressure to the back of Bayden's head. Sliding his fingers through Bayden's hair, he took up a firm grip on the strands. There was no doubt about what would please Axel then, no doubt who was in control and who was following whose lead.

Axel guided him to move more quickly. A few seconds later, Axel began to rock his hips, pushing his cock deeper into Bayden's mouth each time he tugged him forward. It was strong, and certain, but there was little roughness there.

Axel controlled it all, but he didn't go out of his way to make it difficult for Bayden to keep up. His grip on Bayden's hair wasn't painful. He didn't try to force his cock deep into Bayden's throat and make it impossible for him to breathe.

There was real control there, a desire not just to lead but to lead well. Axel didn't need to make a point. He didn't need to hold Bayden there, because he seemed to understand that Bayden had no interest in pulling away.

It was information, not a demand. Axel was showing him what he wanted, what he liked, just like Bayden had asked him to. There was an order in every touch, but it came from a man who knew he didn't need to shout those orders.

Bayden looked up at Axel. Their eyes locked. Bayden had never felt so certain that he was the centre of another man's attention.

Axel's actions grew rougher with impatience, and just a little more perfect, as he got closer to his orgasm. He thrust deep into Bayden's mouth as his cum spilled down Bayden's throat. For a moment, his grip on Bayden's hair was painfully and gloriously tight. Then, as Axel slumped back on the bed, he gentled his hold. He stroked his fingers through Bayden's hair as if deliberately soothing any pain he might have caused, before dropping his hand to the blanket alongside him.

Quick and simple. Bayden could have cheerfully stayed where he was for a lifetime, but he forced himself to pull away before Axel got annoyed with his attempts to linger. He retreated toward the bottom of the bed, not sure if Axel would prefer to be left alone entirely. If different moods called for different things, it was possible he wouldn't want him in the bed, or even in the room.

"You don't have to rush off," Axel said.

Bayden glanced up at him. Axel was wonderfully relaxed after his orgasm. He beckoned Bayden nearer and stroked his lips with his thumb. He smiled when Bayden gave in to the temptation to lick the tip of his thumb.

There was no demand in Axel's touch, but there was acceptance, so much acceptance. It didn't seem to be about a simple willingness to allow Bayden into his space. It felt like more than that; like an offer to let him linger over his attentions in a far more interesting way.

As if reading the idea out of Bayden's head, Axel nodded his approval.

Cautious, aware that humans could be unpredictable even in their most mellow moods, Bayden bowed his head and lapped gently at Axel's softened shaft. A glance up and he saw Axel smile sleepily. Bayden had read the situation right. He was allowed this.

Axel didn't seem to be overly sensitive after his orgasm, but Bayden kept his attentions as light as possible as he pressed gentle kisses and tiny licks against the length of his softened shaft. The scent of Axel's satisfaction was almost as heady as his arousal had been.

Moving down, Bayden mouthed Axel's sac. Axel rearranged his legs, allowing Bayden more room, but Axel barely opened his eyes. He caressed Bayden's cheek with a knuckle and let out a sleepy sigh.

Bayden looked up. Part of him wanted to ask exactly what he had permission to do, but words would have ruined everything. For once, Axel seemed inclined to consider words irrelevant. Bayden couldn't spoil that. He had no choice but to trust and hope that if he did piss Axel off, he'd forgive him.

Bayden moved his head to the left and nuzzled at the skin alongside Axel's crotch. No objection was forthcoming. Axel didn't seem to think there was anything weird about it.

Bayden gained a little more courage. He pressed a kiss there and rubbed his forehead against the dip in the muscle alongside Axel's hip. Moving his head up a little higher, he lapped at the fine trail of hairs between Axel's navel and his crotch.

Gathering confidence, he brushed his cheek against Axel's abs.

It didn't take him long to reach the lowest of Axel's tattoos. He licked the edge of the pattern for the first time. Somehow, he'd expected it to taste different, to feel a different texture against his tongue. There were no differences; Bayden still couldn't resist tracing one of the lines with his lips.

Without warning, Axel slid his hand behind Bayden's neck and tugged him up the bed. Bayden only just managed to keep his balance and not collapse on top of him. With his hands on the mattress either side of Axel, he supported himself as Axel brought their lips together.

The kiss was sweet, and brief, but it still managed to feel like ownership and praise at the same time. Axel didn't offer a second kiss. He smiled and nudged Bayden back toward his explorations.

Bayden turned his attention to Axel's chest. Axel sighed sleepily and shifted to make himself a little more comfortable, but he let Bayden get on with what he was doing without any more guidance.

Bayden traced his way over Axel's skin. When his lips brushed against a pierced nipple, he ran his tongue around the little silver ring. Axel didn't push him away, but Bayden didn't let himself play. If Axel didn't like it, there was no reason to. If he did like it, it wasn't the right time.

Axel didn't want to be turned on. This wasn't about sex. Axel wasn't letting him explore his body so he could get him off. It was so different to how things had been with other humans, or even other wolves.

Bayden kissed his way lower. He kept his hands on the bed to steady himself. The only part of him that touched Axel was his face.

He soon found himself drawn back to Axel's cock. He nuzzled against the soft shaft and kissed Axel's balls. Part of him wanted to keep going and gain as much as he could while Axel seemed so tolerant of his attention, but another side of him didn't want to push his luck too far. Asking for too much and spoiling it all would be sacrilege.

But, the temptation was too great. He dipped his head lower. Axel automatically parted his legs to give him more room, but barely a second later it seemed as if Axel's brain caught up to his body, and he changed his mind. He pulled away. Bayden started to retreat, but all Axel actually did was roll onto his stomach and arrange his pillow comfortably beneath his head.

Bayden waited until he was sure that Axel was settled, then crept closer. It was hard to see Axel's actions as anything other than an invitation. Once more supporting his weight on his hands, Bayden let his lips explore Axel's body. Starting at the top of his back, he pressed a kiss against another tattoo. Just like on Axel's chest, the designs spread down and out from Axel's shoulders. They didn't reach as far down as his waist, or join together in the middle of his torso, but Bayden was sure they would one day. Axel wasn't a man who abandoned a project once he started it.

Even though it hadn't been long since he came, Bayden was once again hard and eager for another round. His cock ached with need, but he was careful not to let it rub against Axel as he leaned over him, especially now that Axel's arse was turned toward him.

He worked his way down toward the small of Axel's back, kissing and tasting him every inch of the way. He let his cheek brush against the curve of Axel's buttock.

He'd come too far to stop. Cautious, he pressed a kiss at the very top of the cleft between Axel's cheeks. Axel moved his legs further apart and Bayden kissed his way down toward his hole.

He kept his tongue's touch especially light then. He kissed, he lapped gently against him, but he was careful not to replicate anything he might hope Axel would one day do with his cock if their positions were reversed. Not without a very clear invitation.

Axel murmured his approval, and reached back toward him. Bayden didn't have time to retreat. Axel caught hold of his wrist and pulled him up the bed to lie in front of him.

The kiss was slow and sleepy. Bayden cautiously returned it, sucking on the tip of Axel's tongue, enjoying Axel's obvious approval almost as much as he relished the kiss.

"Good boy," Axel murmured to him.

He brushed his thumb across Bayden's lips. Bayden's mouth was sensitive after his explorations. He couldn't hold back a gasp. Axel liked that. He caressed his lips again and smiled. "So good."

He ran his knuckles down Bayden's body until his fingertips brushed against Bayden's erection.

"Did you like that, pup?"

A lie would be pointless. Bayden nodded.

Axel wrapped his hand around Bayden's shaft. His hand was much bigger than Bayden's. It made his cock look far smaller than it did when Bayden jacked himself.

"Would a human?" he blurted out.

"The aim isn't humanity; it's honesty," Axel corrected.

Bayden looked down.

"It would be a good thing to like even if a human wouldn't have."

Bayden glanced up.

Axel smiled at him. "Enjoying exploring someone else's body isn't specific to any species, pup." He pulled Bayden closer. Bayden couldn't stop his cock rubbing against Axel's skin. Axel looked down between them. "Neither is wanting something you can't have."

Bayden tried to pull away, but Axel only allowed him to retreat a few inches.

"If shifters could get tattoos, you wouldn't find mine so fascinating, would you?"

He was talking about tattoos? That was what Bayden would never be able to have? He looked down at Axel's chest.

"You don't need permission to touch—with your mouth or your hands."

Bayden trailed his fingers lightly over the cross on Axel's left shoulder. Axel's only response was to trail his fingers over Bayden's shaft, just as delicately.

"You'll be allowed to come again tomorrow," Axel promised.

Bayden nodded his understanding. "I should…" He indicated the smears of cum that still lingered on his own skin.

"Later," Axel said. The fact Bayden wasn't perfectly clean didn't seem to bother him.

Axel arranged them just as he wanted them, with Bayden half pinned beneath him. Part of his weight pressed down against Bayden. His warmth wrapped around him. When Axel pulled a blanket up over them both, the world was as close to perfect as Bayden believed it ever could be.

Chapter Seventeen

"Thirsty, pup?"

Bayden perked up his ears and lifted his head. He began to push himself up onto his paws, but Axel shook his head.

"I'll bring our drinks out here. You can stay there and keep an eye on things. I won't be a minute." He disappeared inside.

Bayden subsided back onto the cushion Axel had put near the lock-up's door, right next to where Axel had spent the last hour working on one of his bikes.

If Bayden had learned anything during his time shifted in front of Axel, it was that Axel talked to him just as much when he was in his wolf form as he did when he was in his human form. The only difference was that Axel filled in Bayden's side of the conversation for him. Bayden stretched and let out a contented little sigh, wondering if there was a way to get Axel to fill in both sides of the conversation when he was in his human shape. It would make life a lot simpler.

The sound of a car pulling into the pub's car park when the pub wasn't open made Bayden's ears perk up. Sometimes the Dragons turned up at odd times on their bikes — one could have easily ridden over to discuss the previous day's ride.

But cars didn't arrive outside pub hours, and this car didn't stop around front. Bayden launched up onto his feet as the car drove into the yard, where only Axel parked.

Bayden looked at the open lock-up. *Keep an eye on things.* It was the kind of order a human might give to a guard dog. It wasn't unlike a command from an alpha to look after the pack's territory.

The convertible sports car rolled to a stop. Bayden's instincts took over. He took several paces forward and barked loudly at the intruder.

In any version of the world where humans were sensible, the driver would have stayed in the car—if not forever then at least until Axel came back out and was able to deal with the situation himself.

A woman got out.

"Well, now, who are you? Axel didn't tell me he was getting a dog." She came straight toward him, obviously not the least bit afraid. The way she talked about Axel made it sound like she knew him really well.

"You're gorgeous, aren't you?" She came closer still. Completely confident, her body language all dominance. In a strange way, she reminded him of Axel. She had the same attitude, the same mannerisms. A few steps closer and he realised there was something familiar in her scent.

He'd smelled it before—very faint, clinging to some of the boxes in the back of one of the less frequently used lock-ups.

She stepped straight into Bayden's space and reached out to him. Unsure what to do, Bayden froze.

If she was an intruder, she should obviously be chased off, but he doubted an intruder would be quite so relaxed. He leaned away from her touch.

"Hey, it's okay. I'm not going to hurt you." She stroked his neck. "Where's your collar, darling?"

Bayden tried to pull back, but she didn't seem to be able to get the hint.

"Sally?" Axel didn't sound angry that she was there, or that Bayden hadn't got rid of her. Bayden leaned to one side and looked around the woman. Axel didn't look angry either.

Sally straightened up when she spotted Axel in the doorway at the back of the pub. "Axe! You didn't tell me you were getting a dog. He's gorgeous."

Axel looked from Sally to Bayden and back again. He chuckled and shook his head. "Go on in, Bayden. I'll lock up and we'll follow you up in a few minutes."

Bayden skirted around the woman and hurried inside. He could hear Axel talking to her as he went, but he was too full of his own thoughts to be able to eavesdrop properly.

Axel always left the doors open when Bayden was shifted. He had a clear path as he rushed up the stairs and through the flat into the bedroom. He switched back just as he reached the door to the en-suite.

His hands were filthy after padding around as paws for the last hour or two, happily tagging along behind Axel wherever he went. He quickly washed his hands and face and headed back into the bedroom to get clean clothes out of his drawer. It wasn't cold, but temperature wasn't the important thing—he added the jumper Axel had bought him and smoothed it into place.

Two pairs of footsteps on the stairs let him know that Axel and the woman—Sally—were on their way up.

Bayden hesitated just inside the bedroom door. Axel and Sally knew each other. They were both alphas. Maybe he should stay in there out of the way.

"Come on out when you're ready, pup." The order solved that conundrum. Bayden squared his shoulders and stepped out of the bedroom.

"You talk to that dog as if he's…" Sally trailed off as she turned to face Bayden. In his human shape he was able to take in a few extra details. She was taller than him, but shorter than Axel. Her hair was long and blonde but wound up and pinned to the back of her head. She was wearing a blue business suit and heels.

Her eyes narrowed as their gazes met and she realised what he was. "Bloody hell."

"Sally, meet Bayden." Axel still had that faint touch of amusement in his voice. He liked that Sally was shocked.

Sally stepped straight into Bayden's space and reached out to smooth his hair, just as she had when he was in wolf form—just as Axel did all the time.

It was just as obvious in human form as it had been in wolf form. She was an alpha. Bayden took a step back.

"Give him some space, Sal." The humour had disappeared from Axel's voice, but she didn't seem to realise that Axel's order really hadn't been a suggestion. She looked over her shoulder at Axel. "He's gorgeous!" She didn't take her hand out of his hair.

"It's not polite to stroke people without an invitation," Axel pointed out.

She turned her attention back to Bayden. There was nothing in her scent that indicated her interest in him was anything other than curiosity, but she was an alpha and she was in his space.

Bayden took a step back and respectfully retreated, making it very clear he accepted that she was more dominant than him, but that he wasn't interested in her being dominant over him. She let him go. Bayden moved to where Axel stood. As tempting as it was to go into his space, he didn't quite dare. Axel solved the problem for him by sliding his arm around him and tugging him closer.

Sally raised an eyebrow. "So, is he bi or are you that besotted you've forgotten he doesn't swing in my direction?"

Axel sighed. "Bayden, meet Salome Carmichael. My sister—and proof that I did something really bad in a previous life and God is still punishing me for it."

Sally laughed and strolled into the kitchen as if she had the right to wander through Axel's territory however she pleased. "He loves me really, Bayden."

She was right. Axel was really pleased she was there.

"Shall I start getting things ready for this evening, s—" He mentally cursed.

"You can call him sir," Sally said, opening the fridge. "I know he's kinky. Do you have any food, Axe? I'm starving."

"You can call me whatever you prefer while Sally's here," Axel said, moving Sally pointedly away from the fridge and nudging her into one of the chairs by the kitchen table. "And there's no need for you to leave the room."

"You can't leave," Sally agreed. "I want to know everything about you!"

It was all Bayden could do to stop the instinct to step back toward the door.

"Grab some coffee and take a seat," Axel ordered.

He hadn't even had time to do that before Sally turned her attention back to him. "So, you're a shifter?"

"Wow, you're quick, Sal. What was your first clue?" Axel asked, over his shoulder as he took three steaks out of the fridge.

She completely ignored him in favour of staring at Bayden.

"Wolf shifter," he agreed.

Age. Job. Bike. Bloody hell—the woman asked even more questions than Axel!

* * * * *

Sisters had their uses, Axel had to admit that. As he joined Sally and Bayden at the table, he'd never felt quite so tolerant of his sister's tendency to bombard any new acquaintance with dozens of questions with no regard for their privacy or inclination to be cross examined.

"What about your family?"

"They live on the other side of the city." Bayden's expression was as hard to read as ever, but his tone of voice was overtly deferential. There were no clipped one word answers here. The guys in the pub might be dismissed with an old-fashioned look, but it seemed Bayden had been brought up to be respectful to women—even women who had to be pissing him off with their impromptu interrogation.

"Brothers and sisters?"

Bayden shook his head. "I don't have any."

"Lucky you," Axel murmured. Sally completely ignored him. Axel smiled, not the least bit surprised.

"What about parents?" she asked.

Bayden hesitated.

"She's not asking if you have parents, she's asking whether or not they have a problem with you dating men," Axel translated.

Bayden shook his head. "Wolves don't care about that."

"Good. So, what do your parents do?"

Bayden gave the question considerable thought as he delicately ate another piece of steak. "My mother used to work with the Danville Project," he finally offered.

"That's the wolf charity, right?" Sally said.

"It's not a charity, it's an organisation." For the first time since Sally arrived, Bayden's voice had an edge to it.

Sally's legal training hadn't been wasted. She noticed the change. She seemed to realise why, too.

"An organisation for..." Axel prompted, not impressed at being the only one who didn't know what was going on.

"They help female wolves who want to move into a different line of work, sir."

"To move out of prostitution," Sally specified. "Mum's church did a fundraising thing for them, when they were her cause of the moment. I wonder if they met."

Bayden shook his head. "My mother did background stuff. She wasn't involved in fundraising or anything like that."

"It's a good cause," Sally said. "I remember mum saying how common it was for shifter women to end up doing sex work."

Bayden tensed up. The change was small. He was obviously clinging to the idea of appearing respectful at all costs, but he was also a wolf who'd taken a lot of financial bets on things that involved sex.

His reaction was subtle enough for Sally to keep going, entirely unaware. "The statistics are crazy and — "

"Sal?" Axel cut in.

"What?" She looked from him to Bayden and back again.

"Pick another topic. There's a good girl." There was nothing subtle about his tone. She got his message loud and clear.

"What about your father?" she asked.

"He's dead." There was no emotion in Bayden's voice. It was scarily close to the way he sounded in a bet, everything blocked out. As changes of topic went, it wasn't an improvement.

"I'm sorry," Sally offered.

Bayden said nothing.

"So it's just you and your mum?" she asked.

"And my grandfather. I don't live with them." And it was important to make that clear, so no one could accuse them of breaking the law.

Axel straightened up in his chair. That was it. Everyone's curiosity had been indulged quite far enough for one day. "That ends the question and answer part of your visit," Axel said.

Sally sighed dramatically and turned to Bayden. "He's just saying that so you don't get the chance to ask me anything about all the embarrassing skeletons in his closet."

"I have nothing to hide. My skeletons all came out when I did," Axel shot back, with a shrug.

"So Bayden knows that all this is just for show?" She waved her hand at one of his tattoos. "Catholic choir boy trying to look all bad and scary and failing miserably."

Axel laughed and leaned back in his chair. "God, it's been too long, Sal."

She nodded and sipped her drink.

"Where was it this time?"

"Last stop Texas, next stop Ukraine," she said.

"Sal's a lawyer—she travels a lot for work," Axel told Bayden. "She only ever passes through here every couple of months."

Sally nodded seriously. "Which means I'm almost as far into my mother's black books as Axe is. I should be settled down with a nice Catholic boy and raising a couple of kids. Which reminds me—Beka's got another one on the way."

Bayden glanced toward Axel for another translation. "Our sister. There's six of us altogether. Four boys, two girls. I'm the youngest, then Sal. Then there's three boys—Josiah, Lazarus and Ishmael. Rebekah's the oldest."

Bayden seemed to have relaxed now that the conversation had moved away from him. He smiled shyly as their eyes met, as if pleased that Axel was willing to bring him in on family gossip. Maybe that was it. Maybe the way to get Bayden to share his secrets was that obvious.

Axel smiled back at him. Yes, sisters did have their uses. As he walked Sally out to her car an hour later, he loved her more than ever.

"He's adorable."

"Yes." Even if it wasn't a word he was going to use out loud about anyone or anything, he couldn't deny it.

"The one thing I hate about having a gay brother," she said, leaning against the side of her car. "You have much better luck with men than I do."

"So that's why you're really here. You've got rid of your latest, so I regain the honour of driving you back and forth to the airport."

"You can't expect me to leave Cherry in the airport car park!" She stroked her fingers down one sleek line of her bright red Ferrari as she spoke.

"Anyone who names their car deserves whatever happens to it."

"From the man who'd sell his soul rather than get a scratch on one of his bikes…"

Axel laughed. "That's different."

She reached up and hugged him. "I'll let you know when the flight's confirmed."

"Sure."

"You should keep him," she glanced up toward the flat as she stepped back and opened her car door. "Seriously, I like this one."

Axel shook his head at her as she drove away, but she was right about Bayden being a sub worth keeping.

Back in his flat, he found Bayden just finishing clearing up after dinner. He looked over his shoulder as Axel walked in.

"I'm sorry I barked at her when she got here, sir. I—"

"Hush." Axel stepped up behind him and pressed a kiss against his temple. "She deserves to be barked at." Sliding his arms around Bayden's waist he encouraged Bayden to lean back against him. "What did you think of her?"

He hesitated, obviously surprised by the question. "She's very nice, sir."

Axel smiled. He'd have probably said the same if she'd been a serial killer.

"You get on better with her than you do with the other Dragons."

"We both know who the more dominant wolf is, sir. That makes everything simpler."

"A female wolf is automatically less dominant?" Axel asked.

Bayden frowned. "I didn't say she was less dominant than me, sir."

Axel ran through the events that day in his mind, trying to remember the tiny clues. She'd got in his space and Bayden had... He'd been polite. He'd lowered his eyes. He'd backed away at the first opportunity. He'd done exactly what he'd said he'd do when approached by a more dominant man who he didn't want to screw.

"You came back to me," Axel remembered. He turned Bayden around in his arms so they stood face to face.

"Because…" He closed his eyes for a moment and tried to think like a wolf. "You were making it clear that, even if she's more dominant than you, you're already submitting to someone else?"

Bayden nodded rapidly, obviously impressed.

Axel was quite impressed with himself too. He was finally getting the hang of the lupine dictionary. "That's why you get on better with Evan and the other lifestyle subs than you do with the doms or the other Dragons."

Evan treated Bayden like a dom. And Bayden was, if not chatty, then always kind to him. The cheap shots and sarcasm were for the doms who tried to lord it over Bayden—who didn't realise he saw himself as more dominant than them. Axel nodded slowly to himself. There was only one anomaly left to discover.

"And you like Hale less than anyone else because?"

Bayden tensed. "Wolves don't have a problem with cops, sir. Cops have a problem with wolves."

Axel met Bayden's eyes. "He has no interest in enforcing anti-pack laws, pup."

Bayden shrugged. Silence fell over them.

"If you have any questions about anything Sal said, you don't need to wait for an invitation to ask them," Axel offered.

There was obviously something, but it took Bayden a little while to get the words out. "She said your family is Catholic, sir."

"That's right."

"They don't like wolves, sir," Bayden blurted out. "I mean, even compared to other humans—even compared to cops."

Yes. Axel remembered that much from Sunday school. "True. But they're not huge fans of gay men either."

"You asked me if my family minded me liking men, sir," Bayden remembered.

Axel took a deep breath, but if he wanted Bayden to tell him things, he couldn't skirt the topic. "Sally has no problem with me being gay. The rest of my family weren't thrilled when I came out. It could have been a lot worse. I was fifteen. They didn't throw me out of the house or anything. Sally stays in touch and keeps me up to date with family gossip. The rest of them, they just...pray for me."

"Praying is a bad thing, sir?"

It was such a tentative question, refusing to answer it would be like a slap in the face.

Axel pointed to the dresser just visible through the door leading into the living room. "Top drawer on the right."

Bayden opened it. "Prayer beads?" he hazarded.

"Rosaries. My mother sends me a couple every year. Birthday, Easter, Christmas. She wants me to come back to the church and save my immortal soul. She thinks I toss them all."

"But you don't, sir."

"No, I don't." He stepped up behind Bayden and nudged the drawer closed, putting them firmly back out of sight. "She means it for the best. They all do."

Bayden turned within the circle of his arms. He stared at Axel's shoulder for several seconds, obviously out of his depth and not sure what to say. Axel wasn't sure what to say either.

Finally, Bayden met Axel's eyes. "I'm glad you like men, sir." He sounded very earnest about that.

It would be rude to laugh at Bayden's attempt to make him feel better. It was far better to kiss him instead.

Chapter Eighteen

"I made you a promise last night, didn't I?" Axel said as they retreated to his flat at the end of the night. Rather than order Bayden to leave his clothes by the door, he led the way straight into the bedroom before turning to face Bayden.

Bayden shrugged, putting a lot of effort into showing that he didn't consider that promise important.

Axel chuckled. "Your memory's better than that, pup."

Bayden swallowed. "You said I'd have a chance to come, sir."

"I did. And I always keep my promises."

"You don't need to—"

Axel silenced him with a shake of the head. "Promises are important." He caught the hem of Bayden's jumper and lifted it up. Bayden co-operated, raising his hands so the soft grey fabric could pass over his head. Axel dropped the sweater on the end of the bed and moved on to the rest of Bayden's clothes.

Bayden soon stood naked in the middle of the room.

Axel stepped back. "Have you ever been tied up when it wasn't for a bet—just because you wanted to be?"

Bayden shook his head. "But it's not a problem, sir."

"Do you like the idea?"

Bayden looked down, unsure again.

"Maybe it's not something you've thought about liking or disliking?" Axel suggested. "Proving the point was the only important thing. How you felt was irrelevant."

Bayden nodded his acceptance of that possibility.

"Tonight, I want you to think about if you like it or not," Axel told him.

"Yes, sir."

"Do you remember your safe word?"

Bayden tensed up.

Axel mentally counted out the seconds while he waited to see if Bayden would try to refuse one again.

"Yes, sir."

Axel nodded his approval.

When Bayden hesitated, Axel waited him out.

"Are you going to use the bed, sir?" Bayden finally asked.

It wasn't quite the question Axel expected. "Yes. Do you have an objection?"

Bayden shook his head. "Maybe I should move my clothes out of the way, sir?"

"Go ahead." Axel went across to the wardrobe where he kept his personal toy collection.

By the time he turned around, cuffs in hand, Bayden had everything folded and put away, and he seemed far more relaxed. Axel couldn't help but smile.

"Sir?"

"You may be the only sub I've ever known who doesn't need to be ordered to keep things clean and tidy."

Bayden looked down.

"That's a good thing," Axel added, in case that wasn't as obvious as it should be. He went over to the bed and fastened restraints to the headboard. "Come here, pup."

With Bayden's co-operation, it didn't take Axel long to have him stretched out on the bed, his wrists bound to the headboard.

Bayden's chest rose and fell as he took a deep breath.

It was hardly the first time he'd been tied up. Axel had seen him restrained often enough himself. But this time was going to be different. He was determined about that.

"Move about and get a feel for them," Axel said.

Bayden looked up at his wrists. In the bets, his aim had always been to remain still and unaffected, not to do anything that would make the other guy think he was getting to him. Now, he tugged gently at the restraints, working out how much slack there was, how much range of movement he was left with. It was the first time Axel had ever seen him moving in his bondage.

"Good or bad?" Axel asked, sitting fully clothed on the bed next to him.

Bayden remained silent but it seemed less like a refusal to answer and more like he didn't know the answer.

"You just think about it, okay?" Axel leaned over and brushed their lips together. Bayden parted his lips, welcoming the kiss, relishing each touch.

When Axel straightened up, he ran his gaze over Bayden's body from top to toe. He was all laid out for him, so perfect, and all his. Axel smiled to himself as he wrapped his hand around Bayden's erection.

Bayden gasped, every muscle in his body tensed. It was a pretty sight, but a little too close to the way Bayden had controlled himself during bets with other men.

"Relax."

Bayden nodded that he'd heard.

Axel moved his hand slowly around Bayden's cock, just passing the time while he let Bayden try to obey his last order.

"Do you remember what I said last night about who controls when you come and what that means?" Axel asked, after a few minutes.

Bayden nodded.

Axel gave him a little while longer. Instant expertise wasn't to be expected. Axel didn't even expect instant enthusiasm, but Bayden didn't make any noticeable attempt to relax or hand over control. If anything, he rushed toward safe ground and the kind of fake submission he'd displayed within his bets.

Axel raised an eyebrow at him, but Bayden's eyes were closed. He was retreating further into bad habits by the second.

There was an easy cure for that. Axel leaned over and calmly took the tip of Bayden's cock into his mouth.

The cuffs rattled as Bayden thrust upward into Axel's mouth. It was easy to ride out his actions. Bayden lifted his head and glared down at him in confusion—his eyes open very wide, his lips parted with shock. Axel dipped his head and let a little more of Bayden's shaft slip past his lips. A spurt of pre-cum landed on his tongue, and Axel's own cock hardened inside his jeans.

Bayden bit his bottom lip and squirmed on the bed, obviously struggling to hold himself back. Confident that he now had Bayden's complete attention, Axel bobbed his head, taking Bayden almost to the base before sliding up until only the tip of Bayden's cock remained between his lips.

He was pretty sure he could read Bayden well enough to have a good chance of stopping before Bayden actually came. And, if he read him wrong, it was hardly the end of the world. Bayden had been right about one thing—sometimes the only thing that mattered was making a point to someone—and making it very clearly.

Bayden closed his eyes. His hands formed into fists above his head as he fought against his own pleasure. He was good at blocking everything out in a bet, but that was about ignoring pain and fear. Axel was sure that Bayden's ability to ignore pleasure was far less well developed.

Bayden might have learned how to give a blow job that bordered on the sublime, but Axel had no doubt that he'd been whipped more often than he'd been sucked off.

Caught off guard, surrounded by unfamiliar sensations, Bayden simply didn't have the skills to hold himself completely in check. Minutes ticked past. Bayden rushed past what Axel had guessed him capable of, but the strain was telling. Axel's own cock ached as he watched Bayden struggle for control.

Bayden gasped for breath. He whimpered and pulled at the cuffs. He tossed his head back and forth on the pillow as he struggled to display a brand of control he'd already been forbidden from practicing. He bucked his hips, pushing his cock deeper into Axel's mouth.

He was so close. A few more seconds would have him coming in Axel's mouth.

Bayden opened and closed his lips, but no words emerged. Bayden tried again and finally found syllables.

"Stop!" Panic filled the word.

Axel immediately lifted his head. "It's okay." He placed his hand flat on Bayden's chest. "You're okay."

Bayden's whole body shuddered as he panted for breath.

"Look at me. Look me in the eye."

Bayden obeyed. Axel held his gaze. "You're fine." Slowly, as Bayden stared into Axel's eyes, he caught his breath.

"Do you want to say your safe word?" Axel asked.

Bayden shook his head. "I…" There was still too much panic in his voice.

"You're okay," Axel moved up the bed and settled his other hand on Bayden's cheek. "Whether you say it or not, nothing will happen until I know exactly what you want." That was important. The sooner he could get that idea permanently welded into Bayden's mind the better.

Bayden stared up at him. His heartbeat was still rapid against Axel's palm, but he'd regained his outward calm.

"Do you want me to untie you?" Axel asked.

Bayden shook his head again. "You said…. I mean… I don't…If you hadn't stopped, I'd have come," he whispered.

"And you didn't want to?" Axel asked.

Bayden frowned. "You didn't give me permission."

"You don't need permission. I told you that last night."

Bayden shook his head. "You don't need to change the rules. I can control—" He flinched at the realisation that that statement wasn't entirely correct.

"Could you learn as much control as any dom, wolf or human, might ever wish you to display?" Axel filled in. "Yes.

I've never doubted that. I could train you. I've done it with other subs. It's not that difficult, but I'm not interested in teaching you that particular skill."

Bayden blinked up at him. Perhaps it wasn't fair to expect him to fully understand new ideas when he was still on the edge, but they could make a start.

"Learning to control your own orgasms and wait for permission is one thing, pup. Most subs can do that. But learning how to really give up complete control of your orgasms, that's something else. I wouldn't even bother trying it with most men." He studied Bayden for several long seconds. "You can do it. It won't be easy for you, but I can take your submission that deep."

Bayden swallowed.

It was the tiny cue that Axel had been waiting for. The idea that he was being asked to do something harder than Axel originally intended would be the thing that sealed the deal.

"Do you want that?" Axel asked.

Bayden nodded rapidly. He licked his lips. "Yes, sir."

"Then from this moment on, you need to accept that you don't get to choose when you come. I make that decision. If I want you to last until I'm ready to come at the same time as you, you will. If I don't want you to get off at all, you won't. And if I want you to come within the first minute, that's my choice as well."

The first two possibilities didn't raise a flicker of response. The third option made Bayden squirm, but he didn't actually protest.

"I think you'd like showing off for me, proving that you can hold back through hour after hour of teasing, wouldn't you? But proving that I can make you come in a few seconds—not letting yourself hold back simply because you don't have permission to exercise that kind of control, that's harder." Axel moved his hand down to Bayden's cock and stroked him, slow and easy, as he spoke. "Holding back is all about having control, but you're not in control now, Bayden. I am. You are my sub, my pup. If I want you frustrated, I can have that. If I want you vulnerable and off balance with a blush staining your cheeks, that's my right too."

On cue, Bayden blushed. He'd never done that during a bet. Axel smiled, more certain than ever that he'd picked the right course of action.

"You won't get in trouble for coming at any point, whatever we're doing. But I want you to be very clear on this, Bayden. I don't want you trying to control yourself when we're together—not in any way. If you try, I'll step in and I'll stop you—every time."

Bayden nodded. His breathing was getting ragged again.

"When we're apart, that's different."

Bayden blinked at him. Axel stilled his hand, giving Bayden space to think a little more clearly.

"When you're not with me I still expect complete self-control. You don't get to sneak away and jack off. If you do, I will find out, and you will be punished."

Bayden shook his head. "I…I wouldn't do that, sir."

It was true. Bayden had far too much pride to sneak some extra pleasure for himself. Axel tightened his grip around Bayden's shaft, making him whimper and rock his hips. "That's a good boy. If you continue to be good, I might let you jack off now and again, when I'm there to watch."

Bayden nodded his acceptance of the possibility.

"Do you understand the rules? If you have any questions about them, now would be the time."

"What if…?" Bayden turned his face away and closed his eyes.

"Go ahead," Axel prompted.

"What if you don't think it should, but it does?"

"If I don't expect something to make you come, but it does?" Axel checked. He already knew the answer, but he took some time to simply enjoy the feel of Bayden's cock in his hand and pretended to give the matter considerable thought, just so Bayden would know that he was serious.

"Getting you off is my right and my responsibility. And if my read on you is off, that's my mistake. I won't be angry with you. I don't expect you to read my mind. If you get the opportunity to come, take it—because you never know how long it will be before the next chance."

Bayden nodded that he'd heard. He didn't seem entirely convinced, but that would come over time, as he gained proof that Axel would be as good as his word.

Axel let silence descend while he continued to toy with Bayden's erection. His own cock was still painfully hard, but he'd been patient for months while he waited for this night, he could be patient a little longer while he made his point.

He watched Bayden, taking in every detail as Bayden fought to hand over control, to relax and simply let what Axel wanted take over his universe. It was an imperfect process, but Bayden was trying. Axel had no doubt about that. Bayden wasn't just paying lip service to the idea, he was struggling like hell to do what Axel wanted—even though it was the complete opposite to his own preference.

If Bayden in bondage was gorgeous, Bayden in submission was exquisite.

Axel couldn't resist taking him closer to the edge, speeding up his strokes until Bayden lost himself in his approaching pleasure. Bayden's lips shaped the beginning of a howl and—

* * * * *

Bayden gasped. He kicked out against the mattress, frantically trying to pull his cock away from Axel's hand. It was impossible to escape. Axel's grip closed painfully tight around the base of his shaft, jolting him from his pleasure and pulling him roughly back from the edge of his orgasm.

"My choice," Axel reminded him. "I could have got you off, but I decided to let you last a little longer."

Bayden swallowed a whimper, but control of his mouth seemed to have slipped away from him along with everything else. The sound was clearly audible, although even Bayden wasn't sure if it was spawned by frustration or gratitude.

Axel stroked his cheek. "Good boy."

Bayden took a deep breath. The air was full of scent. Their combined arousal stole all the oxygen from the room, leaving him breathless.

Axel stood up and stepped away from the bed. Obviously, Axel had the right to go wherever he liked, whenever the mood struck him, but he'd said that he wanted to have sex. He'd said Bayden was good.

Bayden managed not to fidget and pull at his restraints, but he couldn't hold back another whimper. He hoped that the sound might be too high for a human to hear, but Axel chuckled in response to the needy little noise.

Axel pulled his T-shirt over his head and tossed it aside. The rest of his clothes quickly followed, until the only things he wore were his nipple rings and his tattoos.

Bayden licked his lips at the memory of them. Axel ran his thumb over Bayden's mouth and chuckled. "Another time, pup. I have other plans for you tonight."

He opened the drawer in the bedside cabinet and pulled out a tube of lube. The memory of Axel's slicked fingers rushed to the front of Bayden's mind. Being prepared but not actually screwed. Just being toyed with; it had been torture.

Bayden wriggled, but kept his movements as small as possible, waiting for a clear instruction from Axel before he risked doing anything that could be interpreted as an offer.

Axel didn't wait around for an invitation. He pushed Bayden's legs apart—completely confident in Bayden's desire to follow his lead. Bayden stared up at him in awe.

Axel didn't tease this time. In seconds, he had two fingers buried deep in Bayden's arse. He crooked them, making Bayden's mind spin with pleasure.

Unable to hold back without breaking his word, he found himself responding to the slightest twitch of Axel's fingers. His erection throbbed as every movement against his prostate rushed straight to his cock.

Years passed. Bayden wasn't sure what Axel was waiting for. Did he want to make him come like this? It was his choice. If it was what Axel wanted, then it could only be a good thing. Or was there any other reason?

When another possibility occurred to Bayden, he didn't waste time second guessing it. "Sir, do I need to say?"

"Say?" Axel twisted his fingers. Pre-cum dripped more rapidly onto Bayden's stomach as a fresh wave of pleasure rolled through him.

"Say that I'm ready, sir?" Was that what Axel was waiting for?

Axel thought about it, but he didn't still his fingers. "You can always tell me if you're worried I'm rushing you, but no, you can't tell me to hurry the hell up."

Bayden groaned his disapproval.

Axel grinned, obviously enjoying his control of the situation.

Bayden peered up at him. His mind was spiralling. He wasn't sure if he should hope Axel would let him come, or if he should hope Axel would allow him to last a little longer.

Their eyes met. He should hope that Axel would do whatever Axel wanted. And, for once, Axel seemed inclined to do that.

Bayden closed his eyes as everything Axel had said to him settled into place and connected up with everything he'd already known about respecting another wolf's dominance. Submission was different, but it wasn't that different.

Axel was more interested in whether or not Bayden came than a wolf would be, but only because being interested in it meant he could control it. Maybe the difference wasn't because Axel was a human, but because he was an alpha. The possibility knotted hope and perfection together.

"Are you with me, pup?"

Bayden opened his eyes. "Yes, sir."

Axel held his gaze for several seconds. Humans couldn't read people's body language the way a wolf could, but that didn't feel relevant while Axel could stare straight into his soul.

Bayden swallowed rapidly, but couldn't keep back a deep moan of pleasure as Axel crooked his fingers.

Axel took his hand away. Bayden twisted and pulled against his bondage as he gave in to the need to be closer to Axel — to try to get that, even when the bondage made it impossible. Axel took no notice as he moved to kneel on the bed between Bayden's thighs.

Bayden straightened one leg and brushed the inside of his calf against Axel's knee, but Axel's attention was focused elsewhere. He caught hold of Bayden's hips. His grip was strong as he held Bayden in place.

Bayden was as ready as he could ever be. He'd been ready for a lifetime, but he needed Axel's cock inside his arse so badly that he could barely breathe, let alone speak up and tell Axel that.

Words weren't necessary. No questions, no orders. Axel moved Bayden into a position that pleased him and pushed forward, stretching Bayden's hole wide open as he ploughed into him in one harsh movement.

Bayden jerked. He tugged at his bondage. Axel filled him completely, but he wasn't moving. He remained perfectly still, staring down at Bayden.

Bayden couldn't match his control. He writhed against the bed sheet. Axel's grip on him tightened, maybe even hard enough to leave marks. Bayden hoped it would.

Finally, Axel moved. He pushed into Bayden with long, slow movements, making him feel every inch of his cock.

Every thrust took Bayden closer to the edge. There was nothing he could do to make himself come or to stop himself. He was right on the verge when Axel moved one hand to his cock.

To finish him off, or pull him back. As Axel held him in the palm of his hand, it could have easily gone either way. Bayden held his breath until Axel chose his course of action. A squeeze just on the other side of painful stopped Bayden in his tracks. He met Axel's gaze. Success shone in Axel's expression.

No orgasm could have felt better than the wave of pleasure that rushed through Bayden on seeing his alpha so pleased with him.

Axel leaned forward. Releasing his grip on Bayden's hips, he covered him with his body as he thrust deep inside him. His head was level with Bayden's. His lips weren't far away. It would be so easy for Axel to kiss him. Bayden wanted him to so badly.

He wasn't sure if instinct or obedience made him lean up and make it clear how desperate he was for that kiss. Axel dipped his head, as if to grant the request, only to stop just short.

Bayden's breath caught in his throat, but he refused to drop back to the blanket in defeat. Axel grinned before bringing their lips together in a fierce, possessive kiss that made no allowances for anything being any way other than exactly as Axel wanted.

His tongue sparred with Bayden's, not inviting him to kiss him back, but ordering him to.

Axel's thrusts sped up, he pushed into Bayden harder, rougher. The kiss kept pace with every movement of Axel's cock inside him. Bayden fought to keep up as desire raced through him faster and faster.

His orgasm caught him entirely off guard. He tossed back his head, breaking the kiss. His instincts were too close to the surface and too strong to deny. He howled. Ecstasy ricocheted through him, seeming to reach every square inch of his skin before reverberating back deep inside his body.

Bayden was so lost in his own bliss he was only vaguely aware of Axel finding his own climax. The first thing Bayden really registered was Axel's lips against his, leading him into a gentler, more lethargic kiss that lingered delightfully through the minutes.

Axel had time to soften completely before he pulled away and separated their bodies.

It was only the bondage that prevented Bayden from instantly giving in to his instincts, following Axel across the mattress and trying to wrap himself around Axel like an overly friendly python.

Trapped on his side of the bed, Bayden gingerly lowered his legs and stared up at the ceiling. His own cum was drying in ropes on his stomach and chest. As thoughts started to travel ponderously through his brain, Bayden tried to work out if that was a problem or not.

"You'll have permission to go and clean yourself up later," Axel said. "But I will always expect you to wait for permission to leave the bed." He sounded sleepy and sated rather than angry.

Bayden risked a glance in his direction. If that was the only thing Axel thought when he saw his cum, then it stood to reason he'd made Bayden come on purpose. "Yes, sir." His voice was rough.

Axel rolled onto his side facing him. "You howled."

Bayden hesitated. "Yes, sir."

Axel smiled. "I like that." He reached out and lazily ran his hands over Bayden's torso. He didn't seem to be bothered by the way Bayden's semen sometimes smeared under his touch.

There was something undeniably addictive about those idle caresses. Honesty — Axel had offered him that. "I like it when you do that, sir."

Axel didn't take his touch away. "Good."

Bayden would never have admitted that to another man. Enjoying being stroked and petted like a dog was…

"Bayden?" Axel prompted.

Bayden hesitated. Questions were okay. "Is it something a human would like too, sir?"

Axel looked at his hand, as if he'd never considered the question before. "Yes," he said. "Some humans at least—the best ones. It's definitely a good thing to like."

Bayden smiled. Axel smiled back. Bayden had never seen him look quite so satisfied with the world. It was obviously the expression that belonged on Axel's face. Bayden was going to do his damnedest to keep it there.

Chapter Nineteen

Curses scrolled through Bayden's mind as he rode into the car park in front of The Dragon's Lair. The bikes were still there — including Axel's modern Triumph. Axel hadn't given up and started the club run without him.

Leaving his bike at the end of the row, Bayden jumped off it and rushed inside.

Axel looked at him, then at the clock. "Thirteen seconds to spare."

Bayden remembered how to breathe.

"Everything okay at home?" Axel asked. He always asked. Every time Bayden visited, Axel asked.

Bayden nodded. "Everything's fine. I'd have been back an hour ago, but they're doing road works. Not even enough room to overtake on a bike. I was stuck behind a hundred cars."

"Where does your family live?" Griz asked.

Bayden tensed. That was no one's business.

"He wants to know what road the works are on," Axel translated. "We don't want to run into them on our ride."

"They're on the bypass — from the first junction all the way to the old docks, but everyone who's trying to avoid them has backed up on the little roads too."

Hale pulled out his smart phone. "He's telling the truth. All the traffic reports say stay the hell away from that whole side of the city."

"Why would I lie about it?" Bayden asked.

"Does a wolf need a reason?"

"Do you two want to bicker, or do you want to ride?" Axel cut in. "We can head east, skirt around the edge of the city, come back in, cut through the Holborn estate and stop off in the pub at the far end before circling back."

"You want to ride through Holborn?" Bayden blurted out.

Axel raised an eyebrow at him.

"Sir," Bayden added.

"What's the problem with Holborn?"

I grew up there. They'll recognise me. They'll recognise my bike. Bayden dropped his gaze. "It's a rough area, sir."

"Scared?" Hale asked.

Bayden ignored him. "It's not the kind of place you want to ride through, sir."

"We've ridden through there lots of times," Axel said. "We've never had any trouble."

Yes, but you're not a wolf. Bayden bit his tongue.

"I promise, your baby will be fine," Axel said. "If you think the pub's too rough, I'll even let you stay outside and babysit it. But seriously, pup, there aren't that many people who want to pick a fight with twenty men wearing leather."

Bayden met his gaze for a moment. Pushing it any further would be tantamount to challenging his right to take the club wherever he wanted it to go. Bayden's alpha had made his decision. Now, it was Bayden's job to deal with it.

He nodded his acceptance and headed outside with all the others. As he straddled his bike, he took a deep breath. It would be fine. Of course it would. He'd survived nineteen years on that estate. A few more hours weren't even going to be a challenge. It was four years since he'd left. Everyone had probably forgotten him, or had moved away themselves.

Axel led off. Bayden watched the other riders fall neatly into formation as they followed him. Bayden joined the back of the line.

Everything was going to be fine. And, if it wasn't, well, it wouldn't be anything new to deal with. Providing he dropped back a little and made sure he didn't drag the Dragons into any of it, everything would be fine. It would.

An hour later, he'd almost managed to convince himself that he'd been worrying about nothing. Then he saw the police car pull out of the layby where they had always lurked, waiting to catch unsuspecting motorists for traffic stops. A second later, Bayden noticed a second police car join the party.

Bayden's grip on his handlebars turned white knuckled beneath his gloves. He slowed down. Tolmore was riding in front of him. Bayden eased off further, enough to make sure they'd be separated at the next junction, and held his breath.

Luck was with him, Tolmore was out of sight around the next corner before the first police car gave a whirl of its sirens and signalled for Bayden to pull into the next layby. No one from the Dragons would know where he was.

* * * * *

"Where's Bayden?"

Axel looked along the line of Dragons and back toward the turning into the pub's car park. It wasn't like Bayden to lag behind.

Axel pulled his mobile out of his jacket pocket and checked to see if there was a message. Even if Bayden had dropped off the pace for some reason, it shouldn't have taken him long to catch up. It was unlikely he'd got lost, but Axel supposed it was possible. It wasn't a part of the city that a guy like Bayden would be familiar with.

Puncture, maybe?

Anything worse than that was just an overactive imagination, combined with an inclination to feel overly protective toward the boy. Axel leaned back in his seat and checked the view down the road.

Tolmore had been riding in front of Bayden. Axel caught his eye.

"Crossed over the railway line same time as me. Dropped back through the turns. Saw him about three minutes ago, he was keeping up fine."

If something had happened to delay him, he'd have texted Axel to let him know, wouldn't he? Axel frowned as an uneasy shudder raced down his spine.

"There's only so much trouble he could have got himself into in three minutes," Griz said.

"You guys can go in. I'll ride back and see what's happened," Axel decided. Seconds later, he had his helmet on and was rolling out of the car park.

Apparently, he wasn't the only one who thought something serious must have delayed Bayden because a few moments later he was aware of other riders falling in behind him as he retraced their route.

A glance in his mirror hinted that there weren't any Dragons who'd decided to relax in the pub while other men went looking for the stray lamb.

The twisting section of road they retraced might not have been perfect for a newbie, but Bayden was hardly that. It was well within his skill level and —

There! Bayden's bike was in a layby. So were two police cars. A policeman had Bayden up against the side of one of the cars, frisking him.

Bayden looked up as Axel pulled into the layby, followed by all the other Dragons. The look on his face screamed that this wasn't just a random stop. He tried to straighten up but one of the cops pushed him back against the car.

Bayden's bike stood several yards away from the police cars, as if he'd tried to put it at a distance so it would be out of harm's way. Axel rolled forward until he was close to the group and his bike was between Bayden's bike and the cops. He pulled off his helmet.

"What's going on?" He looked at each of the cops in turn.

It was obvious which guy was in charge. He turned and glared at Axel. "It's nothing to do with you."

"Yes, it is. He's riding with us." He nodded toward Bayden.

Bayden tried to straighten up again, but one of the other cops shoved him forward and kicked at the inside of his boots, forcing him back into position. Axel half expected Bayden to drop the guy with one punch, but he subsided meekly against the side of the car. The warning bells that had been going off in Axel's mind went into overdrive.

The cop looked past Axel to the other Dragons. "You're breaking half a dozen anti-pack laws just by existing. Get out of here, all of you, now. Unless you're looking for trouble?" He twitched his wrist.

He was carrying a Taser. Would it pierce a set of leathers? Axel doubted it. Even if they would go through leather and all the cops had one to hand, they weren't going to be any use against over a dozen guys.

Bayden straightened up again, this time he wasn't playing at it. He shoved the cop who'd been trying to keep him against the car out of the way and deftly dodged the other three as he hurried toward the safety of the group.

He was almost there when he stopped and turned back to face the cops, putting himself directly between Axel and the guy with the Taser. "No one's looking for trouble." He put his hands up placatingly. Axel grabbed Bayden's shoulder and tugged him backward, but Bayden planted his feet and didn't budge an inch.

"They aren't breaking any laws," Bayden told the cops. "They're all human. There's no reason to get them involved. They're leaving."

The hell they were!

Axel didn't have time to speak before the cop lifted the Taser and pointed it straight at Bayden. When he'd been frisked, his jacket had been undone. The only thing the Taser would have to pass through was a thin vest.

Axel was bigger and stronger than Bayden—that meant Axel should mind his manners with him. The fact wolves healed quickly didn't give humans the right to be rough. Axel saw the threat, and all those nice polite little ideas went out the window.

He dragged Bayden back, not caring if he pulled him off his feet. Bayden stumbled as Axel pushed him behind him. Other Dragons had got off their bikes. Griz and Drac were at the front of the crowd and caught Bayden before he hit the ground.

"Stay back there," Axel ordered.

Griz and Drac each kept hold of one of Bayden's arms.

The cop with the Taser laughed. "So that's where you disappeared to. You didn't crawl out of the gutter, just slithered along far enough to find someone else to whore yourself out to."

Axel stepped forward. "What did you say?"

The cop smirked. "Oh, did you think you had fresh meat? You're hardly the first guys he's got on his knees for." He looked past Axel to Bayden. "A bitch to a gang of bikers. Your dad would be so proud if he could see you now, wouldn't he?"

The cop knew what the word meant to wolves — Axel saw it in his eyes.

Bayden sprang forward. Axel reacted just in time. He caught hold of Bayden's jacket collar as Bayden tried to pass him, and pulled him back to his side. The moment Bayden realised who had hold of him, he stopped struggling.

Axel glanced back at the other Dragons, but he knew there was no way Bayden would accept being held by any of them. He was damn near vibrating with anger as it was.

"You know him?" Axel asked Bayden.

The cop laughed. "Me and Bayden go way back. You could say I know the whole family."

Bayden tugged at Axel's hold on him.

Hale strode forward, past Axel and Bayden. "Is that your excuse for pulling him over — that you're a friend of the family, Sergeant…?"

"I don't answer to your sort."

"Actually, you do." He pulled out his ID and held it up. "Detective Inspector Hale. You were about to explain why you pulled Bayden over, Sergeant…"

"Granger," the cop muttered. "He was speeding."

"I wasn't breaking the limit, and he didn't pass me," Hale said. His tone of voice was completely expressionless, all business, back on the job.

"Reckless driving. We pulled him over to breathalyse him," Granger bit out. He looked from Bayden to Hale and back again. "You know what wolves are like. Can't stay away from the bottle. His old man was the same, and his grandfather — pure trouble."

Bayden tightened his hand into a fist at his side. Axel strengthened his grip on his shoulder, half sure that Bayden was going to launch himself at the guy, not too inclined to blame him if he did.

"If you really think that, you should breathalyse him. Then we'll all know if you're right. Or would you like to try for another excuse?" Hale asked.

"You must know what wolves are like," Granger spat. "And his family are the worst kind there is. This isn't your patch, you haven't had to deal with them. If you did, you wouldn't be riding with him. If he's not high as a kite it's because he hasn't had a chance to off load the last thing he nicked. The chances are, the stuff's strapped to his bike."

Axel's stomach turned over. He glanced toward Bayden's bike, all three of them were between the cops and the bike. It was perfectly safe.

"And he was riding without…" Sergeant Granger trailed away as saw the look on Hale's face.

"Without insurance? Tax? MOT?" Hale suggested, in the pleasant tone of voice that was enough to let anyone who knew him realise that the whole world was about to hit the fan. "What was he riding without?"

Granger opened and closed his mouth. "You don't know him. I've been dealing with the shit from the Holborn Estate since before you even joined the force."

Axel bit the inside of his cheek, forcing himself to stay silent and let Hale deal with it.

"Bayden's not from Holborn," Hale said.

"He was born there," Granger snapped. His expression changed. He laughed. "Has he taken you in, inspector? Got you caught up in a long con?"

Hale didn't even blink. Con or no con, Bayden was riding with them. It was one thing for Hale to give him hell, another for an outsider to take pot shots at him.

Axel watched as Granger looked from one Dragon to another and finally back to Hale. Gradually, Granger seemed to realise that a shared profession wasn't enough to outrank a shared club.

What Axel had told Bayden earlier was right. There weren't many people who'd go up against twenty guys wearing leather. And, when one of those guys was a higher ranking cop, well some things really were more dangerous than they were worth.

A final twitch of the hand holding the Taser, and Granger took a step back.

Hale led the cops toward their cars. Axel saw him looking at their various ID's and jotting something down in a small notebook. Axel couldn't catch what they were saying. He couldn't bring himself to care either. Hale was better at dealing with people like that, especially when Axel wasn't sure his temper could take being within range of hitting one of the bastards.

Axel tugged at Bayden's shoulder, trying to get him to turn around but Bayden kept all his attention on the cops. Pure hatred shone in his eyes.

"Are you okay?"

Bayden nodded.

"Why did they pull you over?"

Bayden still didn't look away from the knot of policemen. "Cops have never needed a reason to pull wolves over." His voice shook with emotion. Axel placed one hand on Bayden's chest. His heart was racing. For several seconds, Bayden continued to look straight past Axel at the cops.

"Hale's dealing with them. They can't hurt you now."

Slowly, Bayden turned to Axel. Their eyes met. Axel held his gaze as the seconds ticked past and the anger in Bayden's eyes gradually faded. Bayden dropped his gaze.

Axel heard a movement behind him, but he didn't look around. Hale could deal with them, and if he couldn't, there were plenty of other men there. Axel kept all his attention on his pup. Bayden's heart still raced. His breathing was uneven, but he made no move to pull away from Axel.

The sound of the police cars driving away filled the air. A moment later Hale appeared alongside them.

"Is he okay?"

Bayden tensed at the question, but made no attempt to answer it himself.

"Bayden's going to be fine," Axel said, still not looking away from him.

He sensed Hale walk toward his bike.

"Are you hurt?" Axel asked.

Bayden shook his head.

"Can you ride?"

He nodded.

"Then let's get out of here. It's not far to the pub. We can talk there."

Bayden glanced up at Axel. He looked confused, but since damn near everything that had happened in the last hour had confused the hell out of Axel, he couldn't bring himself to be too sympathetic.

He watched Bayden get on his bike. When Axel met Hale's gaze, Hale nodded his understanding. "When I pull out, fall in after me," Axel told Bayden.

"I don't—"

314

"It's an order. The appropriate response is yes, sir."

Bayden dropped his gaze. "Yes, sir."

In the car park alongside the pub, Bayden rolled his bike to a stop next to Axel's. It had taken barely two minutes for them to ride there, but it had been long enough for Axel to get a few priorities straight in his mind.

Fury rolled through him. He got off his bike and took off his helmet. Bayden did the same.

In one movement, Axel pushed Bayden up against the side wall of the pub and pinned him there with a forearm across his shoulders. "What the hell were you thinking?" he demanded.

Bayden made no attempt to push him away or answer.

"You don't ever step in front of me that way again."

Bayden looked up. "What?"

"If I tell you to get behind me, you do it."

Bayden frowned. "You're mad about *that*?"

Axel raised an eyebrow at him.

Bayden studied him for several seconds. "Sir" he added, very softly.

"Yes, that's what I'm mad about. If I give you an order, you obey it."

Bayden swallowed. "Granger didn't have a problem with you, sir."

"And werewolves heal quicker than humans," Axel finished for him.

"Yes, sir."

"I don't give a fuck how quickly wolves heal. You're my sub. And when I tell you to get behind me, you do it."

"I—"

"Would a lupine dom hide behind you?"

Bayden hesitated — that was answer enough.

"Then don't expect me to. You ever do that again, and getting Tasered will be the least of your troubles." He stepped back. Bayden remained against the wall. He didn't look Axel in the eye, but his attention was all on him.

The other Dragons were there, they were all watching. Bayden didn't glance in their direction. Neither did Axel.

He didn't ride with fools, or with doms who didn't know the score. The important thing here was that Bayden could have been hurt.

They might be pissed that Bayden lied to them, but they'd have to be bloody suicidal to act like that was important right then.

"You can all go in," Axel said, still not turning to look at the other Dragons. He heard them file away. Left alone alongside the building, Axel looked Bayden up and down. "Are you hurt?" he asked again.

"I'm fine, sir."

Axel let the silence stretch out. Minutes passed. Finally, Bayden blinked. He glanced toward Axel, but look quickly down. "I should go."

"You don't have permission to leave."

Bayden frowned at the ground just in front of Axel's boots. It seemed like that was all he was either willing or able to do.

"Tell me what happened."

"It...it was nothing, sir."

"Try again, the truth this time."

Bayden winced at the mention of the truth, but he didn't launch into an apology or even try to offer an explanation. "It's no big deal, sir. They just pulled me over."

"For being a wolf?" Axel asked.

Bayden nodded and folded his arms across his chest.

"How did they know while you were riding? There's no way they could have seen your eyes."

Bayden swallowed. "Granger would have recognised the bike, sir. My father used to ride it. He'd have guessed it was me."

"Because what he said was true—you grew up around here?"

Bayden nodded.

"He's pulled you over before?"

Bayden nodded again, a jerky little motion.

Axel narrowed his gaze. "A lot?"

Another nod, Bayden still didn't look up.

"What would have happened if I hadn't come back for you?"

Bayden shuffled his boots against the rough ground. "I'd have paid the fine and caught up with you here, sir."

"How much would...?" Axel's question died as their eyes met. Money wasn't part of that particular deal. Axel shook his head. "Jesus."

"I know your rules, sir. I'd have admitted I broke them."

Axel studied Bayden for several seconds. He didn't see the difference. Nothing could have been more obvious. Bayden honestly couldn't see the difference between willingly screwing around behind someone's back and being blackmailed by a bent cop.

Axel could imagine the conversation. Bayden saying that he'd stopped off along the way to blow a few old friends. That would have been the version of the story he told Axel. It was quite possibly the version of the story that Bayden told himself.

Fury burned through Axel's veins. He knew Bayden would be able to sense it, but he couldn't do anything about that.

"You shouldn't have come back, sir," Bayden whispered.

"Best decision I ever made," Axel snapped.

Bayden dropped his gaze, but not before Axel saw the confusion and the submission swirling in his eyes.

Bayden started fiddling with his keys. It wasn't just nerves. He took both the key to the lock-up and the key to the pub off the ring and offered them to Axel.

Axel didn't take them. "Are you trying to say your safe word?"

Bayden frowned.

"Is this your way of saying you don't want to submit to me anymore?"

Bayden dropped his gaze. "I'm not an idiot, sir. I know that all ended the moment you found out the truth."

"The jury's still out on whether or not you're an idiot. But nothing has ended."

"I—"

"You promised me six weeks. They're not up yet."

"You want—" Bayden broke off, thought for a minute, then nodded. "You'll tell me how the rules have changed, sir?"

"Yes, when we get home."

Bayden nodded.

Axel looked him up and down, trying to convince himself Bayden was okay, when all his instincts screamed he wasn't okay at all. "Anything you need to say before that?"

"You're pissed off with me."

"Yes." Axel made no attempt to soften the answer.

"Maybe, that means I should ride back on my own instead of with the club?"

For a second, Axel thought Bayden was trying to suggest some sort of penance. Then, it seemed more likely that he wanted some time on his own to pull himself together. When Axel worked out the truth, a bitter taste filled the back of his mouth. "You think they'll try to pull you over again on the way back." It was a realisation, not a question. "No. You're not riding back on your own."

"They don't have a problem with you, sir," Bayden said.

Axel pushed Bayden back against the wall. "Anyone who has a problem with you has a problem with me."

Bayden tensed. Axel expected him to try to pull away, but he accepted Axel into his space as if nothing had changed, on his side at least.

"Anyone who'd let a sub deal with that kind of shit on his own has no right to call himself a dom, and anyone who'd let someone who rides with us face off against that bastard on his own has no right to consider himself a Dragon."

He kept hold of Bayden's arm as he led him into the pub. The other Dragons' curiosity was obvious, but so was their wariness. Bayden might have a better read on body language than any human, but Axel was under no illusions. Any species would easily see how livid he was. Even Hale had the sense to keep any inclination to say 'I told you so' to himself.

It wasn't easy for men to tread on egg shells while wearing motorcycle boots, but Axel was sure the Dragons were all doing their best.

Bayden remained silent. Axel kept a careful eye on him. He didn't meet anyone's gaze, but he didn't bow his head with embarrassment either. It seemed that the only person he was ashamed about catching him out on months' worth of lies was Axel himself. The club guys weren't even a blip on his radar.

Chapter Twenty

"Don't get off your bike."

Bayden had already taken off his helmet. He balanced it on his knee and glanced across at Axel. The other Dragons had all peeled away and headed back to their own homes during the return ride. It was just the two of them now in the yard behind The Dragon's Lair.

So, this was it. Axel had had time to think on the ride back and—

"Does he know where you live?"

Bayden frowned. "Sir?"

"The cop—Granger—does he know where you and your family live? Would he go there?"

Bayden shook his head.

"The truth, Bayden. This isn't something it's safe to lie to me about. If he'd go there, I need to know, now."

"He doesn't know where they live, sir."

Axel studied him for several seconds, but eventually, he seemed to be willing to believe him. He got off his bike. Bayden remained where he was, watching him from the corner of his eye so his staring wasn't too obvious.

Axel opened the lock-up where he kept his own bike. He looked over his shoulder and frowned. "What are you waiting for?"

"You said not to…"

"When I thought we'd need to head straight to your mother's place."

Bayden cautiously got off his bike. When Axel put his away, Bayden hesitated to do the same. A raised eyebrow told him that Axel wasn't the least bit impressed.

Bayden put his bike in the lock-up. There were a few other things stored in there. None of them looked expensive, but that wasn't the point, not anymore.

Axel led the way into the pub and straight up to the flat.

Bayden paused by the chair where Axel sometimes liked him to leave his clothes.

"You can leave your jacket there." Axel took his off and dropped it over the back of another chair.

Bayden did as he was told then pushed his hands into his pockets. Axel stood two yards away from him. Bayden didn't have the courage to try to bridge the gap between them, but he couldn't stand the silence. "You're angry, sir."

"Yes. I don't like being lied to—not by someone who works for me, or someone who rides with me. And definitely not by someone who's supposed to be submitting to me."

Bayden swallowed. "A punishment, sir?"

"Not yet. First, you're going to tell me the truth—about everything."

Their eyes met. "Sir?"

"You're going to tell me the truth. Every lie you've ever told me, you're going to fix it. When I know the complete truth, I'll decide what your punishment will be. But I'm warning you, whatever that punishment is, it'll pale in comparison to the one you'll get if you tell me *any* lie from this point on." He stepped forward. "You're being offered a clean slate. It's not something I make a habit of. Don't screw it up."

Bayden swallowed.

"First—what you said about Granger and the other cops not knowing where your family lives, was that the truth?"

Bayden nodded. "I made sure of that, sir. And…"

"And?" Axel demanded.

The truth. "He knows I'll kill him if he goes near them, sir."

"How does he know that?"

"I told him," Bayden said. "He believed me. It was the truth."

"Good." Axel didn't specify if it was good that Bayden had told him the truth, told Granger the truth, or that he'd kill anyone who hurt his family. But the fact that he thought Bayden had done something good was both wonderful and terrifying. Any relief was mixed with a reminder of just how much he needed Axel to be pleased with him.

Axel turned his back on him and went into the kitchen. He put the kettle on, not the least worried that a self-confessed potential murderer stood behind him. Bayden lurked in the doorway, not sure what else to do.

"Is it a human thing, thinking that any conversation is bound to be less stressful if it takes place over tea?" Axel asked.

Bayden blinked at him.

Axel raised an eyebrow.

"Yes, it's a human thing, sir."

"Good boy."

Because he'd told the truth. Bayden swallowed. Axel would consider him to be good if he told the truth. It didn't matter if it was a big truth or a small one, in a way, it didn't even matter what the truth was, Axel just wanted him to tell it.

Axel carried his tea into the living room and motioned for Bayden to bring the other cup along with him. Axel sat on the sofa and indicated the seat next to him. Bayden perched on the edge of the cushion and stared at Axel's boots. It was easier than looking him in the eye. Bayden's heart raced so fast, it hurt the inside of his ribs.

"Start by telling me about Granger."

"He's just a cop, sir." Bayden stared at his tea for a while. "When we lived on Holborn, we were on his...his patch or whatever."

"For how long?"

The truth. Sweat broke out across Bayden's skin. "My father was born there, so was my grandfather. We moved away when I was nineteen."

"Because of him?"

"It got out of hand." Bayden closed his eyes. He was pretty sure he already knew the answer, but he still had to ask. If there was any chance he didn't have to say it all out loud, he had to ask. "How much do you want to know, sir?"

"Everything."

Bayden took a deep breath. There were so many memories, but somehow his mind went all the way back to that first time, back when he hadn't really known the score — back before he'd learned not to care. Bayden cleared his throat. "It was no big deal. After I got my first bike, he'd pull me over every now and again, if he spotted me during a quiet bit of his shift or whatever. I'd…pay the fine." He shrugged.

Axel's grip on his mug of tea was white knuckled. "Did you tell anyone what was happening?"

"They had enough to worry about without me making a fuss. I could handle it. But…"

Axel's right arm lay along the back of the sofa. He moved and rested his fingertips against Bayden's shoulder. Bayden glanced up at him, but Axel didn't seem to want his attention. He'd just done it because he'd wanted to, and maybe because he knew Bayden would think it felt nice.

"Keep going," Axel ordered.

"It started to happen more often. Then, one night he and some of the other cops turned up at our house. They were off duty. They'd been drinking. I convinced them to leave but…" He swallowed. "My mother was there. So was my grandfather." Bayden shook his head, trying to clear their expressions from his memory. "We moved the next day."

"When you say you convinced them to leave," Axel said. "You mean you left with them?"

Bayden nodded. "I didn't care about that. But, if they'd come back when I wasn't there…" He shook his head as other pictures tried to fill his mind. "We moved the following day, and the next time I saw Granger I explained that he needed to stay away from them." Bayden rubbed the back of his neck. The whole truth. "I told him that the only reason I hadn't killed him was because my family didn't approve of wolves making trouble with humans. If anything happened to them, I'd have no reason not to kill him. What he did to me was one thing — but not them."

"What did your family say when they found out what was happening?" Axel asked.

"What could they say?" Bayden whispered into his tea. "It wasn't anything that hadn't happened to them at one time or another."

Silence descended. It filled the room, taking up all the oxygen, until Bayden could barely breathe. He glanced up at Axel. Perhaps it was just Bayden's imagination, but Axel didn't look comfortable with the lack of oxygen either.

"It's not a rare thing, sir. Humans… Wolves…" Bayden sighed. Axel didn't get it. There was no way he could. "My grandfather says that sooner or later a wolf always has to either fuck or fight to survive. It's just the way things are. All you can do is try to make sure you're the one who chooses who you have to do those things with."

Silence returned. Neither of them moved. The only sense Bayden had to work with was scent. That was very clear. Axel was furious; he had the right to be.

"I would have told you, sir." It probably didn't mean much, but maybe it would count for something.

Axel tucked a knuckle under Bayden's chin and made him look up.

"I'd have told you I broke both rules. I'd have taken the punishment. I lied about other things, but never about obeying your rules."

Axel frowned. "Both rules?"

Shit. The complete truth. "The one about other people, and the one about jacking off without your permission."

Axel's frown remained.

"Granger thought making that part of the fine proved I liked what he…"

"Would you have told me that you didn't have a choice?" Axel said. "That's part of the truth too, isn't it?"

"No. I had a choice," Bayden corrected. "It was always my choice."

"No—"

"The wolves in the Captivities didn't have a choice. Free wolves do," Bayden cut in. "Just because there aren't any options you like that doesn't mean you don't still choose one. It doesn't mean you don't own that choice." Axel's knuckle was still beneath Bayden's chin making him keep his head up, but he dropped his gaze. "Sir."

Axel's anger wasn't fading away in the least, and Bayden doubted his tone of voice was helping.

"I don't mean to be disrespectful, sir. But you said the truth—and the truth is I had a choice. I made a choice."

"The truth as you see it," Axel finally said. "You said your mother and grandfather were there when the cops came to your house. What about your father?"

"It was after he died, sir."

"So that was the truth?"

Bayden wasn't sure what Axel would want to know, but he knew he had to offer something. "When I was thirteen."

"That was when your grandfather moved in with you and your mother?"

Bayden nodded.

"And he is ill?"

Bayden forced himself to nod, no matter how much he wished that had been a lie.

"Seriously?"

Bayden took a deep breath. "Wolves are strong, sir. But he's in his eighties and…"

Axel nodded. He moved his hand to rest properly on Bayden's shoulder. "She still lives with him?"

Bayden hesitated.

"Out with it," Axel ordered.

"Wolves would say that he lives with her, sir."

"Because she's more dominant than him?"

"Yes, sir."

Axel nodded his acceptance. "Where?"

"Sir?"

"Where do they live?"

A trickle of sweat ran down Bayden's spine. "What I said about moving out when I turned twenty-one was true, sir."

"That doesn't answer my question."

"I'm not really part of their…I mean, it's not my place to…A wolf shouldn't give out information on another wolf's… It's not right, sir."

"Good boy."

Bayden glanced up at him.

"You could have lied. You didn't. That's a start."

Bayden looked down into his tea.

"You told Sal that your mother does charity work."

"It's not a charity."

* * * * *

"You were very definite about that," Axel remembered. He'd noticed at the time, it had just never occurred to him why. "You said it was an organisation that helps female wolves change careers."

Bayden nodded. "They hire female wolves. There's no charity involved. They all work hard — they earn every penny they're paid, sir." He put his mug on the coffee table, then he didn't seem to know what to do with his hands. "There are residential places, where female wolves can live if they need to. They have a special exemption from the anti-pack laws because there are only female wolves there."

Your mother was one of the women being helped out of prostitution, not one of the people doing the helping. She wasn't some rich woman doling out charity for the feel good factor. She's someone who sold sex. Axel pushed his hand through his hair as he tried to make room inside his head for an entirely different reality than the one he'd thought Bayden lived in.

"She doesn't work there anymore, sir. My grandfather needs someone to look after him," Bayden offered.

He was making an effort, Axel had to give him that. He genuinely seemed to be trying to offer up the truth, however against the grain it went.

"What are they doing for money?"

Bayden tensed up. The answer was obvious. Axel had wondered where all the money Bayden won went for months. Now he knew, but Bayden merely sat there in silence.

"Bayden?"

"I..." Bayden closed his eyes.

"What you said before, about a wolf thinking it's shameful to need help from someone who—"

"They have nothing to be ashamed of." Bayden jerked his head up. "Nothing at all."

Axel held his gaze as the seconds ticked past.

"We never needed help. We always got by. It's only because of the stupid human laws that—" He looked down again.

"If the anti-pack laws hadn't forced you to move out, you'd still live at home, you'd still be part of their pack, and everything would be fine," Axel said.

Bayden nodded.

"As things are, since you moved out?"

Bayden looked down at his hands. His words came slowly. He obviously had to fight against his instincts to force each one past his lips. "It was my fault we needed to move houses. The new place is more expensive. It's not a great area or anything, but…" He took a deep breath. "With three people, between us all, it was okay."

"But it would have been too much for two."

"They shouldn't have to struggle just because human laws are screwed up."

"Agreed."

Bayden studied him very carefully, no doubt searching for any sign of condemnation. Finally, he nodded. "I'm younger than them. It's easier for me to earn money. It was no problem for me to keep paying my share. My mother didn't like it, but…" He shrugged.

"Sometimes you have to look after the people you love in spite of them."

Bayden nodded. It didn't seem to occur to him that it was exactly what Axel had been doing ever since Bayden first walked into his pub.

"When my grandfather got ill and my mother had to stop working…"

"It made sense for you to help out a little more."

The nod was tiny, as if admitting the truth was still hard for him. "It's not their fault, sir."

"I know."

Bayden seemed to remember how to breathe then, but his skin was pale, his discomfort obvious. There was only so far anyone could be pushed in one sitting.

"Any questions?"

"The punishment, sir?"

Axel set his mug on the coffee table. "I'll think about it and tell you later."

Bayden frowned.

"I don't punish people lightly, and I don't do it while I'm angry."

"Until you decide, sir?"

"There's plenty of work to be done downstairs."

Bayden damn near raced down to the pub. Griz was right. If the place got any cleaner, it was going to sparkle.

Axel slumped in his seat and dropped his head to rest against the back of the sofa. He closed his eyes, only to quickly re-open them. He pushed himself up onto his feet. It would be a while before he closed his eyes and saw anything other than the life Bayden had described to him. He shook his head and rubbed at his jaw. So fucked up in so many ways.

It excused a lot. It didn't excuse everything.

Without making a conscious decision, Axel wandered down to the lock-ups. The one on the far left was half storage space, half work out area. Axel didn't bother with wraps today. He pulled on a set of gloves and took a swing at the punch bag hanging from a chain near the centre of the space.

He didn't have Bayden's skill, but he was hardly a novice. His body fell into an easy rhythm as he considered the possibilities. This wasn't a game; it wasn't about sex. Whatever the punishment was, it should ensure that Bayden never wanted to make the same mistake again—that he'd confess any truth in the world rather than risk telling him another lie. It had to be the right punishment.

The chain the bag hung from rattled as he struck the battered leather. Bayden would take it. Whatever punishment Axel came up with, he had no doubt that Bayden would take it without a word of complaint—just like he took the bets without even blinking.

Axel's punches slowed as he concentrated on hitting the bag as hard as possible, putting his full weight behind each blow.

It would have been a hell of a lot more satisfying to have hit Granger. Axel shook his head. If he'd started doing that, he might never have stopped. It would have taken all the Dragons to pull him off the guy, and by that time it would have been too late. There was a reason why he kept a careful rein on his temper.

A noise made Axel look over his shoulder. Bayden dumped a black bag of rubbish into the big wheelie bin in the corner of the yard. He hesitated for a moment then came toward Axel. He offered him a bottle of water.

Axel tugged one of his gloves off and accepted the drink. He took a deep swig.

Bayden glanced at the punch bag but didn't say anything.

It was never easy to guess what would or wouldn't be obvious to a werewolf. "I was picturing Granger, not you."

Bayden shrugged.

"Well?" Axel pushed.

Bayden hid his hand in his jeans pockets. "I don't know what you want me to say, sir."

Axel leaned against the wall of the lock-up. "Tell me why."

"Sir?"

"Why lie about it all? Why the rich tosser act?"

"That's what you called me the first time I came here. I never said I was rich, sir."

"You played up to it. You made sure I went on thinking it."

Bayden looked down.

"You could have told me I was wrong. You told me I was wrong about plenty of other things," Axel pushed. "Why let that lie stand? Are you ashamed of your—?"

"No!"

"Then why?" Axel repeated.

"I liked it," Bayden blurted out.

Axel paused with the bottle of water halfway to his lips. "What?"

"If you'd called me a serial killer, I'd have gone along with that too." Bayden hunched his shoulders as he pushed his hands deeper into his pockets. "I liked the way you treated a silly little rich boy, sir. I didn't want to lose it."

"You thought I liked you because you had money?" Axel demanded, stepping away from the wall.

Bayden stared down at his boots for a long time. "I've had lots of fights in lots of pubs, sir. That was the first time someone accused me of slumming it. And it was the first time anyone stepped in and made sure the other guy paid up. And it was the first time someone tried to patch me up afterwards." He shrugged. "You were nice to me. I liked it."

Axel shook his head.

"I don't expect things to be the same now, sir."

Axel narrowed his gaze. "Because?"

"Because you'd have to be a fool to trust a wolf, because everyone knows that any man who grew up on Holborn is trouble. How many reasons do you need?"

"No." Axel swung Bayden around and pinned him against the wall with one hand in the centre of the chest. "Let's be completely clear about this. You're not the one being insulted."

Bayden blinked at him. "I didn't insult you!"

"Assuming I'd have more respect for a spoilt little rich boy than I would for a man who's doing whatever it takes to look after his family isn't a compliment."

Bayden stared up at him for several seconds. Finally, he seemed to realise that Axel was deadly serious. "I didn't mean to insult you, sir." He looked down. "If you did want money, I could—"

"No."

Bayden hesitated.

Don't you dare offer to whore yourself out for me. The only thing that stopped Axel throwing those words at Bayden was knowing that it was exactly what he'd done for his family. No one deserved to have that sort of sacrifice tossed in his face.

"I don't want your money," Axel said, as calmly as he could. "Finishing that sentence will only make things worse."

Axel released him. Striding over to the other side of the lock-up, he tossed his gloves onto the weight lifting bench. He wasn't going to be able to get rid of any of his extra anger that way.

He stared at an empty patch of wall and tried to think clearly, tried to at least get an idea of how things had been for Bayden before he threw the book at him. If nothing else, knowing how Bayden felt would let Axel know what the punishment should feel like.

If he'd been in Bayden's shoes... If he thought that lying would have made things easier, made the world treat him better, would he have gone along with a lie? Would he have gone out of his way to tell the truth if it had meant risking losing the good opinion of someone he cared about?

Axel shook his head. When he looked at it from that point of view, it didn't take much imagination to come up with an answer.

Shit!

"Go up to the flat. Wait for me in the living room. I've made my decision."

Chapter Twenty One

Everything was going to be fine.

Bayden nodded to himself. He would take the punishment, Axel would be pleased with him, and everything would be fine. Bayden kept reminding himself of those facts as he paced back and forth across Axel's living room.

Clean was good — that was another fact. If Axel wanted to take a shower after working out, that was his right. But, waiting to find out what the punishment would be was driving Bayden crazy.

The sound of the shower stopped. Bayden froze. He didn't move a muscle until Axel walked into the living room a few minutes later, wearing a pair of dark blue jeans and nothing else.

Bayden didn't lower his gaze to admire the view — not even while all of Axel's tattoos were on display. The moment was important. Bayden gave everything he had to studying Axel's serious expression.

It was disrespectful to nag, but Bayden could help himself. "The punishment, sir?"

"There isn't going to be one."

"There has to be."

Axel raised an eyebrow at him. "I decide the punishments, pup, not you."

"You'd punish a human."

"My decision has nothing to do with your species."

Bayden shook his head. "You said you were going to —"

"I said I'd give you my final decision after I had the whole truth from you."

"No. I mean…"

Axel nodded to the sofa. "Sit."

Bayden obeyed. It didn't occur to him to do anything else.

"I won't punish you unless I can look you in the eye and tell you that I would have done better in your shoes. That's not the way it works—not between men who aren't playing games with each other."

Bayden shook his head. "I screwed up. I broke the rule about telling you the truth."

Axel studied him for a few seconds. "Do you think your behaviour was acceptable?"

Bayden shook his head. He'd pissed off his alpha. Worse—it hadn't just been anger in Axel's scent. When Bayden had assumed that Axel cared how much money he had, he'd hurt Axel.

Axel tilted his head on the side. "I won't punish you." He held up his hand again, when Bayden would have spoken. "But I'll offer you the chance to pay a penance."

Bayden nodded quickly.

Axel chuckled. "You have no idea what that means, do you?"

Bayden looked down. "If you'll tell me what I need to do, sir."

"It means choosing to give up one of your privileges for a certain length of time—volunteering to lose something you enjoy, to show that you're sorry."

Bayden nodded.

"Make your choice."

"Me?"

Axel smiled. "Yes, I expect you to pick which privilege you'll lose."

Bayden looked down. At some point he'd wound his fingers together. His knuckles were all white. "You don't want to pick?"

"I'll decide the details, but I want you to choose what to give up."

There was only one real choice he could make. "I should go, sir."

Axel put his hand on Bayden's shoulder. For a second, his expression was angry, then it cleared. "Because being here is something you like?"

Bayden offered a tentative nod.

"That's not what I mean. A privilege is something you do, or I do, that you like. Something you don't want to lose, but not something essential."

Bayden turned his attention back to his hands.

"You don't have to make the right choice the first time. If I don't like one idea, I'll tell you to pick something else."

Thinking through all the things that Axel did, or allowed him to do, Bayden had no idea how to work out what Axel considered important.

What would a human think was important? What would a human want to take away? Bayden's grip on his fingers tightened further. A couple of digits were starting to tingle.

"No ideas or too many possibilities?" Axel asked.

"Too many, sir."

"Tell me what they are. Random order, let me hear them all."

"All of them?"

"Yes."

It was by far the most dangerous order Axel could have given him. List the things you care about. List all the ways a human can hurt you. Make it easy for me to tear your soul out piece by piece. A wolf would have to be a fool to trust a human with that kind of information.

He met Axel's gaze very briefly before looking down. He'd hurt Axel. He should be hurt in return. Telling Axel how to even the score wasn't foolish. But, all the things Axel did...

"I don't want to insult you, sir," he whispered.

"By doing what you're told?"

"If I pick something that's too small." He forced himself to unfurl his hands. "A lot of the things I like, I'm not sure you even think about them, sir. If I pick something that doesn't mean anything to you…"

"It's not about what it means to me."

Bayden rubbed the back of his neck.

"Okay. Give me the list and I'll pick the most suitable thing from it."

Bayden turned his attention back to his hands. "I like that you let me stay here with you," he offered.

Axel nodded, encouragingly. "Keep going."

"I like that you let me ride with your club."

Axel stroked his thumb back and forth over the skin on Bayden's shoulder.

"I like sharing your meals with you at your table and sleeping warm and comfortable next to you in your bed," Bayden admitted. He didn't look to Axel for extra reassurance. Axel shouldn't have to coddle him like that. "I like not having sex with anyone apart from you, and that you don't seem to want to have anyone else either." He took a deep breath. "I like that you trust me with a key and you never think I'm going to steal anything from you. I like that you think I'm good enough to work with you in the pub and that I can be useful. I like that you have a right to be in my space and give me any orders you want. I like calling you sir. I like not being cold all the time. I like that you're okay with me shifting — that it doesn't bother you when I shift. I…"

Bayden shrugged helplessly, knowing that he could keep going in the same vein for hours, but doubting that he would come up with anything more suitable in all that time. They were all things that were big to him, but to someone like Axel — someone who gave so much without ever thinking about it — it had to sound so stupid.

"They're all things you think of as privileges?" Axel asked. "None of them are rights that you never doubted you'd have?"

Bayden opened his mouth to respond but then thought better of it. He shrugged.

Axel stroked a fingertip across Bayden's bottom lip. He'd noticed Bayden's slip. He didn't say anything, but that was the point. Bayden knew Axel wouldn't say anything at all until he'd heard what Bayden would have said.

Bayden cleared his throat. "Wolves learn not to expect too much from humans, sir. It's easier that way."

Axel thought about that for a while. "Sleeping comfortably in my bed with me."

Bayden glanced up.

"Giving up that would work as a penance," Axel said. "All you actually achieved by hiding the truth from me was to make yourself far more uncomfortable than you needed to be over the last few months. Being uncomfortable for a few nights might help you remember not to make the same mistake in the future."

The only thing that really registered with Bayden was that he'd managed to pick something Axel found acceptable.

"One night to represent each month you lied to me," Axel said.

"Yes, sir." Bayden moved to the edge of the sofa cushion. "I should—"

"I told you I'd decide the details."

Bayden subsided back into his seat. "Yes, sir."

Axel smiled, and Bayden guessed that his relief must have been obvious.

"In some ways a penance is similar to a punishment. No one is supposed to enjoy it. It's not supposed to be easy."

"Yes, sir."

"All the usual rules apply, including the one about using your safe word if you need too."

Bayden frowned. The need to deny needing any sort of safety net warred against Bayden's need to do what would please Axel. Finally, the latter won out. He nodded.

That night, when he led Bayden into the bedroom, Axel seemed especially serious. He nodded to the bathroom. "It'll be your last chance until morning."

By the time Bayden returned to the bedroom, Axel had several lengths of leather and chain resting on top of the chest of drawers.

"You can put your clothes away."

Bayden quickly obeyed, but his movements were all muscle memory. His attention remained on Axel.

Axel spread a blanket on the floor. "The best kind of penance replicates the mistake you made and gives you something to think on."

"Yes, sir."

"Lies create distance between people."

Bayden looked at the empty stretch of carpet between the bed and the blanket. "Yes, sir."

"Lie down, on your stomach."

Bayden quickly got into position. The blanket was thin. It didn't provide much cushioning, but Bayden had slept in far worse conditions.

Axel crouched down next to him, and placed the bondage on the floor within easy reach. "You also got yourself tangled up in a lot of half-truths, didn't you?"

"Yes, sir."

"And made yourself very uncomfortable in the process." Axel guided Bayden's hands behind him and fastened leather cuffs around his wrists.

"Yes, sir."

Axel deftly fastened another set of cuffs around Bayden's ankles. Metal rattled. Tension tugged at each of the four cuffs. Bayden looked over his shoulder. A chain connected the pairs of cuffs. Axel hadn't used the full length. He'd purposefully made it a few inches too short, preventing Bayden from straightening his legs.

Bayden frowned. "Am I supposed to tell you the truth even if you don't ask, sir?"

338

"I don't expect you to spontaneously disclose every detail of your life. If I find something you haven't got around to mentioning yet, you won't get in trouble. But if there's something you think I should know, I want you to tell me the first chance you get." As Axel spoke, he checked the fastenings on the restraints.

"Is now a chance?" Bayden checked.

Axel fell still, giving him his full attention. "Go ahead. What is it?"

"It's not that uncomfortable, sir," he blurted out.

Axel chuckled. "You're good for telling me, but give it a few hours and you might change your mind." He ruffled Bayden's hair. "There are two rules I expect you to follow tonight. Disobey either and all hell will break lose."

"Yes, sir."

"Don't shift."

Bayden looked over his shoulder at him.

"I have no problem with the wolf side of you, but now's not the time. I don't know what would happen if you tried to shift in bondage, but we're not going to find out. If you want to shift, tell me and I'll untie you. Any questions?"

Bayden shook his head.

"If you panic, don't try to hide it—let me know."

"I won't—"

"You won't disobey me?" Axel cut in. "Good."

Bayden squirmed at the idea of having to tell Axel anything of the sort. The metal links in the chain rattled.

Axel caught hold of the cuffs and tugged Bayden over to lie on his back, trapping the cuffs and the chain awkwardly beneath him.

"I won't be disappointed in you if you need help, but I will be if you disobey me—very disappointed."

Bayden swallowed. "Yes, sir."

"Good boy." He stroked a fingertip along Bayden's jawline before disappearing to take his turn in the bathroom.

Bayden took a deep breath and let it out slowly. His arms were uncomfortable behind him, but the moment he rolled onto his side, he knew that his own discomfort wasn't the biggest problem. The chain rattled whenever he so much as twitched. He'd have to remain completely still if he wanted to avoid waking Axel up every two seconds.

Axel came back in. He tossed his jeans on the chair in the corner, but he didn't get straight into bed. He returned to Bayden's side and crouched down alongside him.

"You know, you had a perfect opportunity to tell me the truth the first time I patched you up."

Bayden's mind rushed back to that day in the pub kitchen. Axel had been kind to him. "Yes, sir."

"If you'd done that then, I'd be able to take all this off right away. You wouldn't have been uncomfortable for more than a few minutes. You'd be in the bed all warm and curled up next to me under the blankets for the rest of the night."

He left Bayden laying on the floor, got into bed and switched off the bedroom light. The room remained partially lit. Peering over his shoulder, Bayden realised that Axel had left the light on in the bathroom and the door partway open. Even without a wolf's night vision, Axel would be able to see him clearly.

A good penance replicated the situation where he'd screwed up. Axel was watching over him, just like he had when Bayden was taking fights in the yard behind the pub and lying to him about everything. Knowing that just made the comfort and warmth of Axel's bed seem further away.

* * * * *

Axel wasn't actually chilly and uncomfortable in his own bed. That wasn't why he couldn't sleep a damn wink. He was restless because he knew that Bayden wasn't as warm as he liked to be. It had nothing to do with Axel missing his werewolf shaped hot water bottle.

Bayden wasn't wriggling as much as Axel had expected. The chain seldom rattled. But, Axel knew that wasn't because he'd made the penance too easy. A slight discomfort stretched out over hours was harder to take than a whipping—especially when he expected it was something Bayden had been given less opportunity to get used to.

Axel ran the calendar through his mind. It had been just over three months since they'd first met. Call it three and a quarter months by the end of the penance. Three and a quarter nights on the floor.

Halfway through the night, Axel glanced at the clock beside the bed for the millionth time. He pushed back his blankets and swung his legs over the side of the mattress.

Bayden was wide awake, his open eyes clearly visible in the light from the bathroom. Crouching down next to him, Axel checked each of the restraints. Next, he ran his hands over Bayden's shoulders and down each limb, checking how knotted his muscles were.

Bayden's skin was cool to the touch, but he wasn't chilled enough to do him any harm. He was tense, but most of that seemed to come from his confusion at being checked up on rather than his predicament.

Axel touched Bayden's cheek and encouraged him to look up.

"One night for each month," he reminded him. "We're a fortnight in. If you'd told me the truth that night you took the bet with Richards, all this would be over, and you'd be able to come back to bed with me."

"Yes, sir." The words were softly spoken, but they were full of both knowledge and emotion.

Axel pushed his fingers through Bayden's hair in a gentle caress before going back to bed.

Chapter Twenty Two

"This is about the time you started riding with us," Axel said. "If you'd told me then, your penance would only have lasted one night."

"Yes, sir."

After a cold, sleepless night on the floor, Axel wouldn't have blamed Bayden if there'd been an edge to his voice, but there wasn't. He spoke softly, but there was a calmness there.

"You're going to be stiff when you start moving. Take it slow," Axel ordered, as he undid the cuffs from Bayden's ankles and from around his wrists.

"Yes, sir."

Axel helped him to roll over and sit up. "Sore?"

Bayden shook his head. "I'm fi—"

Axel silenced him with a fingertip over his lips.

Bayden cleared his throat. "Not sore enough to want to complain about it, sir."

"That's more like it. Go on." He nodded toward the bathroom. "A hot shower might count as a privilege, but it's not the one you gave up."

Bayden hesitated.

"My choice, not yours," Axel reminded him. "Adding to your penance would be just as disrespectful as trying to skip bits of it." He waited in the bathroom doorway, making sure Bayden set the shower to a suitable temperature before he headed into the kitchen.

Axel let Bayden finish his breakfast before he broke the news of the next item on their itinerary to him.

"When we started this, you set me visiting your place as a limit."

Bayden's fork clattered against his empty plate.

"Because that would have made the rich pillock lie obvious," Axel went on.

He let the silence stretch out until Bayden finally broke it. "Yes, sir."

"Any other reason?" Axel checked.

Bayden shook his head. "It's not a limit anymore, sir."

"We're going to drop by your place today. You can pick up anything else you want while we're there."

"Yes, sir."

When Axel excused him from the table, Bayden got dressed. A few minutes later, he followed Axel outside without a word. He headed to the lock-up, but Axel called him back.

"We're taking my car." Axel nodded to the front passenger side seat as he slid behind the wheel. "You'll either need to give me directions or an address."

Bayden rattled off an address. It wasn't a part of the city that Axel was familiar with. He put the details in the sat-nav and, throughout the journey, the only voice came from the machine.

Twenty minutes after leaving the pub, they pulled up outside a run-down, old building in the worst part of town. By the look of it, the landlord had converted it into bedsits as cheaply as possible a couple of decades ago, and hadn't spent a penny on it since.

Neither of them spoke as Bayden led the way inside.

Axel only managed to get a fleeting impression of the hall as Bayden hurried forward, but it was enough. The wall paper was peeling. Those lights that worked were bare bulbs. Dampness hung in the air.

Bayden led the way up one uncarpeted staircase, then another. Axel automatically reached out to run his hand along the rail, saw the stains on the paintwork and thought better of it.

Bayden unlocked a battered door at the rear of the building and stepped back to let Axel go in first.

There was an obvious division between the public area and the space that was Bayden's responsibility. On one side of it, things were cheap, grubby and obviously uncared for. On the other side, everything was just as cheap, but it had all been scrubbed and fixed up as much as was humanly, or werewolf-ly possible.

A door to Axel's left led to a tiny, but spotlessly clean, bathroom. The rest was just one room. A bed in one corner, a few kitchen cabinets in another. A table and chair, a rickety wardrobe. That was it.

Axel turned around. Bayden's expression was unreadable—just like in a bet. Axel was about to take refuge behind his earlier suggestion that Bayden pick up some things while he was there, when he realised how stupid the suggestion was.

Half the wardrobe's door was missing. There were no clothes left to retrieve, but Axel could easily picture the clothes Bayden had brought to the pub neatly arranged there. Four white vests. A spare pair of black jeans. His leathers. Each item folded with military precision.

Bayden hadn't chosen to travel light when he came to stay at the pub. He hadn't had any option.

Still on a shelf in the wardrobe was what looked like a spare set of bedding. The bed was made perfectly enough to make a drill sergeant weep.

Axel glanced at the kitchen cabinets. He doubted there was more than a meal's worth of food in the place, and it wasn't because Bayden had known he would be spending a few weeks away from home. The cupboard under the sink had probably always contained more cleaning supplies than all the others had food.

A shiver ran down Axel's spine, but it wasn't just because there was an eerie quality to the place. It was freezing in there.

He automatically put his hand against the heater running along one wall. There was a thermostat on the adjacent wall. Bayden hadn't switched it off because he'd be away from home. According to the settings, it should have been pleasantly warm.

"It comes and goes, sir," Bayden said, quietly.

"Does your landlord know about it?"

Bayden nodded.

There didn't seem to be anything else to say. Everything Axel could think of was bound to sound appallingly patronising.

When Axel had believed that Bayden was a spoiled rich kid, he'd imagined that he lived in a posh loft space in the new dockland flats, all clean lines and fancy minimalist decoration. Even since he'd realised that was a lie, Axel had let himself picture Bayden living, if not in luxury, then at least in relative comfort.

They left as wordlessly as they arrived. Bayden paused to lock the door in their wake, but Axel didn't wait. A few moments alone to get his thoughts in order would be a Godsend.

He was halfway down the second set of stairs when he realised he was being watched. A man stood in the hallway. He was in his mid-forties, wearing a stained tracksuit, and had the look of someone who was used to thinking of himself as in charge.

"You're the landlord?" Axel guessed.

"There's one room empty. Same size as that one."

He'd seen who Axel arrived with then. Curiosity got the better of Axel. "How much?"

The man looked him up and down. "Human or wolf?"

"You charge wolves more?"

Something about his surprise filed him as human in the landlord's mind. "No choice," he said. "Got to pay to replace what they wreck. Filthy creatures. Can't trust them to keep up with the rent, either."

A bitter taste filled the back of Axel's mouth. "What are the two rates?"

The man quoted two prices, one roughly double the other.

"Does the higher price always come with faulty heating?"

A creaky stair heralded Bayden's arrival. The landlord turned to him. "If you have a problem with the room—"

"No," Bayden rushed out. "The room's fine. There's no problem."

The landlord's eyes narrowed. "If you're going to be trouble…"

"I'm not." He reached into one of his pockets and pulled out several notes. "Next week's rent."

Axel opened his mouth to point out that Bayden damn near freezing to death in a room he was paying through the nose for was a problem, but Bayden turned to him before he had a chance to utter a word. "It's fine, sir." His tone of voice was as close to a plea as Axel had ever heard it.

There was no reason for Bayden to stay there. It would only take him a minute to pack what was left of his belongings.

"Please," Bayden whispered.

It had taken a lot of trust for Bayden to remove the limit on Axel even visiting the place. As the landlord made a point of double-checking that Bayden had given him enough money, Axel turned on his heel and strode out of the building. It was that or tell the landlord where to shove his room, and to hell with any other consideration.

In the car, Axel stared straight through the windscreen and did his best to calm his temper. Bayden followed him out, but stopped short of approaching the passenger door.

Reaching across the car, Axel opened it for him.

Bayden got in.

Axel sat very still for several seconds. "He has no intention of fixing your heating."

"I know, sir."

"He charges you higher rent than he charges humans."

"I know that too, sir." He said it so bloody calmly.

Axel's grip on the steering wheel tightened. "Why do you stay there?"

Bayden studied the dashboard like there was about to be a test on it. "Most places won't rent to wolves at all. I can't afford wolf-rates in any of the other places that do."

"Wolf-rates?"

"Rents get doubled. Wages get halved." Bayden shrugged.

"I pay you exactly the same as I paid Matt when he worked for me."

"Yes, sir."

Axel's mind raced with so many questions he couldn't decide which to ask first.

"I used to have more," Bayden blurted out.

Axel turned to face Bayden, but Bayden's attention never wavered from the dashboard.

"When I got kicked out of my last place, I wasn't allowed back in to get my stuff. I haven't got around to replacing most of it yet."

He didn't have the money to replace a damn thing. Axel glanced at the keys Bayden held. "You said you garage your bike?"

"About a mile from here, and yes, they charge a wolf more too. So does my mother's landlord."

"Altogether?" Axel asked.

Bayden swallowed. "Between my wages and what I saved up I've got enough to see me through to the end of the six weeks."

After that, it's none of your damn business. Even if Bayden was too polite to say it out loud, it was what he obviously thought.

"I was lucky to find a room anywhere after I had to leave my last place," Bayden said. "If I give it up, I might not find anywhere else willing to rent to me."

And Bayden wasn't ready to trust that their trial period would end with him moving into the pub fulltime. Axel started the car. If he couldn't convince Bayden to trust him by the time those six weeks were up, he didn't bloody well deserve to collar him.

* * * * *

"Spit it out, pup."

Bayden looked over his shoulder. Axel was right behind him. "Sir?"

Axel stepped closer. "Whatever it is you're working your way up to saying, spit it out." Axel chuckled. "Yes, it is that obvious."

Bayden took a deep breath. Axel's scent was strong—it had been ever since he'd took his turn watching over the back room that had been opened to the public that night.

If Bayden leaned back just a few inches, he had no doubt that he'd feel Axel's erection straining against his jeans.

Bayden swallowed. "Do you want…? I know I'm being punished, but I could still…"

Axel slid his arm around Bayden's waist and tugged him back. He was just as hard as Bayden had imagined.

"You could still get me off?" Axel whispered in his ear.

Bayden nodded.

"Are you asking me for something, pup?"

Bayden shook his head. "I wouldn't enjoy it." The moment he realised how that sounded, he shook his head even more vehemently. "I mean, you could do something I wouldn't enjoy, sir." No. That sounded wrong too. "I mean…"

Axel rocked his hips and stroked Bayden's abs. "You mean you're asking for permission to get me off, not to come yourself."

Bayden nodded. It was so much easier when Axel filled in his side of the conversation for him.

Axel turned Bayden around and backed him up against the side of the bar. "Because, it wouldn't be fair for me to be frustrated just because you're under penance?"

Bayden nodded again.

Axel stroked Bayden's hair back from his face and pressed their bodies together—sliding one leg between Bayden's thighs to take away the last vestiges of his personal space. "You're forgetting something, pup."

"Sir?"

"Setting a rule for you doesn't mean I have to follow it too."

Bayden frowned. "I didn't say you did, sir."

"I have options you don't have since you started submitting to me."

Bayden squirmed against the edge of the bar, sure he should be following, but not quite able to.

"I don't need your help to come, pup. I'm not dependant on you for my orgasms. I never will be."

Bayden had been punched in the stomach hundreds of times. Not one blow had knocked the air out of him the way those words did.

He jerked and lifted his head. Their eyes met.

Axel blinked, as if surprised by his response.

Bayden looked down. A human sub wouldn't mind. Or maybe he would, but a human dom wouldn't care if his sub minded. Or…

Axel made Bayden look up. His gaze narrowed as he studied Bayden.

"Yes, sir." That was always a safe thing to say.

If Axel wanted to screw someone else then, yes, sir. What else could Bayden say?

"I told you at the start, if we hit a limit, you're supposed to tell me."

Bayden shook his head. If Axel wanted someone else, he should have them. Whatever Axel wanted, he should have it. "It's not a limit, sir."

"Are you sure, pup?" Axel stroked his cheek. "You can tell me. I won't be angry."

Bayden swallowed past the sudden tightness in his throat. "It's not a limit, sir," he repeated.

"Fair enough." Axel stepped back. He walked away without another word. Bayden caught hold of the edge of the bar to stop himself from rushing after him.

Axel stopped to talk to Griz and Evan.

Bayden tried to turn away, to go back to serving the drinks as if he didn't care what Axel might do, but it was impossible.

Axel wanted him to work there and serve the drinks. No — even reminding himself of that didn't help.

Axel moved on to talk to someone else. Bayden tracked him from one conversation to another. There were lots of men in tonight. Damn near every one of them who called himself a sub would sell his soul to play with Axel.

Bayden's heart raced faster and faster as he wondered which one it would be, which man Axel would take to the back room.

A tiny blond guy with huge brown eyes stepped into Axel's space. No respect, nothing Bayden was willing to call appropriate submission. He demanded Axel's attention as if Axel should be impressed with him, and Axel let him do it. He let the supposed sub damn near hump him in the middle of the room.

He…

Bayden hesitated. Axel let him. He let the would-be sub flirt with him, but he didn't flirt back. He didn't reach out to the sub or pull him closer the way he did with Bayden.

Whoever Axel picked, it wouldn't be that guy.

Eventually, that would-be sub gave up and went away. Barely a second passed before another sub hit on Axel.

Taller, shorter, older, younger. Axel had his pick, and there was nothing Bayden could do but watch while Axel made his selection.

An hour crawled by, then another. Guys started to leave. Axel still hadn't taken one of the subs to the back room. Bayden watched intently as Axel ushered the last few subs out. For the first time since they'd spoken, Axel left Bayden's line of sight.

No one was going to the back room with Axel. Everything was fine. Soon, they'd be alone and —

Bayden stared at the door leading to the pub's entrance as he realised that wasn't guaranteed. Maybe Axel wouldn't walk back in alone. Maybe he'd bring one of the subs back with him. Maybe he hadn't ever intended to take a man to the back room, but he'd always intended to take someone to his bed after closing.

Axel stepped back into the room. Bayden held his breath until Axel closed the door behind him. They were alone — for tonight.

"Leave everything where it is," Axel ordered. "Upstairs, now."

Bayden hurried to obey.

Within minutes, Bayden was naked in Axel's bedroom. Axel looked him up and down, but he didn't reach out to him the way Bayden had hoped he might. He dismissed Bayden to the bathroom.

When Bayden returned, Axel was peering into the wardrobe where he kept his gear, but it was impossible to tell if it was going to be used for pleasure before it was used in his penance.

Axel was still hard. He still wanted to come. He was still thinking about sex. All Bayden could do was hope that for some reason Axel had decided he wanted to play with him in spite of everything.

"How uncomfortable were you last night?"

"It was fine, sir."

"Any time you want to try the truth, feel free."

Bayden winced.

"On a scale of one to ten," Axel ordered.

"Three or four, sir?"

Axel took an extra item from the wardrobe. Bayden didn't see what it was.

"Put the blanket down."

Bayden arranged it on the floor just like the previous night.

Axel moved behind Bayden. "Tonight is going to be more uncomfortable than last night."

"Yes, sir."

Axel slid a harness around Bayden's shoulders and did up the buckles. It wasn't uncomfortable. The lengths of leather lay neatly against his skin, connected by an O-ring in the centre of Bayden's chest.

"Remind me what the rules are."

"No shifting, sir, and I have to say my safe word if I need to."

"Good boy."

Axel turned Bayden around. If he liked the way the harness looked on Bayden, he didn't mention it.

He fitted black leather cuffs around Bayden's wrists and padlocked the chain that linked the cuffs to the harness's O-ring, trapping Bayden's hands in front of his chest.

"Can you reach your cock?"

Bayden shook his head. "I wouldn't, sir."

Axel raised an eyebrow. "That was an order to try, not an invitation to argue with me."

Bayden dropped his gaze. He tried to reach for his cock, but the bondage made it impossible.

Axel nodded to himself and reached for the next item on the bed. It was a spreader bar, but a really short one. "Lie down on your back."

Bayden obeyed. The reason the spreader bar was so short became obvious when Axel fitted cuffs just above Bayden's knees rather than around his ankles. Placed there, the spreader bar forced Bayden's legs wide apart.

There was a ring welded to the centre of the bar. Axel padlocked a length of chain to it and the other end to the harness's O-ring, pulling Bayden's knees up toward his chest.

Unable to close or lower his legs, Bayden's arse was completely exposed. Axel studied him for a long time, but he still didn't say whether or not he was pleased with the sight.

"You can test your bondage," he finally said.

All Bayden could do was squirm a little. He was alone with Axel. Axel's attention was on him, and the scent of Axel's arousal hung in the air. Bayden's cock was hard and leaking pre-cum, it bobbed as he twisted his limbs in an attempt to work out his range of movement.

Axel disappeared to take his turn in the bathroom.

Bayden took a deep breath and let it out slowly. Was it worth trying to offer Axel something when he came back? His bondage did seem to have been set up for sex more than discomfort.

His mind raced as he tried to work out the right words, but he wasn't quick enough. Axel came back. He stripped down to his bare skin, but he didn't head for his bed.

He knelt down alongside Bayden. Without saying a word, he tugged Bayden onto his side, then further over. Unable to straighten his body or move his hands, Bayden found himself kneeling on the blanket with his head down and his arse up. His cheek rested against the blanket, his hands unable to support his weight at that angle.

Axel didn't waste any more time. He slicked his fingers and pressed them against Bayden's hole.

Pleasure shot through Bayden as Axel found his prostate. Biting his lip, Bayden tried to keep his bliss to himself. Axel's fingers slid into him again and again.

Bayden didn't have permission to tell him to hurry up. That gave him leave to simply enjoy Axel's touch without feeling too guilty.

Rocking his hips, Bayden was soon helplessly pushing himself back against Axel's fingers. He whimpered as Axel took him to the edge of his orgasm. Not allowed to hold back, unwilling to risk displeasing Axel by doing that, Bayden desperately tried to relax and let whatever was going to happen, happen.

Axel's fingers disappeared. Bayden gasped with relief. If he was going to be allowed to come, he would much rather it be with Axel's cock buried deep inside him. He would have shuffled his knees further apart in invitation, but they were already spread as wide as they could go.

Axel had used lots of lube, the air felt cold against the slicked skin around his hole. Bayden heard Axel moving around but he couldn't feel Axel touching him any more. Bayden frowned and tried to peer over his shoulder.

Axel moved into Bayden's line of sight. He walked across to the bed and lay down on his back. Bayden's face was turned toward the bed, he had a perfect view as Axel relaxed against the pillows and took his erection in hand.

Axel looked toward him. Their eyes met. Axel had never intended to screw him. Suddenly, that was obvious. Bayden tugged against his bondage. Axel calmly stroked his cock.

"Sir..."

Axel didn't tell him to shut up, but he didn't stop jacking his cock. His hand moved determinedly in long even strokes. There was still lube on his fingers from where he'd prepared Bayden. Pre-cum slicked his touch further. Axel reached down with his other hand, playing with his balls as he got closer to the edge.

Bayden shook his head, rubbing his cheek against the blanket beneath him. Axel took no notice.

He came in just a few minutes but didn't stop stroking his cock as his cum spilled in long ropes against his abs. Axel thrust up against his own palm and moaned in pleasure.

Bayden whimpered. Shaking with need—not for his own orgasm, but to be involved in Axel's. He was overcome by the horrible urge to sob at the sheer injustice of being so close to Axel and yet still so far away from him.

Axel closed his eyes and rested.

His satisfaction filled the room. Bayden crammed air into his lungs as if absorbing enough of Axel's scent might somehow make him feel closer to him. It didn't help. It made him feel emptier. It made him miss Axel's touch all the more.

Axel rolled his shoulders and sat up.

He walked the few paces to Bayden and sat down on the floor next to him. Gripping the harness and the spreader bar, he rolled Bayden onto his back.

"You're not allowed to come unless I make you come — those are the rules you agreed to follow. But I don't have to wait for you to do anything. I'm allowed to jack off whenever I want — whether you're under penance or not."

Bayden closed his eyes. He knew he should feel grateful that Axel hadn't brought someone else to his bed in his place, but in that moment, it wasn't in him.

"I'm not going to screw another guy to punish you — even if you still haven't got the hang of stating your limits." He stroked Bayden's cheek. "But remember this, pup. Half the time you spent lying to me, I spent watching you get screwed by dozens of different men."

Bayden opened his eyes. "I..."

"I know why you did that now but, at the time, all I had was lies. I hated it just as much as you'd have hated seeing me play with someone else tonight, but I hated the idea of you getting hurt even more." He cupped Bayden's cheek in his palm. "When I tell you that I'll look after you even when it's not easy, when I tell you that I'll accept you no matter what, it's not a vague idea. I've already proved I'm as good as my word."

Bayden turned his face into Axel's hand and pressed a kiss against his palm. Axel didn't snatch his hand away. He left it there within easy reach, allowing Bayden to kiss and lick his fingers until a little bit of Bayden's panic eased.

When Axel finally took his hand away, Bayden still didn't have the right words. "I..."

"Hush." Axel pressed a kiss against Bayden's temple before heading into the bathroom to clean himself up.

Bayden squirmed. It only made him more uncomfortable. Even breathing seemed to pull at his bondage, making him all the more desperate to stretch his limbs. It was going to be impossible to sleep for more than a few minutes at a time.

Axel returned. He took something off the bed, where all the bondage equipment had been piled up. He attached it to the chain connected to the spreader bar.

Bayden stretched his neck to see what it was. A jingling noise immediately filled the air. The thing was silver and it looked like a small bell.

Bayden frowned up at Axel. All he got for his trouble was a raised eyebrow. Axel would hear every movement he made in the night. Every time he failed to accept the bondage with absolute stillness, Axel would know he'd screwed up.

Bayden swallowed. "Yes, sir."

Axel went to bed in silence. He didn't say another word until he checked on Bayden in the early hours of the morning.

"We're six weeks in, pup. If you'd told me the truth when you started working for me, you'd have been able to be comfortable from this point on." He slid warm hands over Bayden's body, making it impossible for Bayden to hide how knotted his muscles were.

Axel had been right about that night's bondage being far more restrictive and uncomfortable than the previous night's had been. Bayden closed his eyes. He'd never wished he could go back and fix a mistake more fervently, but that had nothing to do with relief from physical pain. He'd never wanted to share another man's bed more desperately.

Maybe it was the chill or the unrelenting ache in his muscles, or maybe it was seeing the distance between himself and Axel not in vague terms of truth and honesty, but in the physical feet and inches between him and Axel's bed. His mind screamed out that he needed to be wrapped in Axel's arms and completely accepted by him.

In that moment, Bayden would have sold his soul for the ability to go back and tell Axel the truth when he'd first started working for him.

Chapter Twenty Three

Axel glanced at the clock above the bar when Hale strode into the pub looking even more pissed off with the world than usual. It wasn't even noon. They weren't supposed to be open for hours. Hale was still in his work suit. Last time Hale had started drinking that early in the day, it had been a triple murder, and not one of the victims had hit her teens. "Bad day at the office?"

Hale pulled himself onto a stool opposite Axel. "Like you give a toss. Where's the puppy?"

Axel lost all interest in stocking the shelves behind the bar as he realised Hale wasn't there to drink away his woes. "Bayden's out back. He's too busy to eavesdrop."

Hale dropped two books on the bar.

Axel picked up the top one. It looked official. "The anti-pack laws?"

"You want to know what they are." It wasn't a question.

Axel flicked through a few pages.

"I've never arrested a wolf for anything that I wouldn't have arrested a human for," Hale said, all his usual sarcasm absent.

Axel looked up.

"I may handcuff men and order them onto their knees, but not while I'm on the job," Hale said. "And not unless they ask nicely."

Axel flicked through a few more pages. It wasn't a thick book. It felt heavier in his hand than it should.

"I've been asking around. Granger's a sadistic bastard whenever he thinks he can get away with it. He's coming up for retirement in two years, but the rumour is that he won't make it there. He's under investigation."

"For the way he treats wolves?"

"No."

"No?"

Hale sighed and rubbed a hand over his shaved scalp. "Two reasons. One—wolves don't complain, they'd never report a cop. Two—it wouldn't do them any good if they did. Nothing he did to Bayden is against the law. It's screwed up, but that's the way it is."

Axel's grip on the book turned white knuckled.

"I'll only say it once but it has got to be said," Hale announced. "I was right."

"About?"

"Your puppy was lying. He is trouble."

"He was lying," Axel allowed.

"And he's trouble," Hale pushed.

"Because all wolves are trouble, right?"

Hale laughed. "Because he's a brat, and he's got so far under your skin you're stuck with him."

You only think he's a brat because he thinks you're a sub. Axel smiled to himself and picked up the other book.

"There's some sort of campaign to get the wolf-laws overturned," Hale offered. "The guy who wrote that— Kincade—is one of the top guys in it. I think the publisher sent one to every damn police station in the country."

Axel looked at the spine. It hadn't been cracked.

Hale shrugged. "Cops aren't big readers."

Axel turned it over. Kincade Wolf. "The man who wrote it's a wolf?"

"Yeah. A few guys at my station were sent on a course he runs. Community outreach, minority whatever. They all said he scared the hell out of them. A proper—" He cut himself off.

Axel stared at him, waiting for the rest.

Hale shrugged again. "A proper wolf in sheep's clothing. Looks innocent—dressed up in a suit, with a posh accent, and all that. But he's still a wolf at heart. It still felt like he was ten seconds away from tearing someone's throat out. Just like your puppy."

Axel looked down at the book again.

"I'm off. Caught a new case. Haven't slept yet." Hale got off his stool. "You look like you haven't slept either."

"I didn't," Axel murmured, absentmindedly.

"So there are some benefits to keeping a tame werewolf around the place?" Hale asked.

Axel chuckled. Screwing Bayden would have been a far more enjoyable way to pass the night. As Hale headed out, Axel rolled his shoulders.

Bayden having spent a second night in bondage shouldn't make Axel feel like he was the one who'd been stretched on a rack, but it did.

With all his senses on high alert, the bell he'd used to make sure he'd have woken up if Bayden panicked or cramped up had actually woken him up every time Bayden had twitched.

Bayden had to be sore as hell, but hadn't complained once. He'd thrown himself into his work that morning as if he'd had a full eight hours and—

The sound of the pub's backdoor closing made Axel look up.

Bayden stepped toward the bar, only to pause as if unsure of his welcome.

"Okay, pup?"

Bayden came closer. When he was near enough, Axel reached out and pulled him into his space by his belt loops. The kiss was a statement of pure possession—Axel didn't try to pretend otherwise. Bayden was his, and neither Granger nor anyone else was going to lay a hand on him.

Murmuring his approval, Bayden leaned into Axel's body. It almost felt like he was trusting Axel to support him. Axel had never wanted to tug another man down onto the floor behind the bar so badly, but he forced himself to pull back. Bayden ran his tongue over his bottom lip as if trying to catch the tail end of a kiss that had already ended.

He glanced up at Axel, wary and hopeful in equal measure. It would be so easy to order him onto his knees.

Axel ran his finger down Bayden's throat, trying to remind himself why neither of them was going to get laid until after the penance was finished, and failing.

Without any warning, Bayden tensed.

"Pup?"

Bayden said nothing, he just stared at the books on the bar.

"Hale gave them to me."

Bayden swallowed. His Adam's apple bobbed against Axel's touch, but he obviously wasn't thinking about deep throating.

"Anything you want to say?"

"Nothing, sir." All hint of the wolf who'd leaned into Axel's touch was gone. "Is there anything you want me to do?" It was the closest to passive aggressive as Axel had ever heard him sound.

If Axel had known what prompted it, it would have been fascinating. With no idea what was wrong, it was just annoying. "Nothing for now."

Bayden didn't seem to know how to get out of Axel's space without an order.

"I'm going to go up to the flat and read. You can do whatever you want for an hour or two," Axel offered.

Bayden quickly retreated.

"If I want to find you, you'll be…" Axel prompted, when Bayden was halfway out of the room.

"With my bike in the lock-up, sir."

Axel nodded his dismissal. Once he was settled comfortably in his flat, it didn't take Axel long to get a basic idea of the first book's contents.

The anti-pack laws were actually quite simple. Anything that would allow wolves to live in any sort of community, or even maintain any real contact with an extended family was systematically outlawed. A lone wolf was tolerable, but a pack was a threat that humans couldn't allow. Wolves had to be kept weak, they had to be kept isolated. Humanity had to keep them down. Even the pack names had been banned.

Axel frowned. He'd always had the vague idea that wolves all kept the surname Wolf as some sort of statement of species pride. It had never occurred to him that it was illegal for them to use any other surname. The old pack names had died because humans had hunted each one down and slaughtered it.

Axel shook his head. Bayden Wolf. Kincade Wolf. They could be father and son, part of the same pack line, or no relation at all. No one would be able to tell from their names.

He moved onto another section of the book. It was soon obvious that while werewolves had to obey every human law, and dozens of extra ones, they had no redress under the law. It was ridiculously easy for a wolf to be a criminal, but the possibility of one being a victim hadn't even been considered.

Hale was right. Nothing Granger had done to Bayden had been illegal. Nothing the guy who'd choked him halfway to death had done had been against the law either. The man with a knife could have stabbed him without worrying the cops would be on his tail. Axel could put a gun to Bayden's head and pull the trigger, and he wouldn't have broken a single law.

Axel ran a hand down his face as he tried to re-imagine his life if he'd been born a wolf. Memories of family gatherings flittered through his mind. They wouldn't have happened.

His stomach turned over at the idea of losing all those people who'd once been such a huge part of his life, not because he was gay, not because they didn't want to know him anymore, but because humans said so—because having more than two adults under the same roof, even for a few seconds, invited a man like Granger to swoop in and make his life a living hell.

How many times would he have been pulled over? How many fights would he have had to take? How many 'fines' would he have paid to guys like Granger? What would he have done to pay the rent?

Axel rubbed at the back of his neck as he instinctively headed for the lock-ups to check on Bayden.

Bayden was crouched down alongside his bike. He got up when he sensed Axel's approached.

"You don't have to stop on my account," Axel said.

Bayden turned his back on him, but he didn't resume his work.

It took every scrap of his patience, but Axel waited him out.

"You won't find any I've broken," Bayden said.

"What?"

"You can go cover to cover—you won't find an anti-pack law I don't obey to the letter."

Axel caught hold of Bayden's arm and spun him around. Anger shone bright in Bayden's gaze, but there was pain there too—so much pain. "What if I ordered you to break one?" Axel demanded.

Bayden's eyes opened very wide. "You wouldn't!"

"If I don't know what they are, I can't avoid it, can I?"

Bayden held his gaze, studying him very carefully. "That's why you wanted to know?"

"Yes, and you have a new order to follow. If I give you a command which involves you breaking any of those laws, I want you to tell me, straight away."

Bayden hesitated.

"Can you do that?" Axel pushed.

"Yes, sir."

Axel let go of his arm. Bayden didn't retreat, but he looked down. "I should have spoken more respectfully, sir."

"I'll take the truth in a stroppy tone over a lie any day."
Axel ran his gaze over Bayden's bike. It was perfect. Bayden
had it damn near sparkling. *Filthy creatures.* Axel took a deep
breath and leaned against the lock-up's wall.

Axel thought back to Bayden's bedsit. Cheap clothes.
Barely enough food to survive. Bike worth a fortune.

"You said your father used to ride that bike?"

"Yes, sir." Bayden moved back to kneel on the other
side of it.

"You also said it was a gift from your grandfather,"
Axel pointed out. "Is either story true?"

Bayden jerked his head up. "I didn't steal it."

"It never occurred to me that you had."

Bayden looked down. It was obviously something that
had occurred to a lot of other people.

Axel moved around the bike to stand at Bayden's side.
He ran his fingers through Bayden's hair, encouraging him to
look up. The confusion in his eyes tore at Axel.

He crouched down. "You're not in trouble. Forget
about what other people have thought, forget about what you
might have said in the past. None of that matters. Just tell me
about the bike—the truth. You can do that."

* * * * *

You can do that. Axel sounded so confident. Bayden
wished he felt the same way.

Axel slid his hand down to rest on the back of Bayden's
neck. His hand was warm against his skin. It felt good there.
Axel's touch always felt good.

He wasn't like other humans.

"Years ago, before my father was born, my grandfather
had a bike just like this," Bayden whispered.

Axel sat on the floor next to him and nodded
encouragingly.

"They trashed it," Bayden whispered.

"They?"

"Humans."

Axel didn't pull away, he didn't stand up for humans. He slid his hand up and down Bayden's back, caressing him thought his vest.

"Humans don't like seeing a wolf riding this kind of bike now. Fifty years ago, things were so much worse," Bayden kept his tone hushed, as if that somehow made it okay to say it all in front of a human. "They made him watch them while they trashed it. That bike was everything to him. Seeing what they did to it, it broke something in him." Bayden took a deep breath. "When my father was old enough to earn real money in fights, he started looking for a bike that was the same make and model. He finally found this one. But…" Bayden swallowed down a rush of emotion. "My dad thought having the replacement would heal something in my grandfather."

"It didn't work?" Axel asked.

Bayden shook his head. "Some things don't heal. My granddad couldn't bring himself to ride this one. Even now, he can barely look at it."

Axel stroked his fingers through Bayden's hair, very gently.

"My dad thought that letting humans put him off riding a bike like this was letting humans win, so he kept it and rode it himself." Bayden could damn near see him sitting astride it as he spoke, but the image of his father straddling it, so proud, so confident, didn't last. The picture faded away leaving a huge empty space in its wake. "He made my mother and my grandfather promise that if anything happened to him, they'd keep the bike for me until I was old enough to ride it. My grandfather put it out of sight, but when I turned twenty-one, he gave it to me."

"It must have been tempting to sell it when times were tough," Axel said.

"I'd rather die." It was stupid to tell a human that, to tell Axel the easiest way to hurt him, but his desire for Axel to understand how important it was overrode everything else. "My dad wanted me to ride it. He said it was a mark of progress. His father couldn't ride it, but his son would. It was important to him."

Axel stroked his hair back from his face.

Bayden studied the bike through narrowed eyes. "My father died young, but sometimes I think he packed more life into his existence than most wolves who've lived four times as long. That's what I remember most about him—how alive he was. He was so alive, especially when he was riding his bike..." Bayden cleared his throat. "And he wasn't afraid of anyone. A lot of wolves are."

"Afraid of humans?" Axel suggested.

Bayden nodded. "My grandfather's afraid of them. My dad hated them. My mother just wants nothing to do with them—she's even talking about taking a residential place at the Denville project so she'll have as little to do with humans as possible."

"What about you?"

"Depends on the human. You're not all the same." Bayden stared at the ground between his knees and the bike. "There are ones like Granger who I hate. And there are ones like Richards that I don't want anything to do with," Bayden said, weighing each word very carefully.

"And ones you're afraid of?" Axel prompted.

Bayden closed his eyes. Never admit fear. Never let the humans know they've got to you. The truth. "You."

"Me?" Axel repeated, blankly. "You're afraid of me?"

"Yes."

"I won't hurt you, pup."

Bayden looked down. "I'm not afraid you'll whip me, or any of that. That's never bothered me." He let out a short laugh that had no humour in it. God, if that was all it was. He closed his eyes. "My mother was right—it's the humans who seem different that are the most dangerous of all."

Axel touched his cheek and made him turn to face him. "Pup?"

"I'll do anything for you, sir," Bayden whispered. "That's what makes you dangerous. Other humans can't hurt me. I'd never give them the chance. But you… I'd be a fool not to be afraid of you."

Axel pressed a kiss against his temple. Sliding his arm properly around Bayden's shoulders, he tugged him into his arms. He pressed another kiss to the top of Bayden's head and rested his face against his hair.

Bayden leaned into him, unable to even pretend he didn't need Axel's arms around him.

"Good boy," Axel whispered to him. "Good pup."

Any second, Bayden knew that Axel would pull away. He tried to be ready for it, but minutes passed and it didn't happen. Axel stayed right there, just holding on to him.

Gradually, Bayden relaxed against him.

"That's right, pup. I've got you."

Turning his head, Bayden buried his face in Axel's neck.

For a long time, they sat in silence but, no matter how wonderful that was, it couldn't last forever.

"Before, when you were hooking up with wolves, was it always a onetime thing, or was there someone in particular?" Axel asked.

Bayden shook his head, too relieved that the conversation had moved away from his family to worry about where it might be heading instead.

"When was the last time you hooked up with a wolf?"

"Last summer, sir."

"The one when we met?"

Bayden shook his head. "Summer last year. Since then, I haven't really had time. I mean, I didn't want…"

"That was around the time you started taking bets on things that weren't fights?" Axel guessed.

Bayden nodded.

Axel leaned back so they could look each other in the eye, but Bayden wasn't inclined to hold his gaze. He stared down at the cloth in his hand instead. "Most of the time, I didn't have any trouble picking up enough fights to cover everything. But…"

Axel didn't say a word. The minutes ticked past. Bayden reached out and wiped the cloth over the already pristine black paintwork, but it was one of those times when Axel had decided that Bayden was the one who had to speak next.

He had to say something. It had to be the truth. He frowned as he tried to find a version of the truth that didn't give away too much, which didn't leave him too vulnerable in front of a man who already had more power to hurt him than any human should be allowed to have.

Axel settled his hand on Bayden's abs, just above the top button of his jeans. That was it. He just left his hand there. If he'd grabbed his arse or his cock, it would have made sense. If Axel's hand had been shaped into a fist ready to deliver a sucker punch, it would have been easier.

Bayden glanced up at him.

It had to be the truth and, for the man who'd watched him take bets on sex while he hated every second of it, it had to be the complete truth.

"It had been raining forever," Bayden whispered. "Humans don't like fighting in the rain."

Axel still didn't say anything.

"It finally stopped raining the day before the rent was due. There was a pub in the city—I'd picked up lots of fights in the alley behind it in the past. Some of the guys there made huge bets. I thought there was a chance."

Bayden swallowed.

Axel remained patiently silent.

"No one wanted to fight that night, but there were guys back there. One of them offered me twenty quid for a blowjob. I made my choice." Bayden frowned at his reflection in the shining paintwork and rubbed at it with the cloth. "It didn't take me long to realise that the real money came from guys who wear leather. They like using wolves because they don't have to feel guilty about hurting us—it's not the same as beating up a human." He cleared his throat and forced himself to square his shoulders. "And proving to a man like that, that a wolf isn't easy to break, is different from dropping to your knees in a back alley."

He turned to Axel, not sure what to expect.

Some humans didn't understand that it was different. Some humans…

Axel brushed his lips against Bayden's very gently. "Good boy."

Bayden remembered how to breathe. He nodded. Telling the truth meant he was good.

* * * * *

"How uncomfortable were you last night?"

Bayden shuffled his feet in the bedroom doorway. He wanted to lie—Axel would have bet his life on it.

"Maybe six out of ten, sir." He spoke softly, the same way he always did when asked questions like that—as if he didn't want anyone but Axel to hear the answer, didn't want anyone else to know that he was admitting things like that out loud.

Axel nodded that he'd heard. Bayden could take a more uncomfortable bondage arrangement. He'd do that before the end of the penance, but not tonight. Tonight Axel had a different kind of discomfort planned for him.

He dismissed Bayden to the bathroom and took several items out of the wardrobe where he kept his toys. When

Bayden came back and stood naked in front of him, Axel wasted no time.

"Sit down."

Bayden sat on the blanket Axel had spread out on the floor.

Axel quickly fixed the black leather wrist and ankle cuffs in place. They were padded and designed to be comfortable. Bayden watched in silence as Axel completed the arrangement by sliding a short length of chain through the D-rings on each cuff and padlocking it in place. Bayden's hands and feet were all staying close together for the rest of the night.

"Eight weeks in — you'd been working for me for two weeks," Axel said. "You knew me pretty well by this point — well enough that you should have realised that I don't judge a man by how much he has in his wallet." He didn't give Bayden time to answer before he took his turn in the bathroom.

When he came out a few minutes later, Axel went straight to his bed without even glancing in Bayden's direction. Making himself comfortable, he picked up one of the books from his night stand and opened it to the old envelope he'd used as a bookmark.

Bayden hadn't tried to lie down and make himself comfortable. He sat exactly where Axel had left him, staring at Axel with an intensity that made it difficult for Axel not to squirm.

Forcing himself to focus on the book, Axel did his damnedest to pretend that he was completely oblivious to Bayden's presence. Minutes ticked past. He turned the page and began a new section of the book.

Bayden continued to stare. His attention was like a physical pressure against Axel's skin. Another few pages. A new chapter. Bayden didn't move, didn't stop staring, didn't speak.

"If you have something to say, pup, you'll have to say it out loud. I'm not a mind reader." For the first time, Axel set his book down and turned to face Bayden.

"There's nothing I want to say, sir."

Axel smiled. More likely, Bayden thought everything he wanted to say to him was too rude to be considered respectful. "If you want to read them after I'm done, you're welcome to."

"No!"

Axel rolled onto his side and propped his head up with his hand.

Bayden looked down. He took a deep breath. "No, thank you, sir." His voice trembled with the effort it took for him to adopt a polite tone.

"Oh?"

Bayden shifted his weight in an effort to find a more comfortable position on the thin blanket. It took him a long time to find a response. "I already know what human books say about wolves."

Axel glanced at the book he'd been reading. It had been written by a wolf. It spoke about wolves with respect. But what he was actually reading wasn't as important as what Bayden thought he was reading. "Tell me what the books say."

Bayden glanced pointedly at the book laying on the bed in front of Axel. Axel pretended not to notice.

"It doesn't matter. It's not important," Bayden mumbled.

"That doesn't answer my question."

Bayden's jaw twitched as he clenched his teeth. "It all happened a long time ago."

"You're thinking about what the books say about the Captivities?" Axel asked.

Bayden nodded.

"This book hasn't mentioned them yet."

"It will say the same as all the human books say about the Captivities. It was all very wrong, very *unfortunate*, that humans hurt the wolves they caught," Bayden spat the platitudes out with obvious contempt. "But then they'll go on to say it all worked out for the best — that it's because of the Captivities that wolves are able to live among you today. If wolves hadn't been tamed by humans, we'd have been too dangerous. Really, you did wolves a favour."

"That's what the books I studied in school said," Axel admitted.

Bayden stared down at his bound wrists. He took a deep breath and let it out very slowly. "They're wrong."

"Anyone who defends the Captivities is wrong."

Bayden shook his head. "I mean about who modern wolves are descended from. They never managed to breed us. Werewolves don't breed in captivity — no matter what the humans do to them, no matter what they make wolves do with humans, with other wolves, with…" He closed his eyes.

"After they were freed," Axel began.

"No. The things they did to those wolves. Even after they were freed, none of them were in any condition to breed."

Axel straightened up.

"They wanted to make sure the male wolves they freed would be as docile as possible. They called it gelding." He met Axel's gaze for a moment. "The female wolves…that wasn't so intentional, but there's a limit to how much cruelty even a wolf's body can heal from."

Axel sat up and dropped his feet over the side of the bed. He tossed the book on his bed-side cabinet. Forget how long ago it had happened, the pain Bayden felt was there right now.

* * * * *

372

Bayden tensed as Axel got to his feet. With the worst of human's cruelty right in the front of his mind, he had no idea what to expect from Axel. Could a man who shared a species with the people who had done all those things really be so different?

Axel sat down on the floor next to him, just as naked as Bayden was.

Bayden's heart raced. Sweat trickled down his spine, but he didn't flinch when Axel reached out to him.

His hand was gentle against Bayden's cheek. Axel slid his fingers through Bayden's hair and pushed it back off his face. He was going to say it was okay. Bayden braced himself for it, hoping like hell he could nod and agree without Axel calling him on lying. Because, it wasn't okay, nothing that was anything to do with the Captivities had been okay — it never would be.

But Axel didn't say that. He didn't say anything. He just sat there, with only a few inches between them, occasionally stroking his fingers through Bayden's hair.

Slowly, Bayden felt his heart stop racing. His breaths became more regular. Anger began to burn less fiercely inside him. The tension in his muscles eased.

Bayden glanced up. Their eyes met and Bayden realised that Axel had been aware of it all, had somehow known that a gentle presence would help more than lies and platitudes.

Axel moved away, but only far enough to lean back against the chest of drawers. He beckoned Bayden closer. Moving with his hands and feet bound wasn't an elegant process, but being close to Axel was the only thing that really mattered. When Bayden got to him, Axel guided him to sit between his legs, curled in against his chest. Bound as he was, Bayden couldn't reach out to Axel, but that became irrelevant when Axel wrapped his arms around him and held him close.

"You were telling me that today's wolves are all descended from the wolves who remained free, the ones who were never captured," Axel reminded him after a few more minutes had passed.

Bayden nodded, taking the chance to rub his face against Axel's tattooed skin in the process. "My dad used to say that was a tactical error on humanity's part," he whispered.

Axel stroked Bayden's side, encouraging him to snuggle against him.

"He said that what doesn't kill a species makes it stronger. Humans caught the weakest, the slowest, the least intelligent wolves. They saw to it that only the fittest ones survived, that modern wolves are stronger than any of the previous generations were."

"What do you think?" Axel asked.

"I don't think every kind of pain makes people stronger. Some pain just hurts," Bayden said. "Nothing good comes out of the way humans treat wolves." He glanced up at Axel. "At the way *other* humans treat wolves."

Axel pressed a kiss against his temple. "One of the books Hale gave me was written by humans about the anti-pack laws. The other one was written by a wolf."

Bayden glanced across to the book on the bed side table.

"His name's Kincade Wolf," Axel said. "Have you heard of him?"

Bayden shrugged.

"He's leading a campaign to have the anti-pack laws overturned."

The campaign wouldn't do any good. Nothing would change. Humans would still be humans at the end of it. But, Bayden leaned a little more firmly into Axel's embrace, enjoying the way Axel's voice reverberated through his chest as he spoke, even if the topic he wanted to talk about wasn't of particular interest to him.

"If he's successful, wolves would only have to obey the same laws as humans," Axel went on. "Humans who committed crimes against wolves could be charged."

Bayden took a deep breath, inhaling Axel's scent, loving the way the warmth of Axel's body wrapped around him.

"Is that something you'd like to be involved in?"

Bayden blinked, wondering if he'd missed a whole segment of the conversation while he'd been relishing Axel's closeness.

Axel smiled, obviously realising that Bayden had been distracted and by what. "Would you like to get involved with the campaign to overturn the anti-pack laws?"

"No!" The moment he realised what Axel was suggesting, Bayden blurted out his answer—almost as vehemently as he'd been when he rejected the idea of reading Axel's books. "No, thank you, sir," he corrected a moment later.

Axel stroked his cheek. "You don't want to?"

Bayden's hands tightened into fists. "I don't want any trouble, sir."

Axel nodded slowly. "Okay. Nothing that could cause any trouble for us." Bayden frowned, but Axel raised an eyebrow at him. "Anything that causes trouble for one of us, causes trouble for both of us."

Bayden rested his head on Axel's chest. He could hear Axel's heartbeat, slow and steady. He listened to it as his own pulse gradually slowed and his panic at the idea of getting involved in that campaign faded away.

Axel didn't rush to say anything, but it didn't feel like he was waiting for Bayden to speak. Axel just held him, idly caressing him as if to remind Bayden he had the right to touch every bit of him. It was perfect, but such silence couldn't last forever—humans enjoyed talking far too much for that.

"You've been very good today. You told me the truth about a lot of things."

Bayden snuggled into Axel in response.

"I'm proud of you, pup. I know it wasn't easy for you." He pressed a kiss against Bayden's hair and slid his hand up Bayden's thigh.

Bayden didn't have much room to move in his bondage but he kept his legs even closer together than he had to. Axel noticed. He looked down and immediately saw what Bayden had been hoping to conceal.

Axel chuckled. "You won't get in trouble for getting turned on, even if you are still under penance."

Bayden slowly let his legs fall apart as far as the cuffs allowed. Axel trailed a fingertip up Bayden's flourishing erection.

"You never need to hide enjoying my touch. I'll never be mad at you for it." He caressed Bayden's cock very gently, teasing him with soft sensations, and tapping the tip to make the whole shaft bounce and bob for his amusement.

Bayden watched Axel toy with him. The bondage made it difficult to move, but it was his submission that really kept him there, feeling vulnerable and cosseted in equal measure.

"Such a good boy," Axel murmured.

Bayden had to ask, even if he didn't have the right words. He tilted his face up and hoped. Axel granted him his kiss—a gentle touch of the lips, far more chaste than Bayden would have preferred, but still enough to send tingles down his spine.

"Do you want me stay here with you while I finish the chapter?"

Bayden glanced at the book. "You'd be more comfortable—"

"I didn't ask where I'd be more comfortable."

Bayden took a deep breath and nodded.

"Good boy." Axel brushed their lips together briefly before reaching across and snagging the book.

Bayden closed his eyes and rested his head on Axel's shoulder. Unsure how long it would take Axel to finish his chapter, he refused to waste time worrying about the words Axel might read. It was far more important to enjoy being held close.

Chapter Twenty Four

It would be so easy to end the penance early.

As Axel led the way up to the flat at the end of the third day of Bayden's penance, he'd never been more tempted to say to hell with all other considerations. He was the dom. It was his decision. Bayden wouldn't complain about being allowed to skip the final part of the penance.

Axel stared at the patch of carpet where Bayden's blanket had been spread out the previous three nights. It had taken all his self-control to force himself to leave Bayden there when he'd finished the chapter he'd been reading and was due to go back to his bed.

Bayden had accepted his punishment so well, he deserved to be let off early for good behaviour, didn't he? Axel looked over his shoulder. Bayden stood in the bedroom doorway, patiently awaiting an order.

Axel bit back a sigh. What Bayden really deserved was a dom who would stick with his decisions and see punishments and penances through to the end, no matter what his personal feelings might be. He hated punishing Bayden, but that wasn't a good enough reason to turn into the kind of wishy-washy dom who'd never deserve Bayden's respect.

"Tonight's bondage is going to be a lot more painful."

"Yes, sir." Not even the slightest hesitation.

By the time Bayden returned from the bathroom, Axel was ready. He'd laid all the necessary bondage neatly alongside Bayden's blanket.

"Kneel here."

"Yes, sir."

Axel crouched down behind Bayden. One caress to remind Bayden how pleased he was with him, and Axel got down to business. He began with Bayden's arms, pulling them behind his back and sliding a black leather sleeve over both limbs at the same time. As Axel did up the buckles, working from those by his wrists up towards those around his biceps, Bayden's arms were tugged closer together, straining his shoulders and stretching his muscles.

The buckle closest to Bayden's hands was fitted with a D-ring. Axel padlocked a chain to it. Arranging Bayden on the blanket, laying on his side, Axel fastened the other end of the length of chain to one leg of the chest of drawers below the window.

They were halfway there.

Axel moved around Bayden and carefully fastened a ball stretcher around Bayden's sac. The two inches of black leather forced Bayden's nuts down away from his body. Axel had worn similar toys himself. It wasn't comfortable, but it wouldn't actually hurt Bayden — not yet. There was a D-ring on the ball stretcher too. Axel clipped a length of chain to it and ran it toward the base of the bed.

He tugged, very gently. Bayden obediently squirmed on his blanket, moving his crotch closer to the base of the bed. The chain behind him rattled. When it grew taught Bayden had to strain his arms, lifting them away from his body in an effort to position himself as Axel demanded.

Axel attached the end of the second length of chain to the bed frame, leaving just a fraction of slack. He checked the arrangement carefully. From that moment on, Bayden had a choice, he could move back and release the strain on his shoulders, but in doing so he'd cause the ball stretcher to pull painfully at his sack.

There was no escape from pain, just a choice between two forms of it — each of which would grow more intense as time passed.

Even now, it had to send discomfort twisting through Bayden's body. Axel wouldn't have expected a human to tolerate it for long, but Bayden was nothing if not tough —

physically at least. Everything he'd gone through had made his body resilient, even if it had taken a psychological toll.

His penance would be real. It would take him to the edge and make him determined not to lie again. Maintaining the position would test him, but it was a test he could pass.

Axel took his turn in the bathroom. By the time he returned to Bayden's side, it was obvious that Bayden had realised just how much of a battle of endurance he was in for. There was no way he'd be able to sleep a wink.

"Okay, pup?"

"Yes, sir."

"If you'd told me the truth when you started submitting to me, you'd be in my bed right now."

Bayden closed his eyes. "Yes, sir."

Axel got into bed, but he didn't try to sleep. He remained wide awake, watching Bayden choose one type of pain over another again and again. At first he remained relatively still. As the minutes ticked past at glacial speed, he had to switch tactics more frequently.

By the time the clock reached the next hour, Bayden couldn't remain still for more than a minute at a time.

Axel threw back his blankets.

The chains only took seconds to undo.

"Sir?"

"It's okay," Axel said, undoing the quick release tabs on the bondage sleeve. "It'll hurt when you first move your arms, but that won't last long."

"I didn't ask you to untie me, sir." There was just a touch of uncertainty in his voice, as if he'd considered doing that so many times, he wasn't entirely sure he hadn't succumbed to the temptation.

"Hush."

Axel tossed the sleeve aside. Bayden gasped as Axel guided him to put his arms in front of him. Axel moved on to the ball stretcher. As much as Bayden tried to co-operate, he was stiff and clumsy. It was pointless to order him to his feet.

Axel simply picked him up and carried him the few paces to the bed.

Quickly tugging the blanket up over them both, he beckoned Bayden closer.

"Sir?"

"Yes, pup?" Axel reached down between them and cupped Bayden's balls in his palm, gently massaging them to ease the way they had to ache.

"I don't understand, sir?" Bayden whispered.

"One night for every month you lied to me. Three and a quarter months," Axel reminded him.

"Three and a *quarter* nights," Bayden realised.

"If you hadn't told me the truth when you did, you'd still be down there."

A shiver ran through Bayden. He didn't feel chilled enough for it to be an entirely physical reaction, but Axel pulled Bayden closer anyway, letting him share his body heat.

Bayden hesitated for a moment.

"You can come as close as you want," Axel said.

A moment later, the only way Bayden could have got any nearer would have been to climb inside Axel's skin with him.

"That's right," Axel murmured. "I've got you." He rubbed Bayden's biceps and shoulders to coax the stiffness out of them.

Bayden snuggled in against him. The punishment had taken him so close to the edge he was past hiding how much he needed Axel's praise and comfort. He murmured his pleasure at each touch, making Axel smile.

"See how good everything is once we tell each other the truth?" Axel whispered to him.

Bayden nodded, and took the opportunity to burrow his face into Axel's shoulder at the same time.

Axel slid a hand down his back, welcoming him back to his side with every touch. "Good boy."

Bayden's cock hardened against Axel's thigh. Axel's body quickly responded in kind. Bayden pushed out his arse when Axel's hand slid over his buttocks.

"It's late, and you're exhausted," Axel chided.

"I could suck you off if you prefer, sir. And I can make it quick if—"

Axel hushed him. "Tomorrow," he promised. "We'll do everything there is to do, tomorrow. Just rest now."

Bayden had snuggled down so far under the blankets, his face was inaccessible. Axel pressed a kiss on top of his head. A second later, Bayden placed a tentative kiss on Axel's collarbone in return.

"Good pup." Axel grinned with relief. They'd both had enough punishment. Tomorrow it would be time to play.

* * * * *

Tomorrow.

Obviously it was Axel's choice what they did and when they did it— and Bayden had no doubt that was exactly the way things should be. But, Axel had said they would have sex tomorrow, and it was tomorrow.

By the time the pub was due to open for business that evening, Bayden was starting to really wish he'd asked Axel to specify a rough time of day.

Axel came around the bar and stood behind Bayden. He chuckled as he slid his arms around Bayden and encouraged him to lean back against him. "Impatient, pup?"

The truth. Bayden nodded. He'd been impatient first thing that morning. After an entire day on edge hoping that Axel hadn't changed his mind, he was little short of desperate. "If I've done something to make you not want to—"

"I'd tell you," Axel cut in. "Mind reading isn't part of the deal. I still want everything I've wanted since the first time you walked into this pub."

Bayden nodded.

"Tonight, after everyone's left. No distractions, no cutting things short because we have to open the pub. Just you and me." Axel dipped his head to whisper against Bayden's ear. "It's going to be so good, pup. So good."

Then, Axel was gone to open the pub's front door and welcome in the first customers of the day.

Bayden managed to hold back a whimper, but there was no way he could convince his cock to soften. He was still hard and aching when Axel locked the door after everyone at the end of the night.

Bayden stepped out from behind the bar and started to collect up the empties. He'd just put the first lot on the bar when Axel caught hold of his shoulder and spun him around.

They stared at each other in silence for a long time.

"Anything you want, sir," Bayden whispered.

"Anything at all?" He slid his fingers through Bayden's hair and took a tight grip on the strands.

Bayden nodded, tugging at Axel's grip on his hair. Axel didn't slacken his hold in the least, and Bayden felt something inside himself relax. Axel was in charge now — not just the way he always was, but in a way that meant Axel intended to control each inch of Bayden's body and every corner of his mind.

Axel smiled, as if he sensed Bayden give up every detail. He slid his hand out of Bayden's hair and back to his cheek.

Bayden kissed his hand, just as he had when Axel had sat naked on the floor next to his bound body, explaining exactly how much he'd hated watching other men screw him. Axel's smile broadened. He stepped forward, making no allowance for the fact that Bayden was already in that space. Bayden quickly yielded and stepped back.

"I want you upstairs, naked and waiting for me in the living room. Now."

Bayden raced up the stairs and took off every stitch as quickly as he could without ripping the seams. Axel was still downstairs when he was finished. Bayden absentmindedly folded his clothes and set them neatly on the chair while he waited. His hands were shaking with need. His cock curved up in front of him, painfully hard.

He'd seen human submissives kneeling with perfect poise while they waited for a command, but they were other men, submitting to humans who weren't Axel.

Axel stepped into the flat. He didn't glance in Bayden's direction—not even to check that he'd followed his orders. He went through to the bedroom, but he didn't invite Bayden to join him. Shuffling his weight from one foot to the other, Bayden remained by the door.

Axel returned with a set of cuffs and stopped under the beam on the other side of the room. "Come here. All the way to me," he specified, before Bayden had a chance to pause outside Axel's space.

Axel put the cuffs around his wrists. As Bayden watched Axel's hands move confidently at their task, he couldn't help but think back to the way Axel had bound his fists before fights.

But he wasn't going to fight this time. They were going to play. That was what humans called it. The most serious thing in the world, and they called it play. Bayden glanced up. Axel didn't look like he thought this was a game. His lips smiled, but his eyes were serious.

"Here are the rules," Axel said. "Your safe word is still the same. If you don't like what is happening, I expect you to say it."

Bayden nodded.

"And remember that you're not allowed to try to control when you come."

"I could—"

Axel put a fingertip to his lips. "It's my choice. You'll come when I want you to. That might be in five hours, it might be in five seconds."

Bayden felt the heat rush to his cheeks at the second possibility. Axel caressed the flushed skin with his knuckles, apparently pleased with that reaction. He picked up the chain linking the cuffs at Bayden's wrists and lifted it to loop it over a hook on the beam above them.

Bayden stretched up onto his toes to make it easier for Axel. The chain settled into place. Bayden tried to lower himself down, but he was too short. His weight remained forward on his toes, his body stretched out taut.

After the last four nights, part of Bayden expected Axel to step away and go to bed.

Axel did move—but only to stand at Bayden's side. "I'm not going anywhere." He put his right hand against Bayden's arse. Bayden tensed, as much in expectation as anything else, but Axel just rested the cupped palm against him and settled his left hand similarly against Bayden's stomach.

"I…"

"It feels different when you're not left on your own in the bondage, doesn't it?"

Bayden nodded.

Axel began to move his hands slowly over Bayden in a casual display of ownership. Bayden did his best not to wriggle in an effort to lean into every touch, but it was so tempting.

"You don't have to keep yourself still. That's what the cuffs are for."

Bayden glanced up at Axel.

"Whenever you're in bondage, you're always allowed to move as far as the bondage allows. It's there to tell you what the limits are—to help you."

He cupped Bayden's balls, just letting the heat from his hand soak into his skin as his other hand roamed. It was so much like the first time Axel brought him up to his flat to have sex.

Bayden closed his eyes. His hopes had been just as high that night, but his need now was so much greater.

"You've never been spanked unless it was part of a bet, have you?"

The answer Axel expected was obvious. Bayden only hesitated for a second before he shook his head.

"The truth," Axel pushed. His right hand rested motionless on Bayden's arse. Bayden knew there was no way in hell Axel would move it until he got his honest answer.

"The bets, sir... The whole point of using a wolf is so..." Damn it, there wasn't a way to say it without insulting him. "Spanking wasn't really something they..."

"If a man wants a wolf specifically because wolves heal quickly, he's more likely to whip him than spank him?" Axel translated.

Bayden nodded.

"Because a spanking isn't hard core," Axel went on. "It would be a waste of a convenient punch bag."

"I..."

Axel stroked Bayden's abs. "Hush. There's nothing wrong with telling me what some idiots think."

Bayden swallowed.

"It's never been your ability to heal or your willingness to take a beating that's interested me."

Bayden parted his lips, but he couldn't bring himself to ask what it was about him that did interest Axel.

Axel finally moved the hand resting on Bayden's arse. He squeezed the muscle and rubbed his palm in circles against it. The first tap was so light it was hard to see it as anything other than an insult.

Bayden pulled away as far as his bondage allowed.

"This isn't a punishment. It's not a test to see how much you can tolerate. I want to know if you can enjoy it," Axel whispered in his ear. "We're going to start slowly and build it up."

Bayden licked his lips.

"If you want to stop, you can say so at any time. But you're not allowed to tell me that I don't need to take my time with you. I've been looking forward to this for months, pup. I'll be damned if I'm going to rush it."

Bayden remained silent.

Axel brought his hand down on Bayden's arse again, just a fraction more firmly. "Concentrate," he whispered, soft as a secret. "Think about exactly how it feels. Don't just let sensations happen, go and find them, meet them halfway. Let me in, pup."

Bayden frowned as he tried to do what Axel said.

Another tap, again just a tiny bit harder. There was no pain. There was barely any sensation at all. Axel was right, Bayden had to work at it, had to try to amplify it all and make the most of what little Axel was willing to offer him.

Axel spanked him again.

Bayden let out a frustrated moan. There was so bloody little to react to.

"Forget about everything you've done before. This isn't a bet. It's not a punishment — it means any kind punishment is over. I'll only ever spank you because I'm pleased with you, not because you've done something wrong. There's no winner here, no loser. There's just you and me."

Another spank. A tiny flare of heat spread through Bayden's left buttock. He'd never been so damn grateful to feel anything. He closed his eyes, concentrating, unwilling to waste it.

Again. Bayden chased after the fleeting moment of heat Axel's palm offered him.

Axel brought his hand down on Bayden's right buttock this time. A rhythm called to Bayden as Axel moved his hand from one side of his arse to the other, offering him those infuriatingly gentle taps. Bayden rocked with them, pushing back into each contact as if he could somehow convince Axel to turn the teasing taps into real spanks that way.

Heat gradually built in Bayden's buttocks. Relief rolled through him, and with it came a curious kind of pleasure. The sensations were from Axel—so they were by their very definition a good thing. And Axel wouldn't offer them to him if Bayden hadn't pleased him in some way. Axel wouldn't go out of his way to send twisty shots of sensation through his veins unless he thought Bayden had earned them.

Bayden rocked his hips. It wasn't like pushing back against a man's cock when he bottomed, but the action called to the same part of him. It was all about acceptance, about acknowledging that he was allowing another man to do things he would only be willing to accept if he considered that man to be entirely dominant over him.

"That's right. That's good."

Pleasure peaked and eddied inside him as Axel's voice seeped into his mind. Bayden tugged at the cuffs above his head, rising further onto his toes as the heat in his buttocks spread through his body, making his breaths turn ragged and his pulse race.

He pushed back against the next spank, but Axel's hand wasn't there.

Bayden whimpered. He blinked open his eyes. He shook his head, knowing that it couldn't happen, not again.

"You stopped." Bayden looked over his shoulder. "Sir, you…you stopped!"

"Hush. Not for long." A moment later, Axel slid slicked fingers between Bayden's buttocks.

Bayden peered up at him. Axel's fingertips rested against his hole. When Axel stopped doing something, he didn't always go back to finish what he started. Twice before, he'd prepared Bayden only to change his mind. Bayden didn't know if he would survive one more unfinished game.

Their eyes met. Axel's fingers remained perfectly still.

Not pulling away ceased to be enough. If Bayden wanted this, he knew he'd have to make it clear. If he was willing to risk being prepared then abandoned for a third time, he had to ask for it.

He shuffled his legs further apart, making his arse more accessible, even if it meant only having tentative contact between his toes and the carpet.

Axel pushed two digits deep inside him and immediately found his prostate. Bayden moaned and rocked his hips more desperately.

"Does that feel good, pup?"

Bayden nodded.

"Do you like the way my fingers feel inside you?"

"Yes, sir." He'd like Axel's cock even more.

"Do they feel hot?"

Bayden frowned. Yes. They were hotter than they should be. It wasn't just Bayden's arse that had been heated by the spanking. Axel's hand had come down against his buttocks just as often as his arse had felt its impact. Humans weren't as resilient as wolves. He looked up. "You're hurt?"

Axel stroked his left hand up and down Bayden's chest as he worked his fingers deeper inside him. "No. It feels good."

Bayden nodded, all his worries relieved. "Good," he repeated. The spanking did feel good. It was nothing like a whipping. It was hot and tingly and it made him want to squirm and push his arse back against Axel's crotch as Axel screwed him hard and frantic. Unable to do all that, Bayden just did his damnedest to ride Axel's touch.

When Axel took his hand back, Bayden held his breath. If Axel walked away now…

His breath rushed out as a yelp as Axel struck his arse with his open hand. It was harder than the previous spanks. It was all Bayden could do not to howl in pleasure as he jerked against his bondage.

The spanks came faster and harder. There was no time to process them, but Bayden still followed Axel's order to look for every scrap he could find. He couldn't switch that instinct off. Sensations threatened to overwhelm him, and still he scrambled for every crumb.

He gasped for breath, his mind reeling with unfamiliar pleasure.

As suddenly as he'd resumed the spanking, Axel stopped it again. Bayden tried to turn to him, but Axel didn't give him the chance to move. Axel reached up and unhooked the cuffs from the beam.

The next moment, Bayden's feet left the floor. Axel tossed him over his shoulder as if he weighed nothing. He strode into the bedroom and threw Bayden unceremoniously onto his bed. The cuffs were still fastened together. They made Bayden clumsy, but he managed to roll over and get on to his hands and knees.

He heard Axel undoing his fly, and he spread his knees further apart on the bedspread in an entirely instinctive offering.

Words. Axel liked words. Bayden found one. "Please..."

It was a magical word. Axel immediately caught hold of his hips and pushed into him. He didn't stop until he was buried in Bayden's arse to the hilt. Lowering his head toward the mattress, Bayden supported his weight on trembling forearms.

It was dangerously close to the position he'd been bound in during the second night of his penance. Bayden closed his eyes. Tonight was different. He wasn't discarded on the other side of the room unworthy of being screwed. He was in Axel's bed. Axel's grip was tight and their bodies joined together as thoroughly as any could be.

Axel held Bayden still as he swayed away, only to push into him again with deep, purposeful thrusts.

Each time their bodies met, new pleasure burst through Bayden. It felt like a lifetime since he'd last been allowed to come. He'd been hard off and on all day, wondering what

Axel had planned for him. His arse was sensitive after the spanking.

He wanted it to go on forever. He wanted to still be hard and desperate to come when it was all over, so Axel would know it had never been about Bayden looking for pleasure for himself. But what he wanted wasn't as important as obeying Axel's orders.

Bayden relaxed, holding nothing back from his alpha. A few thrusts were all it took before Bayden tossed back his head and howled as his orgasm tore through him. Pleasure ricocheted within him, seeming to reach every square inch of his skin before reverberating back deep inside his body. He clawed at the blankets in an effort to keep hold of the world. He gasped for breath. And the whole time, Axel's rhythm didn't even falter.

He ploughed into Bayden, almost hard enough to push him off balance on every thrust. Completely spent, there would be no more peaks of pleasure for Bayden that night. It was all about Axel now. Bayden tightened and relaxed his internal muscles, working his hole around Axel's shaft as he pushed back into each thrust, trying to give Axel the best ride ever.

Axel had to come. He had to. Bayden couldn't fail him again. The idea that Axel might not get off on screwing him, that he'd end up finding his pleasure in his own hand again, made Bayden whimper.

A harder, rougher thrust and Axel finally came. There was no howl to mark the occasion, but Bayden moaned with a dizzying combination of relief and pleasure.

A few moments later, Axel stilled, then moved away to collapse on the bed alongside him. It took everything Bayden had in him not to instantly follow Axel across the mattress and try to wrap himself around him.

Gingerly lowering himself down to rest flat on the bed instead, Bayden buried his face in the blankets. His wrists were still cuffed together. His buttocks throbbed after the spanking. His cum had created a wet patch on the sheet beneath him.

It felt like someone had taken a sledge hammer to his mind. His psyche had shattered and lay in sparkling, broken pieces across the bedspread. Against all logic, he didn't find that possibility in any way worrying.

He lay there, breathing deeply, simply enjoying the scent of their combined pleasure until Axel reached over and undid the cuffs. He nudged Bayden to take the bathroom first.

Bayden quickly cleaned himself up and completed his usual nightly routine. There was a mirror above the sink in the bathroom. Bayden turned his back to it and rose up on his toes, trying to see what sort of marks Axel's spanking had left on his skin. It was impossible. All he could do was peer awkwardly over his own shoulder and catch glimpses of the top inch or two of reddened skin.

"Furthest wardrobe door on the left," Axel said, as Bayden stepped back into the bedroom.

Just because an order was incomplete and made no sense, that was no reason to disobey it. Bayden opened the specified wardrobe door. On the inside was a full length mirror.

He glanced toward Axel.

"You don't want to see your spanking in a reflection?" Axel teased. "Go ahead."

Bayden turned his back to the mirror and peered over his shoulder into the glass. He'd imagined that there would hardly be a mark on him after how gentle Axel had been but his arse flushed bright red — the colour concentrated more intensely toward the centre of each buttock and gradually fading out as it reached the edge.

A movement warned Bayden that Axel was approaching, but he couldn't tear his gaze away from the mirror. Axel stopped toe to toe with him. Bayden watched in the reflection as Axel reached around him and palmed his arse. A gasp echoed through the room.

"Sore?" Axel asked.

"Good," Bayden corrected. It felt fantastic. It looked amazing too. Axel's hand prints on him, marking him out as belonging to Axel, just as if he was Axel's mate.

Bayden felt the cheeks on his face turn a similar colour to his buttocks. He stopped looking over his shoulder and stared at Axel's collar bone instead.

"Like or dislike?" Axel asked, softly.

"Like, sir," Bayden whispered. He liked it so much.

Axel palmed Bayden's arse more firmly. Bayden glanced up, but Axel was still studying the reflection.

"Do you, sir?" Bayden blurted out.

"Do I what?"

Bayden hesitated.

"Did I like spanking you?" Axel guessed. "Yes, pup. I loved it, almost as much as I loved screwing you afterwards. And I love the way your arse looks."

Bayden smiled. There was no doubting Axel's honesty.

When Axel decided that the reflection had been admired for long enough, he took his turn in the bathroom.

A glance toward the bed reminded Bayden that he couldn't spend all his time peering in the mirror. He worked quickly and had almost finished changing the bed before Axel came in.

Axel raised an eyebrow when he saw what he was doing.

"I…When I came, I…" Bayden hesitated. "Should I have asked for permission, sir?"

Axel shook his head. "No, it's fine." He seemed amused. That wasn't a very logical reaction, but it was better than him being angry. Bayden didn't question it.

As soon as the bed was re-made, Axel arranged them so Bayden spooned in front of him, his heated arse aligned with Axel's crotch and the blankets pulled up high to keep out any drafts.

After the previous nights on the floor, it was closer to heaven than ever.

"Too sore?" Axel asked, as he encouraged Bayden to press his arse back against him more firmly.

Bayden shook his head rapidly. "I like it, sir."

There was power in those words. They weren't a mistake. They didn't mean a human could use that knowledge against him at the first opportunity. Not with every human. Not with this human.

Chapter Twenty Five

"You really do heal quickly, don't you?"

Bayden looked over his shoulder. Axel stood in the bedroom doorway, studying Bayden's backside.

Bayden had already checked in the wardrobe mirror. There wasn't a single mark left after the previous night's spanking. "Are you disappointed, sir?"

Axel shook his head. "I have no problem applying new coats as often as necessary."

As Bayden walked past him into the living room, Axel swatted him on the arse—not hard, but maybe just enough for a tiny touch of colour to spread across his skin.

When Bayden looked up, Axel winked at him.

If he wanted the colour to stay there, he'd have to spank him a lot. At least once every day. The idea of Axel's hand falling against his arse that often went straight to Bayden's cock. Naked since he got up, he had no way of hiding how enthusiastic he was about that possibility.

"So you really did like it?"

Axel stepped up behind him. Bayden wasn't the only one who was hard. As Axel reached around and stroked Bayden's cock, he rocked his hips and rubbed his own erection against Bayden's arse.

The world faded away as Bayden closed his eyes and pushed himself helplessly against Axel's palm. Axel tightened his grip around Bayden's shaft. He stroked him faster, using Bayden's pre-cum to slick his touch.

Bayden leaned back against Axel, unable to do anything except accept whatever Axel chose to do with him and—

Axel's hand disappeared. "Later," Axel whispered in his ear. He stepped away, leaving Bayden blinking in confusion.

It was Axel's choice. Just because he'd chosen to let him come quite consistently so far, Bayden knew that there was no guarantee it would always be that way.

After a penance, it was time to play. Axel had meant it—he really was in the mood to play—and to tease. By the time they were due to open the pub that evening, Bayden had lost count of how many times he'd been taken to the edge, only for Axel to stop at the last moment.

Straightening up from where he'd been crouched down, checking over his bike, Bayden turned toward the pub only to realise Axel was coming from the other direction.

Neither of them said anything as Bayden locked his bike away, but he could feel Axel's gaze following his every move. He hadn't even had time to put his keys in his pocket before Axel kissed him.

Bayden parted his lips, welcoming him in, easily following Axel's lead.

Axel pushed him back against the wall alongside the lock-up's roller door and pinned him there. Bayden made a pleased little noise in the back of his throat as Axel rubbed their bodies together. Catching Bayden's wrists, Axel trapped them against the rough concrete.

Bayden bucked against him, meeting every movement and—

A wolf whistle cut through the air.

Axel broke the kiss and looked around. Bayden was just tall enough to peer over Axel's shoulder. Hale, Griz and Drac all stood in the yard. They'd obviously left their bikes around front. Bayden had been too distracted to hear them arrive.

"Don't stop on our account, we're enjoying the show," Griz called out.

Axel sighed and pulled away.

"What, is he suddenly shy?" Hale demanded.

Axel tossed the keys to the pub's front door to him. "Bugger off, the lot of you."

Bayden waited until they were all out of sight. "I'm not shy, sir."

Axel smiled. "I know."

If that wasn't the reason, then... Bayden looked down. "Pup?"

"I wouldn't embarrass you in front of them, sir."

Axel raised an eyebrow.

"You can treat me the same as a human sub, whoever's there. I wouldn't show you up, sir. I won't do anything lupine in front of them."

Axel studied him seriously. "You're new to this—just like every human is at some point. You're still learning. You don't really know what your kinks are yet, and you sure as hell don't know what your limits are."

Bayden shook his head. "I wouldn't disobey any order you gave me, sir. I wouldn't say my safe word."

Axel shook his head. He stroked Bayden's cheek. "Still learning," he repeated. His voice was off, it sounded like he was reminding himself of that, not Bayden. Suddenly, he smiled. "Anyway, I have plans for us later. Ones that don't involve an audience. I don't want any distractions."

Bayden nodded his acceptance of Axel's decision.

Axel slid his arm around Bayden's shoulders as he led the way back into the pub. "You've said that you'd like to pretend that we're the same species lots of times, haven't you?"

Bayden nodded cautiously, hardly daring to hope.

"Stick around, pup. You're going to get the chance to do exactly that."

* * * * *

Bayden had barely returned from locking the pub's front door at the end of the night when he realised the atmosphere had already changed. 'Later' had finally arrived. Axel was ready to play.

"Do you remember what your safe word is?"

"Yes, sir."

"You're not *allowed* to say it if you need to. You're *required* to."

That was fine. It's what Axel would tell a human too. "Yes, sir."

"We're going to play. We're going to go back to the first night you walked in here. But we're going to pretend that one thing was different. We're going to imagine that we're the same species."

Bayden nodded. His palms were slick with nervous sweat. He wiped them on his jeans. "You'll tell me if I do the wrong thing, sir, something that isn't entirely human?"

"No."

Bayden pushed his hands into his pockets. "I don't want to just be *close enough*. I want to get it exactly right for you, sir."

"We're not going to pretend you're human. We're going to pretend that I'm not."

Bayden frowned. "Sir?"

"We're going to pretend that, the first night you came in here, it wasn't a human working behind the bar. It was a shifter."

Bayden swallowed.

"You're going to pretend that I'm a wolf." Axel came out from behind the bar.

Bayden remained frozen in place as the gap between them gradually disappeared.

"You're going to act exactly as you would if you were with another shifter, apart from one thing. If you want to do anything that a wolf would understand as meaning no—that you want to stop—"

Bayden shook his head, denying the possibility.

"Then you do that," Axel went on. "But you say it, too. No, or stop, or your safe word — whichever you prefer."

He stood directly in front of Bayden, just outside his space. Bayden stared up at him. Axel wouldn't step forward unless he gave him his word. If Bayden didn't want to play that particular game, he had an easy out.

But if Axel was a wolf, if everything could really be that simple... If there was any chance of that, Bayden couldn't say no. He nodded.

Axel raised an eyebrow, obviously far from impressed.

"Yes, sir. I understand the rules." He took a deep breath. "I'll obey them."

"And, tell me, Bayden. What would a more dominant wolf do with you?"

"Whatever he wanted, sir," Bayden whispered.

Axel stepped forward.

If Axel was a wolf, if Bayden wasn't trying to control his own reactions and make them what a human expected, what a human would understand, then...

Bayden dropped his gaze and tilted his head down, just the way he would if he wanted to acknowledge the dominance of another wolf.

Axel moved closer. Bayden held his ground as well as he could, but Axel pushed up against him, forcing him out of the space he occupied. Bayden was about to take another step back when Axel slid his hand behind his head and held him in place.

There was no attempt to coax. Axel wanted Bayden's head to stay where it was, and that was what was going to happen. The kiss was harsh, almost ruthless.

Bayden parted his lips, welcoming Axel in, offering him everything he had. Axel wasn't holding anything back. Bayden was free to act like a wolf, but somehow, that had given Axel permission to act like himself.

Still pushing forward, Axel forced Bayden back. Bayden had to grab Axel's shoulders just to keep himself on his feet.

A wolf wouldn't have minded — Axel didn't seem to mind either. Even when Bayden's back hit the wall, and he had no excuse for keeping his hands there, he held onto Axel's shoulders.

Axel nipped at Bayden's bottom lip. His tongue thrust against Bayden's, warring with him, making it clear that there would be no quarter given, no peace treaty offered.

Bayden whimpered, making his attempts to kiss Axel back gentler, more overtly submissive as he felt Axel step up and take the alpha's role as his right.

Axel pulled back. He frowned.

He thought Bayden was saying no. Panic shot through Bayden at the idea of so much perfection being taken away.

"Yes." He tugged at Axel's T-shirt, begging him to understand. "Yes." He said again, as if saying it often enough might drown out the no that Axel had imagined hearing. "Yes."

Axel's frown cleared. Then, against all logic, he pulled away even further.

Bayden tried to keep hold of Axel's T-shirt. Axel ignored that as he reached for the base of Bayden's vest and pulled it up. No words, no orders, but Axel wasn't stopping, he was getting Bayden naked.

Axel didn't ask for Bayden's assistance, or for his opinion. He was completely focused on making things happen just as he wanted them to. Bayden was mesmerised. He'd barely lowered his arms before Axel roughly twisted him around and shoved him up against the wall.

Bayden braced himself against the paintwork.

Axel reached around Bayden and undid his fly. His touch was impatient. Bayden half expected the denim to tear, but his jeans were still in one piece when Axel pushed them down.

The denim bunched up around his legs. Bayden tried to crouch down and take off his boots, but Axel pushed him up against the wall again.

Scrabbling at the paint, Bayden tried to hold himself still as Axel's hands roamed possessively over his body. Available — that was all he needed to be — available and willing. There was no need to communicate anything beyond that.

Axel wrapped his hand around Bayden's erection and jacked him roughly. Caught between human rules and lupine experience, Bayden wasn't sure if he should hold back or not. He glanced over his shoulder. Axel liked it when he didn't hold back. If Bayden knew what a more dominant wolf preferred, there wasn't a question what he'd do.

He did his damnedest to relax his body and simply let Axel make the choice for him.

Axel made a noise in the back of his throat that sounded like pure triumph. He released Bayden's cock, his query apparently answered. Bayden glanced back in time to see Axel take a bottle of lube from his pocket.

Bayden tried to shuffle his feet apart. His bunched up jeans made it impossible. All he could do to show willingness was stress his submission.

Axel slicked his fingers and slid them between Bayden's buttocks. His touch wasn't painful, but there was far less concern. Axel was starting to trust him not to mind a rougher touch — to enjoy a rougher touch.

Reaching past Bayden, Axel put his hand on the wall. His palm covered Bayden's fingers where he braced himself. Axel's arm was right there, in easy touching distance.

If Axel didn't like what Bayden did when he responded like a wolf, then he would… Bayden hesitated. If that happened then, Axel would probably, finally throw his weight behind the idea of Bayden learning to act more like a human.

Either way, Axel would end up getting a submissive who behaved the way he wanted.

Bayden let his instincts take over. He whimpered, nuzzled against Axel outstretched arm and silently prayed.

Axel's fingers stilled inside him, as if he was thinking. He didn't say anything but, when he moved again, he thrust his fingers deeper. Bayden whimpered his approval. He couldn't stop himself rocking his hips and pushing back against Axel's fingers, but he concentrated on nuzzling at Axel's arm and shoulder—at whatever bit of him he could reach.

He shuddered as Axel's fingers rubbed against his prostate, taking him to the edge of his orgasm once more. Without warning, Axel took his fingers away.

Bayden whimpered. He moved his weight from foot to foot, damn near wiggling his arse in invitation.

The sound of a fly being drawn down made Bayden moan with impatience. It was a short zip. It couldn't take that long to undo it, but years passed before Axel pressed the tip of his cock against Bayden's hole.

Bayden froze. That was fine and natural and just as it should be. But, Axel froze too, and that was so many kinds of wrong.

Bayden whimpered, a high keening noise.

Axel remained perfectly still.

Bayden looked over his shoulder, desperate to work out what was wrong. "Yes," he offered, just in case there was any doubt about that. He met Axel's gaze but couldn't hold it. He rocked his hips, frantic to work himself back onto Axel's cock but not quite able to take the initiative.

Axel grinned. He didn't just seem to know how much Bayden needed him to screw him, he obviously thrived on knowing it.

Bayden dropped his head forward. He wanted to beg, but he knew he wouldn't have begged a wolf—not with words. Bayden pressed a kiss against Axel's arm, not telling

Axel that he wanted him to screw him, but telling him that, even if he didn't screw him before he sent him mad with frustration, he'd still love him anyway.

Bayden hesitated mid-lick. He'd love him anyway…

As if that was the realisation Axel had been waiting for. He pushed forward, sheathing himself in one strong motion. Bayden didn't have room in his mind for thoughts then.

Axel's rhythm was fast, his thrusts almost harsh enough to knock Bayden off his feet. He gasped. His hands slid against the wall as he sought to steady himself while still rocking back and meeting every movement of Axel's hips.

Axel held Bayden's sides, gripping him hard enough to make his skin bruise and his soul sing out with pleasure. Bayden wasn't sure if Axel wanted him to come or not. It felt more like Axel didn't care any more, as if Axel was in the moment and the only orgasm he cared about was his own.

Bayden moaned his pleasure as he gave himself up to a world in which he had no need to think. His instincts were more than enough until Axel suddenly jerked away from him.

His cock slid out of Bayden's arse. His hands deserted Bayden's hips. Before Bayden could look over his shoulder, Axel spun him around.

Off balance with his jeans trapped around his ankles, all Bayden could do was slump back against the wall and relish every moment as Axel kissed him hard enough to risk bruising his lips. Bayden clung to Axel's shoulders and returned each harsh kiss with a tender one of his own.

Without warning, Axel pulled back again, but he didn't leave Bayden behind. Axel tugged Bayden forward. The jeans hobbled him. Axel only seemed to realise that when Bayden stumbled.

Lifting him off his feet like a human bride on her honeymoon, Axel carried him the few paces to the nearest table. Flat on his back on the table, Bayden peered up at Axel, completely enthralled, but he still wasn't capable of parting his legs when Axel tried to step between them.

* * * * *

Axel cursed when he saw Bayden's jeans. He didn't have the patience to undo boot laces.

Bayden let out a frustrated little whimper and peered up at Axel as if he fully expected Axel to be able to fix the problem with a look. Well, maybe not with a look, but...

"Stay."

Axel reached over the bar and grabbed one of the knives from the block there.

It took him less than three seconds to cut through the centre of Bayden's jeans, separating the legs from one another.

Bayden spread his legs and tugged at Axel's wrists, pulling him forward.

Axel didn't need to be coaxed. Throwing aside the knife, he caught hold of Bayden's hips once more, and held him in place as he slid deep inside him. Bayden stared up at him, every emotion and reaction flashing across his face. There were no lies now, nothing hidden.

Bayden tilted his head, bearing his neck.

Axel leant forward and sucked at the skin directly over his jugular to create a deeply coloured love bite.

Bayden jerked as he came, no warning, no holding back, and completely perfect. He writhed against the table as his cum spilled over his stomach. His howl echoed around the room as Axel straightened up.

Bayden settled his hands over Axel's as he gradually came back to himself, not holding his hands in place, but petting them and welcoming the tight grip Axel had on him. He slid his palms up Axel's arms, braver and more tactile than he'd ever been when he was focused on Axel being a human.

When Axel moved his right hand up to Bayden's shoulder, Bayden's fingers traced higher up his arm. Bayden's touch became even lighter, but there was nothing tentative about it. There was more genuine confidence in it than Axel had seen him show before.

Bayden slid his hand over Axel's chest, caressing him through his T-shirt. He paused with his palm over Axel's heart and kept his hand there as Axel thrust into him harder and faster than ever. Their eyes locked. It was obvious that Bayden didn't find it easy to meet his gaze, but he worked at it. His fingers trembled, his breath caught in his throat, but he didn't look away until Axel came deep inside him.

Pleasure hit Axel like a truck. He had no idea what a wolf's orgasm felt like, but pretending to be a shifter had put his own human senses on high alert. Bliss burned through his veins. The room swirled with vivid colours as he fell still and fought to catch his breath.

A few moments passed, and Axel moved his hand from Bayden's shoulder up to his cheek. The kiss Bayden pressed against his thumb was feather light. Sliding his hand behind Bayden's neck, Axel pulled him up to be kissed properly.

The urgency was gone; Axel allowed this kiss to be gentle. Bayden hesitated. Axel instinctively tightened his grip on his hair, reminding his pup that he was being gentle because he chose to be, not because he'd lost the ability to be strong.

Axel hadn't realised it was possible for a wolf to purr in approval, but there was no other word for the sound Bayden made.

Finally, Axel broke the chain of tender kisses. "Okay, pup?"

Bayden nodded. His attention settled somewhere around the centre of Axel's chest, until Axel made him look up.

His expression was off. Axel stroked his fingers along Bayden's jaw as he tried to work it out.

Bayden dropped his hands to the table on either side of him. He no longer reached out to Axel. The perfect trust had gone, but Axel knew it was possible now. In time, he had no doubt he could make it permanent.

Stepping back, he helped Bayden off the table. He smiled to himself as he took in the state of Bayden's jeans. He'd ripped a few seams in his time, but that was the first time he'd resorted to completely obliterating someone else's clothes.

"I'll get you a new pair of jeans," he promised, just in case Bayden didn't realise it should go without saying.

Bayden shook his head. "It's fine, sir. I can —"

"I'm not saying I don't think you're capable of buying your own clothes. But, if I wreck something, I replace it."

Bayden glanced up at him. He nodded, although he still seemed far more bothered by the idea of Axel buying him a new pair of jeans than Axel cutting a pair off him.

"I...I should clean up." Bayden pushed his hand through his hair and blinked at the room as if he'd never seen it before.

Axel didn't know if wolves experienced sub space, but Bayden seemed more than a little out of it. The separated legs of his jeans were around his knees. Bayden tried to pull them up, but there was no way they'd stay in position. He frowned at them, apparently unable to work out a solution that would leave his hands free.

"Don't throw them away," Axel ordered.

Bayden blinked at him. Axel settled his hands on Bayden's hips, holding the denim up and considering the possibilities. "A little bit of trimming, add a belt, and they'll make an interesting alternative to chaps."

When Axel looked up, Bayden was studying him seriously.

"Was pretending we're the same species as hot as you'd thought it would be?"

Bayden nodded.

"What aren't you telling me, pup?"

Bayden shrugged. He made no effort to reach out to Axel the way he had during the scene. It was as if he'd been thrown back into a world where he didn't know the rules. A slight colour stained his cheeks. He looked unexpectedly innocent.

Axel tugged him forward and pressed a kiss to his temple. "Leave the cleaning up until tomorrow. The only place you need to be right now is in my bed."

Chapter Twenty Six

Axel smiled when he spotted Bayden at the sink behind the bar washing something or other. Lately, he found himself smiling at Bayden almost as often as he found Bayden cleaning something.

"Okay, pup?"

Bayden glanced briefly over his shoulder as Axel joined him and leaned against the counter next to him. Bayden took a knife out of the hot soapy water and carefully dried it. His attention was all on his task, he didn't seem to have any to spare for his dom.

"Bayden?"

"It had been on the floor, sir."

Axel's cock hardened at the memory of tossing it aside in his haste. A glance around the room showed that Bayden had already cleared away any other evidence of the scene they'd enjoyed the previous night.

Axel slid his arm around Bayden and encouraged him to lean against him, but Bayden remained tense.

"You said before that it was okay for me to go out, sir."

"I said it was okay for you to ask—but that you need permission before you can go anywhere," Axel corrected.

"And that permission is a formality if I want to go to see my family, sir." His voice was off.

Axel encouraged him to turn around within his embrace.

"My mother called. It's been a while since I…" He glanced up at Axel. His expression was wary, but it was hard to tell if that was because he wasn't sure his dom would be pleased with him for wanting to go out, or if his mother had made it clear on the phone that she wasn't pleased with him for not dropping by more often just because he had a new boyfriend.

"She's right," Axel said. "It has been a while. You should go to see her today."

Bayden glanced toward the store room where he usually started his morning duties. "I haven't…"

Axel shook his head. "Go."

Bayden shuffled his boots.

"That was an order, pup."

A few minutes later, Bayden had retrieved his jacket from the flat and was heading out the door. He didn't seem enthusiastic about his venture. He obviously expected to receive a lecture when he got to his mother's place.

Axel chuckled as he watched him go, already planning a few fun activities to cheer him up when he got back. Bayden's visits home rarely lasted over an hour or two. They'd have plenty of time to play before the pub opened. Maybe it was time to explore one of the back rooms with him. Bayden would look stunning bound naked to the spanking bench.

It was one of the Saturdays when the back rooms would be open later in the night. Watching over the novices would be a lot more erotic if he had a few mental images of Bayden to superimpose on their scenes. The idea of Bayden working his shift in the pub with a spanking hidden under his jeans had Axel hardening even further.

Six hours later, as Axel opened the pub alone, his amusement with the situation was non-existent. He strode across the car park in front of the pub and looked along the road toward the city. Forget any plans involving a back room. Bayden was cutting it fine for his shift.

As he walked back into the pub, the sound of a motorcycle caught Axel's attention. Drac pulled into the car park and rolled to a stop. Axel nodded to him. How's business at the tattoo parlour? Working on any interesting designs?

Axel went through small talk on autopilot. For once, tattoos held no interest for him.

As he walked back inside, Axel checked his phone. No voice messages. No texts. He tapped his phone against the bar and considered his options. A glance at the clock and he saw the hands tick to the hour. Bayden was officially late.

Axel rattled off a quick text to him and pushed his phone into his pocket.

Drac looked around as he pulled up a stool at the bar. "Where's the puppy?"

"He went to visit his mother. He should be back any time."

A few minutes later, the door swung open. Griz stepped in. It was a couple of hours before he'd be needed to man the door. Apparently, Bayden was the only one who couldn't keep track of time today.

Axel ground his teeth together.

"Hoping to see someone else?"

Axel put Griz's drink in front of him and marked it down on his tab.

Griz looked around. He laughed as he put together the pieces. "That's what comes from letting the boy wander around without a collar. Never know what kind of trouble he'll get himself into."

Axel said nothing.

Griz stopped laughing. "Damn, Axe. The boy can look after himself."

Yes. Unless he got pulled over by a cop who didn't like wolves, or crashed his bike, or... Axel bit back a sigh and checked his phone again.

"Where's Bayden?"

There was part of Axel that was pleased to realise just how accepted Bayden was, how damn near every one of the Dragons considered him a permanent feature. Most of him was too pissed off to give a toss about anything other than finding out where the hell Bayden was. "He's running late," Axel snapped.

Hale laughed. "I'm working tomorrow so I was only going to stay for a quick drink, but I might stick around, just to see the puppy get his comeuppance. Should be a good show."

"Yeah," Griz said. "What's the plan?"

"That depends on his excuse," Axel said.

Hale gave a disbelieving huff. "You're getting soft in your old age."

"I vote for a spanking," Griz said. "One spank for each minute he's late."

Everyone automatically checked his own watch, then laughed as they realised every one of them was doing the same maths. Bayden was coming up to an hour late. A few of the more sympathetic doms winced in sympathy. Evan's eyebrows disappeared behind his fringe.

Axel forced himself to relax. They were right. Any minute, Bayden would rush in, stumbling over his words in his rush to explain. And, unless there was some very believable reason for him being unable to get back to the pub, or contact him by any possible means, then yes — Axel's only real concern would be deciding on the most suitable punishment.

A spanking wouldn't work as a punishment for Bayden. He'd taken too many whippings for cash. Any dom stupid enough to try to punish him that way would just blur the line between a good dom and a punter. A spanking would always be praise between them — a sign that a punishment or a penance was over and it was time to play.

"I think, whatever the punishment is, it should be public," Drac said.

"Can't get a sub of your own, so you want to perv on mine?" Axel shot back, but his heart wasn't in it.

His phone rang.

Axel pulled it out of his pocket. *Bayden.*

Axel remembered how to breathe. He opened the call. "Pup?"

"Sir?" His voice was off—not just because it was mangled by a bad line.

Axel's relief faltered. He hushed the guys at the bar and put his hand over his free ear. Something about his tone got through to them, they fell silent with uncharacteristic obedience. "What's wrong?" Axel demanded.

"I…" Bayden cleared his throat. "I'm sorry I've missed my shift, sir."

Axel's heart rate doubled. "What's wrong?" he repeated.

"Nothing. I'm fine."

"Bollocks," Axel snapped. "Are you hurt?"

"No. I…I'm fine." It would have been more believable if his voice hadn't come so close to cracking.

"Where are you?"

"I'm…He…" Bayden cleared his throat.

Axel's grip on his phone turned white knuckled. "Tell me where you are. I'll come and get you."

"I need permission to be away from the pub overnight, sir."

Axel shook his head. "That's not happening. Tell me where you are. Who are you with?"

"I…He…" His voice cracked.

"What he? Bayden?"

"I'm sorry, sir. I'll explain in…in a few days." The words were barely rushed out before he hung up.

"Bayden?" All Axel heard was the dialling tone. "Bayden?"

He quickly hung up his end of the call and auto-dialled Bayden's number. It went straight to voicemail. Axel cursed. "Bayden. Call me back. That's an order, not a suggestion, pup. Call me back."

When Axel looked up, everyone was staring at him.

"What's going on?" Hale asked.

Axel frowned at his phone. "I don't know." All he knew was that there was a 'he' involved, and that he'd never heard Bayden sound that shaken—not even that night he'd arrived cut up and half choked to death.

"What did he say?" Griz asked.

Axel rubbed his temple. His mind was a complete blank. "He said he's fine."

"Where is he?" someone else asked.

"I don't know."

"You said he went to see his family, right?" Griz prompted.

"That was hours ago." Axel pushed his hand through his hair. "He could be anywhere by now."

"Call them."

"I don't know their number. I don't know where they live." Axel stared across the bar at his friends. He had no idea how to find Bayden's family. He didn't even know what their first names were.

"What exactly did he say?" Hale demanded.

"He said he's fine, but he was lying. He wants a few days before he comes back."

The other guys exchanged glances.

"Have you done anything that would make him bolt?" Griz asked.

Axel's gaze went to the corner where they'd played the night before. It had been different. It had pushed Bayden. It had shaken him a bit and demanded he do something he didn't find easy, but he'd been okay about it.

The scene hadn't been rough. Bayden wasn't hurt. His jeans hadn't survived, but...

Axel looked at the knife in the block. He knew of at least one scene where seeing a man pulling a knife hadn't gone well for Bayden.

No. Axel took a deep breath. He'd have known if Bayden was that freaked out. The only thing that had been difficult for him had been giving in to his instincts as a wolf.

And today, he'd gone home to wolves who'd always told him not to trust humans.

At least, he'd probably gone home to wolves. He hadn't said he was going home until Axel reminded him that he needed permission to go anywhere apart from that.

"Axe?" Griz prompted.

Axel opened his eyes. He met Griz's gaze. "We did a scene. It pushed him."

"How did he sound on the phone?"

Hurt. Scared. Guilty. Axel took a deep breath.

"Do you know where he lives?" Hale asked.

Axel didn't answer. He picked up his keys and headed out. Hale was hot on his heels. Axel went toward his bike but checked the instinct. Bayden hadn't sounded in any condition to ride. Axel changed course and got in his car.

Hale jumped in the passenger seat without waiting for an invitation. "Griz and Drac are going to stick around here. They'll call us if he turns up."

Axel drove in silence as Hale spoke into his mobile. When he pushed his phone into his pocket a few minutes later, he turned to Axel. "No accidents that match his description, or his bike's description. No arrests involving a wolf all day."

"Nothing official," Axel muttered.

"Granger's on duty, but I checked in with a cop I know I can trust. Granger hasn't been out of the station all day. He hasn't had a chance to make trouble for anyone."

Hale fidgeted with his phone some more. "It would be easier to try to track his family down if wolves had proper surnames."

"They had pack names."

"What?"

Axel's grip on the steering wheel turned white knuckled. "Wolves had pack names, but it's against the law for them to use those names. It's against the law for them to have any surname other than Wolf. It was in that book you gave me. It's one of the laws Kincade is trying to get overturned."

Axel pulled up outside Bayden's place and led the way inside.

They were barely two steps into the hallway when the door to the landlord's room jerked open.

Axel went straight to Bayden's room. He knocked on the door. He managed to keep the first knock polite, the second one not so much. "Bayden?" There was no sign of light under the door. Bayden wasn't someone who'd hide inside if he knew his dom was calling his name, but Axel hadn't thought Bayden would hang up on him either, or disappear without warning.

Axel's heart hammered against his ribs. Kicking the door in wouldn't help. He stepped back and turned to Hale. "You've got your notebook with you?"

Hale handed it over.

Axel scrawled a note and pushed it under the door before heading back downstairs.

The landlord was still in the hallway. He eyed them both suspiciously.

"When was the last time you saw Bayden?" Axel demanded.

"Why?"

Axel didn't grab him by the neck and toss him against the wall, but it was a near run thing. "When?" he repeated.

The landlord took a step back. "When he was here with you."

Axel looked the guy up and down, he looked intimidated enough to have given in to honesty. Axel wrote his phone number down on another piece of paper from Hale's notebook and handed it to the landlord. "The moment you see him, you call me."

"Why?" The guy repeated.

"There's money in it for you if you do."

The landlord's eyes narrowed. "How much?"

"Two hundred," Axel said, almost entirely at random. "If he comes here, you phone me straight away."

The landlord's expression turned considering.

"If you see Bayden, you call me. You don't tell Bayden, you don't see if he'll offer you more money not to phone me. You call me straight away."

"And if I don't?"

"You'll find out just how much more dangerous than a wolf a human can be."

The landlord scrambled crabwise into his flat, slamming and locking the door in his wake. He'd phone.

Out in his car, Axel sat staring through the windscreen. He'd thought things were screwed up last time he'd sat there, but at least Bayden had been with him then, Bayden had been safe.

"Can you remember anything about where his family lives? He got caught in traffic on his way back from there, didn't he?" Hale asked. "Before one of the club rides?"

Axel tried to think. "Not a good area. Better than Holborn, but not by much. West side of the city, probably."

"We could get a list of all the wolves living in that area," Hale suggested.

"From police records?" Axel shook his head. "He said he'd made sure Granger wouldn't be able to find out where they lived. They're under the radar. And he won't still be there anyway. Three adult wolves under the same roof, he won't risk it."

Hale rubbed his hand over his shaved head. "Would he have gone to a nightclub, or to another pub?" Hale asked.

"That's against the rules."

"And?"

"No, he doesn't break them, not usually," Axel said. "Not until today. Unless..."

"What?"

"If he needed to make quick money. If he went to his mother's and she needed money fast, he might..." He shook his head, as if that would make him less likely to throw up at the images that flashed through his mind.

"Do you want to start checking the clubs?" Hale asked.

Axel nodded. "I'll drop you off next time I see a taxi rank."

"No. I'm going with you."

Axel shook his head.

"If he's in trouble, I'll be able to help."

Axel considered the possibility that a cop might be useful.

"I can stop you getting done for murder," Hale offered.

"I won't kill him." He was just going to handcuff Bayden to his wrist and never let him out of his sight again, that's all.

"I'm not worried you'll kill the damn puppy. But, if someone's hurt him, I'm probably the only one who has a chance of stopping you from murdering the man."

"And you think that's going to make me more likely to keep you around?" Axel muttered.

Hale huffed.

"If someone's hurt him, you won't stop me from killing them," Axel said. There wasn't anything that would stop him from doing that.

* * * * *

Bayden closed his eyes very tightly. Legs pulled up in front of him, he folded his arms and balanced them on his knees. Bowing his head he hid his face against his forearms.

He tried to take a deep breath, but it stuck in his throat. He shook his head. What kind of a man couldn't even breathe without giving way to emotion?

The room was dark but, when he lifted his head, he could make out the outline of the bed. Approaching it wasn't an option. He stayed on the floor in the far corner of the room, as if that would make it all less real.

His jacket lay on the carpet at his side. His mobile was in the pocket. It would only take him seconds to phone Axel. Then everything would be fine. Somehow Axel would be able to make everything okay and —

Bayden shook his head. This wasn't Axel's problem. It was his problem. He was responsible for it all, and he would deal with it. Axel was...

Axel was going to be so mad at him for breaking the rules. Even if Axel could magically turn up, take control and make everything better, Bayden had given him no reason to want to do that.

The chances of Axel even being willing to take him back after this were tiny, and —

Bayden's throat closed up. He shook his head. No matter how angry Axel was with him, Bayden still wanted Axel with a deep ache that filled his body, mingling and intertwining with other kinds of pain.

He glanced at the pocket his phone was in, but he didn't reach out to it. He wanted Axel, but he'd learned a long time ago that what a wolf wanted and what he got were always two very different things.

* * * * *

Axel stared at his mobile. It was all he seemed to do anymore. Forty-eight hours. If anyone had told him that being away from any guy for forty-eight hours would turn his brain into mush, he'd have laughed.

Laughing wasn't an option any more. He paced from one side of the living room to the other.

He'd lost count of the number of messages he'd left for Bayden, how many texts he'd sent him, and how many clubs and pubs each Dragon had gone to, calling in every favour they had in an effort to track down any trace of him.

If Bayden turned up in any place where men wore leather, someone would let them know. Probably. When a guy like Bayden offered himself up on a platter, with no limits and no survival instincts, Axel suspected phone numbers were all too conveniently forgotten.

Axel had also lost count of the number of scenarios that he'd considered.

If his mother or grandfather had needed money, Bayden would have done whatever it took to raise it—no hesitation. He could be somewhere trapped in a mockery of a scene, with the kind of man who wouldn't let him safe word out of it.

Axel paced into the bedroom. He'd already been through the drawer where Bayden kept his stuff—carefully unfolding each item and going over every inch before gently replacing it. There weren't any clues.

There was no money in there, but he could have taken that with him in case his mother needed it. It didn't mean he wasn't coming back. He wouldn't have left his clothes there if he'd gone with no intention of returning.

Axel went back to the drawer. There was so bloody little in there. He should have known better than to wreck his jeans in that last scene. Bayden was careful with his things. Damn it, he didn't even let his clothes get creased, let alone cut up.

And what kind of idiot pulled a knife out in a scene without any warning? All the work he'd done teaching Bayden that he could trust him, and he'd thrown it away because he was too damn impatient to undo some laces.

But, if the scene they'd done together had scared Bayden, he could just be holed up somewhere, licking his emotional wounds. It was one of the less terrifying possibilities. Maybe nothing bad had happened to Bayden. Maybe he was perfectly fine and he just needed some space. He'd said he wanted a few days before he came back. That was fair enough, wasn't it?

Bayden had always said that the sub left the room if he didn't want to submit to a dom who was in his space. Maybe this was just a wolf's way of making it clear they'd stumbled on a limit.

Closing Bayden's drawer, Axel paced back into the living room. Without thinking about it, he found himself heading for another drawer.

No God worth believing in would be punishing him for being gay. But, a punishment for being an arrogant arsehole and forgetting how careful he needed to be with someone like Bayden? Devine retribution seemed to be pretty fitting in those circumstances.

Axel opened the drawer.

His mother hadn't bought the rosaries in bulk. Each one was different. Some were obviously expensive, some less so. Different materials, different styles. He shook his head.

If Bayden was listening to the messages Axel had left for him rather than simply deleting them on sight, he'd have heard some of the angrier messages Axel had left for him on the first day. Maybe he was scared to come back.

The later messages that had promised forgiveness, change and damn near anything else Axel could think of, should have levelled things out. But, that wasn't guaranteed, not if Bayden had stopped listening to them.

Axel dipped his hand into the drawer and picked up one of the rosaries at random. At this point, he'd take any help he could get.

Chapter Twenty Seven

"Axel!"

Axel spun around. Griz's eyes were wide open. He pointed to the monitor behind the bar as if he'd seen—

Bayden.

For several seconds Axel couldn't do anything but stare. It was raining hard, but neither Bayden nor his bike could be mistaken. If someone else hadn't pointed out the image, Axel would have been inclined to think that he was imagining it.

As he watched the screen, the image of Bayden took off his helmet, got off his bike and walked toward the pub's front door.

Axel turned around when Bayden left the security camera's field of vision. He held his breath as the door opened. Bayden stepped into the room. He was dripping wet, his hair plastered down against his scalp, his jeans sodden. Axel had never seen a more beautiful sight.

Axel wasn't even aware of moving. One moment he was behind the bar, the next he was across the room, and he had Bayden pinned against the wall next to the door. All thoughts of gentleness and feverish apologies temporarily forgotten, Axel couldn't help but grip him tight.

Bayden was pale and shivering, but he was there. Axel gasped for breath as relief rushed through him. Bayden made no attempt to struggle, or to lift his gaze.

"Tell me," Axel demanded, his voice hoarse.

"He…" Bayden closed his eyes.

Axel's heart lurched. "Bayden!"

"He died."

Axel's blood turned cold. "Who died? What happened? Were you in a fight?"

Bayden shook his head. "My grandfather. He…He died." He looked up. The pain in his gaze filled the world. If the only water on his checks came from rain, it was through sheer force of will. "He died."

Axel slid his hand behind Bayden's head and pulled him forward, into his arms. He let him tuck his face into his shoulder while he simply relished the fact that Bayden was there, close enough for him to hold on to.

"He died," Bayden repeated.

Axel closed his eyes and held Bayden as tight as he could. For once, he didn't worry about Bayden being small enough to crush. Axel held him so tight his own muscles ached under the strain.

"He died."

Instinct took over. Axel's anger was still there, harsh and biting, but Bayden's pain somehow pushed it down to be dealt with later. Axel made a soothing noise in the back of his throat, the same kind mothers used when rocking a fretting infant.

Bayden's shoulders were shaking. It was impossible to tell if it was cold, shock or emotion. Axel just held him.

"He died." There was obviously no room for anything else in Bayden's world beside that fact.

Axel rubbed Bayden's back through his leather jacket. He was sure that whatever he asked Bayden, those were the only two words he'd get in response. He pulled back and peered down at him.

Bayden took a shaky breath. He cleared his throat and found a new sentence. "Do…do you want me to leave?"

Axel tightened his grip on him. "Leave? What?"

"I broke your rules. You're angry. If you don't want to let me come back, I…I understand. I just…I said I'd come and explain. I can go if…" He broke off. It was difficult to tell if that was because he'd run out of words or because he was afraid of bursting into tears.

"You're not leaving."

Bayden nodded.

A noise behind him reminded Axel that they weren't alone. It was impossible to tell how much the other guys had already overheard, but they didn't need to hear any more.

"Upstairs. Wait for me there."

"I…"

"Now," Axel said. "Give me your keys, and go."

Bayden's hands shook as he gave up his keys. Every man in the pub watched Bayden leave the room. Axel remained where he was. When Bayden was out of sight, all attention turned to him. Ignoring most of the staring, Axel went to the bar where the Dragons were sitting. After everything they'd done to help him try to find Bayden, they deserved some sort of explanation.

"He said his grandfather died," Axel said.

Hale stood. "Go up with him. We'll get rid of everyone and lock up."

Axel nodded. "Thanks."

Griz clapped Axel on the back as he followed Hale up to the bar.

"Put Bayden's bike in his lock-up and drop the keys back behind the bar for me?" Axel asked, handing him the keys.

"No problem."

Griz would look after the bike like it was a delicate new born, but the fact that Bayden hadn't objected to leaving his bike out in front of the pub showed just how off balance he was.

Axel wasn't sure what state he would find Bayden in when he pushed open the door and stepped into his flat. He did his best to be mentally prepared for anything.

Bayden stood next to the chair where he had so often left his clothes. He hadn't taken them off tonight, even though he was dripping wet. It was hard to tell if he was waiting for an order, or if he was simply lost in his own thoughts.

"Leave your clothes there." Axel remained barely six inches away from Bayden as he stripped down. His hands were clumsy. Whether through cold or nerves, it took him several attempts to undo his laces. He'd left his leathers in the drawer in the bedroom. His jeans were so wet he had to peel them off an inch at a time.

But, there was one fact above all others that Axel focused on. There wasn't a mark on him. It didn't actually let Axel relax — he could have been hurt and healed in the time he was away, but it allowed the image Axel had carried around of Bayden beaten and bloody to fade toward the back of his mind.

Leaving Bayden by the door, Axel went into the bathroom and grabbed a huge bath towel. Bayden looked confused but Axel wasn't in the mood to pretend towels were important.

Bayden dropped his gaze and co-operated while Axel wrapped the towel around him and rubbed it against his skin to take the worst of the damp and chill off him.

Once he was satisfied the boy wasn't in imminent danger of freezing to death, Axel nudged him into a chair at the kitchen table. "When was the last time you ate?"

Bayden blinked at him. He didn't look capable of keeping anything down.

Axel put the kettle on out of pure habit. While the water boiled, he studied Bayden.

"Before you decide if I'm allowed back, sir. I…"

Axel waited with more dread than patience.

"I need… I won't ask if I'm allowed to come back if…" He swallowed rapidly. "The rules about me taking bets. I need to take one."

"On a fight?" Axel asked.

Bayden shook his head.

"No."

Bayden had his arms wrapped around his torso holding his towel in place. His grip on himself tightened when he heard the anger in Axel's voice.

"You disappear for three days. And the first thing you can think of to say is that you want permission to screw around?"

"I can't..." Bayden closed his eyes.

"This isn't a good time to be trying to negotiate," Axel said.

"I need the money," Bayden rushed out.

Catching Bayden's chin, Axel tilted his head back and stared down at him.

"I said I'd get the money to him by the end of the week."

"Who?" Axel demanded.

"The man who..." Bayden swallowed. "He arranges the engraving, on the stones."

"The headstone for your grandfather," Axel realised.

Bayden nodded. "I can't raise that much money that quickly with just fights. If I could have permission to do just a couple of bets that look like scenes, then—"

"How much do you need?"

Bayden swallowed. "Seven hundred pounds." He cleared his throat. "I could do the bets somewhere else. I could stay away until any marks other men left on me were gone, and—"

"No. No bets."

Bayden nodded slowly. For several seconds he remained perfectly still, his eyes tightly closed. "I...I understand. I should go. I—"

Axel put his hand on Bayden's shoulder and kept him in his chair. "I'm not telling you to leave. I'm saying you don't need to do any bets. I've got the money."

Bayden shook his head very rapidly. He tried to back away and almost fell off his chair. Axel caught hold of his other shoulder to steady him.

"I'm not asking you to—"

"You don't need to ask," Axel said.

Bayden shook his head again. "I can get the money myself. I just—"

"No."

"I don't want your money."

"You'd rather take it off some guy in a bet?" Axel demanded.

"Yes."

"Why?"

"He wouldn't be important. You are. I don't want your money." By the time he was finished, panic filled his words.

Axel guided him back into his chair and crouched down in front of him. "You understand that I'm not talking about paying you for anything, right?"

Bayden closed his eyes. "He's not your grandfather. He's not part of your pack. It's not your responsibility."

"You're my sub. You're my responsibility." Axel pushed Bayden's hair back off his face. It was starting to dry and go fluffy around the edges.

"I didn't come back to you because I want your money."

"No. You came back because this is where you belong—here with me," Axel said, with complete confidence.

"I'm not asking for—"

Axel put a fingertip against Bayden lips. "The money's not a problem. And even if it is, it's not a problem that needs to be solved tonight."

Bayden hesitated.

"There'll be a headstone. It will be paid for on time. We'll sort out the details tomorrow. It's not a problem for now. I've made that decision. You don't need to think about it anymore tonight."

Bayden nodded. He blinked, his eyes flooded with relief at someone else making a decision for him. Axel felt a similar wave of relief rise up inside him. Bayden was back.

Everything was under control. There weren't any problems Axel couldn't fix now. As his fear faded, some of his anger went with it.

"Good pup."

"What...what are the problems for now?"

He sounded so scared, so uncertain about the world. Axel slid his hand through Bayden's hair. "There are questions I need you to answer before I can work out what the problems might be."

Bayden nodded.

"I expect you to be completely honest with me, even if you don't enjoy doing that."

Bayden nodded again.

"Do you have any questions?" Axel asked.

"Yours are more important," Bayden whispered.

"Ask."

It took Bayden a full minute of silence to come up with anything. Then, in a very small voice, "I'm allowed to come back?"

"Yes."

Bayden took a deep breath. He obviously hadn't really believed he'd be welcome. "Am I still supposed to call you sir?"

"Why wouldn't you be?"

"That was just while you wanted me to submit to you."

Axel stroked his cheek. "You're still my sub. That hasn't changed."

"When you said I can come back. I know I can't... I broke the rules. I don't expect...I don't expect anything. I just..."

"Don't get ahead of yourself." Axel stood up. Wrapping his arm around Bayden's shoulders he led him into the living room and guided him to sit down with him on the sofa. "Tell me what happened. From the beginning."

"He died."

Axel wrapped his arm a little more tightly around Bayden's shoulders. "From the beginning, pup."

* * * * *

The beginning. Bayden wasn't sure where that was anymore.

"My mother called. She said my grandfather was having a bad day, that I should try to go and see them," he hazarded.

Axel didn't correct him. He'd found the beginning.

Bayden swallowed. "He…he's been ill for a long time. I knew that he… I just didn't think that he'd actually… But, he died."

"Did you get there in time to say goodbye?" Axel's voice became softer—gentler.

Bayden nodded. He closed his eyes, but that just made it so much more difficult to believe he sat anywhere other than at the side of his grandfather's bed. He bit down hard on his bottom lip, but emotions swirled ever faster inside him.

Axel's arm tightened around him, pulling him back to the here and now. Bayden opened his eyes, but he couldn't lift his gaze.

"Your mother was there too?"

Bayden nodded.

"Where is she now?"

Bayden fidgeted with the edge of the towel Axel had wrapped around him.

"Bayden?"

"She's taken a residential place at Danville. It's not a charity." Bayden forced himself to look up and meet Axel's eyes so he'd know that was the truth.

"It's an organisation," Axel agreed. "No charity involved."

"She didn't have to go there. She wanted to. I could have looked after her. She knows that I could have."

Axel stroked his hand up and down Bayden's back. "That's where she is, at one of the Danville projects?"

Bayden nodded. "They picked her up today."

Axel continued to gently caress his back. "Is there going to be a funeral?"

"It's done. We buried him this morning. It's all paid for apart from the stone. There has to be a stone. It's the law."

Axel nodded. "There'll be a stone. You don't need to worry about that."

For a few seconds, silence descended. Bayden took a deep breath. He could still smell Axel's anger. It wasn't as strong as it had been. There were lots of other emotions mixed in with it, but it was still there. "You're angry."

"That you needed time away from here to make arrangements after your grandfather died, no." Axel stroked his hair back. "That you didn't tell me where you were or what was going on, yes."

Bayden nodded. He folded the edge of the towel between his fingers. The reason for the emotion wasn't that important. The fact Axel was angry with him was all that mattered.

Axel caught hold of Bayden's chin. "For all I knew, you were the one who'd died."

Bayden shook his head.

"It didn't occur to you that I'd be worried about you? You could have crashed your bike and been lying in a ditch somewhere. You could have been pulled over by someone like Granger. You could have been at a club doing the kind of bet that would likely get you killed."

Bayden frowned. Axel wasn't just angry. He was afraid too. He'd been scared — really scared. "I'm sorry, sir." Bayden looked down. "That doesn't fix anything."

"No, it doesn't. But it's a start."

Bayden peered at his grip on the towel.

"You said you paid for the funeral," Axel said.

Bayden nodded.

"How?"

"The money I'd saved up for the rent and things, I used that."

"You haven't earned any money while you've been away?" Axel pushed.

Bayden shook his head. "I have to ask for permission to do that."

"Including to fight?"

"I'm only allowed to take fights here," Bayden reminded him. "I didn't break the rules—not those rules."

Axel's whole body tensed up. "Which rules did you break?"

"Not being back here at night. Missing my shift." He thought very carefully, not wanting to miss anything out and lie by accidental omission. "Going places other than my mother's without your permission."

"Places like?"

"There's a burial ground. There was an undertaker's."

"The only places you went were to do with the funeral?"

Bayden nodded.

"What other rules?"

Bayden thought about it very hard.

"Did anyone lay a hand on you?" Axel asked. "And I don't mean did you give your mum a hug."

Bayden shook his head very quickly. "I'd tell you if I broke those rules, sir. I would."

Axel nodded. He seemed to believe him.

The silence stretched out until Bayden had to break it. "There has to be a punishment, sir."

Axel stroked his fingers through Bayden's hair again, cradling him close. "Yes, there does."

Bayden braced himself. He nodded, ready for whatever it would be. He straightened up and squared his shoulders, determined not to let Axel down.

"You understand what you'll be punished for?" Axel asked.

"Breaking the rules, sir. Being away. Missing my shift."

"No." Axel was quiet for a long time. "You'll be punished for not telling me where you were or what was going on. If you'd stayed on the line and finished the phone call, I'd have given you permission to stay at your mother's for as long as you needed to. You wouldn't be in trouble for anything at all."

Bayden swallowed.

"Why did you hang up?"

Because if I'd stayed on the line another few seconds, I'd have burst into tears. He felt like doing the same thing right then. "I had to…" He stared down at his hands. "I had to… He died, and…" He bit down hard on his bottom lip.

He was not going to break down. He wasn't. Not on the phone and not in person. That was not going to happen.

"I had to sort everything out, sir." He glanced toward Axel. The way Axel frowned was almost the last straw. Bayden jerked himself to his feet and paced over to the window, turning his back on Axel before he proved just how right his mother was to doubt his ability to lead even the tiniest of packs.

Blinking rapidly, he brushed at his eyes to check. Tears hadn't fallen. They weren't going to fall.

He heard Axel get up and leave the room. Bayden closed his eyes and managed not to run after him. He didn't know if the punishment had started, if not being close to Axel was part of it. Bayden gripped the towel tightly. He wanted to be close to Axel so badly. He didn't deserve to be held close, but he wanted it so much he could barely breathe.

Axel came back. Bayden turned toward him. If Axel had just gone to get something to punish him with, maybe there was still hope.

Axel went into the flat's kitchen, then returned to the living room. He had a bottle in one hand and a glass in the other. He sat on the sofa.

"Come here."

Bayden sat next to Axel, but he couldn't meet his gaze. He watched Axel pour a large glass of clear liquid, but his brain was so sluggish he couldn't work out how it would fit into any punishment.

Axel held out a glass. "Drink."

Bayden automatically took the glass.

"Toss it straight back in one. Do as you're told."

He obeyed. The liquid hit the back of his throat. It was the same thing that had made him choke when he drank most of the top shelf. He barely managed to swallow it down before he started coughing so hard tears sprung to his eyes. Still coughing, he rushed to wipe them away, but it was as if the first few drops had broken the damn.

His coughing stopped, his tears didn't. He covered his eyes and tried to turn away, but Axel caught hold of his shoulder and pulled him back. The next thing he knew he was curled up in Axel's arms and a few stupid tears had turned into a flood.

"I..."

"Hush. Let it out."

Bayden shook his head.

"Don't argue with me, pup. Do as you're told. Let it all out." Axel's words were gentle, but his tone allowed no room for argument.

"He died," Bayden blurted out.

Axel held him tighter, rocking him gently.

Bayden pushed against Axel's chest, trying to get away, but Axel's grip was too strong. The only place Bayden could hide his tears was in Axel's shoulder.

"He died. And she's gone. And it wasn't supposed to happen. He wasn't supposed to die. I never wanted him to die—never." The tears weren't the only things that flowed faster than he could control. The words were unstoppable. He had no idea how many Axel could make out through the tears, but Bayden was powerless to stop them from tumbling past his lips.

When he finally managed to silence both his tears and his garbled explanations, the room was eerily quiet. His whole body trembled.

Bayden's mind slowly came back on line. He pulled away. This time, Axel allowed it. "I…"

"Yes, you did, pup. And the world's still spinning."

Bayden blinked at him.

"That was why you hung up on me, so I wouldn't hear you cry."

Bayden glanced at the glass. Axel had known what would happen. He'd made it happen on purpose.

"I don't care about tears. And I don't care if you blush over them," Axel said.

Bayden cautiously lowered his head onto Axel's shoulder. Axel let him do that. "It wasn't just that. I…"

Axel just stroked his palm over Bayden's back. The towel had slipped. It pooled around his lap, leaving his back bare and nothing between him and Axel's touch.

"I couldn't risk it, sir."

"Me knowing where you were?"

"You ordering me to come home." Bayden ran his fingers over the edge of a tattoo just visible past Axel's T-shirt sleeve. "It was my responsibility. I had to sort it all out. I couldn't just…"

"You thought I'd have ordered you to do that, that I'd expect you to obey that kind of order?" Axel asked.

"I wanted to. It was all falling apart and…" He shook his head. "And all I wanted to do was walk away, to come back to you and pretend that it wasn't happening, that it wasn't my responsibility. What kind of a wolf does that?"

Axel pushed his fingers through Bayden hair. "It never occurred to you that I could have helped if you'd told me what was going on?"

"It wasn't your responsibility. He wasn't part of your pack. I should have been able to handle it." Bayden cleared his throat and tried to pull himself together once more. "You didn't say what the punishment is, sir."

"I'll make my decision and we'll discuss what it is closer to the time."

"Sir?"

"There'll be a punishment, but not while you're still grieving," Axel said.

"I can—"

Axel shook his head. "The decision's been made."

Bayden had missed that certainty so much. He looked down. "Until then, sir?"

"Everything is exactly the same as it was before."

Bayden nodded.

* * * * *

"One last question then we'll be done for now." Axel hesitated, only in part because he wasn't sure how much more Bayden could take that night.

Bayden looked up. He had dark circles under his eyes. His hair was all messed up. His skin was pale.

Axel had never seen anyone look so fragile, but he had to know. "The scene we did the night before you left—did it make you less likely to contact me?"

Bayden fidgeted with the edge of the towel. The answer was obvious.

Axel bit back a curse. He stroked Bayden's jaw, making him look up. "The knife?" he asked. He supposed that was better than some of the other possibilities that had occurred to him. He still didn't know how he could have been so stupid.

Bayden frowned, as if he thought Axel was an idiot for not having known it would bring up bad memories for him.

Axel stroked his fingers along Bayden's neck, where one of the cuts had broken his skin.

Bayden jerked back. Before Axel could react, Bayden was out of the room.

Axel rushed after him, only to hesitate when he realised Bayden had gone into the kitchen rather than head for the exit.

Bayden hurried back in with a knife in his hand.

He held it out, the handle pointing toward Axel. When Axel didn't take it, Bayden proffered it more intently.

A quick dart forward, Bayden caught hold of Axel's wrist and pushed the knife's handle against his palm.

"Bayden?"

"You can."

Axel looked down at the kitchen knife. "Pup?"

"You can, sir," Bayden rushed out, pulling his towel back around him as it started to slip. His hands were shaking.

Axel carefully put the knife on the coffee table, never taking his eyes off Bayden. "I can?"

"You think I didn't like it. That I don't think you should have. That I'm afraid of it," Bayden shook his head. "I'm not. You can. We can do whatever you want."

Axel put his hand on Bayden's cheek and gently hushed him.

"Whatever you want, sir. Please?"

"What scared you if it wasn't the knife?"

"I wanted to come back, sir. I wanted that so much."

Axel narrowed his gaze. "You liked it so much, it made it more tempting to leave your responsibilities and come back to me?"

Bayden looked down.

"Because in that scene you felt…"

Bayden remained silent for a long time but Axel waited him out.

"Right," Bayden finally whispered, barely loud enough for Axel to make out the word. "Safe. Yours." Heat rose to his cheeks.

"Mine," Axel agreed. Bayden had felt like he belonged to him. It had been an entirely accurate sensation. Axel brushed their lips together. He let the first few seconds be about pure reassurance.

"I liked it, sir," Bayden whispered, when Axel pulled back. His grip on Axel's T-shirt was white knuckled.

Axel nodded. Bayden had liked it, and he wanted it again.

"Last time, how you acted, that's how a wolf shows that he likes his lover being more dominant with him?" Axel asked.

Bayden hesitated. "It means something different to a human, sir?" He sounded heartbroken over the idea.

Axel thought back to that night, the soft tenderness of every touch. "It could mean a human sub was trying to gentle things down, that he was worried his dom was being too rough with him."

Bayden shook his head, very rapidly. "I won't do it again, I—"

"Yes, you will."

Bayden shook his head again.

"I'll be very disappointed if you don't."

Bayden glanced up at him. "You liked it too, sir?"

"Pup, I actually cut your clothes off. That doesn't mean I was going through the motions." He kissed him again, very gently. "Give me your instincts, show me what you'd show a wolf."

Bayden stared at the way he held Axel's shirt. He nodded. Dipping his head, he pressed a kiss against his shoulder and nuzzled against his skin. His actions were hesitant, he evidently expected to be knocked back for his cheek, but the move was obviously honest too. He wasn't doing anything because he thought it was what Axel wanted.

It wasn't even about what Bayden wanted — it was pure need driving him now.

Axel led him into the bedroom. It took a fraction of a second to discard Bayden's towel, and barely a few more moments for Axel to have himself just as naked.

Bayden's vulnerability was so close to the surface. His need for reassurance was so obvious. Words weren't enough. The kind of comfort and acceptance he needed wasn't to be found in syllables. It had to be wrapped around him, completely possessing him.

The relief in Bayden's eyes when he realised that Axel didn't intend them to simply sleep in the same bed confirmed every one of Axel's suspicions.

Quickly preparing Bayden, Axel arranged him on the bed on his stomach. Bayden tried to get up onto his hands and knees, but Axel hushed him back into place. As he pushed into Bayden and brought their bodies together, Axel completely covered Bayden's smaller frame.

Bayden's hand rested on the bed sheet alongside his head. Axel caught hold of his wrist but he kept his hold on him gentle, just letting him have the reassurance of knowing he was being held.

Bayden twisted and offered up his other hand.

Taking Bayden's other wrist in a similar grip, Axel pushed into Bayden again and again; one slow, deep thrust after another.

Bayden was back, and Bayden was his, and everything was fine. For the first time in days, Axel could breathe. He rocked his hips, not inclined to rush now that he had Bayden safe where he belonged.

Bayden tugged at Axel's hold on him — a tiny movement. Bayden's cheek rested on the pillow, his profile was clearly visible. He didn't look scared or uncomfortable.

A few seconds passed and Bayden tested his hold again.

Axel stilled. He saw a flash of emotion in Bayden's eyes and made a leap of faith.

"Are you trying to say your safe word, pup?"

Bayden shook his head very quickly. "I—"

"Because that's the only thing that will convince me to let you go. Squirming is only going to make me hold you tighter, keep you closer, safer."

Bayden whimpered. He pulled more firmly against Axel's grip on him.

Tightening his fists around Bayden's wrists, Axel let a little more of his weight rest on Bayden, pinning him firmly in place.

Bayden gasped. A moment later, he smiled. Relief flashed across his face.

Axel rocked his hips more deliberately. It had been days since they screwed, but there was no desperation there, only determination. Bayden was his. Axel thrust deep inside him, doing his damnedest to let Bayden feel his possession of him, all the way through his body.

Bayden murmured his pleasure. Every so often, he would fidget within Axel's grip again, asking to be held even tighter. Axel's hands started to cramp. He would never have risked holding a human that tight, but he gave Bayden what he asked for, trusting him to follow his instincts and know what he needed.

The skin beneath Axel's fingers turned white. Bayden's breathing became shallower and more rapid. He jerked beneath Axel, unable to move far enough to even scrabble at the sheets as he came.

As far as Axel could tell, Bayden had made no effort to hold back. He'd done exactly what Axel's rules demanded.

Axel relaxed his hold on Bayden, but a whimper quickly convinced him to resume the painful grip. He thrust harder, letting his body take over as his mind gradually released all the fears that had consumed him over the last few days.

He came, pinning Bayden down hard against the mattress. As pleasure faded, Axel refused to pull away. Instead, he allowed more of his weight to rest against Bayden. Minutes ticked by. Finally, he convinced himself to move to lie next to Bayden rather than directly on top of him.

"Good boy," Axel murmured.

When Bayden hesitated, Axel tugged him closer. Bayden's hand came to rest on Axel's chest as he curled in against his side.

Axel checked his wrist. It was already marked. By the morning, he had no doubt bruises would encircle his skin. "Sore?" he asked.

"Good, sir," Bayden whispered. "Yours. Safe."

Axel brushed their lips together and held him a little more tightly. "Good boy." Nothing had been resolved. They still had to deal with everything that had happened, but Bayden was there in his bed and in his arms. Axel could breathe, and everything else could wait until tomorrow.

Chapter Twenty Eight

"I can get the money myself, sir."

Axel opened the safe in his office at the back of the pub and started to count out notes. "You're sure there's nothing apart from the headstone?" he asked. "Think it over carefully so we can take care of it all at the same time."

"There's nothing else," Bayden said from the doorway. "But you don't need to pay for anything at all."

Axel ignored the last bit.

"If you'll just give me permission, sir," Bayden said again.

"Not going to happen." Axel made sure the money was right and held it out to Bayden.

Bayden didn't take it. "You could punish me for it, sir."

"I could give you permission, then punish you for doing what I gave you permission to do?" Axel checked.

Bayden looked down. "Yes. Or punish me for needing to ask for permission in the first place, or…"

Axel rubbed the back of his neck. He could punish his sub for needing money to bury his grandfather. What the hell kind of man did Bayden think he was? He frowned as he considered that line of thought more carefully. There were other people whose opinion Bayden cared about, and being a dom didn't give Axel the right to think the whole world revolved around him twenty-four hours a day. "Your grandfather wouldn't want me to pay for it, would he?"

Bayden swallowed. "He'd say it's not your responsibility, sir. He'd be right." He pushed his hands deep into his pockets. "He was right about a lot of things."

"Things about humans?" Axel guessed, wondering if he was about to find out another reason why Bayden hadn't rushed back to a human's side.

"No. About what it means to be a good wolf. He was." Bayden looked up. "He was a good wolf, sir. The best. I'd have given up anything for him to have been okay. I would have."

Axel stroked Bayden's hair back from his face. "What if we call it a loan? I won't *give* you the money. I'll just lend it to you. You can pay me back. You and your grandfather will both know that you were the one who really paid for it."

Bayden nodded. "I can pay you back quickly. I'll—"

"You won't do it by taking a bet that looks like a scene."

Bayden nodded and sighed as if the entire weight of the headstone had been lifted off his shoulders.

When Axel smiled, Bayden smiled back. For the first time since he'd returned, the expression didn't look forced.

"You'll pay me back slowly. No rushing. No deadlines. Understand?"

When Axel held the money out again, Bayden took it.

"I need permission to leave the pub to pay for the stone," he admitted.

"I'm driving you there."

"I can..." Bayden trailed off when their gazes met and he apparently realised he would never win that argument. He remained silent as Axel led him out to the car.

The funeral parlour that Bayden directed Axel to catered to humans as well as wolves. There was no need for Axel to ask if humans were welcome or if he had to wait in the car while Bayden went in on his own. He didn't actually need to work up the self-control to let Bayden out of his sight. As soon as he realised that, Axel felt much better about the world.

Bayden took his sunglasses out of his pocket as they left the car, then he seemed to realise they weren't necessary. He pushed them back into his jacket pocket. Inside was a marble floored lobby with a receptionist's desk. Axel hung back while Bayden approached the woman at the desk. He kept his voice down in deference to the sombre surroundings. Axel didn't hear what was said.

Bayden nodded and returned to Axel's side.

"I'm sorry, sir. I'll need to wait until Mr James is free to see me."

"It's fine." Axel shepherded him toward a row of chairs on the other side of the lobby.

Bayden turned to the exit instead. "I can wait outside."

Axel couldn't blame him for wanting to get out of the place. "Okay. I'll tell the receptionist we'll be out there."

"She knows, sir."

Outside, Bayden seemed to breathe a little easier. Axel led the way to a bench and nudged Bayden until he sat down. The sun was shining. The building was set back from the road and surrounded by well-kept gardens. It was almost possible to believe that they sat in a park and that there was no reason to consider their surroundings to be melancholy.

"After we finish here, do you want to stop by the cemetery?" Axel asked.

"It's not the same one humans use, sir."

"We can still go, if you'd like."

Bayden nodded, but he didn't speak. Axel would have bet the entire seven hundred on that being because Bayden was worried about how much emotion would be audible in his voice.

A few other mourners came and went. When two separate sets of people seemed to have jumped the queue in front of them, Axel got up. "I'll check they haven't forgotten about us."

"Humans get seen first." Bayden stared at his hands. "They won't keep a human waiting while they deal with me."

"They told you to wait outside," Axel realised. They weren't out there because it was depressing as hell in there. They were outside because of, what? Some screwed up no dogs inside rule?

"You don't have to wait, sir. I can make my own way back to the pub. I won't go anywhere else. I'll just—"

"There's no need for that," Axel cut in.

Bayden glanced up at him. "You're angry."

Bloody furious would have been closer to the mark. "Not at you."

Bayden stood up. "I don't want any trouble, sir."

"What?"

"You're not used to it, sir. There's no reason why you should be. But..." Bayden looked down. "I don't want any trouble. Not here."

Axel stared at him, completely speechless.

"There has to be a stone, sir."

And if Axel caused a scene they might refuse to make it. He swallowed down his anger as best he could. "Sit down."

Bayden obeyed, but his movements were wary. He didn't entirely trust him not to storm in there and screw everything up for him.

Axel sat down next to Bayden and rested his hand on the small of his back. "I'm not going to create a scene. There's not going to be any trouble."

Bayden nodded. "Thank you, sir."

Axel managed a smile, but it wasn't easy, not when Bayden apparently lived in a world where he thought that was something he had to be grateful for.

Bayden rubbed his knuckles together. The sleeve on his jumper slipped back. Axel's predictions had been accurate. There were bruises around his wrist from where Axel had held him the night before.

Axel ran his thumb over the discoloured skin, remembering the last time he'd seen bruises around his wrists.

"I like them, sir."

"What?"

"The marks, I like them."

"Why?"

"Because you left them on me." He watched with apparent fascination as Axel caressed the bruises. "I'd like any marks you left on me."

"Because they mean you belong to me?"

Bayden focused on them even more intently. "These ones do. The marks from the bets didn't mean that."

"No, they didn't mean a damn thing." Axel slid his arm further around Bayden's shoulders. Maybe he had to keep his tongue about anti-werewolf bullshit, but he'd be damned if he'd tiptoe around and be wary of any homophobes hidden in the bushes too. Bayden was his.

Several more human clients came and went. It was another hour before the receptionist appeared in the doorway and signalled that they were temporarily allowed in the building. The actual meeting took all of two minutes. Bayden checked the wording he wanted on the stone once. Mr James checked that Bayden hadn't short changed him twice, and they were back out in the fresh air.

Axel rolled his shoulders. He'd never realised that simply standing in the background and watching an undertaker act like a bigoted wanker could be so bloody exhausting.

"Which way?" Axel asked, as he drove out of the funeral home's car park.

Bayden shook his head. "We don't need to go to the burial, sir. It's already taken longer than—"

Axel put his hand on Bayden's knee. "Just give me the directions, pup. Unless you want to stop off somewhere first. Flowers for the grave, is that something your grandfather would like?"

Bayden shook his head. He gave the directions quietly, almost as if he was afraid to interrupt Axel by uttering them.

The lupine burial ground was set right on the other side of town, near an old industrial park. Axel pulled into a layby not far from a set of heavy iron gates. There were no other cars in sight.

Bayden got out without a word. He didn't say anything about Axel following him in. There were no headstones, or at least none that stood upright. The stones all lay flat on the ground, line after line of them. There was moss growing on some, making the marble and granite slabs blend into the ragged strips of grass between them.

Bayden pushed his hands into his pockets and kept his head down. He seemed to know where he was going. Axel fell into step beside him. There were no flowers, no trees, no benches. There wasn't anything to look at apart from the inscriptions on the gravestones that flanked the path.

Every surname was the same. No way to tell which wolves were related or what pack they belonged to. Most of the stones were about six foot long by three foot across, but every so often there was a smaller one. They were halfway across the grave yard before Axel realised why. They were the graves of children. The gravestones were smaller because the graves they covered were smaller.

Axel looked along the rows again. There were far too many small ones.

Bayden came to a halt, but he didn't approach a particular grave.

Poor little sod. "It's easy to get turned around and lose track," Axel offered.

"I know where he's buried, sir," Bayden said. "I just have to wait until they go." He nodded to a couple standing about a hundred yards away.

"They're at your grandfather's grave?"

Bayden nodded.

"Do you know them?"

"A little, sir."

"You could go and talk to them."

Bayden shook his head. "I'll wait until they're gone."

"If lupine families are anything like human families I'm guessing that part of the family stopped talking to another because what his auntie said about her cousin when they were at so and so's wedding forty years ago?"

Bayden smiled, but shook his head again.

Axel touched his cheek. "What if I give you some privacy to talk to them on your own?" It would be easy enough to be out of earshot without having to actually let Bayden out of his sight. Axel could manage that.

"You're not the problem, sir. It's three wolves that people object to," Bayden reminded him.

Axel looked around them. The couple at the grave were the only people within sight. "Who'd know?"

"It's better not to take the risk."

Axel frowned.

"After you get caught a couple of times, you learn it's better not to take the risk, sir."

"What about you talking to one of them?"

"It's fine, sir. I'll wait. Or, we can go back. It'll be time to open soon and —"

Axel slid his arm around Bayden's shoulders. "We'll wait."

Bayden cautiously leaned into him, just slightly, as if he was desperate for comfort but wasn't sure if it would be snatched away at an unexpected moment.

Axel took Bayden properly in his arms and encouraged him to rest his head on his shoulder while they waited. Whether it was coincidence or because they were aware that someone else wanted to approach the grave, the other couple didn't linger for more than a few minutes.

It was the only grave with freshly turned over earth still visible. Every other one was covered by a stone.

When Bayden knelt down near the base of the disturbed area of earth, Axel remained a few steps back.

"He was a good wolf, sir," Bayden suddenly said.

Axel moved closer and crouched down behind Bayden, resting a hand on his shoulder.

"He always said that a good wolf's aim should be to die peacefully in his sleep of old age. Not many wolves of his generation managed it, but he did." Bayden ran his fingers over the weed strewn grass. "You keep your head down, you don't cause trouble, and you survive. He was right."

Axel squeezed his shoulder. "He lived with you and your mother for a long time?"

"Since my dad died. My father, he…wasn't the kind of wolf who would ever die of old age."

"Is his buried here too?" Axel asked.

Bayden nodded.

"Do you know where?"

Another nod.

"Do you want to visit his grave as well?"

"No." The word was sharp. Bayden glanced over his shoulder. "I'd prefer not to, sir. Today's not about him."

"That's fine, pup." Axel ruffled his hair.

"It's only wolves that are buried here?" Axel asked, when Bayden had been quiet for a long time.

Bayden nodded. "My granddad would have enjoyed that, being surrounded by wolves."

"I'm sorry I didn't get the chance to meet him."

"You'd have liked him, sir."

"I don't doubt it."

The minutes ticked past. Axel's feet started to fall asleep, but he remained crouched down beside Bayden.

"He'd have liked you too, once he got to know you," Bayden whispered. "It's just that other humans, so many other humans are… He was scared of humans, sir, but he had a right to be. You're different than the others. He'd have seen that in time."

Axel pressed a kiss to the top of Bayden's head.

The time when the pub should have opened came and went. Axel shifted his weight far enough that a little bit of blood could reach his toes and slid his arm more comfortably around Bayden's shoulders.

He had no idea if Bayden was aware of the time passing. He seemed lost in his own world. Axel could easily imagine the days when he was away from the pub passing the same way. Or in waiting until all the humans were seen first.

Bayden glanced up at him. "He was a good wolf," he said again.

"So are you," Axel said.

"No, I'm not. Not the way he was."

Axel pushed Bayden's hair back from his face. He wanted to kiss him gently on the lips, purely for comfort, but he doubted it would be considered respectful given their location. He kissed his temple instead. You couldn't get more chaste than that. Hell, he'd have done that in front of Bayden's grandfather when he was alive.

Bayden turned his head and pressed a kiss against Axel's hand—his first real movement since his hands fell still in the grass over an hour earlier. It was cautious, but not the least awkward due to their location. Axel stroked his cheek in praise.

They walked out of the graveyard arm in arm and drove back to the pub in silence.

There were already a couple of Dragons outside. Sometimes a short submissive was a blessing. Axel shook his head and shot a look at them above Bayden's line of sight. Whatever they'd intended to say, they stowed it away for later.

Inside, Axel nudged Bayden to go on ahead. Griz waited until Bayden was out of hearing before he spoke up. "I was starting to think he'd disappeared again."

"We were visiting his grandfather's grave."

"His grandfather really died?"

Axel nodded. "Old age. I think it was pretty expected, but still." He started taking the chairs down from on top of the tables.

Griz followed alongside him, automatically taking on half the job. "They were close?"

Axel nodded.

"Close enough to give him a free pass on disappearing?"

"There's no such thing as a relationship that close. I'll deal with it when he's out of mourning."

"Can we watch?"

Axel chuckled. "It won't be that kind of punishment." He thought back to Bayden's list of things that he considered important privileges, the things that really mattered to him. Whatever the punishment was, it would likely take place entirely inside Bayden's head.

Bayden looked up from his work when Axel joined him. "I should have asked if it was okay for me to…"

Of course, he'd listed working there as a privilege. Axel slid his arm around Bayden's waist. "I told you that the time isn't right for any kind of punishment, didn't I?"

Bayden looked down. "I can take—"

Axel kissed him gently on the lips. It was a pleasant way to silence him.

"When the time is right, we'll talk about it. Until then, you carry on exactly as you did before, with one exception."

Bayden glanced up at him, obviously trying to appear prepared for anything.

"You either stay behind the bar, or within my line of sight. If you want to go anywhere else, you ask me first. I don't care if you just want to take a leak during your break. You don't leave my sight without permission."

Bayden shifted his weight from one foot to another.

"It's not a punishment, it's a new rule." Axel stroked his arm. "Rules aren't bad things, are they?"

Bayden shook his head. "Rules are good."

Axel stared down at Bayden. When he whispered the words to himself that way, it sounded like rules were the only things keeping him together.

Would more rules help? Axel pressed a kiss to Bayden's temple. He had a strong suspicion that the only thing that would really help Bayden recover from the shock of his grandfather's death would be time. Axel could give Bayden as much of that as he needed, but it didn't really feel like enough.

He stroked his fingers up the side of Bayden's neck, picturing a collar there. That would help too. Soon, he promised himself. Soon.

Chapter Twenty Nine

Bayden ran his fingers over the inscription on the polished surface of the gravestone. It was damp after the previous night's rain and felt even colder than it should. "Do you know why we have to have gravestones like this, sir? Why the humans made it a law?"

"Yes." Axel crouched down behind him and put his hand on Bayden's shoulder. "I read about it in the book by Kincade."

Bayden nodded. Axel loved those damn books. They were both starting to look dog-eared, the number of times he'd read them. He always specified which book he was quoting though—if it was the book written about wolves or the book written by a wolf.

"Humans used to think that werewolves could come back from the dead," Axel said.

Bayden nodded.

"I wish it was true too," Axel whispered to him.

Bayden swallowed. If humans could have been right about that one thing, it would have made all the lies they told about wolves worth it. If his grandfather could come back…

"There's nothing I wouldn't give up for him to come back," Bayden whispered. It was true. The fact that he'd gained certain options when his grandfather died didn't mean he'd wanted him to die.

"He was your dad's father, right?"

Bayden cleared his throat. "Yes, but they weren't very alike…"

"You said your father wasn't someone who would ever die of old age."

"Yes, sir."

"How did he die?"

"He didn't think it was fair that wolves took home half the wages humans were paid for doing the same job in the same place. He stood up to owners." Bayden sighed. "Well, not really. He just caused trouble." Bayden ran his fingers over the gravestone once more. His grandfather had always had more sense than to cause trouble.

"He was murdered." Axel shock was obvious.

Bayden laughed, caught off guard by how little Axel still seemed to know about what it was like to be a wolf, no matter how often he read those damn books. "You have to be human to be murdered. Wolves are slaughtered, or put down, or maybe culled."

"Did they find who did it?" Axel demanded.

"Granger and his friends?" Bayden tugged up a few of the blades of grass he'd been toying with. "It was right at the top of their priorities."

That was the way things were—even Axel's books acknowledged it. If a wolf had any sense, if he was a good wolf, he learned to accept that. He kept his head down and didn't cause any trouble. If his father had been half as sensible as his grandfather then…

Bayden shook his head. That was no way to think about his dad. A man couldn't be blamed for who he was. An alpha couldn't be blamed for losing his temper with humanity.

Bayden looked up at Axel. He smiled when he saw the fury burning as brightly in Axel's eyes as it had ever burned in his father's. Yes, alphas were alphas. Different rules applied.

As Axel led him back to the gates of the burial ground, Bayden wrapped his arms around himself. It felt a lot colder than mere temperature suggested it should. Even when they got back to the pub, Bayden couldn't quite convince himself that the air around him was anything other than frigid.

With the jumper Axel had bought him on beneath his leather jacket, he should have been sweltering inside the pub. It was all he could do not to shiver.

Men came up to the bar, bought their drinks and went away. The noise gradually built up as more and more people arrived. It wasn't the busiest night, but it felt like all of Bayden's senses were on high alert. Every word echoed around the room.

Info and stats on different bikes bombarded him. Stories about rides and rallies collided with gossip about who wanted to whip who.

"Do you think they do puppy play?"

Bayden glanced along the bar. Two men promptly stopped staring at him. Subtlety was obviously not their strongest point.

Bayden wiped down the bar in front of him, but now that he'd noticed the men's conversation, it was bloody difficult to turn his senses elsewhere.

"They must do. Boy's been following him around like an honest to God puppy ever since he came back. Never more than the length of a lead away from him."

Bayden mentally cursed. They were right. It had been over a week and a half since he got back, and he'd been staying close at heel the entire time. He peeked at Axel out of the corner of his eye.

Rules about staying within sight didn't mean Axel wanted to be tripping over him all the time. Axel hadn't complained, but it must have been getting on his nerves.

"He's hot. And werewolves are bloody good lays."

Bayden took a deep breath and let it out slowly. He'd have to do a hell of a lot more than get Axel off if he wanted Axel to keep him around.

"More trouble than he's worth."

Bayden wished that was wrong, but he had a horrible suspicion that the guy was right.

"Okay, pup?"

Bayden looked up. Axel was right there.

"I should take some of the empty bottles out back," Bayden blurted out.

Axel nodded his permission.

Grabbing one of the plastic containers of empties, Bayden headed out to the big recycling bins.

Halfway across the yard, he paused, looking at the lock-up where he kept his bike.

His grandfather had been right about a lot of things. Good wolves got their priorities straight. The Triumph had always brought trouble with it. It was too flash, it drew too much attention. Riding with The Black Dragons was good, but he'd already ruined two separate club runs.

Bayden stared at the lock-up door. His father had ridden it, but maybe his father wasn't the wolf he should be emulating. His dad hadn't been the kind of man, or the kind of mate, Axel would be interested in. And it was what Axel wanted that was important.

Bayden swallowed. Without a wolf within reach that he could claim any kind of pack connection to, Axel wasn't just important, he was everything, and—

Bayden spun around when a hand landed on his shoulder. "Sir!"

"I thought you'd got lost," Axel said.

"I…" Bayden shook his head, trying to clear it. "I'm sorry, I…"

"Come on." Axel took the container from him and carried it across to the bin.

"I can do that, sir."

"Hush." He held the box as Bayden pulled empty bottles out and tossed them into the bin. "What were you thinking about?"

How I can be less trouble and more worth keeping around.

"The truth doesn't need thinking time, pup."

Bayden frowned at the bottle in his hand. "Just some things I heard the other guys talking about in the pub, sir. It's not important."

"For example," Axel ordered.

"What subs are supposed to be like and what they're expected to do."

"Specifically?"

"Earlier, I overheard one of them say that cooking is subs' work, sir." That was true enough.

Axel laughed. "Everyone's entitled to his opinion, even if it makes him sound like a wanker. My brothers used to think that cooking made a man look gay."

Bayden peeked up at him. Axel didn't look even the slightest bit offended.

"Any dom who lives his life by the rules another man sets doesn't really understand what the label is supposed to mean," Axel said. There were only a few bottles left in the container. He picked them up and tossed them in with the others. "Dragons get a vote in club matters. Subs get to state their limits. A collared sub gets to state his preferences in a lot more things than anyone else. But, when it comes down to it, a dom does what he wants without worrying about things like what some idiot considers to be subs' work—or what his family thinks makes him look gay."

"I…"

"You're right to tell me if you hear something that worries you; that's good." He put his arm around Bayden as he led him back into the pub.

Bayden leaned into Axel's side. Yes, it was definitely Axel's opinion that was the important thing. He'd just listen to Axel, and everything would be fine.

* * * * *

Axel watched Bayden carefully as he took off his clothes and placed them neatly on the chair just inside the door.

Bayden didn't look in his direction, but he didn't look lost in his thoughts the way he so often seemed to be since his grandfather's death, either.

For a long time, Bayden stood naked and motionless, just staring down at his clothes. A tiny movement and Axel realised that Bayden's attention had moved to his wrist.

The bruises Axel had left there were long gone.

"Pup?"

Bayden looked up, his expression full of longing. What he needed was obvious.

"Go into the bedroom," Axel ordered. "You can take your clothes with you and put them away. Look in the toy cupboard. There's a pair of black leather gloves on the second shelf, bring them back here."

Axel made himself comfortable in the arm chair. Bayden quickly returned to his side and lowered himself to his knees as he offered Axel the gloves.

Axel put them on. They were nothing like his motorcycle gloves. The thin leather moulded itself to his hands, quickly warming up to body temperature. He checked each fingertip before calling Bayden up to sit on his lap. A few nudges had him sitting astride Axel's legs, facing him.

Axel put his hands on Bayden's shoulders to steady him. Bayden frowned as Axel ran his palms down, then up, Bayden's arms. Whether he liked leather or not, he didn't seem impressed with anything getting between him and his dom's touch.

Axel altered the angle and stroked his fingertips down Bayden's arms. Bayden gasped and peered at the skin Axel had just caressed. Thin scratches decorated his arms.

Axel held up his gloved hands so Bayden could inspect the fingertips. He turned his hand and let the tiny mental points catch the light. Bayden looked from them, to the light pink scratches on his arms. Suddenly, Bayden seemed far more willing to tolerate the gloves.

Placing a fingertip on the centre of Bayden's chest, Axel drew a line along his skin, pressing harder than he had before. The scratch was deeper. The colour it left in its wake was a few shades darker.

"Does it hurt?" Axel asked.

Bayden shook his head.

"Good. Marks don't have to mean pain."

Bayden looked up and met his gaze. He nodded slowly as he realised what Axel was offering him and why.

Bayden looked down at his own body as if he'd never seen it before, or perhaps as if he was re-imagining it as a canvass that Axel could create some glorious work of art upon.

Turning his palms up, Bayden held his arms away from torso, making every inch of skin as accessible as possible.

Axel ran his gloved hands up Bayden's thighs. He didn't let the tips touch his skin just yet. He made his pup wait, aware that he was holding his breath in expectation, but not about to rush.

As Axel worked his way over Bayden's body, Bayden's cock hardened. Axel felt Bayden's muscles knot with tension, too, but he was sure that it had nothing to do with Bayden wanting to come. No, what Bayden really wanted were the marks. He wanted to belong to someone more desperately than anyone Axel had ever met.

Axel smiled as Bayden squirmed. Bayden could do without an orgasm, but to be held on the edge of being possessed was far harder. Bayden swallowed rapidly but didn't ask.

A bead of pre-cum formed on the tip of Bayden's cock. Axel swiped it up with a leather covered knuckle and offered it to Bayden's lips. He lapped up the taste. A slight hesitation and he pressed a kiss against the glove, thanking Axel even when he hadn't been given anything he really craved.

Moving his knuckle to Bayden's chin, Axel coaxed him to look him in the eye.

Need. So much need, but complete acceptance of Axel's right to deny him what he needed too.

"I don't like being ignored."

Bayden frowned.

457

"Don't look down. Keep your eyes on me."

"Yes, sir."

Axel slid his hands down Bayden's back, dragging the metal tips along his skin, all the way down to his buttocks.

If there was a way for Bayden to earn praise, it was by holding Axel's gaze, and he threw himself into that task as if his life depended upon it. He didn't even blink.

"Good boy."

Axel didn't need to look down to see what he was doing. He knew Bayden's body so well he could have played the game blindfolded, except that would have meant missing the look in Bayden's eyes too.

A calm gradually settled over Bayden. He couldn't keep Axel's gaze the whole time, but he managed to keep his attention on Axel's face—dropping his gaze to Axel's lips every time looking Axel in the eye became too much for him.

It made Bayden look simultaneously submissive, obedient and desperate for a kiss.

Bayden's back, his thighs, the outside of his upper arms and finally his chest—Axel calmly claimed each bit of him. When he looked down to admire his work, Axel made it obvious what he was doing, reminding Bayden that one of them didn't need anyone's permission to do that.

None of the scratches were deep, none of them drew blood. Axel trailed one fingertip over Bayden's torso as he considered his options. Bayden's cock was flushed with arousal, the head peeking past his foreskin. Axel ran a finger up the length. Bayden stopped breathing. Axel traced the same line again, letting the metal tip touch Bayden's cock this time, but only as a tease. Axel made him wait until the third caress before he actually allowed him to get any benefit from it.

Bayden's head dropped back. He did his best to keep his gaze on Axel's face, peering at him from beneath lids that were heavy with pleasure, but his eyes kept fluttering closed.

Bayden's cock jerked under Axel's feather-light touch. Bayden pushed his hips forward, desperate for more. His arse rubbed against Axel's cock through the thin layer of denim separating them.

Axel wrapped his gloved hand around Bayden's cock. Tensing and relaxing each finger in turn, he gently milked his shaft.

"Move for me."

Bayden blinked at him. He swallowed rapidly. He tentatively rocked his hips—pushing his cock gently against Axel's palm.

"You can do better than that, pup."

Bayden took a shaky breath and thrust properly into Axel's grip.

"Good boy. You can put your hands on my shoulders to steady yourself, but I don't want you to stop moving until I give you permission."

"Yes, sir." Such a soft whisper. Bayden settled his hands on Axel's shoulders just as tenderly.

"That's right," Axel whispered. He looked down, watching Bayden's cock slide against his hand. The tip of his cock appeared past the black leather channel with each thrust. More and more pre-cum leaked from the tip and smeared against Axel's glove.

"Do you want me to…?"

"I want you to concentrate on obeying my orders, nothing else."

Bayden could hold back. Axel had no doubt about that. If he'd been allowed to show off his self-control, Bayden could have kept going without coming for hours. But that wasn't the challenge.

Their eyes met. Bayden thrust forward again. Then once more. He threw his head back as he came, exposing his throat in that now familiar way. His grip on Axel's shoulders tightened and Bayden clung to him as if Axel were his only anchor in the roughest of storms. Barely a minute after Axel first ordered him to move Bayden's cum spilled against Axel's hand and T-shirt.

Bayden's howl wasn't as loud as usual. His breathing was ragged. Heat rushed to his cheeks. But he didn't stop moving.

Axel remained silent, watching Bayden struggle to keep going as his cock started to soften and thrusting into Axel's palm had to bring more pain than pleasure. So gorgeous.

"You can stop." Axel kept his hand around Bayden's cock as he slid his other hand into Bayden's hair and guided him forward to be kissed. "So good," Axel whispered to him. "So hot."

Bayden murmured against Axel's lips. His hands gripped Axel's T-shirt very tightly by the time Axel finally broke the kiss.

Axel didn't give him time to pull himself together. "Undo my fly, pup."

For a second, Bayden looked confused by the order. Then he seemed to realise what Axel was talking about. He quickly fumbled at Axel's clothes, tugging them out of the way while still obeying Axel's order not to look down.

"Good boy."

Axel's only contributions were to lift his hips so Bayden could move his clothes out of the way, and to ensure that Bayden didn't fall off his lap. Working by touch with clumsy hands, Bayden eventually freed Axel's cock.

"There's lube on the side table."

Bayden blindly rummaged around in the bowl of odds and ends there until his fingers wrapped around the little bottle of lube. He didn't wait for another order. He smeared the lube down the length of Axel's shaft.

Axel's guess had been right. Even though he'd come, Bayden's need was still obvious. Being topped wasn't just about the chance to get off for Bayden. A nod was the only encouragement he needed. He lifted himself up and guided Axel's cock inside him.

For the first time, Bayden was in control and free to set the pace himself, but Axel only allowed that freedom to last for a few seconds. He caught hold of Bayden's hips, forcing him to slow down and give himself time to relax. Cum smeared against Bayden's hip. The metal fingertips pressed against Bayden's skin, drawing a gasp from him.

"Patience, pup. There's no rush."

Bayden squirmed and rocked his hips, obviously incapable of stilling himself. His hands fluttered mid-air as he struggled to work out where to put them.

"On my shoulders."

Bayden didn't obey instantly.

"A little bit of lube won't kill me, pup."

Bayden delicately placed his hands on Axel's shoulders

"You're allowed to touch me. I'd tell you if you weren't."

"Yes, sir." The words were barely breathed. Bayden rocked his hips again.

"Good boy." Axel thrust up into him. "Move for me."

Bayden set up a careful rhythm. Maybe it was because he wasn't used to riding another man, but every time Axel let the metal tips scratch his skin, Bayden lost his coordination.

He was a stubborn little bugger, though; he kept trying to follow the order. Watching that was almost as erotic as the way his hole tightened and relaxed around Axel's shaft as he rode him. Bayden was his. Even if he wasn't wearing Axel's collar around his neck, he belonged to him as thoroughly as any man ever could.

Axel ran his gaze down Bayden's body. His cock was hardening again, but Axel wasn't inclined to grant him another orgasm that night.

Instinct begged Axel to move, to thrust up into Bayden again and meet each movement, but he held himself in check, making sure Bayden was the one who did all the work tonight.

But, that was the only way Axel held back. Being able to last a lot longer than Bayden wasn't a point he needed to make that night. Axel didn't try to make it difficult for Bayden to ride him over the edge. The look of bliss on Bayden's face when Axel came was just as intense as when Bayden had come. Axel half expected another howl to fill the air.

He tugged Bayden forward and brought their lips together.

The kiss was far sweeter than it had any right to be while Axel's cock was still buried deep in Bayden's arse.

Even when the kiss ended, Axel wasn't inclined to separate their bodies. He guided Bayden to sit up straight. Bayden still didn't have permission to look down, but Axel considered the marks he'd left on Bayden very carefully.

When he looked up, Bayden was still trying to catch his breath.

Axel stroked his cheek. Another scratch appeared, a very light one.

Bayden swallowed, drawing Axel's attention to his throat. The need to put a collar on him was getting more intense by the day. Axel drew another line with his fingertip, all the way around Bayden's throat. Damn, but his cock tried to harden at the sight. Finally, Axel separated their bodies, although he kept Bayden on his lap.

Bayden still didn't look down, but he took one hand from Axel's shoulder and gently touched the inside of Axel's wrist, just above the line of his glove. Axel nodded. Bayden guided Axel's hand up to his lips and began to delicately lap up the cum, methodically cleaning the leather surface.

"Carefully," Axel warned, when Bayden took one fingertip between his lips. "I don't want any scratches on your tongue. It's far too talented to put at risk like that."

Bayden blushed at the mild praise. His actions became more confident. When the glove was cleaned to his satisfaction, he cautiously leaned forward and lapped at the traces of lube he'd left on Axel's T-shirt when he grabbed his shoulders.

Axel made no comment. That was apparently encouragement enough.

Bayden dipped his head, tying his body in knots in an attempt to remain on Axel's lap and simultaneously lean down far enough to lick up the cum that had landed on Axel's T-shirt.

Axel grabbed a cushion and dropped it on the floor between his feet. Bayden moved silently down to kneel there. He still hadn't forgotten the order to keep his attention up on Axel's face. Even when the angle made eye contact impossible, Axel was still sure of the direction of Bayden's gaze.

No rush, no hesitation. Bayden lapped deliberately at Axel's T-shirt, dampening the T-shirt with his tongue as he cleaned up his own orgasm. He kept working until Axel pulled the T-shirt over his head and tossed it aside.

Sliding his fingers through Bayden's hair, Axel made it clear that he didn't want him to stop. Bayden's tongue danced against his skin, checking that none of his semen had seeped through the thin cotton.

Gradually, he made his way down Axel's body.

Axel was completely soft.

Bayden pressed a kiss against Axel's pubic hair just above his cock. Staring down at him, Axel saw that smudges of lube and smears of cum were the only things visible on his shaft. Bayden didn't look down to check before he kissed his way to the very tip of the shaft.

Inch by inch, Bayden worked his tongue over Axel's cock. So gentle, so submissive. Axel stroked his hair back from his face. "Good pup."

Bayden smiled, but he didn't stop. He was soon murmuring his pleasure; his lips reverted to kisses. As much as he loved to see Bayden enjoying himself, it was too soon for Axel to want to get hard again. He coaxed Bayden back up onto his lap and settled him in position.

"You can look down at yourself."

Bayden gasped when he saw the patterns Axel had traced out on his body.

"Sir?" A word spoken so softly, it was just on the edge of hearing, even when they were mere inches apart.

Axel stroked Bayden's cheek with a knuckle. "You're always allowed to talk to me, pup."

"Just because I…"

"No, pup. Not just because you said you like it. I like it too. It would be a strange dom who didn't like marking his territory, wouldn't it?"

Bayden smiled. He ran his fingertips very gently over the scratches on his chest.

They wouldn't last. The way Bayden healed, every single one of them would have disappeared by morning. The memory of them would last far longer.

"Yours," Bayden whispered.

"Yes."

Bayden glanced up, obviously not aware that he'd spoken out loud. He nodded when their gazes locked. "Yours."

Chapter Thirty

Bayden hesitated at the door to the office at the back of the pub. Axel sat in front of the computer, but he was staring at his phone rather than the monitor and looked deep in thought. Bayden stepped back. Their conversation could wait. Axel obviously had more important things on his mind.

Just then, Axel looked up. He smiled. "You can come in."

Bayden stepped into the office. "Have you decided what the punishment should be, sir?"

Axel set his phone down and beckoned him closer. Bayden tried to kneel as he stepped into his space, but Axel stopped him short and arranged him to stand in front of him, leaning back against the edge of his desk.

"The punishment for not telling me what was going on?" Axel asked.

Guilt rolled inside Bayden. "And for anything else you think I should be punished for, sir."

Axel studied him carefully for a few minutes. "We'll talk about it all closer to the time."

Bayden shifted uncomfortably against the edge of the desk. It was Axel's choice. Everything was Axel's choice. But… "You don't have to wait on my account, sir. I'm fine now. Whatever the punishment is, I can…" He closed his eyes for a moment.

Axel stroked Bayden's side through his vest, warming every bit of skin he touched.

"Is having to wait part of the punishment, sir?"

"No." Axel sounded very certain about that. "It's about giving you the chance to deal with one thing at a time. You're grieving for your grandfather. Everything else can wait."

"But—"

"Everything else can wait. That includes any punishment."

Bayden stared down at the way his own hand had curled into a fist. He knew Axel had noticed the gesture, but he didn't comment on it. Bayden folded his arms, tucking his hands out of sight. "It's been three weeks since he died."

"Yes."

"And it's not as if I hadn't had time to settle in to submitting to you by then. I'd already been doing that for three weeks..."

"Yes."

Bayden moved his weight from one foot to the other, not sure how much further he could push the conversation without sounding like he was demanding something or challenging Axel's dominance.

"It's six weeks since you agreed to submit to me." Axel's tone made it obvious he'd only just realised that.

Bayden nodded. "I thought you might want to punish me today. Before I..." He looked down, not quite strong enough to finish his sentence.

Axel straightened up in his seat. His scent changed. "Before you what?"

"You said I could try to submit to you for six weeks. You kept your word. You gave me six weeks." He swallowed.

"Before you what?" Axel repeated.

Bayden's heart raced. "You said at one point that my job wasn't anything to do with that, so if you're still okay with me working here..."

"Before you what?" Axel repeated.

"Leave," Bayden blurted out.

"I never said that I expected you to leave after six weeks."

Axel rolled his office chair forward. Bayden edged sideways to give Axel more room. Axel put his elbow on the desk alongside Bayden. His other hand still rested on

Bayden's waist. Axel was now firmly between Bayden and the door.

Bayden looked past Axel, wondering if it was just his imagination that made him wonder if Axel was worried he was going to run away.

"Did you always think you'd leave after six weeks?" Axel asked. He was doing that thing where he spoke very slowly, giving himself plenty of time to think and select each word with care.

Bayden nodded.

"It never occurred to you that you might want to stay here for longer than that?" He frowned, but not because he was angry—his expression came from the ferocity with which he was studying Bayden, trying to read him in a way which was first nature to a wolf but so difficult for humans.

"I…" Bayden unfolded his arms and pushed his hands into his pockets.

Axel waited.

"What I wanted wasn't important. I'd only saved up enough for six weeks, sir," Bayden admitted.

Axel nodded slowly. While he thought, he stroked Bayden's side. Bayden closed his eyes, relishing the idle gesture.

"A few things have changed since you started submitting to me."

Bayden opened his eyes as he forced down a fresh wave of guilt. Things had changed, but they hadn't changed for the better. This wasn't the way he'd wanted things to turn out. A bitter taste filled the back of his mouth.

"Is there anything that would stop you from being able to stay with me for as long as you wanted to now?" Axel asked.

Bayden cleared his throat, but he still couldn't get a word out. He shook his head.

"Originally, we spoke about re-negotiating after six weeks, but we're going to defer that."

Bayden forced himself to look up.

"Any renegotiating can wait until other things are settled." Axel didn't make it a question, it was a statement of fact. "It's not something you need to think about right now. Things will continue exactly the way they are. Your wages cover the rent on your flat, don't they?"

Bayden nodded.

"So there are no decisions you need to make today. Everything can wait. That applies to both the punishment and the renegotiation. One thing at a time," Axel reminded him.

Unsure his voice would come out steady, Bayden took refuge in another nod. He could stay. The knowledge spiralled through his mind leaving a joyful, glittery vapour trail in its wake, but shame rushed through him in the wake of every positive emotion, obliterating any relief he might have felt. What kind of wolf felt happy when a member of their pack was barely cold in the ground?

Axel's phone made a noise. He reached past Bayden and picked it up from his desk. He read something off the screen and sent back a text, his thumbs moving too rapidly for Bayden to decipher the words.

"That was Sal," Axel said, putting the phone back on the desk. "She called earlier to say she's flying out tonight and wants a lift to the airport. She just texted me the times. It will be during opening hours."

Bayden said nothing.

"I'll give you a choice. You can come with me, or you can stay here."

"Whatever you prefer, sir."

"I prefer to give you the choice."

Bayden shuffled his feet. He couldn't keep following Axel around like a puppy forever. Axel should be able to meet his sister without someone tagging along and getting in the way. The last thing he wanted was for Axel to regret inviting him to stay on just a few seconds after he'd granted that permission. "I'll stay here, sir."

Axel stood up. He brushed their lips together, but he didn't linger for a longer kiss. It was about praise not sex. "That's fine. You'll be in charge when I'm gone."

"Me?"

Axel chuckled. "Yes, you. Who else? Some of the other Dragons will be here. One of them will take over behind the bar when you take your break, and they'll jump in if you need a hand. There'll be plenty of guys who'll back you up if there's any trouble."

"You wouldn't prefer one of them to be in charge, sir?"

"Because they're doms?" Axel asked. "Because they're full members of the club? Or because they're human?" Any humour that had been in his expression disappeared when he reached the last option. "You work here. You live here. You're my sub. I don't expect you to take orders off anyone but me and, yes, when I'm not here, you're in charge. The other guys will help you, but they all know better than to play the dom with you or to tell you what to do—they all know you won't get in trouble with me for disobeying any of them."

"I'm sorry, sir." He seemed to be saying that all the time lately.

"You're still learning." He stroked Bayden's cheek. "Tonight's not a test. You just do what you always do, and it will be fine."

"Yes, sir."

Just do as you always do. It was a clear order; Axel always gave clear orders. But it wasn't an easy order to follow. The minute Axel walked out of the pub to fetch his sister, the world tilted beneath Bayden's feet.

Axel not being there changed everything. Bayden needed Axel—even if he couldn't quite put his finger on what he needed him for.

He didn't need him to be able to do his work behind the bar. That was easy. He wouldn't need help from the club guys when he was serving drinks. He wouldn't need anyone if there was trouble either. He could look after himself.

He stared down at his knuckles as he absentmindedly served another customer. Even if he hadn't been in a fight for a while, a wolf didn't forget those kind of skills just because life got easier for a few weeks.

Bayden could still fight. It was one of the very few things that hadn't changed since he first rode into The Dragon's Lair. He could still drop any human he needed to.

If he'd needed to go back to earning his living with his fists, now that his six weeks were over, he could have done it. No one would have had to force him, or even ask. He'd *wanted* to go back to doing that at the end of his six weeks—he had.

He'd have taken whatever bets he needed to. He'd have supported his mother and his grandfather without any hesitation. He didn't need to be with Axel so much he'd been willing to wish his own blood dead in order to be able to stay with a human.

No wolf would do that, no good wolf.

Several more customers came and went. Bayden glanced at the clock above the bar.

It was stupid to miss Axel when he'd only just walked out of the building. Bayden could look after himself. He'd have been able to look after his mother and grandfather too. He'd have been more than willing to give up his time with Axel. It was what wolves did, wasn't it? They put the other wolves in their pack first—always.

Thoughts swirled through his head faster and faster, until they overlapped each other in their rush to remind him of all the ways he'd screwed up. If his grandfather was still alive he'd have… If his mother had stayed away from Danville and let him look after her, Bayden would have… If there were still bills that needed to be paid, he'd…

"Bayden."

He moved down the bar and served another drink. As soon as the customer turned away, Bayden's thoughts came rushing back.

If it had been necessary, he'd have… He shook his head at himself. Who was he kidding?

He'd failed to be a good wolf in so many ways.

Bayden swallowed. Was that what had killed his grandfather in the end? Had he realised just how poor a representative of their species his grandson was? He'd been so ill, that kind of realisation could easily have been the final straw.

Bayden's throat tried to close up. He'd been trying so hard to be a good wolf for so long — proving that he could pay his way and be a good member of the pack. Had his grandfather realised it was all a lie — that he was too selfish to deserve to be called a member of any pack? Bayden's hands shook as he took empty glasses off the bar and set them on the counter behind him.

He couldn't keep screwing up. Panic pounded through his veins. It was too late to impress his grandfather, or even convince his mother that she wasn't better off at Danville. But he could fix things with Axel.

That had to be possible, because he couldn't lose Axel as well. His heart faltered even thinking about it. His breath stalled in his lungs. He gripped the edge of the bar.

One thing at a time — that's what Axel had said.

Remembering the order let Bayden push his panic aside.

One thing.

He hadn't been able to stop Axel paying debts that were nothing to do with him. He couldn't alter when Axel was willing to punish him for his mistakes. But he could control some things. He could control…

Bayden's mind went blank. He racked every corner of his brain. He'd handed over the decisions about so many parts of his life, but he could still control…

When he paid back the money he owed Axel. Yes! The moment the idea hit him, he knew that he'd stumbled on the one mistake he could fix that very moment.

Seven hundred pounds. He looked at the clock again. A straight forward bet on a fight wouldn't do it—not if he wanted to be able to hand Axel the money as soon as he got back to the pub. But the right bet with the right person...

Bayden assessed the men in the pub, discounting one possibility after another. Finally, he spotted a familiar face at the table in the corner. That particular man hadn't been around much since their last bet. Even now, he only lurked on the edges of the crowd, aware that he wasn't really welcome.

The right bet with the right person.

Another glance at the clock and Bayden headed to where Drac, Griz and Hale were sitting with a few other men, playing poker.

"Axel said one of you would cover the bar while I take my break," Bayden said.

Drac drained the last of his pint and scooped up his chips.

Griz indicated the seat Drac had been using. "Grab a stool. I'll deal you in."

Bayden shook his head.

"Don't have the balls for it?" Hale asked.

Bayden didn't have time to waste rising to that kind of bait. "There's something I need to do."

He went straight to the table in the corner, aware that he'd attracted some attention but not inclined to care. It wasn't the kind of bet he liked taking, but maybe that was as it should be. It would hurt, but he deserved to hurt after screwing things up so badly and being such a poor excuse for a wolf.

With the terms of the bet set, he headed toward the back of the pub. Griz and Hale had abandoned their card game and were hot on his heels.

"What's going on?" Hale demanded, as they caught up with him halfway along the corridor that led to the back rooms.

"A bet," Bayden said.

Hale caught hold of his arm and pulled him back. "What?"

"A bet," Bayden repeated. One that would let him earn enough to pay Axel back that night.

"No."

Bayden looked up at Hale. "It's nothing to do with you."

"You think Axel will agree with that?"

Bayden frowned. "Yes."

"Then you're an idiot. And if you think I'll believe Axel signed off on this, you must think I'm an idiot too."

"Axel doesn't think I'll do what you tell me," Bayden said. "He's never said I have to obey you."

Anger filled Hale's scent. "If you're going to be riding with us—"

"Then I should prove that I'm capable of seeing through any bet I make."

Bayden tugged his arm out of Hale's grip. He turned and ran straight into Griz.

"Bayden, slow down and think for a minute. Okay?" Griz's tone was mellow. He wasn't ordering anyone about. He was being friendly and reasonable. He also had hold of Bayden's arm.

"Let go of me. If you don't do that when I ask politely, I'm allowed to insist. Axel's very clear about that."

Griz and Hale exchanged glances.

"Axel's going to freak," Griz said.

Bayden didn't bother to disagree, but that wasn't because he thought that Griz was right. Bayden knew how things worked. Money was important. A wolf proving that he could pay the bills—that he would do whatever it took in order to do that—was important, too.

One thing at a time. It would have been better to prove that he could be a perfect human submissive or that he could take whatever punishment Axel wanted to dish out. But,

Bayden wasn't above scrabbling for crumbs. Proving he'd do what it took to pay his debts would be a start.

He turned to the man who'd taken his bet.

Proving this particular point would involve a certain amount of pain, but that wasn't a problem. Bayden was used to that kind of pain.

* * * * *

Griz was lurking in the pub doorway when Axel drove into the car park. Axel's blood went cold. He jerked the car to a stop, not caring how badly he parked, and jumped out of the car. "What happened?"

"You need to keep your temper," Griz said.

Axel tried to step past him, but Griz blocked his path.

"Get out of my way."

"Axe. Listen to me. You need to keep your temper. He's not himself at the moment. You said it yourself—he's still grieving."

"Is Bayden in there?" Axel demanded.

"Yes."

Axel's pulse slowed slightly. "Is he okay?"

Griz hesitated. He was a big guy—but not so big he couldn't be moved aside when adrenaline spiked in Axel's veins. Axel shoved Griz out of the way and damn near threw himself into the pub.

Bayden was behind the bar. He had his back to the door, but he was there, working away as if it was just any other day.

Jesus—Axel was going to kill Griz for scaring the hell out of him that way.

Bayden turned around.

It felt like someone had punched Axel in the stomach.

"He took a bet," Griz said from somewhere behind him.

"A bet," Axel repeated blankly. One of Bayden's eyes was swollen shut. His lip was split. A vivid purple bruise covered his jaw. Dried blood crusted on his temple, matting into his hair.

"He lost," Griz said.

"Bayden doesn't lose bets." Axel could barely breathe well enough to get the words out. Bayden didn't lose bets. It just didn't happen. Bayden had his jacket on and done up, hiding his body from the neck down. Axel's gaze went helplessly from one facial injury to another.

Bayden stared across at him. He made no move to close the gap between them. Even if he was physically capable of it, Axel knew Bayden wouldn't approach a more dominant wolf.

A bet was a werewolf's way of reminding humans how difficult it was to break them. Axel had never seen a man closer to being broken than Bayden had been since his grandfather's death. Poor little sod.

Axel crossed the room and stopped just in front of Bayden. Up close, the wounds looked even more painful. It took Axel years to make words happen but, when he finally spoke, he sounded impossibly calm. "What happened?"

"I took a bet, sir, on a fight."

"You lost?" Axel frowned as he struggled to make sense of it. Bayden didn't lose. The way he fought, it was impossible to think of any human winning against him. Unless it wasn't a human. Bayden wasn't the only wolf in the world. "A fight with another shifter?"

That was better in a way. It wouldn't cut Bayden's pride so deep. He'd survive that far more easily. But Bayden shook his head.

Bayden's hand rested on the bar. Axel caught hold of his wrist and studied his knuckles. There wasn't a mark there. "You didn't fight back." *I know better than to hit a cop.* Possibilities clicked together. Bile rose in Axel's throat. "A cop?"

Bayden shook his head again. He reached into his jacket pocket with his free hand and pulled out a thick fold of notes. He offered them to Axel. "For the gravestone."

"You lost the bet," Axel reminded him.

"I didn't win the fight, but I won the bet, sir." His words were slurred by his injuries, but there was no mistaking them or their meaning.

"You bet on the other guy. You threw the fight? You…" Axel managed not to throw up, but it was a near run thing. "What was the bet?" he demanded.

"That we could fight for three minutes without me landing a single blow." There was no emotion in his voice. He wasn't a scared little pup who'd been cornered into a horrible bet and needed his dom to tell him everything was okay. He wasn't someone who'd come face to face with a bent cop and done whatever it took to survive.

All the fear Axel had felt when he first saw Bayden's injuries cooled into unadulterated fury. "Who set the terms?"

Bayden hesitated.

"Who suggested that as a bet?" Axel repeated.

"I did, sir."

Part of Axel had already known what the answer would be. The confirmation still hit him like a right hook. Axel had been angry the moment he saw the first bruise, but that had been directed at a nameless faceless spectre that had hurt his pup. Now, Axel knew who was responsible, who had made this happen.

"Get out."

Bayden tried to pull away.

Axel tightened his grip on his wrist. "Not you—*you* stay." He turned to the men on the other side of the bar. "Everyone else, get out—now."

The Dragons started ushering men out, with varying levels of politeness depending on the Dragon.

When everyone else was gone, Griz and Hale came back, Evan trailing along in Griz's wake.

"I said everyone out," Axel told them.

"Sir?"

Axel glanced at Evan. The boy looked up at Griz, big blue eyes full of concern.

"That's not something you have to worry about," Griz promised.

Evan looked from Bayden to Axel and back, apparently not convinced. Axel turned his attention to Bayden. As far as he could tell past the bruises, Bayden didn't share Evan's worries.

"Um…" Evan cleared his throat. "Bayden?"

Bayden glanced at him, but he didn't even seem to understand what Evan was asking.

"He wants to know if you feel safe being left alone with me," Axel translated through gritted teeth.

"Of course I do."

"If you're sure," Evan said. Griz led him away a few seconds later.

Only Hale remained there. Axel glared across the bar, knowing that Hale was judging the grip he had on his temper. "Do you have doubts too?"

"On you keeping your temper? Yes."

"If you think I'd —"

"I think he's a bloody hard man to track down if you say the wrong thing and scare him away," Hale cut in.

Axel looked down at the grip he had on Bayden's wrist. "Neither of us is going anywhere."

"Is that right, Bayden?" Hale asked.

"I won't leave if I'm allowed to stay," Bayden said.

Hale seemed to accept that. The room was very quiet when he left. Axel stared at the door for what felt like hours before he turned back to Bayden.

Bayden offered him the notes once more.

Hale was right about one thing. Throwing a tantrum wouldn't help, it would just risk scaring Bayden away. Axel temporarily caged his temper as best he could. "There's no doubt that you're allowed to stay, you understand that?"

Bayden nodded. It was a cautious action, but it wasn't obvious if that was because he was wary of committing himself or because his head had to hurt like hell.

"You need my permission to leave the pub while you're submitting to me, and nothing I say is going to equal permission for you to leave. If something makes you doubt that, you ask — you don't leave."

Bayden nodded again. He glanced down and offered the money yet again. He really didn't seem to get why Axel wasn't taking it.

"Did you have this planned before I left?" Axel demanded.

Bayden shook his head. He fidgeted with the money. "You said I'm allowed to take bets on fights, sir."

"If you thought I'd have given you permission to do this, why did you wait until my back was turned?"

Bayden shuffled his feet but failed to volunteer any information.

Axel ground his teeth together. "Who was the bet with?"

"Ford. Everyone saw him lose the first time I came here. He —"

"He has no idea what being a Dragon means," Axel bit out. "He actually thought this would impress us."

"Hale threw him out," Bayden said. "But…"

The idea of hearing him defend Ford made Axel sick to his stomach, but he couldn't seem to make his lips move to stop him.

"It was just a bet, sir. He didn't do anything wrong."

Axel grabbed hold of Bayden's arm and spun him around so he faced the mirror behind the bar. "You don't think this is wrong?"

Bayden seemed to try to frown at his reflection, but his eye was too swollen to allow for much facial expression. "The bet was—"

"Would you have kept hitting someone who looked like this?" Axel demanded.

Bayden swallowed.

"Would you keep hitting someone who wasn't hitting you back?"

Bayden shook his head.

"That's why he'll never be one of us. And it's why Hale got rid of him before I got here." If he'd still been there, Axel would have done his damnedest to kill him. The only way Ford would have walked out of there alive would have been if the other Dragons had managed to physically restrain Axel.

Bayden met Axel's gaze in the reflection as best he could. Axel took another deep breath. His own anger would have to wait. Standing behind Bayden, looking over his shoulder into the reflection, he forced himself to consider the injuries as objectively as possible.

"Has anyone looked you over?"

Bayden hesitated.

Axel wasn't in the mood for that. "Well?"

"Tolmore wanted to, sir," Bayden said.

"But?"

"It was the end of my break."

"And?" Axel prompted.

Bayden looked down. "You said I don't have to submit to anyone else, sir." *And I'd never trust anyone but you to patch me up.* The unsaid words rang through Axel's head more loudly than the ones Bayden whispered.

Axel turned Bayden toward him. He forced as much emotion out of his voice as possible. "I'll bet Griz and Hale tried a few orders too."

Bayden nodded.

Axel ran his thumb as gently as possible over the bruise on Bayden's jaw. "They told you to wait until I got back and that you shouldn't take the bet?"

He nodded again. "But your rules say I'm allowed to take bets on whatever fights I want—as long as I take them here and when there are other people around to make sure everything stops if I say the word."

"The difference between your previous fights and this one didn't occur to you?" Axel asked, with forced patience.

Bayden shook his head. He seemed genuinely confused.

Axel stepped back. "Upstairs. Now."

In the flat, he led Bayden straight into the en-suite off the master bedroom.

"Undress."

Bayden offered him the money once more.

Axel folded his arms rather than take it. A few moments of hesitation and Bayden put the notes down next to the sink.

As Bayden stripped off his clothes, he revealed the full extent of the beating he'd taken. His whole torso was a motley of different colours. There were scrapes where he'd obviously hit the ground hard. A particularly dark bruise on his ribs had to have been inflicted by a boot.

Most of the hits that Bayden had allowed to land had been body blows. Pictures flashed through Axel's mind, each one worse than the last. Bayden had had the skill to end the fight whenever he'd wanted, and he'd chosen to let Ford land every one of those blows—he'd preferred that than let Axel lend him a few hundred quid.

Axel nodded to the shower.

Bayden stood under the water apparently unconcerned by the hot spray hitting his injuries. If the soap stung against the cuts and grazes, he didn't mention it. He scrubbed himself down exactly as he usually did, but when he reached for his towel, Axel stepped forward.

Grabbing the first towel to hand, which happened to be one of his own, Axel started to dry Bayden, checking him over inch by inch in the process.

"You'll get blood on it, sir," Bayden protested.

"You should worry less about getting blood on things and more about the fact you're bleeding," Axel growled.

Bayden pulled back. He dropped his head. It was as if someone had flicked a switch. Axel had never seen such a rapid display of submission from him.

"Come here." His best efforts failed to gentle his tone.

Bayden stepped closer, but he didn't glance up. He didn't look defensive; he looked vulnerable. Axel gritted his teeth. Instincts warred inside him, half wanting to throttle Bayden, half wanting to wrap him in cotton wool and make sure he never got hurt again.

Unfortunately, neither option was viable.

Bayden remained very still while Axel worked his way over him. The beating was worse than the result of every fight Axel had seen him in put together, but Bayden didn't flinch or make a sound.

Once Bayden was dry, Axel led him into the kitchen. Bayden was nothing if not persistent. He didn't try to pick up any clothes, but he brought the money with him and tried to hand it to Axel again.

Axel scrubbed at his own face with his hand. "You really don't get why I'm mad at you. Do you?"

Bayden glanced at the money. "It's all there, sir."

"I don't doubt it." Axel got out the first aid kit and sat down at the table. He indicated the other chair to Bayden.

The routine had become unbearably familiar.

Bayden sat in silence as Axel worked on him. He didn't react to anything, until Axel ran his fingers very lightly over a bruise high up on his ribs.

Bayden gasped.

"That hurts?" Axel's eyes narrowed. He hadn't pressed hard and Bayden's pain tolerance was through the roof. It shouldn't have been that tender unless his ribs were completely demolished.

Bayden shook his head. "The marks — they don't mean anything unless they're from you, sir."

Axel went back to work. "They don't mean you belong to anyone else, but that doesn't mean I like them."

"I can still do whatever you want me to, sir."

"You're in no condition to play," Axel snapped.

Bayden moved to the edge of his chair, obviously relieved to think he'd finally worked out what the problem was. "I can, sir." He thought for a moment. "If you're behind me, then—"

"You're in no condition to play," Axel repeated. "You were in no condition to be left alone here tonight, either." And that was the real problem, wasn't it? God, what had he been thinking, letting Bayden out of his sight?

"I'm fine."

"If you were fine, you wouldn't have done this." Axel ran a fingertip over one of Bayden's many bruises. "Would you?"

"Wanting to pay you back doesn't mean there's something wrong with me. I always paid my own way. Whatever money we needed, it was never a problem. I might not be as good a wolf as my grandfather was, but I've always paid my way. I…" He took a shaky breath. "I should have been able to handle it from the start. You shouldn't have had to—"

"I had no problem paying for it," Axel cut in, unable to pretend that the money was in any way important.

"He wasn't your responsibility. He's wasn't part of your pack!"

"But you are."

Bayden opened his mouth. He closed it. Words didn't happen. He stared at Axel as if he'd risen from the dead following crucifixion.

Axel's eyes narrowed. "You're part of my pack," he repeated.

Bayden just stared at him, but for the first time in what felt like a long time, there was a light at the end of the tunnel. Bayden's desperation for the word finally gave Axel something to catch hold of.

"Do you doubt you're part of my pack?" Axel demanded.

Bayden looked down. "I..."

"You've felt like you're part of my pack for a long time, haven't you?" He pushed.

Bayden didn't deny it.

Axel scrolled rapidly through everything he knew about packs—everything Bayden had let slip, everything Kincade had written about in his book.

"I treat you like you're part of my pack, don't I?"

Bayden nodded.

"Since when?"

"The first day." Bayden cleared his throat. "Since the first day we met."

"Yes."

Bayden swallowed. "I...I was, or I am, sir?"

"You *are* part of my pack. The club—The Black Dragons—they're my pack, and you're part of that. It will take the jacket to make it official, but everyone knows that you're one of us, that you're part of my pack."

"Humans..."

"Are just as capable of forming a pack as wolves." Axel held Bayden's gaze, daring him to think differently. "And we're just as capable of taking a mate."

Bayden didn't move, didn't blink.

Axel's confidence soared higher with every second that passed. "When everything is sorted out, you will be a formal part of this pack, and you will be my mate. I've known that's where we've been heading for a long time. I think you have too."

"I thought…" Bayden met his gaze.

"You thought you were the only one who wanted that?" Axel asked. That had to be the problem, because there was no way anyone could doubt that Bayden wanted it with a ferocity that Axel had never encountered in another sub.

"I…"

"Just because humans use different words, that doesn't mean we aren't talking about exactly the same thing."

Bayden cleared his throat. "You want…"

"Yes." Axel let his complete certainty fill the word.

"Even though I screwed up again?"

"Yes." No doubt. No hesitation.

Bayden looked at the money resting on the table between them.

"I said you'd be allowed to pay me back, and I'll stand by that," Axel promised. Bayden reached out to the money, and Axel knew Bayden was going to try to hand it to him. "But I won't touch a penny you earned this way. You can pay me back out of your wages, or whatever, but not this money."

Bayden stared at the folded notes. "What do you want me to do with it?"

Axel shrugged. "Keep it. Toss it. Put a match to it for all I care. It's nothing to do with me."

Bayden put the money back on the table and dropped his hand onto his lap. His disappointment was palpable.

Axel couldn't give way to sympathy. "There are plenty of other things that need to be dealt with," he announced.

"Yes, sir."

"Like the punishment you still have outstanding."

"You said I wasn't allowed to be punished yet, sir."

"I was wrong. Waiting isn't helping you. You'll be punished now. The punishment starts tonight." Even as he said it, Axel knew it was the right choice—the only choice at that point. Sympathy, patience and understanding were only part of what Bayden needed to receive from his would-be master. It was now time for the other part.

"Yes, sir."

Axel was silent for several seconds.

"Do you want me to get anything for it, sir?" Bayden asked, once more moving to the edge of his seat.

"Like a whip?" Axel suggested.

"Whatever you want."

"It's not going to be that kind of punishment."

"I can take it, sir."

"I know you can. I don't think you even care about that kind of pain anymore. I'm the only one who cares if you get hurt—that's why this bothers me far more than it bothers you." He stroked a knuckle under Bayden's injured eye.

Bayden leaned into his touch, so desperate for reassurance. Axel forced himself to take his hand away.

"The punishment will be losing your privileges, and it will last until every injury has completely healed."

Bayden nodded.

Axel let silence fall, forcing Bayden to make the next move, to actively come to him for the punishment rather than just accept what was thrown at him.

"Am I allowed to ask which privileges, sir?" Bayden asked, very softly.

"All of them."

Bayden tensed. "You said I had to tell you if you said something that made me think you want me to leave, sir."

"Living here isn't a privilege, that's part of being my mate, and that will never change. But, everything else we spoke about before your penance—all those privileges are gone, no exceptions."

"Yes, sir." He sounded calm. It was obvious that he had no idea what that would be like in practice.

"This punishment is going to be a lot harder than your penance was, but you'll get through it," Axel promised him.

Bayden nodded.

Axel stood up. "It's time you went to bed."

485

Bayden stood up, moving as if he was entirely unaware of his injuries. He turned toward the master bedroom. Axel forced himself to wait until Bayden was about to step inside before he called for him to stop.

"You'll sleep in the guest room during your punishment."

Bayden looked through the master bedroom door to the floor where he'd slept before.

"I told you this would be harder," Axel reminded him.

Bayden wrapped his fingers around his opposite wrist. He looked up at Axel, but didn't manage to put words to his question.

"Bondage is a privilege." Axel led Bayden to the guest room. "In the bed, under the covers," he specified.

Bayden stared at the bed with obvious disapproval. It was a perfectly nice bed. It was also where he'd slept those nights he'd stayed at the pub, back before he'd been anything more than a bartender to Axel. That knowledge would make the punishment far more effective than any physical discomfort could.

Bayden looked up at him once more.

"You're allowed to let me know if there's something wrong. You can say your safe word if you need to. You can ask questions if you're not sure about something. But this is it—the punishment starts now."

"Yes, sir."

"No."

Bayden frowned as best he could with his current injuries.

"That was one of the privileges you listed. Until the punishment ends, I'm not sir to you, I'm Axel."

Bayden jerked back as if he'd been slapped. He nodded his understanding, but Axel couldn't allow that to be enough. He waited for a real answer.

Bayden closed his eyes when he realised that Axel was going to make him say it. He whispered the words very softly, each one dripping with pain. "Yes, Axel."

Chapter Thirty One

Bayden sat on the edge of the bed with his knees pulled up toward his chest and his arms looped over them. The sun was up, but there wasn't a clock in the spare bedroom, and Bayden had no idea what time it was. Hours seemed to pass before Bayden heard Axel moving around the flat.

Bayden went quickly to the bedroom door. Hand on the handle, he took a deep breath before slinking out of the room. His clothes were all in Axel's bedroom. He wasn't sure if wearing them counted as a privilege. It was possible he'd spend the next few days nude. Either way, his inability to get his clothes without being given permission to enter Axel's bedroom reassured him he wasn't making the wrong decision by seeking Axel out while naked.

Axel was in the kitchen. His hair was damp from the shower. He was fully dressed. He looked over his shoulder as Bayden paused in the kitchen doorway.

Axel looked him up and down, but his gaze was assessing rather than admiring. Bayden tightened his hands into fists as he fought against the urge to cover the worst of his bruises.

The silence was unbearable. "I wasn't sure if the shower counts as a privilege, sir."

"The shower doesn't. Hot water does. And it's Axel, not sir."

Bayden took a step backwards. Axel raised an eyebrow.

"Yes, Axel." The words tasted like ash in his mouth. He retreated into the bathroom off the guest bedroom.

The water was frigid. Bayden's breath caught in his throat as he stepped beneath the spray. It was hardly the first time he'd needed to wash under cold water. Back at his bedsit, there had rarely been any warm water. A shiver ran through him as he scrubbed at his skin, not inclined to be gentle against bruises that had made Axel so angry.

It was so damn difficult to get really clean when the water was cold. Bayden shook his head. Axel had been too kind to him for too long. He was getting weak, taking things for granted and starting to rely on them. What kind of a wolf was he? He muttered a curse and scrubbed harder. He stayed under the spray until he was as clean as he could get.

His shivering had stopped by the time he'd dried himself and headed back to the kitchen.

Axel was dishing up breakfast. Bayden faltered on the threshold, not wanting Axel to think he was there expecting to be fed. A few days without food wouldn't do him any harm. He watched in silence as Axel plated up his own breakfast.

Axel turned away from the counter. For the first time, Bayden realised Axel had been dishing up two plates of food. Axel held one out to him. Bayden stepped forward, desperate for any excuse to be closer to Axel, but he kept his hands at his sides.

"Don't argue. I've no intention of starving you."

Disobeying that tone of voice wasn't an option. Bayden took the plate and turned to the table.

"You can sit on the sofa in the living room while you eat."

Bayden looked at the kitchen table. He'd said it. He'd made it part of the list of things he liked. He'd labelled eating there with Axel as a privilege he enjoyed.

Bayden looked down at the breakfast. It would have been easier if Axel had decided to starve him.

Not sure what to say, Bayden turned away in silence. He was halfway to the door when Axel spoke again.

"Yes."

Bayden turned back to him.

"You want to know if I'll keep twisting the knife? Yes, I will." Axel stepped forward. "This isn't a game. It's not easy.

It's not supposed to be fun. It's supposed to make sure you never make the same mistake again."

"It won't, s—Axel. If I'd realised you'd be worried about me, I'd have found a way to let you know I was okay."

"This too," Axel said, stroking the bruise on Bayden's jaw. "I don't know if you were trying to punish yourself for borrowing money or punish me for insisting you let me lend it to you—"

Bayden shook his head. "I wouldn't do that, sir. I mean, Axel, I—"

"I don't care which it was," Axel cut in. "It's never going to happen again." He put his knuckles under Bayden's chin and made Bayden look him in the eye. "Never again." He nodded his dismissal.

Bayden went into the living room. The sofa. It wasn't the order he'd wanted, but it was a specific order. It was something. In a world that suddenly ceased to contain all the things he'd unthinking come to rely on, that he'd unthinkingly fallen in love with, Bayden clung to it.

Axel wanted him to eat. A knife and fork rested on the plate alongside the food. Bayden balanced the plate on his knees and forced himself to work his way through the breakfast. His bruised jaw throbbed. His throat kept closing up. The split on his lip stung. The food turned cloying and stuck to the roof of his mouth. He forced himself to swallow it down anyway.

He'd only just finished when Axel came out. He took the plate off Bayden and went back into the kitchen. Bayden heard him washing the dishes. That was his job. Even if Axel never let him prepare food, cleaning up was his job. Bayden closed his eyes tightly, ignoring the shooting pain in one side of his face. Lost without an order, Bayden remained where he was until Axel returned.

"You can get dressed."

Bayden rushed to obey. He tried to go so fast his hands turned clumsy. Axel had to think he was wasting time on purpose.

"And your jumper," Axel corrected, from the doorway.

"Yes, sir."

"No."

Bayden glanced up at him. "Axel," he corrected. "I'm sorry, I'm not trying to disobey…"

Axel turned away. Bayden hurried along in his wake, just like he had those first few days after he'd come back, unwilling to let Axel out of his sight.

Downstairs, Bayden made a determined effort to pull himself together. Glasses and bottles littered the tables, most of them half full after the Dragons had rushed everyone out the previous night. Bayden grabbed a tray and started to collect them.

"You can sit at the bar."

Bayden froze. No. He looked at Axel, then at the amount of work there was to do. No. He turned back to Axel. "I meant that a job that paid this much was a privilege, sir. Being paid human rates rather than wolf rates. Not working here altogether. If you don't pay me then—"

"The next time you lie to me, I'm adding an extra day to the end of the punishment."

Bayden met Axel's gaze. Anger burned in his eyes.

"You have thirty seconds to correct the last lie, or that one counts."

"I…" Bayden closed his eyes. "It's being allowed to work with you and feeling useful that I like. That's what I consider a privilege, sir." He winced. "I mean, Axel."

Axel nodded. "Sit at the bar," he repeated, indicating the stool that Bayden had used when he'd first visited the pub.

Bayden couldn't help but think back to that first day. As Axel moved around the room, cleaning up, doing work that he'd let Bayden do for weeks, Bayden stared at the door leading back toward the kitchen where Axel had patched him up, and he thought about the previous night when Axel had cleaned his wounds, for the eighth or ninth time.

He couldn't have let Tolmore treat his injuries, even if the guy was a paramedic. It would have felt as much like cheating on Axel as it would have if he'd let Tolmore screw him.

Bayden took a deep breath and turned his attention to the patch of bar directly in front of him, thinking about the things he'd listed as privileges, and those he hadn't.

"The list wasn't complete," he stuttered.

Axel moved to stand directly opposite him. He didn't speak, he just stood there waiting to see what Bayden had to say for himself.

"When we talked about privileges, I didn't list everything. There are other things that I didn't expect, that I didn't think of as rights."

"Such as?"

"Most pubs don't like wolves inside at all," Bayden offered.

Axel leaned against his side of the bar, removing a bit of distance from between them. "That's why you kept trying to take your drink outside the first few weeks?"

Bayden nodded.

"Whether you expect it or not, you do have the right to be treated the same as any human who walks in here. And I definitely have the right to keep you where I can keep an eye on you."

"I just—"

"You were right to tell me," Axel cut in.

Bayden took a deep breath. He'd actually done something right. It felt like the first time in years he hadn't made things worse.

"Telling me what you like goes against all your instincts, doesn't it?" Axel asked.

Bayden shifted uncomfortably on his stool, so tempted to lie. "No, it's not an instinct. Instincts are different." Bayden could feel Axel studying him, but he kept all his attention on the bar. "My instincts have always told me to trust you and tell you the truth," he whispered.

"And you've been ignoring your instincts because?"

Bayden swallowed. "Because I was obeying my family rather than you." He forced himself to look up.

The anger he expected to see in Axel's expression wasn't there. Bayden waited, hoping that Axel would respond, or ask a question, anything; but Axel remained silent, making Bayden do all the work.

Bayden licked his lips as they went dry with nerves. "They always said that if a wolf tells a human what's important to him, the human will use it against him. Use it to control him, to hurt him."

"Do you think that's what I'm doing?"

Bayden closed his eyes. "You have the right," he whispered. "If I'm submitting to you, then you have the right to know everything, and to do whatever you want with that information."

Axel was quiet for a long time. Bayden was sure that Axel expected him to say something and was desperately trying to work out what that was when Axel broke the silence himself.

"They were right."

Bayden looked up at him.

"Whichever member of your family told you that I'll use any information you give me about what you like and dislike to punish you — they were right."

The breath caught in Bayden's throat.

"And, when the punishment is over, I'll use the same information to make sure you know everything is fine between us."

Their gazes locked.

"I'll use it to punish you and to praise you. I'll use it to remind you what's important, to bring us closer together, and to make sure you're happy and safe in your submission. This isn't a silly little game with cookie-cutter roles. What you want is important. Who you are is important." Axel made sure he held his gaze as he went on. "Whatever you tell me about what you like and dislike, I guarantee that I'll pay attention to every word. I'll remember what you say, and I'll use that information to mould what we have into something as strong and as perfect as anything can be."

Bayden swallowed rapidly. "Yes." That was the only word he managed to say. Yes to everything Axel offered. Yes to everything Axel could ever ask of him in return.

Axel nodded once, turned away, and went back to his work.

He hadn't said Bayden was good. It wasn't until the words failed to hit the air that Bayden realised he'd come to expect them. When he did something right Axel said he was a good boy, or sometimes that he was a good pup, but always that he was good.

Bayden looked down. He'd obviously have to do a lot more things that were right before he could be considered a good anything again.

* * * * *

Axel had to chuckle when he saw how wary Hale and Griz looked when they walked in that night. It didn't feel like a coincidence that they'd turned up at the same time.

"There was no way either of you could have stopped him."

Axel glanced down the bar to where Bayden was sitting, and his amusement died. The swelling had gone down somewhat overnight, but the bruising on his face was still painfully vivid.

"What's going on?" Griz asked, with a nod toward Bayden.

"He's taking a break until he's healed up," Axel said.

"As a punishment?" Hale asked.

Axel dipped his head once in acknowledgement.

"I thought you said you were waiting until he was over his granddad."

"Things change." He glanced toward Bayden again. Axel already seemed to have spent half the day doing that. Just because Bayden needed to be punished now, that didn't mean he was ready for it, or that it was safe to pile huge amounts of pressure on a wolf already close to breaking point.

Enough pain to make sure Bayden learned never to make the same mistake again, but not enough to break him. Axel rubbed the back of his neck. It had taken so much courage for Bayden to give him the information he needed in order to make it an effective punishment. He had to get the balance just right—to prove he was worthy of Bayden's trust, because one wrong move, and it would all go to hell.

Over the last couple of months, Axel had got used to Bayden doing more than his fair share of work around the pub. Doing both their jobs kept Axel busy, but the shift still crawled past. Bayden remained on his stool and barely moved a muscle—Axel glanced in his direction every other minute, but he never saw him fidget.

"You want a hand closing up?" Griz asked, as everyone started heading out at the end of the night.

Bayden jerked his head up. Axel considered his options. Bayden obviously hated the idea of anyone else being allowed to help when he wasn't, and a punishment had to hurt.

Axel nodded. "You can have Evan collect the empties."

Griz nodded to Evan, and the boy set about it. Axel turned his back on the room and started cashing up.

"He'll forgive you." That was Griz's voice and it came from just alongside Bayden's stool. Axel didn't turn around to listen, but he didn't turn his attention elsewhere. Bayden didn't say anything in response, but that wasn't surprising, and it wasn't enough to put Griz off. "Back when I was drinking, I borrowed one of his bikes—sweet little job with custom paintwork that had barely had a chance to dry. I crashed it into a solid brick wall. It was a complete write off. If he'll forgive me for that, he'll forgive you for this."

Axel smiled down at the register as he remembered the rather interesting little chat he and Griz had had when Axel had found out what happened to his bike. But he didn't find much to smile about during the following twenty-odd hours.

By the time they got within a few hours of closing the next night, Axel felt like smiling belonged in a different universe. The constant need to balance everything just right, to consistently enforce a set of rules that he hated almost as much as Bayden did, it was like the perpetual screech of nails on a chalkboard. Pushing the boy away when he wanted nothing more than to pull him close and tell him everything was okay, was like thumb screws—the real things, not some kinky toy the manufacturers wanted to sound hard-core.

"How much more do you think he can take?" Griz asked.

"He can take it," Axel said. If it was done carefully. If he kept his eye on him and tweaked things just right, Bayden could take it.

Axel glanced at his watch. It was a few minutes since he'd given Bayden permission to visit the gents. As fragile as he was this soon after losing his grandfather, there was no such thing as keeping too close an eye on him. And, as hard as Bayden was finding it not to be useful, it was easy to imagine him giving in to the temptation to sneak in a bit of unobtrusive service while he was out of sight.

Axel stepped into the bathroom. His guess hadn't been far off. It wasn't the room Bayden was struggling to clean to his standards. His hands were red from being scrubbed under the cold water.

"Sorry. I didn't realise I'd been too long." His voice wasn't steady. He didn't look up as he turned around.

Axel stepped up behind Bayden, and turned him back to face the sink. Reaching past him, Axel turned on the warm water tap.

"I'm not allowed," Bayden reminded him.

"I'm allowed." Axel checked the temperature and guided Bayden's hands under the water. His skin was icy cold. Even tepid water would have to feel scalding. Bayden jerked, but he didn't try to pull his hands away. He obediently allowed Axel to hold his hands there until they warmed up. Axel reached for the soap.

Bayden glanced over his shoulder at him, so wary, so close to breaking.

"It's important to be clean, to be seen to be clean," Axel quoted. And going over forty-eight hours without being able to wash under hot water and feel really clean was worse than a whipping for a wolf who needed the whole world to know that wolves weren't filthy creatures.

Bayden swallowed. "What you want is more important."

"Tell me the difference between a scene and a bet," Axel ordered, as he carefully washed each of Bayden's fingers in turn.

"It's not a battle. No one wins in a scene," Bayden whispered.

"That's right, because in a scene we're both on the same side," Axel agreed. "A punishment is just the same. It's not about breaking someone."

Bayden looked down at his hands.

"You'll get through it," Axel promised. "I'll get you through it. You won't break. I'll never let that happen." Standing behind Bayden and reaching around him, Axel almost had Bayden in an embrace, but he resisted the temptation to turn it into a real hug.

"Thank you, sir."

Their eyes met in the mirror. Axel shook his head.

Bayden flinched. "Axel."

Axel grabbed a paper towel from the dispenser and dried Bayden's hands, letting him feel fussed over for a few more minutes.

Bayden leaned toward him, only to sway back. He peered up at him all need and uncertainty.

It took all of Axel's self-control to resist pulling him properly into his arms and promising to never let him go. "You're doing fine." He ran a finger down Bayden's cheek. "You're healing well."

Bayden swallowed. He nodded.

It was true. It looked like he'd had a fortnight to heal rather than a couple of days.

The bruises on his face were fading more quickly than those on his body, as if Bayden hadn't allowed Ford to land such heavy blows there. But, by the time Bayden had spent his third night in the guest room, even the worst of the bruises on his ribs were starting to yellow around the edges.

It was impossible for Axel to tell how much pain any of the injuries caused because Bayden never complained of any. Axel's only real information came from studying him each morning before he gave him his clothes. Bayden never mentioned the bruises and the longer the punishment went on, the less inclined Bayden was to speak at all — even to Axel.

Each night in the pub, Axel watched Bayden. He tolerated the other Dragons making occasional small talk with him, and he was polite to any lifestyle subs who approached him, but he barely looked up when any other doms spoke to him.

So, when Axel saw Bayden exchanging several sentences with one of the doms who lingered on the edge of the regulars, the conversation received his complete attention.

* * * * *

"What's the deal with you and Axel?"

Bayden glanced up. The guy was tall with scruffy brown hair. Bayden vaguely recognised him as someone he'd served drinks to in the past.

"I heard you're available for scenes again."

Bayden tensed. He glanced down the bar toward Axel and realised that he was observing them with interest. "Who did you hear that from?" Bayden managed to ask the guy.

"Common knowledge. You screwed everything up with Axel. You're back to playing with other doms."

Common knowledge. Bayden took a deep breath. Axel obviously thought his injuries had enough time to heal.

"Is that right?" the guy pushed.

"Something like that," Bayden said.

"So…" The guy put his hand on Bayden shoulder.

Bayden managed not to flinch. "You just need Axel's permission."

"What?"

"Check with Axel. It's his decision. You need his permission to do a scene with me," Bayden repeated.

The guy looked down toward Axel. "You're sure he's not still screwing you?"

Bayden swallowed down a bitter taste. "Not since I messed up."

The guy thought about that for a moment before heading down the bar toward Axel.

Bayden had known it would happen sooner or later. All his privileges—no exceptions. The only reason he hadn't had to give this one up before was because Axel thought he was too beaten up.

Bayden clenched his jaw. All he had to do was find the place he used to go inside his head when he did bets with other guys, it shouldn't be too hard. He'd had lot of practice at not caring who he had sex with.

"Bayden?" Axel nodded toward the back rooms.

When Axel stepped into one of those rooms, Bayden followed hot on his heels, determined that Axel wouldn't see him hesitate or falter. Bayden quickly glanced around the room. There was no one else there. Axel slammed the door, keeping everyone out, for now.

"For a moment, I thought you'd actually bought a clue."

Bayden lifted his gaze; Axel didn't look pleased.

"But you haven't, have you?" Axel demanded.

Bayden peered up at Axel, but he didn't know what he wanted him to say.

"I thought you sent him over to me because he was bothering you, and you wanted me to get rid of him. But, no, you actually thought there was some chance in hell I'd let him fuck you."

"It was part of the list, sir—I mean, Axel."

Axel's eyes narrowed. "It was one of the privileges you listed—you like not having to have sex with anyone but me."

Bayden nodded.

"And you thought I'd let someone else screw you to prove a point?"

"You said all of them, no exceptions, and..."

Axel stroked his cheek and made him look up.

Bayden swallowed. "You haven't liked most of the things we've done over the last couple of days. What you said about us being on the same side, you meant it. Just because you don't like the idea of someone screwing me, that doesn't mean..."

Axel sighed. He slid his hand back so it rested on the back of Bayden's neck.

"Pup, I don't know how to make this any clearer. As possessive as I feel toward you, you don't need to worry that I'll let anyone else play with you. You need to be bloody grateful you're still allowed to shake hands with people." He pulled Bayden closer. "I won't let anyone near you, not to prove any point on the planet."

The heat from Axel's body called to Bayden. He managed not to snuggle, but he had to relish being held so close.

"You are mine, and I don't share." Each word was more like a growl than the last.

Bayden nodded, not above enjoying the way the gesture made Axel's grip tug at his hair. He took a deep breath, but he had to know.

"The list. Part of it was you choosing not to..."

"I'm not going to screw someone else just to make you feel bad," Axel confirmed. He pulled Bayden away and looked down at him. "That's not the way things work, not for us."

Bayden nodded.

Axel moved his hand up to stroke his fingers through Bayden's hair. "You'll understand one day, pup. I promise you that—you'll understand what a good dom is like. I'll teach you all about it."

Bayden nodded again, not quite willing to spoil the moment by uttering a verbal response that couldn't include the word sir.

They were almost out of the room before Bayden spoke up. "What you said before, I don't mind."

Axel raised an eyebrow at him.

"Not shaking hands with people I mean. That's more of a human thing anyway."

Axel smiled. "Don't tempt me, pup. Start accepting rules like that, and I'll have you in a bubble with no one allowed to come within six feet of you."

Or in a collar and lead. That was what Axel really wanted. A collared submissive. Bayden reached up and ran his fingers along his neck. When Axel talked about that it never sounded like treating someone like a dog—he made it sound like it was part of treating someone like a mate.

* * * * *

Bayden took his clothes off with even more care than usual. Axel frowned.

Bayden was tense. His movements were jerky. That was wrong. He shouldn't be in pain at this point. However hard he'd found going without his privileges, his injuries were nearly all healed and —

Axel straightened up. There had been faint marks on his ribs that morning, but with the extra time to heal during the day, they'd vanished.

He stepped forward. Bayden froze, his fly undone, his jeans barely hanging on his hips. Axel ran his fingers over Bayden's torso. Five days. The longest five days in Axel's life, but they were over.

"Perfect," he whispered.

When he looked up, he found Bayden studying him intently. Leaving his hand resting on Bayden's abs, Axel met his gaze.

"You know what you did wrong?"

Bayden nodded.

"Tell me."

"I should have told you what was going on when my grandfather died, and I shouldn't have suggested the bet with Ford."

"What do I want you to do differently next time?" Axel asked.

"Tell you what's going on and not take bets."

"No bets like that," Axel specified, stroking Bayden's hair back from his face. "You don't let anyone hit you if you can stop them."

"Apart from you," Bayden added.

"Me?" Axel frowned wondering where the hell that came from.

"I like it when you leave marks on me," Bayden whispered.

Axel's lungs remember how to function. "The right kind of marks. Not the kind that bet left on you. I've never given a lover a black eye in my life, and I'm not going to start now." Axel thought about that as he stroked Bayden's hair, relishing being able to pet him that way without needing to hold back. The complete truth—if he demanded that off Bayden, Axel had to offer the same in return. "Actually, that's not strictly true. I did give a sub a black eye once—Fisher, years ago."

"I don't mind. You—"

Axel covered his mouth with his hand. "That's not something I want to hear you say." He held Bayden's gaze until Bayden realised how serious he was and dropped his eyes in submission. "And the black eye I gave Fisher—that was because neither of us had good enough balance to have shower sex while we were that drunk. We fell over before we even got started. I elbowed him in the face as I went down and gave him a hellish shiner. But, since he kneed me in the balls when he landed on me, I'd have happily swapped for the black eye."

Bayden smiled behind Axel's hand.

"I won't leave those kind of bruises on you. But some marks, the right kind of marks, they can be arranged. A spanking. Paddles, whips, canes, crops. There's plenty of marks you can have."

Bayden nodded. "Yes…" He stared up at Axel, so much pleading in his eyes.

"Sir," Axel finished for him.

Bayden closed his eyes. "Yes, sir." The punishment was over. The look on his face when he opened his eyes, Bayden wouldn't have been able to last through another minute of it.

Dipping his head, Axel brought their lips together. Bayden leaned into the kiss. He even reached out to Axel without any extra prompting and placed his hand delicately on Axel's chest.

"Tonight, sir?" Bayden whispered, as Axel ended the kiss. He stared at Axel's shoulder. "Please?"

"A hot shower and bed," Axel whispered into his ear.

Bayden nodded. It obviously wasn't what he'd been asking for, but he didn't complain. Axel sent him into the bathroom and let him linger under the hot spray for as long as he wanted, getting as warm and clean as it was possible for a wolf to get. Bayden needed that, but it wasn't all he needed.

While Bayden was in the bathroom, Axel stripped down to his bare skin. He opened the toy cupboard and examined his options. He'd spent a lot of time over the last few days thinking of ways to celebrate the end of Bayden's punishment. All he had to do was pick which one would be best for them.

Bayden came into the room, his hair still damp from his shower. He looked from Axel's face, to the toys, to Axel's flourishing erection. His expression perked up considerably.

Axel chuckled. "You didn't think we were going straight to sleep, did you?"

Bayden smiled. Within what seemed like seconds, his cock was just as hard as Axel's. It looked like it would only take a single caress to take him over the edge. Axel smiled as he thought back to the night when it had taken little more than that to make Bayden come.

Axel closed the door on the wardrobe without taking anything out to play with.

"Sir?"

"No bondage tonight," Axel said.

He guided Bayden onto the bed with him. Axel kept their kisses gentle, slow, and almost sweet. All he really wanted was to pin Bayden to the bed and remind him that he was never going to let him go, but he forced himself not to.

Bayden was quick to lean into every touch, but he remained tense.

When Axel pulled back and looked down at him, Bayden frowned. "I don't understand, sir."

Axel ran his hands over Bayden's skin. "There's nothing to understand, pup. If I have an order for you, I'll let you know."

Bayden nodded.

Axel patiently re-explored Bayden's body, as if something significant might have changed in the last few days. It hadn't — Bayden was as perfect as ever, and as responsive, too. He leaned into every caress, so eager for whatever Axel was willing to offer.

After a few minutes, Axel felt a tentative touch to his shoulder. Pleased with Bayden's willingness to ask, Axel quickly nodded permission for Bayden to explore.

For a man without a single piece of ink, Bayden had one hell of a tattoo fetish. He traced them over and over again, first with his fingers then with his lips and tongue. He paid special attention to the tattoo on the outside of his right arm, a copy of the patch all The Black Dragons wore on their jackets.

Eventually, Axel guided Bayden's mouth down to his cock. Bayden damn near purred his pleasure as he wrapped his lips around Axel's erection. Axel rested his hand on the back of his head, guiding his movements, letting him know exactly what to do this time.

Bayden moaned around the head of Axel's cock as he teased it with the tip of his tongue. It had been days since Axel had come. Closer and closer to the edge. Bayden whimpered, begging Axel to feed him his cum. At the last second, Axel tugged him back, pulling Bayden's mouth away from his cock.

"Sir!" Bayden's eyes opened wide. He shook his head. "I..."

There was no way he could work out what mistake he'd made when he hadn't done anything wrong. Axel had left it until the last moment — he didn't have time to explain.

He pulled Bayden up the bed and brought their lips together. Rolling over and finally allowing himself to pin Bayden to the bed, Axel slipped his hand between them. A few strokes was all it took for ecstasy and relief to make Axel's whole body shudder above Bayden.

Bayden gasped into the kiss as Axel's cum landed on his skin. Axel kept his hand moving until every last drop of his semen spilled against Bayden's body.

Completely spent, he looked down Bayden's torso. As he caught his breath, he admired the pattern the lines of cum created.

"Sir? Did I do something that...?"

"Hush." Axel ran his fingers through the trails of semen before wrapping his hand around Bayden's cock.

Bayden jerked, trying to push his erection against Axel's hand, but Axel wasn't interested in jacking Bayden off tonight. He took his hand away, leaving Bayden's shaft coated in his cum.

He glanced up. Bayden was watching him with fascination. Axel repeated the process, this time he rubbed his cum over Bayden's balls, working it into the short, dark hairs. Another swipe across the ropes of cum and he nudged Bayden's legs apart.

He smeared his semen against the cleft of Bayden buttocks, and used it as lube when he slipped one finger into his hole, marking him there as well. Bayden whimpered.

Axel looked up again. He'd wondered if Bayden would have needed an explanation, but, no, a wolf knew when a man was marking his territory. The knowledge shone bright in Bayden's gaze.

If Bayden had rushed to clean up after himself whenever he'd come against Axel, Axel set about doing the exact opposite. Bayden was his—every bit of him. Making sure that Bayden knew that Axel wanted to claim and mark his territory was just as important to him as it had been for Bayden to prove that he hadn't been trying to state his dominance.

Axel caught up a final smudge of cum and stroked it onto Bayden's cheek. "You're mine."

"Yes, sir."

Axel ran a fingertip along Bayden's erection. "You'll be allowed to come at some point." He wasn't inclined to be any more specific than that.

Bayden nodded.

"You can shower again in the morning, but tonight you're sleeping like this."

"Yes, sir." He looked at the tiny strip of blanket between them, then up at Axel.

"As close as you want," Axel allowed.

Bayden shuffled nearer, then glanced down at Axel's hand. He touched the inside of Axel's wrist. Axel's fingers were more than a little sticky. A few moments work with Bayden's tongue solved that. Another few licks to Axel's cock to lap up any cum that had lingered there, and Bayden cautiously rested his head on Axel's chest.

"Good boy."

Bayden took a deep breath and let it out as a contented little sigh. He was asleep in seconds.

Chapter Thirty Two

Axel had given Bayden permission to leave the main bar room in order to complete his morning's duties, but Bayden knew that the moment he was finished Axel expected him to return to his side.

That wasn't a problem. Being with Axel all the time was a comfortable kind of perfection, but Bayden was increasingly aware that it couldn't go on forever. He paused as he entered the main bar room and looked across at Axel.

Moving closer to Axel was easy and instinctive, but it took all Bayden's courage to speak up when he reached the bar. "Do I still need permission to be out of your sight, sir?"

"Yes." Axel's tone wasn't in the least bit angry, but it invited no debate on the matter.

Bayden shuffled his feet. "Can I ask for permission, sir?"

Axel looked up from the beer invoice he'd been frowning at and smiled. "Of course. You can always ask, pup. But I won't always say yes."

Bayden hesitated, still on the customer side of the bar. "Am I allowed to stay here when you go out for your ride later today, sir?"

Axel set the invoice down. "Is there something wrong with your bike?"

Bayden shook his head.

"Are you ill?" Axel came around the bar and put his hand against Bayden's forehead.

Bayden didn't pull away from Axel's touch, because, well, it was Axel's touch, and that was always something to be appreciated. It was only a few days since his punishment had ended; frequent casual contact was still something to be cherished, even if it came in a form that didn't make a lot of sense to a wolf. "I'm fine, sir."

Axel's eyes narrowed. "We're not going anywhere near Holborn, and even if we were, Granger would have to be suicidal to try to touch you when you're riding in the middle of the club."

Bayden shook his head. "It's not that. I just..." He looked down at his boots.

"Is there somewhere else you need to be today?" Axel asked.

"No, sir. I could just stay here." Bayden glanced up. "I wouldn't leave. I wouldn't break any of the rules. There's plenty of work I could do while you're out."

Axel took his hand away. He folded his arms. "Unless you can give me a good reason, no."

Bayden pushed his own hands deeper into his pockets. "I just think it would be better, sir."

"Way too vague to count as a reason, good or bad."

Bayden didn't sigh. That wouldn't have been respectful, and respect was important. There were going to be no more screw ups, no more reasons for Axel to punish him. "It's not important, sir."

"What isn't?"

"Riding with the club. It's not important."

Axel's frown returned. "Today in particular or in general?"

Bayden couldn't push his hands any further into his jeans pockets without his trousers falling down. "In general. It's not important."

Axel didn't look any happier.

"*You* riding with them is important," Bayden rushed out, as he realised that what he said might be open to misinterpretation.

"But you riding with us isn't?"

"I'd prefer not to, sir."

Axel leaned back against one of the bar room tables. "Why?"

He was actually going to make him say it. Bayden glared at his feet for a few seconds. "I don't want to ride with the Dragons anymore, sir."

"Lies again?"

"It's not a lie!"

Axel raised an eyebrow at him.

"I'm not lying," Bayden repeated, more politely. "If you're worried I'll leave when you're out, you could padlock the door behind you." As hard as he tried, he couldn't stop the words from speeding up, until they tripped over each other in their haste to be said. "Or, if you don't want me in here when you're not here, I could wait outside until—"

"Enough." Axel stepped forward. He caught hold of Bayden's shoulders, steadying him with a tight grip, and the world became a much better place. "That's enough," Axel repeated, more firmly.

"I don't want to lose you too," Bayden blurted out.

Axel's frown deepened. He moved one hand to the back of Bayden's head.

"The club, riding with them, it's not important, sir. This is."

"This?"

"This. You." Bayden placed his hand gently on Axel's chest. "I...I don't want to lose you too."

"That won't happen."

Bayden looked down.

Axel's grip tightened on his hair, tugging at the strands, making Bayden look him in the eye. "That won't happen."

Bayden swallowed. "I don't want to screw up again, sir."

Axel's hand gentled in his hair, but Bayden had no doubt it would tighten again if he tried to move without permission. He was tempted to move just to make it happen.

"You made a few mistakes. You accepted your punishment. It's time to stop feeling guilty, pup."

Bayden looked down. "Do you want me to ride with you?"

"Yes, always." No doubt. No hesitation.

Bayden nodded. Even if his suggestion was a good one, his timing had obviously been wrong. He'd offer again when the time was right. "Yes, sir."

* * * * *

"That's the trouble with wolves. You can't trust them. Disobedient as hell."

"What do you expect from something that's half wild animal?"

Axel glanced along the bar. The two guys sitting at the other end weren't trying to keep their voices down. Bayden had to have heard every word they said, but he was no fool — he'd apparently decided that they weren't worth paying attention to.

"Wolf-boy."

Bayden tensed. For several seconds, he simply stared at the bar he was wiping down. Axel smiled to himself, knowing that Bayden wouldn't answer to that. He never had. The silly tossers could die of thirst waiting for him to—

Axel's smile disappeared as Bayden went to the other end of the bar and served the guys without either a word or a growl.

Bayden went back to his duties. The guys went back to their conversation.

"Looks like Axel's got him well trained."

"I still wouldn't trust him."

"I don't know. I wouldn't mind taking Axel's bitch for a ride if he's broken him in."

Axel had no doubt that Bayden was still listening to their conversation, but apart from his grip on the cloth he used to wipe down the bar turning white knuckled, he still didn't react—not even to the one term that always made him want to lynch the whole human race.

Axel stepped up behind Bayden and put his hand on the small of his back. "Pup?"

Bayden turned to him, his expression entirely blank. "Sir?"

"Take the empties out back while it's quiet."

"Yes, sir."

Axel watched him go, then went down to those two guys at the end of the bar. "Something to say?"

Apparently taken mute, they shook their heads in perfect unison.

"You both had plenty to say a few moments ago."

He met one man's gaze, then the other's. Neither of them uttered a word. Axel knew them as people who were on the edges of the scene. They often turned up on the nights when the back rooms were open to the public, but only to gawp, not to actually show off their own skills.

"Didn't mean any offense," one of them finally muttered.

"When you insult a sub, you insult his dom. You'll learn that if you ever try playing rather than just watching. Bayden might have the patience to put up with your bullshit, I don't." He looked from one man to the other. "Any questions?"

They once more shook their heads in sync. A moment later, they'd hastily swallowed what was left of their drinks and headed for the exit.

If Bayden noticed they'd gone when he came back into the room, he didn't mention it. Axel didn't say anything about it until the pub had closed for the night.

"Any particular reason you didn't tell those guys where to shove their opinions?" Axel asked once they were alone in the room.

Bayden didn't pretend not to know who they were talking about. He shrugged. "It wasn't important, sir."

"What people think of wolves, what they call wolves, what they call you, none of that is important?"

Bayden shook his head.

"Since when?" Axel demanded.

Bayden picked up some of the empty glasses and carried them to the bar. When he tried to walk past Axel with another handful of empties, Axel stopped him short.

Bayden looked down at the glasses. "Do I need permission, sir?"

Would you prefer Evan help you? Bayden didn't actually ask that, but Axel wouldn't have blamed him if he had.

"To clear up, no—you don't need permission—it's part of your job. But to avoid my question, yes, you would need permission, and you don't have it."

"I don't want any trouble, sir."

"With me?"

Bayden stared at the empties. "With anyone."

Axel took the glasses out of his hands and set them aside. Bayden tensed.

"No one else is going to clear them away," Axel promised. He tugged Bayden closer by his belt loops. "Tell me what's wrong."

"Nothing, sir."

As lies went it was probably one that Bayden told to himself as much as to Axel.

"Maybe I was too hard on you," Axel mused, out loud and entirely for Bayden's benefit.

Bayden shook his head. He even reached out to Axel, placing both his hands on his chest.

"You're not acting like yourself since your punishment. I let that bull about not riding out with us slide, but wherever this is going, it stops now."

Bayden stared at his hands resting against Axel's black T-shirt. "Maybe I'm acting more like the kind of wolf I should be, sir," he said, very softly.

"What kind of wolf is that?"

"The kind that would make you happy," Bayden said. He frowned, obviously giving a great deal of thought to each word. "One that would put his mate and his pack first. More like him, sir."

"More like your grandfather?"

"Yes, sir."

Axel slid an arm around him and gathered him close. He sighed and pressed a kiss to the top of Bayden's head. Hearing someone scream under the lash was one thing. The pain in Bayden's voice was almost enough to bring Axel to his knees.

Axel had no idea how to fix this kind of pain. He led Bayden up the stairs and settled them on the sofa in the living room, trying to project confidence and certainty even though he was completely out of his depth. "Tell me about him," he hazarded.

"He was a good wolf," Bayden whispered. "You'd have liked him."

Axel weighed his options. "Liked him, yes. Respected him, yes. Preferred him to you, no."

Bayden turned and snuggled into Axel's side more comfortably. He always seemed smaller when they were alone together, so much more in need of his protection.

"Maybe if I was more like him, she would have trusted me to look after her," he whispered.

"Your mother."

Bayden nodded.

I can't lose you too.

Because when she moved into Danville, he'd lost his mother as well as his grandfather. Everyone he'd thought of as being his pack had gone, and he'd been left scrabbling for whatever he could keep hold of. Axel stroked Bayden's back as he carefully slotted puzzle pieces together in his mind.

"So, all the things you're doing differently are to make me happier?" Axel asked.

Bayden nodded.

"You think you riding with us makes me unhappy?"

"I've already ruined two runs," Bayden whispered. "The club, it's important to you—it's your pack. You should be able to ride without worrying that I'll get pulled over, or that the pub you want to stop at won't let me in, or…" He sighed and tucked his face into Axel's shoulder.

"What about what you want?"

Bayden shook his head, rubbing his cheek against Axel in the process. "Not important."

"It's important to me."

Bayden hesitated, obviously unsure what to do about that.

"Letting bastards mouth off in the pub, it's the same thing, isn't it? Keep your head down, don't make a fuss."

Bayden nodded again, and traced the line of one of the tattoos on Axel's opposite arm.

Axel sighed. Ever since that last punishment, Bayden had been—

No. Not since the punishment, before that. Ever since his grandfather died, Bayden had been off balance, acting out of character, trying to be someone he wasn't—

"Your grandfather would have taken a beating off Ford." The realisation hit Axel so suddenly, he didn't have time to stop it leaving his mouth.

"Sometimes it's more important to be able to take a beating than to win a fight. Part of being a good wolf is knowing that. I thought…"

"That I'd think you were good for getting the money?"

Bayden shrugged, but it was obvious that was exactly what he'd thought. He still didn't get why it hadn't worked, why Axel seemed to be working from a different definition of what a good wolf was.

Axel scrabbled through his memories, trying to drum up something about wolves that wouldn't simply reinforce such screwed up ideas. Neither book could offer him any help. The only glimmer of hope came from a whispered conversation in a graveyard. "Would your father have taken a beating off Ford?"

Bayden shook his head. "It's different, sir. He was an alpha."

"Was he a good wolf?"

"He was a good alpha, sir. It's different." Bayden looked down. "A good wolf puts their pack first—alphas do that in a different way."

"Your mother and father were together until he died, weren't they? He was nothing like his father, but she obviously trusted him to look after her and—"

"Wolves bring home half the money humans do," Bayden cut in. "And maybe that's not fair. But, dead wolves don't bring home a penny. A good wolf keeps his head down and doesn't cause trouble. He doesn't get himself killed fighting battles he has no chance of winning."

Axel stroked Bayden's hair back from his face. So much pain. Axel helplessly pressed a kiss to Bayden's temple.

"If my grandfather hadn't moved in and helped..." Bayden shook his head. "My grandfather was a good wolf. Maybe if they could have trusted me to be a good wolf too..."

"But you think you're more like your father?"

"She always said I was getting more like him all the time."

Silence settled over them. Axel let it linger, more because he wasn't sure how to break it than because he thought it might inspire Bayden to offer up any extra information, but eventually Bayden did speak.

"It's not always easy being a wolf. Being an alpha who can't form a pack, that's worse. An alpha can't be expected to accept things the way they are, but other wolves should. I need to work on that."

No. The word screamed through Axel's mind. The idea of Bayden working on getting better at taking a beating, at living scared, made Axel want to put his fist through a wall.

Bayden looked up at him, obviously aware that something was wrong.

Axel brushed their lips together, playing for time while he desperately tried to work out how the hell he could convince Bayden that he shouldn't try to be like a man he was still in mourning for.

When he lifted his head, Axel pushed his fingers through Bayden's hair, stroking it back off his face. "Where your mother's staying, at Danville, can the women there have visitors?"

Bayden nodded. "She said I can go and see her."

"What about human visitors?"

A confused little frown furrowed Bayden's forehead. "Sir?"

"I think it's time I met your mother, pup."

Chapter Thirty Three

"It's stopped raining, sir."

Axel turned away from the kitchen window. He hadn't been checking the weather so much as staring into space, but Bayden making the effort to initiate small talk was something that should always be encouraged.

Axel held out his arm, welcoming Bayden in to his side. "It's turned into a nice day, but we'll still take my car rather than ride."

Bayden glanced up at him.

"You're not sure she's happy there, are you?" Axel asked.

Bayden shrugged.

"If your mother doesn't want to stay at Danville, she can come home with us today. We'll fix the rooms above the garage into a little flat so she can have her own space but still be here with you."

Bayden studied him very carefully. "I don't..."

He seemed caught off guard by the idea, but Axel had had plenty of time to plan it out since Bayden had agreed to take him to visit his mother. "She could stay in the spare room while we do up the flat. You'd have to remain dressed while she's visiting, but it wouldn't take us long to do the work—the guys would all help."

"I..." Bayden shook his head. "Three wolves can't live together, sir."

It took Axel a few seconds to realise who Bayden was thinking of as the third wolf in that scenario. Part of him wanted to simply stand there in silence and relish the fact Bayden considered him so different to the bad humans he'd met, he'd unconsciously started thinking of him as a wolf.

Eventually Axel forced himself to speak up. "It would be two wolves and a human, pup," he corrected, ever so gently.

Bayden's eyes opened very wide as he realised his mistake. "I—"

"Hush. It's a compliment, not an insult, pup. Don't backtrack and spoil it." Axel stroked his thumb across Bayden's lips.

Bayden looked down.

"You consider her to be part of your pack, right?"

Bayden nodded.

"So, if you're part of my pack, she is, too. A package deal."

Bayden glanced up at him, his expression so confused, as if he couldn't believe he'd actually muddled up what he considered to be such a defining characteristic.

"It's just an option," Axel said. "If she's not one hundred percent happy there, she can come home with us today."

"I didn't ask for..." Bayden whispered.

"You're not asking for anything," Axel said, very firmly. "I'm telling you. It's not a case of choosing between wolves and humans. You never have to choose." He stroked Bayden's back through his jumper. "Talk to your mother about it today. Find out what she thinks."

Bayden nodded. He trailed his fingers along the tattoo on Axel's arm as Axel checked his watch.

"We should get ready to leave."

Bayden followed Axel into the bedroom, but he didn't say anything. It was unlikely Bayden's mother would like tattoos as much as Bayden. God knows Axel's mother hated every one of them. Axel dug out a black, long sleeve shirt that covered all his ink.

Bayden sat on the bed and watched.

"Do you want to get anything for your mother on the way?" Axel asked.

Bayden shook his head.

"Nervous?"

He shook his head again.

It was one of those lies he told himself. Axel took a deep breath, not inclined to admit that he was nervous as hell too. "What's her name?"

"Sir?"

"Your mother—what do I call her? Is it Mrs Wolf, or do I call her by her first name, or what?"

"Her first name's Miriam," Bayden offered, but he didn't seem entirely sure what Axel should actually address her as. He appeared just as out of his depth as Axel felt.

On the way out of the flat, Axel paused. He glanced into the kitchen. The money Bayden had won still sat on the kitchen table. They'd been edging around it ever since Bayden began his punishment, neither of them willing to touch it.

"Sir?" His tone made it clear that he'd noticed what Axel was looking at.

"Your mother might find some extra cash useful," Axel pointed out.

Bayden shuffled his feet.

Axel made himself step forward and pick it up. He held it out to Bayden, but Bayden seemed frozen in place.

"It's okay, pup."

Bayden glanced up at him. He took the money and pushed it deep into his jeans pocket, as if it would contaminate his hands if he held it a second longer.

Axel let the matter drop. He was meeting his boyfriend's mother; there were only so many things he could worry about at one time. "You said before that wolves don't usually prefer men or women," Axel reminded him, as they drove out of the pub's car park a few minutes later.

"Yes, sir."

"So, your mother's not going to have a problem with you turning up with a…boyfriend rather than a girlfriend?"

Bayden shook his head.

Axel tried to pretend that meant everything was automatically going to be okay. Unfortunately, he was already pretty sure that any objection Bayden's mother would have to him would be based on species rather than gender.

* * * * *

Don't be nervous. He'll know if you're nervous, so will his mother. Every wolf in the place would know if Axel wasn't entirely confident and at ease, just from his scent. Thinking about that fact didn't help Axel feel in the least bit less anxious.

He adjusted the little visitor's badge he'd been issued at the kiosk at the edge of the car park after the woman inside had checked his ID.

"Sir?"

Axel smiled down at Bayden. "Am I the only one fascinated by the idea that someone might mistake either of us for one of the women who live here unless we have little badges on?"

Bayden smiled back at him, but he still seemed to be watching him warily.

In an effort to appear far more relaxed than he felt, Axel turned his attention to the building they were about to enter. From the way Bayden spoke about the place, Axel had expected something sterile and austere—a cross between a prison and a factory.

It was actually an old manor house set well back in its own grounds. It looked like one of the stately homes his school had taken kids to on field trips.

A stately home that didn't trust its visitors to be well behaved, Axel mentally corrected, as another security guard checked their visitors' tags and their ID's, before ticking their names off a list.

Axel ran his eyes down the list of expected visitors as they waited. *Axel Carmichael.* His name stood out from all the others—easy to spot because it was the only one that didn't end in Wolf.

Bayden kept pace with Axel as they made their way down a path along the outside of the building to another door where their visitors' badges were once more checked.

The woman doing the checking smiled politely. "Miriam knows you've arrived, she'll join you shortly."

The woman ushered them into what Axel guessed was some sort of visitor's room. There were lots of tables and chairs arranged around the space. A hatch at the far end of the room appeared to offer refreshments. The windows looked out onto the garden. There was a door on the other side of the room with another security person manning it, who would, presumably, let the women from inside the building through to meet their visitors.

The room was spotlessly clean—just as Axel assumed any place inhabited by wolves would be. The furniture was functional, but there was a reasonably cheerful air to the place. The women who'd come out to greet their guests all looked happy and healthy.

China rattled as someone carried a tray away from the serving hatch. Muted conversations filled the air. It seemed more like a quaint little tea shop than a prison visiting room. The worst of Axel's fears faded somewhat.

Axel waited to see if Bayden wanted to pick a table, but he stood motionless with his hands shoved in his jacket pockets. He didn't look interested in making any kind of decision for himself.

Axel led him across to a table near a window. "Have you been here before?"

"No, sir. Not inside." He pulled his hands out of his pockets as he sat down, and rested his hands on the table.

"You don't have to call me sir while we're here."

Bayden jerked his head up.

Axel put his hand over Bayden's. "Pay attention. I said you don't have to, not that you're not allowed to. I'm telling you that you don't have to call me sir in front of your mother if you prefer not to, that's all."

"I'm still allowed to?"

"Yes."

Bayden nodded to himself. "Yes, sir." There was just a bit of defiance in the way he said it. He obviously hadn't appreciated the offer of discretion one little bit. Axel left his hand over Bayden's, allowing the contact to linger for as long as Bayden might be able to take some comfort from it.

Bayden's fingers twitched under Axel's palm. He turned to face the door but didn't pull his hand away from Axel's.

A woman stepped into the room. She was about Bayden's height and had the same colouring as him, with long dark hair plaited over her right shoulder. She was dressed simply, like all the women there, in a long dress with a loose fitting cardigan over it.

Axel turned his attention to Bayden and found him studying his mother very carefully. He still didn't pull his hand away. Axel stood up, letting their hands separate naturally. Bayden jerked to his feet alongside him.

Miriam smiled when she saw her son. Putting his hand on the small of Bayden's back, Axel gently nudged him forward.

Hugs between Axel and his own mother had become awkward the moment he'd come out. Bayden turning up with a human hadn't had the same effect on his relationship with his mother. When they embraced, it was as natural and honest as breathing. Several seconds passed before they stepped back. Bayden held her at arm's length for a few seconds, still studying her carefully.

She wasn't easy for Axel to read, apart from those times when her expressions matched those Axel was familiar with from Bayden. As far as Axel could tell, she was worried about Bayden, but not as worried about him as he was about her.

Bayden glanced over his shoulder. "This is Axel."

Miriam glanced toward him and nodded slightly.

"He asked what he should call you, but I wasn't sure," Bayden added.

As any intention Axel might have had of hiding how wary he was of saying the wrong thing died swiftly at Bayden's feet, Miriam met his gaze. She took half a step forward and held out her hand. "Miriam."

Not wanting to stress his humanity any more than necessary, Axel skipped any attempt at small talk. Greetings done, he settled down to observe mother and son in silence.

"You look less tired," Bayden said.

She smiled. "I am less tired."

Bayden nodded, his gaze quick and assessing. "You're happy you moved in here?"

"Yes."

Axel was pretty sure that a dozen different messages passed from one wolf to the other that he was entirely unaware of. Body language. Scent. He was a novice at deciphering the first and oblivious to the second.

"We sorted out the gravestone. It wasn't a problem."

We. It wasn't a word a wolf used by accident.

Miriam turned to Axel, studying him with increased interest. "You've visited our burial ground?"

"Yes, when I took Bayden to visit his grandfather's grave. It's very peaceful." Respectful tone. Remember that a wolf always says the dom takes the sub places, not the other way around. Keep the answers short and sweet. Axel wasn't sure he had lupine speech patterns down perfectly, but he did his damnedest, unwilling to lose whatever ground he'd made so far.

"Everyone's being kind to you?" Bayden asked his mother.

Miriam nodded. "You don't need to worry about me, love."

Bayden didn't nod in response. He didn't do anything.

The moment seemed right. "Why don't you go and get your mother something to drink?" Axel asked, nodding to the serving hatch.

Bayden hesitated. He looked from his mother to Axel and back again, but he went without protest. Axel watched Bayden until he was out of ear shot, then turned to Miriam.

Unsure how much time he'd have, he didn't waste any. "I'm not going to bother with a whole speech about how well I'm going to treat your son or how happy I'm going to make him. Mostly because I don't think you'd believe a word of it."

She blinked at him, just the way Bayden did when he said something that was so unexpected, or so human, it took a wolf's mind a few seconds to work out what the suitable reaction might be.

"I don't expect you to like me or to approve of me. Over time you'll see for yourself how I treat Bayden and make up your own mind. But…" Axel sighed. There was no easy way to say it. "He thinks you moved in here because you don't trust him to look after you."

"Bayden and I spoke about my reasons for taking a residential place here." It wasn't a correction as such. She spoke the same way Bayden often did, as if he didn't want to imply that humans were stupid, but it was kind of obvious they were.

There wasn't time for subtlety. "He thinks he's let you down and ended up losing both his grandfather and his mother within a few days. He's tying himself in knots trying to work out how to be a better wolf — a wolf who'd have been worthy of your trust."

She glanced across to where Bayden was queuing for refreshments. Her eyes weren't the amber colour that gave away a wolf's species, but they were still a lot like Bayden's, just as watchful, just as assessing.

"I can't fix that," Axel pointed out.

She turned back to him.

"If I need to find a way to convince him that he's a good wolf on my own, I'll do it. But it's not my opinion on that which is bothering him—not really."

Bayden came back. He had two cups and two cakes on a tray. He placed one set in front of Axel and one set in front of his mother. As an expression of divided loyalties went, it couldn't have been clearer. The pieces of cake were exactly the same size. They even had the same number of pieces of strawberry on top.

"Thank you." Axel stood up.

Bayden began to do the same, but Axel put his hand on his shoulder.

"I'm only going to see what all those notices say," Axel said, pointing to the notice board on the far side of the room. "You stay here and have a chat with your mam."

Axel was acutely aware of two sets of eyes watching him walk across the room, but he kept all his attention on the notice boards. All he could do was hope.

If Miriam didn't offer her son her approval, there was nothing Axel could do about that. Axel pushed one hand into his pocket. His fingers brushed against a rosary that he'd put in there that morning without really thinking about it. He'd take any help he could get.

* * * * *

"Axel's worried that you think you've let me down somehow."

Bayden stared at Axel's retreating back until he couldn't put off facing his mother any longer. "You don't need to be here."

She reached across the table and stroked the back of his hand. He turned his hand over, letting her put her palm against his

"Everything happened very quickly. It always does when a wolf reaches the end. Maybe I was wrong to…"

"You didn't do anything wrong," Bayden said, very firmly.

His mother smiled at him, the same way she had when he was a little boy and she'd thought he was trying to grow up too quickly. "Do you really think I took the residential place here because I was scared you wouldn't look after me?"

Bayden looked down.

"You'd have led a pack well, you'd have looked after any wolf who was part of your pack. I've never doubted that. That's not what me moving in here was about, love. I've told you that before."

Bayden pushed his free hand through his hair. "You want to live trapped in here, doing what humans say all the time?" He kept his tone respectful through sheer force of will, and tried not to think about how horrific it would be, being forced to obey a human who wasn't Axel.

She smiled.

Bayden didn't see anything to smile about.

"Is that what you think it's like? I've never said that."

Bayden met her gaze. Good wolves didn't complain, and she was a good wolf.

She shook her head. "I like it here, love. It's..." She looked around the room. "You think the security makes it a prison, I think it means that everyone in here is safe."

"I can keep you safe."

"It's not so much about me being safe anymore. Some of the women here, they have reason to be worried about specific people coming here to find them. I haven't had to worry about that for a long time."

Bayden met her gaze. "Dad made sure of that."

"Yes, he did."

Even if no one had ever wanted to give him the whole story, he'd put together enough on his own. Before she'd met his father there was a human pimp who'd controlled her. After she'd met Bayden's dad, that had stopped being a problem. "I could too."

She sipped her tea. "These days, so could I. I'm not the girl who got mixed up in all that anymore. I can look after myself, and I can help the women who are just starting to learn how to do that. I'm not here to get help from humans. I'm here to help other wolves."

Part of Bayden wanted to believe it. He'd never seen his mother look so relaxed, so confident in her surroundings. Her scent, her body language, it all told him she was fine, but another part of his brain just refused to go there. "I…"

"If I'd moved in with you, it would have been impossible for you to find a mate," she pointed out. Her scent made it clear she was humouring him. "You wouldn't have brought a third wolf into the house, and you wouldn't have asked me to leave when you found a mate either."

Hope flickered. "Axel's not a wolf. He said you can come to live with us and —"

"I wouldn't have been able to ask you to leave if I found a new lupine mate either," his mother cut in.

Bayden looked up. "You've found a new mate?"

She hesitated. "Maybe."

Bayden automatically looked over both his shoulders, as if this possible mate might jump out at any moment.

"She's not here today. But, perhaps there will be a time when I'm the one introducing my new mate to you rather than the other way around."

Bayden's eyes narrowed. "You didn't say you wanted to move in here to be with your mate."

"No, I moved in here because I thought it would be the best for you and for me, and because I thought I could do some good here. I hadn't met her then." She set down her cup. "If I didn't know you were a good wolf—a strong wolf who can take care of yourself and anyone else who needs your help, I would never have accepted a place here. I'd have wanted to," she stressed. "I would have regretted not being able to be here, but I wouldn't have left you unless I knew you were strong enough to thrive. And I think that's exactly what you're doing."

Bayden turned his attention to his knuckles and studied them for a while.

"That's nothing to feel guilty about, love."

He met her eyes.

"That's the real problem isn't it?" she said. "Things have worked out in a way that let you get on with your own life and be happy, but you feel guilty."

Bayden closed his eyes. Six weeks. If his grandfather hadn't died, if his mother hadn't taken a residential place at Danville, he'd have had six weeks with Axel before he'd have had to give it up and go back to taking the kind of bets Axel would never have let his sub take.

Now, he might never have to give Axel up, but the price other people had to pay to make that possible. He shook his head.

"You're allowed to be happy."

"It's just…"

"Stop trying to punish yourself. He'd have wanted you to be happy. You're not respecting his memory by making yourself miserable. Throwing away what you could have with Axel isn't going to bring him back."

Bayden pushed his hand through his hair.

"Would he be disappointed that I've found a place where I can be happy and comfortable, where I can help other people?"

"Of course not."

She smiled. "The same goes for you finding a good home with Axel. Accepting that things changed when he died and moving on isn't the same as being glad he's dead, love."

Bayden swallowed. "He always thought I was too much like dad. He was right."

"You're very like your father in a lot of ways."

Bayden looked down.

"But in one way you're more like me. You're not destined to be an alpha, love, but you'll make a good mate for one."

Bayden hesitated.

"You're not wrong to see that in him. It's there. He's just as much an alpha as your father was. You're right to think he cares about you a great deal, too."

Bayden glanced across to Axel. "I love him." He whispered it softly, as if Axel might overhear him if he said it just a fraction louder. "I didn't mean to, but…"

"You didn't mean to fall in love with a human?" she asked.

Bayden stared at Axel's back. He nodded.

"That's nothing to feel guilty about, either."

Bayden took a deep breath. They were supposed to be talking about her, not him. "Is your mate an alpha too?"

"We'll talk about her another time," she promised. "Your mate is waiting to come back to the table."

Bayden knew that tone of voice. He might technically be the most dominant wolf at the table, but only one of them was the mother. He was halfway to his feet when Axel glanced across at them and met his gaze.

When Axel re-joined them, Bayden was aware that Axel was trying to read his body language. Bayden smiled up at him, trying to make it easier for him. Axel set his hand on the small of Bayden's back as he sat down. It felt nice. After a moment's consideration, Bayden put his hand lightly on Axel's thigh in return.

When Bayden looked up, his mother was smiling at them.

Half an hour later, as they got to their feet and said their goodbyes, Axel once again left Bayden alone with his mother.

Bayden took the money from the bet out of his pocket.

"Bayden."

He smiled at the chiding note. "I know you don't need it. But, maybe one of the other women here could use it — one of the women you're helping."

"Or you could use it yourself," she pointed out gently.

"It's... Axel doesn't like how I earned it." Bayden looked down at the money. "He has a point."

She hesitated.

Bayden shook his head when he realised what she had to assume. Even if he'd never told her what he'd done to earn money, he knew she'd guessed a long time ago. "I just threw a fight. He doesn't like it when I get hurt."

She took the money and slipped it into her pocket.

"I'll see you again soon?" Bayden asked.

"Whenever you want." She smiled. "Both you and your mate."

* * * * *

"Well?" Axel asked, as they got into his car.

"She likes you. She said we can visit whenever we want."

Axel nodded. He'd hoped Bayden would say more, but he fell silent. Axel gripped the steering wheel tightly and tried to keep his scent calm while he waited. They were halfway home and the steering wheel was close to getting permanent fingertip impressions in it before Bayden was finally ready to speak.

"She's met a new mate." His tone gave away nothing.

"That's good?" Axel hazarded.

"She's helping a lot of the other women who live there."

"Good."

"She said she can look after herself. She's there to help wolves, not to get help off humans."

"That's good, too," Axel said, a little more confidently.

Bayden nodded. "She's a good wolf, sir."

Axel changed gears and took a risk. "Is she good in the same way as your father or the same way as your grandfather?"

Silence descended again. Several minutes passed.

"Good in her own way. I think, maybe there's more than one way to be a good wolf," Bayden said, very softly.

Axel nodded, but the knife-edge still remained.

Several miles passed before Bayden spoke again. "She said my granddad would understand that adapting to the way things changed when he died isn't the same as being glad he died. He wouldn't think that made someone a bad wolf."

Axel's grip on the steering wheel finally eased.

Chapter Thirty Four

"I hear there's going to be a bike up for sale."

It wasn't about someone wanting another beer. It wasn't exactly an unusual topic of conversation. Bayden let the words flow around him as he dried one of the glasses he'd just washed and set it back on the shelf.

He glanced across to where Axel was working at the other end of the bar and smiled slightly. Maybe his mother was right—it was okay to smile. It was okay to be glad that he could have more than six weeks with Axel, even if he hated the event that made that possible.

"Bayden."

He turned around. Tolmore and Hale sat next to each other at the bar.

"Is it true that Axel's putting your bike up for sale?" Tolmore asked, his voice just a fraction too innocent to be believable.

"No, it's not true," he said, with forced calm. Tolmore was just trying to wind him up, that was all. Being an arsehole was pretty much Tolmore's default state. Bayden's fist still tightened around the cloth at the idea of anyone talking about his bike that way.

"So you're not his sub? You just call him sir because you work for him?" Tolmore asked, in that same fake casual tone.

"I'm his sub," Bayden corrected. His knuckles turned white.

"A real sub rides on the back of his master's bike. That's why it's called a bitch seat. Seems kind of suitable for a werewolf…"

Bayden knew that it wasn't just Tolmore who was waiting to see what kind of reaction he'd get. Hale was taking in every detail. A cop was paying attention. Axel's friend was listening.

A hand landed on Bayden's shoulder. "Time for your break."

It wasn't anything of the sort, but Bayden didn't argue. He followed Axel into his office.

"I didn't growl at him, sir." Bayden offered. That counted as progress of a sort, didn't it? Surely, it meant he was a little closer to acting like a human, even if he wasn't all the way there yet.

"Why not?" Axel demanded.

Bayden hesitated.

"Why didn't you growl at him?" Axel asked again. "Because a good wolf wouldn't, a good sub wouldn't? Because you didn't think I'd like it if you did?"

Bayden shrugged.

Axel leaned against the edge of his desk. "A few months ago, you'd have had him by the balls for calling any wolf that word."

"That was before, sir."

"Before you started submitting to me?"

Bayden nodded.

"I may not have liked the rich tosser act, and I hated the lies. But I never had a problem with your attitude. I've never told you not to stand up for yourself. I think that part of the act was actually a damn sight closer to the real you — to what you'd be like if you weren't checking your instincts all the time."

Bayden pushed his hands into his pockets.

"You said before that you could tear any of their throats out whenever you wanted."

Bayden stepped forward. He put his hand on Axel's arm the way he knew Axel didn't mind. "I wouldn't do that, sir."

Axel waved away the reassurance, even as he slid his arm around Bayden and welcomed him close. "Is there a middle ground?"

"Between being a wolf and a human?" Bayden asked.

"No, between killing them and letting them talk shit whenever they feel like it."

Bayden frowned.

"Can you make it clear there are certain things that a human can't call a wolf without seriously hurting one of them?"

Bayden ran his fingers over Axel's T-shirt—so familiar with Axel's body he could easily trace the line of a tattoo that was hidden away. "I've had a lot of fights with humans. I've never lost my temper. I've never killed one."

"Can you make your point without risking you getting hurt at all?"

Bayden nodded.

"At all," Axel stressed.

He looked up. "Yes, sir."

"Do it."

Bayden's fingers fell still. "A wolf can't react every time a human says something stupid, sir." Memories rushed through his mind. It was a nice fantasy, but a wolf couldn't do it. He shook his head. "It would cause too much trouble, draw too much attention."

"In my pub, a wolf can do whatever I give him permission to do." The tone was pure alpha.

Bayden met his gaze.

"I'm not telling you that you have to throw down with every idiot in the world, pup. But if you're going to be part of this club, part of this pack, you need to be able to make sure the other guys know when they've screwed up. Maybe in other pubs we have to be more careful, but not here. Here, it's safe for you to be a wolf."

It was a fantastic tone of voice. It sent a shiver down Bayden's spine and blood rushing to his cock. Bayden was pretty sure Axel didn't intend it to be erotic, but, God, it was.

"Any questions?" Axel said.

Just one. "Why?"

"Because there are some lines they have to learn not to cross. They push—you push back. If you can make damn sure they never make the same mistake again, all the better."

He was teaching Bayden how to be the kind of sub he wanted—what a human expected off a member of his pack, regardless of species. It was what Bayden had wanted for so long. "Yes, sir."

"Just remember that I meant what I said, pup. I'm giving you permission to make an example out of the next person who calls you that, not to kill anyone off entirely."

Bayden nodded. He was halfway to the door when he paused. "Is it like bets and fights, sir?"

Axel raised an eyebrow.

"Not when I'm on the clock?" Bayden specified.

"No. You can do it whenever you want."

Bayden nodded to himself. He went back to work. Axel did the same. One glance at the men on the other side of the bar and Bayden knew that most of them thought that Axel had taken him out of the room to read him the riot act.

Be polite to customers. Be polite to club members. Be polite to doms.

The only ones who didn't seem so sure that the lecture had taken that course were Griz and Hale. They looked from Bayden to Axel and back again. Griz smiled into his drink. Hale rolled his eyes.

Tolmore, apparently oblivious to all that, sat up straighter. "Setting a price on your bike?"

Bayden looked him up and down as far as possible from his side of the bar. "There are some things it's a really bad idea to call a wolf." His words were softly spoken and calm. He met Tolmore's gaze and held it.

It was a clear warning. Tolmore had heard it. He was sober enough to understand it.

"I'm terrified," Tolmore drawled.

Bayden shrugged. He'd warned the man. It wasn't his fault if Tolmore was too stupid to take it.

Tolmore laughed. "That's it? That's all you're going to say. Bloody hell, you should at least talk a better game. Even a dom's bi—"

Axel's orders hadn't stopped in Bayden's human mind. It was permission from Bayden's alpha and it had sunk in, right down to the instinctive wolf part of his psyche. Bayden didn't stop to think. He didn't even wait around to hear the second half of the syllable.

Anger rushed through Bayden, and for the first time in so many years, he didn't try to check it. He launched himself across the bar, shifting mid-air. Tolmore toppled as Bayden's paws connected with his shoulders.

Tolmore hit the floor, hard. Bayden landed on top of him. A growl reverberated in Bayden's throat, but it was nothing like the noise he made with a human voice box. This sound came from an entirely lupine throat.

Most of his clothes had fallen away as he shifted. He shook away the tattered remains of his vest. Tolmore tried to push him off and scramble to his feet. Another growl from Bayden killed that idea in its tracks.

Tolmore froze, and power rushed through Bayden. He hadn't lied to Axel. It would have been easy to tear Tolmore's throat out. There would be no more stupid statements then.

Bayden's self-control wasn't as strong when he was in lupine form. Even if he wasn't allowed to bite, he couldn't help but stare at Tolmore's jugular.

He was so focused on Tolmore's throat, it was hard to pay too much attention to the commotion around him. There was a certain amount of shouting and swearing. A lot of it was directed at him, but none of it was in Axel's voice, and that made it irrelevant.

Panic flooded Tolmore's scent. He scrabbled at the floor. Lifting one hand, he tried to push Bayden away. Bayden easily caught Tolmore's hand in his mouth. He let sharp teeth press against the flesh, but stopped just short of breaking the skin.

Tolmore's babbling turned more rapid and higher pitched.

"That's enough."

Bayden looked up. Axel had come around the bar. Bayden was about to release Tolmore when he realised that Axel wasn't talking to him, he meant the shouting.

Silence fell over the room.

"Can't you call him to heel?" someone demanded.

"Yes, if I feel the need to."

"The need—!" Tolmore fell silent as Bayden growled around his hand.

"He's your boy so he gets to run riot through the club?" Hale asked, quite conversationally all things considered.

Bayden watched Axel turn toward him. "He's mine. But, as far as the club's concerned, he'll be held to the same standard as everyone else."

"And this is fine with you?" Griz asked. He didn't sound any more worried than Hale.

Axel glanced down to where Bayden continued to pin Tolmore to the floor. Bayden's eyes met his, and Axel smiled. "Well, if Tolmore insists on starting fights he can't finish…"

Bayden watched Axel turn to the men around them. His posture was all alpha. There wasn't a hint of anger or uncertainty in his voice. "Next time he tells you there's something a human shouldn't call a werewolf, you all might want to listen."

Bayden knew that other people spoke, but he found it very hard to take his attention away from Axel to care about what they said. Axel was pure perfection, and out of all the men there, he'd chosen Bayden to be his mate. Even in his wolf form, the knowledge made Bayden's breath catch in his throat.

"I'm still down here—if any of you give a toss. Axe, he's your b—" Bayden pressed his teeth more firmly against Tolmore's hand. "Boy! I was going to say you're his boy!" It was a lie, but one that hinted he'd realised his mistake. "For God's sake, Axel—call him off!"

Axel chuckled. "Okay, pup. You've made your point."

Bayden dropped Tolmore's hand and leapt neatly off the prone figure. He trotted across to Axel, still in his wolf form. Axel crouched down to greet him. He scratched the top of Bayden's head and stroked his ears while Tolmore scrambled to his feet.

"You can switch back whenever you want to."

Bayden remained where he was, his head still under Axel's hand as he returned to his human form. He ended up on his hands and knees at Axel's feet. It was a good place to be. With his instincts closer to the surface than ever, it felt quietly sublime, but Axel soon helped him up.

"Dizzy?"

Bayden shook his head.

Axel brushed their lips together. Bayden wasn't sure if the kiss was praise or just Axel's way of welcoming him back to his human form. Either way, Axel didn't linger over it.

When Axel nodded his dismissal, Bayden made his way around the bar, completely naked. As Bayden pulled his jeans on, he was aware that all the men in the club were watching him, some with a new kind of caution, some with admiration that had nothing to do with his shifting skills.

His vest was only good for rags. With just his boots and jeans on, Bayden washed his hands, picked up a cloth and wiped it over the bar where the dregs of Tolmore's beer had spilled in the commotion.

"That was all because he called you Axel's..." Griz trailed off, obviously not inclined to tempt fate.

Bayden nodded. He silently served Tolmore a beer to replace the one he'd spilt.

"Any other landmines we need to be aware of?" Griz asked.

Bayden shook his head. Human words weren't easy then. There was still a touch of growl in his voice when he spoke. "Just that one."

That seemed to mollify the other men.

"Fair enough, but you could have killed him," Drac said.

Bayden shook his head. "Wouldn't do that. Axel told me not to."

A burst of laughter from the other side of the bar made Bayden smile. It was probably best that they thought it was a joke. A glance toward where Axel was talking to Hale further down on the other side of the bar, and Bayden realised three things.

Axel had heard what he'd said. Axel knew it was the truth. And Axel was okay with both those facts.

* * * * *

"What the hell?" Tolmore demanded as he moved down to where Axel stood, still on the customer's side of the bar, talking to Hale.

Axel chuckled. "He did warn you."

"He..." Tolmore waved a hand at where Bayden had pinned him to the floor.

"He was far more polite about it than I thought he would be," Axel mused, more to himself than Tolmore.

"Polite!"

"Oh, grow a pair. There's not a scratch on you."

"That's not the point. He..." Once more words failed Tolmore. He shook his head.

Axel grinned.

"Subs aren't supposed to do that!"

"Doms aren't supposed to wind up other guys' subs and insult their species."

Tolmore made a strangled sound in the back of his throat. "Your boy needs to get a sense of humour."

"How funny is it when straight men make jokes about gay men? I wouldn't expect him to take jokes about wolves off me. I sure as hell don't think he has to take them off you."

Tolmore pushed his hand through his hair. There were slight marks on the back of his hand where Bayden's teeth had pressed against the skin, but Bayden hadn't drawn blood. Axel leaned against the bar, idly wondering if that was only because Bayden didn't want Tolmore bleeding everywhere and making a mess. He wouldn't put it past his pup to have considered that.

Tolmore's hand was shaking. "Bloody werewolves." He shook his head. "Did you know he could do that?"

Axel smiled as he remembered that Tolmore hadn't been one of the Dragons who watched Bayden shift before. "He turns into his wolf form for a few hours most days. You get used to it."

Tolmore looked down the bar toward Bayden. Axel followed Tolmore's line of sight. Bayden was stripped to the waist and completely unselfconscious about that fact, but more than a few guys were getting a good look. Those who had turned up too late to see what exactly had destroyed Bayden's vest were being far less subtle about it than those who'd witnessed his shift.

"You know," Tolmore pointed out. "Really good whiskey is supposed to help with shock."

He'd been a reasonably good sport. Axel made his way back behind the bar and poured him a reasonably good whiskey.

Further down the bar, Axel spotted a couple of guys approach Bayden. They each took their time getting a good look. Axel followed their gaze. Bayden was still lean. His ribs didn't show quite as clearly now, but each line of muscle was still beautifully delineated.

"You're the shifter, aren't you?"

Bayden dipped his head once in acknowledgement.

"The one who'll whore himself out to anyone for a bet?"

Bayden didn't blush. He didn't even blink. "I used to do that." His voice had already lost most of its growl.

"Used to?" the guy demanded, his plans for the evening obviously ruined.

"I'm submitting to Axel now."

The guy's frown deepened. "Just him?"

"That's right."

"Must be costing him a fortune," the guy sneered. His friend laughed.

For the first time, Axel noticed Bayden tense. "The only thing he pays me for is the work I do behind the bar. Do you want a drink or not?"

Beers ordered, the first guy put his cash on the bar. When Bayden went to take it, the man put his hand on top of it, pinning it in place.

"How much would that have bought me if you were still whoring yourself out?"

Axel straightened up. There were risks attached to letting Bayden draw a line in the sand. Axel had been aware of that when he gave him permission. There was no guarantee they had the same definition of what was acceptable and what wasn't.

Bayden would come to heel if Axel called, but...

Bayden leaned forward and calmly inspected the notes on the bar. "Twenty quid? It might have got you a blow job if my rent was due."

He sounded calm. He was in his human form and still on his side of the bar. Axel stayed where he was, forcing himself to let Bayden play it out on his own while those two facts remained.

"How much would it cost me to outbid Axel?"

Bayden turned his back on him. "I told you, he's not paying me."

"Come on, everyone knows what wolves are like. There's no such thing as a former whore. A higher bid, and you'd be off like a shot."

Bayden's shoulders tensed up. He turned around very slowly.

Axel tensed too, not entirely sure what was about to happen. He was vaguely aware of all the other Dragons focusing their attention on the conversation too.

"If you'd come in here a few months ago, you could have whipped me, or screwed me. You could have had me obeying your every order and dropping to my knees every time you clicked your fingers. If you'd put down the cash, you could have had anything you wanted. I was never fussy about who I took a bet from. Whatever you'd wanted, I'd have done it—if I needed the money really badly, it probably wouldn't even have cost you much."

Axel's hand furled into a fist. His heart rate doubled. It was the truth. He knew that. He'd seen it with his own eyes. But, he couldn't feel as calm about it as Bayden sounded.

"Now, Axel can get me to do whatever he wants. The difference is that I won't take a penny off him."

"Yeah, right," the guy who'd tried to proposition him muttered.

"Yeah," Bayden echoed. "Right. But even that's not the most important difference."

Axel tore his gaze away from Bayden for a second. His pup had everyone's complete attention. There wasn't another conversation in the entire pub.

"He doesn't need to pay me, he doesn't even need to ask. Whatever he wants, it's his—any time, any way he wants it. I'll do anything for him, but I won't look for payment afterwards, I'll get down on my knees and thank him for the privilege."

"Everyone knows he's been babying you and—"

"He could beat the hell out of me, or whore me out to every man in this pub, and I'd still crawl at his feet and beg to know what else I could do to please him." No hesitation, no doubt. It was a simple statement of fact from Bayden's point of view.

The guy fell silent, but Bayden was on a roll.

"You think I looked like a good lay when I was going through the motions to win a bet?" Bayden shook his head and laughed. "You have no idea what a wolf's submission is like. The only person in this pub who does is Axel—and it's not because he pays me; it's because he's the kind of guy I'd never take payment from. That's the difference between a real dom and someone who has to pay a man to get on his knees— that's the difference between Axel and you."

There was anger there, but it obviously wasn't because Bayden didn't like reality as he saw it. Apparently, it was one thing for some idiot to call him a whore, but another to call his dom a punter.

Bayden turned away from the guy, dismissing him as if he was less than nothing in his eyes. One of the Dragons clicked back into life and ordered a beer. Gradually, conversations resumed.

Axel made his way down the length of the bar. He stopped directly behind Bayden. Sliding his arm around him, he settled his hand on Bayden's bare abs.

"Just so there are no misunderstandings, I neither want nor need you to stand up for me. I can fight my own battles. Looking after my reputation is not your job."

Bayden looked down. "I'm sor—"

"That said," Axel cut in. "Your little speech was the hottest thing I've heard in my life." He tugged Bayden back so their bodies were pressed tightly together, and Bayden would have no doubt just how turned on he was.

Bayden relaxed. "It was just the truth, sir."

"I know."

Bayden remained perfectly still for a few seconds. He glanced at the men around them, then shuffled his feet further apart, spreading his legs and making it perfectly clear that he had no problem with Axel screwing him right there, in front of everyone.

"Later," Axel corrected.

* * * * *

"Go upstairs. Put your old jeans on."

Bayden looked down at the ones he was wearing. He hadn't damaged them when he shifted. At least, he hadn't thought he had. He studied them more carefully, trying to work out what had displeased Axel, wondering if that's why he hadn't wanted to screw him when the pub was still open.

"They're all in one piece," Axel said. "That's what's wrong with them. I want you to wear the ones that aren't."

"The ones you cut?"

"They're in your drawer. There's a belt with them. Come down to the back rooms when you're done." He didn't sound like he wanted to be kept waiting.

Bayden hurried up the stairs. The jeans were just where Axel had said they'd be. Bayden hurriedly pulled his boots and his jeans off. He grabbed the old pair and tugged them on. The original cuts had been all about easy access. Axel had improved on them since then.

The seat of the jeans was gone, leaving Bayden's buttocks exposed. The front of the trousers was half there, but the denim had been trimmed back, leaving his cock and balls free.

Bayden slid the belt Axel had left with the jeans through as many of the belt loops as still remained, and did it up. The strip of leather finished off the frame. He looked down his body, then over his shoulder. It shouldn't be possible for clothes to make him look more naked than he'd been when he wasn't wearing anything.

His erection curved up, standing proudly away from his body, the flushed tip peeking past his foreskin. His cock bobbed with each step he took on the way down the stairs.

A door leading into one of the back rooms was open. Bayden stepped inside.

Axel had tossed aside his T-shirt and was inspecting the contents of a cupboard on the far side of the room. He turned when he heard Bayden walk in and looked him up and down. "Turn around."

Bayden turned on the spot, letting Axel get a good look at his altered jeans. Axel's scent made it clear he liked the view, but, just in case there could have been any doubt, Axel whispered his approval under his breath. "Perfect."

He pointed to the spanking bench.

Bayden climbed onto it, settling his knees on the widely spaced supports and bending over. With his torso resting on the padded surface, his backside was offered up for Axel to do with as he pleased. The denim covering his legs only made him more aware of how bare and vulnerable his arse was.

"Would you have liked being put on display in front of everyone like this?" Axel stepped up alongside him and ran his fingers over Bayden's exposed buttocks.

"Yes, sir."

"Letting them see what I can do with you?"

"Yes, sir." It was exactly what he wanted.

"Demonstrating how much pain you can take to please your dom?"

Bayden nodded rapidly. "Yes, sir."

"Showing off how I can make you come less than five seconds into the game?"

Bayden stopped himself from nodding just in time. He looked over his shoulder.

"The rules wouldn't have changed just because we had an audience. You'd still have come when it pleased me, not when it would impress them. That could have been five hours into a scene, or five seconds. That's always my choice."

Bayden looked down.

"I don't care whether or not we play in public, pup. I have nothing to prove to anyone. But make no mistake, if we do play in front of other men, I'll make damn sure the only man you're focused on impressing is me."

Axel moved around the spanking bench, fixing restraints around Bayden's wrists and ankles. "Your safe word is the same as it's always been."

Bayden stared at the floor just in front of the bench.

"I expect you to say it, if you need to. That would remain the same whether we're alone or in a crowd."

Bayden swallowed. "Yes, sir."

Axel ran his hand over Bayden's back as he walked toward the base of the spanking bench. "You're allowed to move however much you can. Remember, the bondage is there so you don't have to think about it."

"Yes, sir," Bayden repeated. He glanced over his shoulder. From that angle, it wasn't easy to see Axel's face. He traced one of the tattoos up Axel's arm, but didn't try to twist around and see Axel's expression clearly.

The scent of leather and arousal hung in the air. Axel didn't smell angry, but it was hard for Bayden to believe he wasn't.

"I shouldn't have asked."

"About what?" Axel ran his palm in circles over Bayden's arse.

"About doing a scene in front of them." Axel was the alpha. It was Bayden's job to follow, not lead. All his big talk, about how good a sub he was. It was a mercy Axel hadn't laughed at the idea in front of everyone.

"I'm not angry with you."

Bayden squirmed against his bondage.

"You only get marks when I'm pleased with you, right?"

Marks? Bayden looked over his shoulder again, this time he made the effort to look Axel in the eye.

Axel smiled. "Unless you don't want them?"

"I want them!"

Axel chuckled. "Good boy." He brought his hand down against Bayden's right buttock.

It wasn't hard enough to hurt, but Axel wasn't teasing him the way he had last time. There was a wonderful sting to it. Axel swiftly struck Bayden's left buttock just as hard.

"I knew these jeans would look good on you."

Bayden closed his eyes, picturing it—Axel standing over him, tall and strong, with all his tattoos on display. And, in front of Axel, himself bound with his arse on display, so safe and yet so vulnerable at the same time.

Axel found a rhythm he liked. Bayden couldn't help but rock within his restraints, pushing back into each spank.

"You did good today." Axel didn't let up for a second.

Bayden's breaths were already ragged. He didn't try to answer, but pleasure rolled through him just as quickly as the heat from the spanking.

"I was proud of the way you handled them." His hand came down again.

Bayden's arse had been red the last time Axel had spanked him. This time felt far more intense, maybe even harsh enough that there would still be marks to admire the following morning. The cheeks on Bayden's face flushed just as brightly as he relished Axel's praise—whether he believed he really deserved it or not.

When Axel stopped the spanking as suddenly as he'd started it, the only sound was Bayden's panting.

Axel didn't say anything as he slid slicked fingers against Bayden's hole. Bayden closed his eyes and prayed. Axel wouldn't leave him hanging this time. He wouldn't get him ready only to change his mind about screwing him. He'd said Bayden was good—and he wasn't the kind of human who set a wolf up for a fall. He wouldn't have said it unless he thought it was true, and if it was true, there was no reason not to screw him.

Bayden's mind blurred in a kaleidoscope of pleasure as Axel's fingers worked deeper inside him. Axel took his hand away; all the colour faded from Bayden's world. His thoughts congealed.

Axel took up a tight grip on Bayden's hips, but Bayden's mind remained blank until he felt the tip of Axel's cock pushing into him.

Axel didn't stop until his cock was buried as far inside Bayden as was physically possible. He ground his hips against Bayden's spanked arse, drawing a pleasure filled moan from him. Bayden still couldn't catch his breath. He tugged at his restraints just the way Axel had said he could.

The need to move, to demand Axel move too, was unbearable. Axel knew what he wanted—Bayden had no doubt about that. But Axel made him wait, remaining perfectly still until Bayden knew he was going to lose his mind.

Finally, Axel yielded. He once more picked whatever rhythm suited him. Bayden had as little control over it as he'd had when Axel was spanking him.

All Bayden could do was accept, but what raced through Bayden's psyche was Axel's acceptance of him. He was Axel's. Neither of them had any doubt about that. Maybe Axel intended him to come at that moment, maybe Axel was too concerned with his own orgasm to care if Bayden came or not. Either way, Bayden was helpless. Lacking permission to hold himself in check, he could only give in to his own need.

The world swirled around Bayden. Just a moment later, he felt Axel spill inside him. Axel tightened his grip on Bayden's sides as he came and Bayden smiled down at the floor just in front of the spanking bench. He might have just gained a few marks that would last through the night.

Axel pulled away. He straightened his clothes. Bayden remained in place. His only contribution was to murmur his approval when Axel ran his fingers over both the spanking and where his fingertips had pressed against Bayden's sides.

"I like the marks, sir."

"Would you like some which will last longer?" Axel asked.

Bayden nodded.

Axel moved forward and stroked his fingers through Bayden's hair. "Don't you want to know what kind of marks I'm offering before you get too enthusiastic?"

Bayden shook his head.

"It'll hurt," Axel warned, amusement filling his tone.

"Whatever you'll give me, sir."

Axel walked away. Bayden took a deep breath and let it out very slowly. Axel wasn't leaving him, he wasn't the type to walk off in a huff. True to form, Axel only stopped briefly at the cupboard he'd been looking in when Bayden came down stairs, then he came back.

"It took a lot of trust for you to follow my orders today. You've earned some stripes."

Axel didn't stand as close as he had when he spanked Bayden. He had something in his hand but Bayden didn't crane his neck to try to see what it was. Trust. Axel liked it when he trusted him.

Bayden closed his eyes and finally managed to settle his breaths into a slow, easy rhythm. All that good work ended in a gasp.

Bayden tossed his head as lightning shot through his spanked buttocks. A line of pure fire flared from one side of his arse to the other.

"Count for me, pup."

"One, sir." Bayden's voice was rough but level.

Seconds ticked past. Bayden forced himself to relax when every physical instinct wanted him to tense up.

Another bolt of scorching heat travelled along a line just below the previous one.

"Two, sir." Bayden closed his eyes, focusing on the sensations the way Axel had asked him to once before. "Three, sir... Four... Five..." Bayden counted each one out. His voice was a little rougher each time Axel set another line of flames burning across his backside. "Six, sir!"

He pulled helplessly against his bondage. Holding nothing back from Axel, Bayden let his mate see exactly what each strike did to him.

Bayden had barely stilled himself when he felt Axel's fingers trace over his skin, from the base of his right buttock all the way to the top, passing over six raw strips of skin.

"The cane feels nothing like a spanking," Axel observed.

Bayden couldn't argue with that.

"Do you think the marks will be worth it?"

Bayden nodded rapidly.

Anything that marked him out as Axel's was worth it.

Chapter Thirty Five

Axel grinned when he saw Bayden walk out of the pub to join him in the lock-up he used as a mini gym. Bayden stark bollock naked was always something to grin about.

Bayden walked across the yard at the back of the pub, entirely at ease with his nudity. He only paused when he saw that Axel had stopped working out to admire the view. "You said not to get dressed before I came out to keep you company, sir."

"True."

Bayden sat down on the thickly cushioned mat Axel had placed in the corner for his use. That wasn't unusual. Technically, it wasn't unusual for Bayden to be undressed when he did that either.

"Any reason why you haven't shifted today?"

"You didn't order me to, sir."

"I've never ordered you to."

Bayden shrugged.

Halfway through a set of crunches, Axel remained perfectly still, and waited.

"They'll disappear quicker if I shift, sir."

Axel beckoned him closer. Once Bayden was within reach, he turned him around to get a good view of his arse. The lines the cane had left on his buttocks yesterday were still visible, but they'd already paled significantly. Axel ran his fingers over them. Bayden looked over his shoulder.

"I like them too," Axel said. "But you know, if they disappear, I have no problem putting some new marks in their place. Rapid healing isn't a bad thing."

Bayden nodded.

"But neither is having you wander around naked. You don't need to shift unless you want to." He released Bayden and sent him back toward the cushion with a light tap on the arse.

Axel went back to his work-out, but while having Bayden rest in the corner of the room looking exactly like a wolf had become quietly companionable, having a naked and willing submissive sitting around in his human form was as distracting as hell. Axel sped up his work out, casting frequent glances in Bayden's direction.

If he caught Bayden watching him with admiration more than a few times, he spotted him frowning at the wall of the lock-up just as often. Axel glanced at the wall. It was bare and boring. On the other side of it was the lock-up containing Bayden's bike.

At the end of his third set of press ups, Axel sat back on his heels and wiped his face with a towel. "Pup?"

"What they said about selling my bike, sir. It—"

"Was bullshit," Axel cut in.

Bayden turned his attention back to the wall.

"It's yours, pup. I don't sell things that don't belong to me."

"I could sell it," Bayden said softly. He stared at his hands. "It draws attention—makes things more difficult than they need to be."

"It was important to your father."

"He was my alpha," Bayden said, placing the stress firmly on the word was.

Axel tossed the towel aside and grabbed his water bottle. "What he wanted isn't important anymore?"

"It's not the most important thing."

Axel remained silent.

"It would make a lot more than seven hundred pounds, sir."

"The fallout if you sold your bike to pay me back would only be slightly less dramatic than when you let yourself get hurt to pay me back."

Bayden looked down at his fingers. He'd entwined them so tightly the tips were turning white. "The bike was important to my old pack, to my old alpha."

"And now you're ready to have a new pack and a new alpha?"

"If that's what you still want, sir."

Axel joined Bayden on his cushion. It was barely big enough for both of them. Snuggling wasn't optional. Axel guided Bayden to curl into his side and rest his head on his shoulder. He hadn't intended them to have that particular discussion today, but he couldn't lie about it. "I've wanted that for a long time—it just took me a while to translate what I wanted into words we both understand."

Bayden took a deep breath and let it out very slowly.

Axel stroked the nape of Bayden's neck, trying to work out if Bayden was ready for the next step or not, and what stumbling blocks might be in their way. "Did you mention the possibility of being my mate to your mother when we visited her?" he asked.

Bayden nodded.

Axel controlled all his reactions as best he could, not wanting Bayden to know how nervous he was. "Does she approve?"

Another nod.

Axel smiled. "Would your grandfather have approved?"

Bayden didn't respond immediately.

Axel left it a while to see if he was just trying to find the right words, but eventually he had to prompt him. "Pup?"

"I wouldn't have asked for his approval, sir."

Axel tried to think like a wolf. "Because your mother was the more dominant between them, if she approved, his approval went without saying?"

Bayden curled in closer to Axel's chest and Axel automatically tightened his hold on him. Even as he frowned, trying to work out what was wrong, Axel stroked Bayden's back and pressed a kiss to the top of his head.

"Because if he was still alive, I wouldn't be here," Bayden finally whispered. "I couldn't have looked after him and obeyed your rules about how I earn money. I'd have had to stop submitting to you after the six weeks were up and—"

"Bayden," Axel cut in. "Did you think you would have gone back to—" He stopped himself short with the word prostitution hanging from his lips. "To taking bets that looked like scenes?"

Bayden nodded.

Axel made him look up. "That was never going to happen. I know I told you before that saying your safe word would be able to stop *everything* between us. But, that wasn't entirely true."

Bayden tried to look down but Axel refused to give him permission to do that.

Bayden cleared his throat. "If you'd still wanted me sometimes, I'd never have said no to you, sir."

Axel stroked Bayden's hair back from his face. "That's not what I mean. You can decide you don't want to have sex with me. You can decide you don't want to submit to me. You can say your safe word, or say no, or whatever—there are lots of ways you can stop those kinds of things. But you can't just decide I should stop caring about you. A word can't make me stop looking after you. That's not the way it works—not between men who aren't playing games together."

"I can look after myself," Bayden whispered. "I wouldn't have expected you to—"

"Your family didn't expect you to help out, but you did, even after they told you not to."

Bayden pulled away. "It's different. I wouldn't have taken money off you."

Axel let Bayden sit upright, but he put his hand on his thigh, knowing that the lightest touch would be enough to keep him where he wanted him. "You wouldn't have taken cash off me to pay your bills, but there are ways I could have made sure you could earn enough yourself, without needing to do things like that."

Bayden tensed. His leg twitched under Axel's fingers. Bayden didn't go so far as to pull away, but when he spoke, his anger was obvious. "If there was any other way, I would never—"

Axel shook his head. "Being human means I have options you won't have until the anti-pack laws are overturned."

Bayden folded his arms across his chest.

"Did you know Tolmore inherited his uncle's house last year? He's talking about renting out some of the bedrooms. If your mother and grandfather had moved in with him, he wouldn't have charged them wolf rates. If your mother had been willing to do more than her fair share around the house, that would have meant even less rent. Tolmore's gay, so you wouldn't have had to worry about him bothering her—they'd have both been perfectly safe." He studied Bayden's expression carefully and weighed each word before he spoke. "You could have covered their bills from your wages here— you wouldn't have needed to take a penny off me that you hadn't earned."

Bayden nibbled on his bottom lip.

"If you didn't like that idea, then Drac is talking about doing up the flat above his studio. They could have moved in there with a similar deal."

Axel stroked Bayden's cheek.

"If you didn't like that plan, Griz is always complaining he needs someone to sort out his workshop—between doing that and your work in the bar, you could have probably covered all the bills even if they kept paying wolf-rates where they were living before."

Bayden bit his bottom lip. "I…"

"Is that why you've been feeling guilty—because you thought it was his death that meant you could stay with me?"

Axel shook his head and stroked Bayden's cheek, very gently. "Between us we would have found a way to keep your family safe without you needing to do any bets that broke the rules. You're not here because your grandfather died, pup, you're here because this is where you belong."

Bayden slowly unfolded his arms. He closed his eyes. Axel watched as Bayden swallowed several times in quick succession. Without opening his eyes, Bayden leaned forward and rested his head against Axel's chest again.

"Good boy, I've got you."

"I can learn to be just like a human for you, sir, and —"

Axel put his hand over Bayden's mouth. "Not an offer I want to hear."

Bayden waited patiently until Axel took away his hand. "It would be easier for you. It would mean —"

"It would mean I don't deserve you in my pack," Axel cut in, allowing no room for argument in his tone. He stroked Bayden's cheek, just to make sure he knew he wasn't angry with him. "Telling someone you'll accept them as long as they pretend to be someone they're not — that's not real acceptance. And saying you'll love someone as long as they lie about part of who they are — that's not real love, pup." Bayden tensed at the word love being uttered out loud for the first time. Axel smiled and pressed a kiss against Bayden's temple. "I won't be someone who does that."

Bayden pressed a return kiss against his shoulder, as shy as ever but with just a little bit more confidence this time.

"I love you pup — every bit of you. You'll never need to lie to me about anything, or to hide anything from me. That's what real love is all about."

"I love you too." He whispered the words into Axel's shoulder, as if he was too shy to lift his head and say them to his face.

"Enough to agree to be part of my pack?" Axel asked.

"Yes, sir."

Even though he knew the answer, Axel's soul still soared at it being acknowledged properly between them. "And my mate?"

"If you want me to, sir," Bayden whispered.

Axel coaxed him to lift his head. "And my submissive?"

"Your collared submissive," Bayden specified.

Axel studied where his fingers had automatically slipped down to rest against Bayden's neck. "Is that a problem?"

Bayden took a deep breath.

It was always going to be their most likely stumbling block. Axel had known that from the start. Asking Bayden to wear something that was more likely to be worn by a dog than a wolf was always going to be hard for him. If wolves had been made to wear them during the Captivities, he'd have been brought up to hate the very idea.

Bayden swallowed. His Adam's apple bobbed against Axel's fingertips. "Would it have to be tight, sir?"

"Tight?" Axel echoed blankly, thrown completely off his stride.

"You said I'm not allowed to try to stay human all the time," Bayden reminded him.

"That's right."

Bayden put his hand to his throat. "I think my neck's bigger when I'm in my wolf shape. If it was looser, I think I could shift with it on and..."

"And it would never have to come off," Axel finished for him. He nodded, instantly in love with that possibility. "I'll get one that will fit you all the time—whatever shape you're in."

Bayden smiled. A few seconds later, he followed it up with a nod.

Axel stroked his fingers against Bayden's neck again, finally letting himself enjoy the image of a collar laying there without forcing himself to remember that he might have to learn to live with the fact it could be a reasonable limit for a wolf. His cock hardened, his soul cried out with pleasure, but he did his damnedest not to let either reaction distract him. "You know some things will change once you're collared?"

"Whatever you want." Bayden said it with perfect confidence, as if it was the most natural thing in the world for him to submit to Axel in every way there was.

"I want you to give up your place and move in here properly."

Bayden glanced up at him. "After the collar?"

"No. There's no need to wait. As soon as we get time to fetch anything you want from there."

Bayden cautiously placed his hand on Axel's chest. When Axel didn't object, Bayden fell into his habit of tracing his tattoos while he thought. "I can pay you the same as I paid for my bedsit, and the garage I rented. You could—"

Axel shook his head.

"I'm not here because I want your money, sir."

Axel moved his hand to the back of Bayden's neck and stroked the hair at his nape. "I know that."

Bayden moved on to one of the tattoos on Axel's arm. "I always paid my way. When I was living at home, I never lived off anyone else."

"I won't play the landlord with you, pup. You can't pay to live here." Bayden tensed. Axel could feel the desire to pull away get stronger by the moment. So many men had paid him to do so many things. A landlord wouldn't be the worst role he could be cast in. "Of course, if you're just telling me you want to chip in for household expenses, that would be different. There's nothing wrong with that."

Bayden looked up.

"Part of your wages can go in the bills pot," Axel allowed. "And you can keep the rest to spend on whatever you want."

Bayden nodded.

"But I decide what proportion goes where," Axel added.

Bayden stopped nodding.

"Alpha's prerogative," Axel said. Just as he suspected, that idea sealed the deal. Bayden wouldn't argue with his alpha unless he had to.

Axel smiled down at Bayden. The way they were snuggling against each other already had them both hard and eager to play.

"What about the money I still owe you?" Bayden said, softly.

"We'll sort that out before the collar goes on," Axel decided, pulling his own brain back above his belt once more, with only a little extra difficulty. "A clean slate."

Bayden smiled up at Axel. His obvious relief left Axel in no doubt that he'd made the right decision. Waiting would be worth it if it let Bayden come to him without anything hanging over his head.

"But that doesn't mean you're allowed to do anything crazy to get the money," Axel reminded him.

"I won't let you down again, sir."

Axel brushed their lips together. "There's no rush. I'll need time to get a collar that's just right for you. The thing about wolves not liking silver — is there any truth to it?"

Bayden shook his head.

Axel ran his hand down Bayden's back and over his caned arse, but he stopped short of starting anything. "If you're going to be my mate as well as my sub, is there anything else I need to get?"

Bayden looked up at him with a mix of curiosity and confusion.

"Are there any lupine traditions — gifts one wolf gives another when they become mates?" Axel checked. "Or is there a ceremony — like when humans get married?"

Bayden shook his head. "The only thing that matters to us is both wolves knowing who their mate is." He paused for a moment. "What about you, sir?" The words were soft and cautious.

"Me?" Axel asked.

"What about the other side of the human traditions, sir? I get a collar, you get…"

Axel grinned. "I get you."

* * * * *

"Do I still need permission to go out, sir?"

Axel looked up from where he had the pub's accounts spread out across the desk in his office. Bayden had showered and dressed after spending the last couple of hours shifted. It was once more hard to remember that he could ever look anything other than human.

"Go where?" Axel asked.

"Out," Bayden repeated.

"Do you want to visit your mother?" Axel guessed. "We could…"

Bayden shook his head.

Axel leaned back in his chair and studied him. Bayden stood in the doorway making no effort to actually enter the room. He had his hands pushed deep into his pockets, the way he did when he wanted to make sure he didn't fidget.

"It's been a while since we paid our respects to your grandfather," Axel said.

"It's nothing like that, sir. I'd just… I'd like permission to go out."

He'd been cooped up for a while. It wasn't unreasonable for him to want to kick off the dust and get some air. Hell, after the way he'd wanted to avoid riding after all that bull with Granger, Axel was sure he should be celebrating rather than questioning him. "It's a couple of hours before we need to open, we could go for a ride —"

"On my own, sir."

No. Axel bit back the instinct and forced himself to be reasonable. This wasn't a kinky little scene. It was real life. As much as he loved the idea of never letting Bayden out of his sight for the rest of his life, it wasn't realistic long term. "Where do you want to go?"

Bayden shuffled his boots. "It's not somewhere you'd disapprove of, sir."

"But it is somewhere you don't want to tell me about."

Bayden shrugged.

"What do you want to do there?" Axel tried.

"Nothing that's against your rules, sir."

Axel stretched his legs out and crossed his ankles. It had been three days since they spoke about the collar. A certain amount of boundary testing was to be expected. Bayden wanted to be sure that he would be allowed a reasonable amount of freedom before he made that commitment—he wanted to know that Axel would trust him. There was nothing strange about that.

Axel smiled reassuringly. "If you tell me where you want to go and what you want to do, you'll probably get my permission."

"Hello?" Griz's voice called through from the door at the back of the pub.

Bayden looked over his shoulder.

Axel got up. He ruffled his hair as he went to meet Griz. "We'll talk about it later," he promised.

Bayden said nothing.

Outside, they found Griz looking very pleased with himself. There was another man with him, still straddling an old Royal Enfield bike. The guy took off his helmet as they approached. Evan.

"You got his bike running?" Axel asked Griz. At the same time, he nudged Bayden toward Evan. "Go on."

Bayden joined Evan as he got off the bike. Axel kept an eye on them while he listened to Griz rattle off a list of things they'd done to the bike to bring it up to its current standard.

Evan pointed to something on the bike. Bayden had never held a grudge against the boy for helping out in the pub during his punishment. He paid attention to everything Evan said. After a while, Bayden even went so far as to utter a few sentences himself. In werewolf terms, that counted as exceptionally friendly.

Bayden crouched down alongside Evan as they studied a bit of the bike that Evan was apparently especially proud of. Axel couldn't hear what they said to each other, but the fact a real conversation had developed was promising. Friends among the lifestyle subs, and particularly with one who might well join the Dragons in the future, could only be a good thing for Bayden.

When the bike had been admired to everyone's satisfaction, they went inside. Bayden headed behind the bar just as instinctively as Axel. "Sir?"

Axel slid his arm around Bayden's waist. "Pup?"

"You said we could talk later."

Axel glanced across to Evan and Griz. "We can."

"Would it make a difference if I took Evan with me?" Bayden rushed out.

Axel nudged Bayden around to face him.

"You could ask him if I broke any of your rules while we were out. You could trust him to tell you if I did—he's a really bad liar."

He was offering to take a babysitter with him. For a man as proud and as inclined to be self-reliant as Bayden, it was a huge concession. "It's that important to you?"

Bayden's shrug was as good as a yes.

"How long?"

"Sir?"

"How long do you want permission to be out for?"

Bayden studied Axel carefully. "An hour and a half, sir."

"And what does Evan have to say about this? That's what you were talking about out by his bike, right?"

"He said he doesn't need permission from Griz—their rules don't work that way. If you'll give me permission, he's willing for us to go whenever it's convenient to you."

Axel stared down at Bayden for a long time. Doubts niggled at the back of his mind. Echoes of the terror he'd felt when Bayden disappeared on him before sent a shiver down his spine, but he'd have to show that he trusted his pup out of his sight sooner or later. "You have an hour and a half. Take your phone. If you run into any trouble, call me."

Bayden glanced at the clock above the bar. "My shift starts in an hour, sir."

"You have an hour and a half," Axel repeated.

Bayden nodded. Within a few minutes, he and Evan were gone. Back inside the pub, Axel looked at his watch and wondered what the chances of him keeping his sanity for the next eighty-nine and a half minutes were.

"Do you know where they're going?" Griz asked as he settled himself at the bar.

"No."

"Well, don't look at me," Griz said. "Evan's a pretty little sub, but I'm screwing him and helping him fix up his bike, not collaring him. Unless he's in handcuffs, he goes where he wants."

Axel poured them both a drink.

"Talking about collars..." Griz said.

"Yes. Soon."

"Oh, bloody hell, man. What are you waiting for?" Griz demanded. "If you don't get him on a collar and lead soon, he's going to drive you insane."

Axel chuckled. "He borrowed some money off me when his grandfather died so he could pay off the last of the funeral stuff. He wants to pay me back before I collar him. It's a reasonable request."

"Seven hundred pounds, right?"

Axel raised an eyebrow at him.

"The bet he took with Ford — it was for seven hundred pounds. Bikers gossip, and the kinky ones are the worst of all, you should know that by now."

"And you should know me well enough to know that I'd cut my hand off before I accepted money he earned taking that kind of beating."

"Fair enough."

Axel looked at his watch again. Less than five minutes had passed. Bloody hell.

* * * * *

The door swung open three minutes before opening. That wasn't unusual. Every one of the Dragons and half of the regulars had proven themselves incapable of telling the time at one point or another.

Evan stepped inside.

Axel looked past the boy but there was no one walking in behind him. "Where's Bayden?"

"He's putting his bike away around back." Evan came up to the bar. He looked nervous. That wasn't good. He took a deep breath and glanced from Griz to Axel. "Bayden asked me to speak to you."

Axel frowned. Evan's nerves didn't improve.

"He said you'd want to ask me if he broke any of your rules when we were out. He—"

Axel held up a hand. "That's enough."

Just that moment, Bayden came in from the back of the pub. He paused, apparently sensing that all wasn't well.

"Come here."

Bayden joined Evan and Griz at the bar.

"Did you break any of the rules when you were out?"

Bayden looked toward Evan.

"I'm asking you not him."

Bayden turned back to Axel. "No, I didn't break any, sir."

Axel nodded. "That's all I need to know. You don't need anyone else to vouch for you. Any questions?"

Bayden shook his head.

"Your shift's about to start." Axel nodded for him to come around to his side of the bar. As Bayden washed his hands at the sink, Axel stepped up behind him. "When you want to tell me what today was all about, I'll listen. But, I'm not going to go around asking other men to tell me what my sub is doing."

"I didn't mean it as an insult, sir."

Axel tightened his hold on him for a moment. "I know. But the only checking up I intend to do will happen tonight. I'm going to go over every inch of you to make sure there's not a mark on you that I didn't put there myself."

Bayden turned and put his hand on Axel's shoulder. It was still wet and soapy. The water quickly soaked through Axel's T-shirt.

Axel shook his head before Bayden had a chance to protest.

"I'm talking about having you naked and tied up, completely helpless when I work my way over every inch of you. I won't find any new marks, but I'm definitely going to enjoy the inspection. And if you're good, you might even get a few more marks from me as a reward."

Bayden smiled. "I'll be good."

Chapter Thirty Six

"If you're ever going to join The Black Dragons properly, it's time you showed us what you're made of."

Bayden looked up. There were more members of the club in than was usual for a weeknight. They were all staring in Bayden's direction. It didn't feel like a coincidence that they'd all turned up together. Bayden looked down the bar toward Axel, wondering if he knew what was going on. Axel had obviously caught the words, but he didn't seem to be ahead of that particular curve.

Hale stood up. "I've been thinking about all those fights you took when you started drinking here. You won, fair enough. But it's not like that proved much. There wasn't a single guy who was a real challenge. If you want to prove you have what it takes to join the Dragons, you're going to have to do better."

Hale wasn't saying that he couldn't join Axel's pack. He wasn't Axel and he didn't have the right to say anything like that. But, all the very logical things that went through Bayden's mind were no competition for his instinctive panic at the prospect of losing another pack before he'd even officially joined it.

"Hale." Axel stepped up alongside Bayden. "What's going on?"

"A simple bet. A few of us reckon Bayden doesn't have what it takes to win a fight against a man who knows what he's doing and we're willing to put our money where our mouths are." He turned to Bayden. "What do you say wolf-boy?"

Bayden swallowed. He could take down any member of the Dragons—hell, he could take down any member of the species if he needed to. If he had permission to…

Bayden looked down. His father would turn in his grave, but it wasn't his father's opinion that was important. "You'd win," he said—forcing himself to say the words clearly, no matter what the cost.

Hale couldn't have looked more shocked if Bayden had slapped him.

"I don't have permission to take bets anymore," Bayden said. "So, you're right—I'm no match for you. You'd win by default, all of you would."

"Who said you don't have permission?"

Bayden turned to Axel. *You.* Axel had said it, except it felt like pointing that out would have meant contradicting him in front of his whole pack. Bayden bit his tongue and stayed silent.

"I said you don't have permission to bet on the guy you're supposed to be fighting. You don't have permission to throw a fight and get the crap beaten out of you. A fair fight taken here—one where you actually fight back—that's not against any rule I've set for you."

Bayden stared up at Axel, trying to work it out. Axel hated it when he took fights, he'd always hated it. He had no reason to grant him permission to do that.

"There goes that excuse," Hale chipped in. "So unless the real truth is that you don't have the balls for it…"

Bayden never took his eyes off Axel. His scent was off but Bayden couldn't work out why. He didn't seem angry. There'd been no doubt in Axel's voice when he said that Bayden had his permission.

"One hundred each says you can't beat any one of us in a fair fight," Hale said.

"I'll cover your side of the bet," Axel offered.

Bayden hesitated. He was almost afraid to hope, but if Axel was giving him permission, it was just possible. "Will you take whatever money I win, sir?"

"Money earned like this, in a fair fight when I'm there to keep an eye on things, yes."

Bayden immediately turned to Hale. "Whenever you're ready."

Within minutes all the Dragons were out the back of the pub and anyone else who'd tried to tag along and watch had been banished back inside, with the exception of Evan. Bayden stripped to the waist and Axel began binding his knuckles.

"Are there any Dragons you can't beat?" Axel asked.

"You."

Axel chuckled. "Only because you wouldn't let that happen."

Bayden tried to shake his head, but Axel stroked Bayden's cheek and stopped him short. "My ego's not that fragile, pup."

Axel glanced over his shoulder at where the other Dragons were congregating, before turning back to Bayden. "You fight fair. You fight to win. But you remember that these are the guys you're going to be riding with—they're going to be your pack. This is about finding your right place in the pack, not about anyone trying to break anyone else. They're not out to get a wolf. They're hazing the new guy, just like they would if you were human."

Bayden nodded. Nervous energy pumped through him, making him desperate to fidget, but he forced himself to give Axel his whole attention.

"You knock them down, but when the fight's over, you help them back up." Axel thought about that for a second. "But carefully. Some of them aren't above sneaking in a late blow."

Bayden rubbed his covered knuckles together. "If one of them leaves a few bruises, sir…"

"You won't get in trouble for that. Letting someone land one hit is different from letting someone keep on hitting you long after any decent man would throw in the towel himself, rather than keep on going."

Bayden met his gaze.

"Yes, I know you always let guys think it's a closer fight than it ever really is." Axel chuckled. "It's a strange brand of politeness, but I can live with it for today."

Griz came across to them. "Any problem with me holding the money and playing referee?"

Axel took out his wallet and handed him one hundred pounds without the slightest hesitation.

Griz went back over to the other guys. Bayden saw Drac offer him a few bank notes.

"Everyone know the rules?" Griz asked.

"No one's allowed to shape shift," Tolmore called out. Everyone laughed.

Bayden nodded his willingness to go along with that rule. He ran his eyes over the group of Dragons. There were nine men present, not counting Axel. It was hard to distinguish one man's scent from another when they stood so close together, but as a group they smelt nervous.

Axel brushed his lips against Bayden's. "Go on, pup."

Bayden stepped into the middle of the yard. Drac joined him. It was surreal, standing there, facing off against one of Axel's friends. Adrenaline raced into Bayden's veins, the same as before any fight, but the anger he usually felt wasn't there.

When he looked at Drac, Bayden didn't see hatred, or even contempt for what he was. Drac wasn't just a human, he was one of the guys who rode with Axel. More important still, he was the guy who did Axel's tattoos.

Bayden glanced across at Axel. He loved those tattoos. Bayden made a mental note to make sure that Drac's hands came out of the fight completely unscathed. If that meant making sure Drac didn't land a blow with his hands, so be it.

Win. Don't get badly hurt. Keep Drac's hands safe. The thoughts scrolled lazily through Bayden's mind as his body fell into a familiar routine. *Circle the other guy. Dodge, block, land a hit.* It wasn't complicated.

Drac knew how to fight. He was quite good for a human. He was bigger than Bayden, but he was also more than a decade older, and Bayden guessed that he'd done most of his fighting years ago.

Drac went down hard, but he got back up. He got up the second time, too. The third time he half sat up and rubbed at his jaw, but he didn't rush to his feet. Bayden met his gaze and held it. The fight was over. All he had to do now was wait for Drac to admit it. Then Bayden could prove his point and make sure everyone knew which species had come out on top.

Bayden glanced towards Axel. Pack. One member of a pack didn't rub salt into another pack member's wounds. He didn't rub sarcasm into a loss either. Bayden stepped forward and offered Drac his hand.

* * * * *

"You're one man short."

Hale and Griz turned away from the fight as Axel joined them.

"Seven guys. Seven fights. Seven hundred pounds so he can pay off the money he borrowed from me. That's the idea, isn't it?"

Griz smiled. Hale shrugged, but the scheme had his name written all over it.

"He won't fight Evan," Axel pointed out, as he watched Bayden sidestep a neat attempt to sweep his legs out from under him. "He won't fight any man who already knows he's less dominant than him."

"No one's ever mistaken me for a sub," Hale said. "You?"

Hale nodded, just once. "Me." He'd turned back to the fight and was studying Bayden's technique with far more focus than any casual observer should display.

Axel looked from Hale to Bayden and back again. It probably wouldn't help to point out that Bayden really did see Hale as less dominant than him.

"Problem?" Hale asked.

Axel watched Bayden help the fifth man he'd beat in a row onto his feet.

Tolmore turned to Axel. "Remind him he's not allowed to turn into a damn wolf this time."

"He won't shift during the fight," Axel promised.

Tolmore sighed and approached Bayden. He didn't look at all enthusiastic about the fight.

"Do you have a problem with me fighting your sub?" Hale asked as Tolmore and Bayden circled each other.

"He might not be willing to fight you," Axel said.

"Why?"

"He learnt a long time ago not to hit cops back." Axel studied Bayden. He had the grace of a dancer as he dodged a clumsy attack from Tolmore, but it was hard not to picture how he'd have looked taking that beating off Ford or how he'd have acted when faced with Granger.

"If he's going to ride with us, he'll have to learn to see all of us as Dragons, first and foremost."

Axel nodded. Hale was right. And he wasn't the kind of man who'd hit a man who didn't fight back. Unease still prickled up and down Axel's spine.

Tolmore didn't last long. He'd done his best. They all had. None of them had *let* Bayden win. They weren't giving him the money, merely the chance to win it. Just like they wouldn't give him a place in the club, only the chance to earn it.

"Time for a break," Axel called out. "Everyone take five."

Bayden retreated to his corner. He fell still as Axel joined him and checked his injuries. There was a bruise on his temple and a scuff on his jaw, but most of the blows Bayden had allowed to land were body blows and almost all of them were glancing impacts.

"Sir?"

"You're doing well," Axel said.

Bayden looked up at him warily, as if he couldn't quite believe the praise was justified.

He stood very still, but the energy and adrenaline pumping through him was unmistakable. The only reason he wasn't bouncing on the spot was his desire to show respect.

"There's only one more guy who thinks he's a match for you."

Bayden nodded. His eyes sparkling with pleasure at being able to earn the whole seven hundred in one shot.

"Hale."

Bayden flinched as if he'd been slapped. His face went expressionless.

"It's your choice, pup."

Bayden looked down. "I don't want trouble."

"There won't be any trouble."

Bayden nodded. He looked over to Griz and Hale. Axel traced his line of sight. Hale was handing his money to Griz. The last hundred Bayden wanted to earn.

Bayden nodded. "Okay."

"You remember the rules, pup?" Axel checked.

He nodded again.

This time, when Bayden headed for the middle of the yard, the atmosphere was different. Everyone knew it wasn't a friendly fight. They weren't men who'd ever said a kind word to each other.

"What are the odds?" Griz murmured to Axel.

"Bayden might go easy on him. He still doesn't want to get in trouble for beating up a cop."

"Or?"

"Or Hale will say the wrong thing, and Bayden will wipe the floor with him. He won't kill him, but he could easily make Hale wish he was dead."

Hale feinted, stepped in close, then swung a left hook. It caught Bayden in solar plexus. A human would have doubled over, Bayden didn't even flinch. The world went from slow motion to fast forward. It was hard to see individual moves. Both men knew what they were doing, and they both knew they were fighting someone else with real skills.

Bayden twisted, swiped with his legs and used Hale's own body weight to topple him. Hale hit the ground hard, but rolled away without missing a beat.

Bayden crouched down a yard away, ready to pounce.

Hale got up onto one knee, but he didn't launch himself immediately to his feet the way Axel expected him to. He swiped at his split lip.

"Every wolf I've ever met is a criminal." The words carried clearly across the yard.

Bayden tensed. So did Axel. Hale had always been good at pissing people off. If there was anyone who could make Bayden lose his temper, it was him. Now was not the time for this kind of bullshit.

"Most of the humans I meet are criminals too," Hale added. "Part of the job,"

Bayden was still couched down, muscles tensed, ready to pounce.

"I've arrested plenty of wolves, but never for anything I wouldn't have arrested a human for."

Bayden didn't even seem to breathe.

"Honest cops don't have anything to do with honest wolves. Of course, that means the only cops honest wolves meet are bent."

Bayden still didn't speak.

"Granger's not going to bother you any more."

That broke the spell. Bayden only shifted his weight an inch, but it was enough to let Axel breathe.

"We couldn't get him for what he did to wolves, but we did get him. He's been charged. He's going to be convicted. He'll do time—I'll make sure of that."

Bayden's ribs shook as he took a deep breath.

"There's one thing I learned about wolves on the job that is true," Hale said. "Wolves are good fighters. Better than any human is."

Truce.

Hale was admitting that he couldn't win. The wording was impersonal, an acknowledgement of species differences without any reference to the dominance of particular individuals. For a man like Hale, it was still an olive branch the size of the ark.

Bayden pulled himself to his full height so he loomed over Hale. He stepped closer and held out his hand.

The moment Hale was upright, Bayden snatched his hand away. He retreated out of Hale's space in silence and headed straight to Axel.

Axel slid an arm around him and pulled him in close. Bayden was so tense, he couldn't even lean into the embrace, but Axel kept him there, letting him feel their bodies pressed against each other while he pulled himself together.

The other guys headed inside. Another ten minutes passed before Bayden finally leaned forward and rested his head on Axel's shoulder.

"You did good," Axel whispered to him.

"I didn't kill him."

Axel smiled. "Yes, that was definitely a good thing."

"I wasn't sure if I could. Once I hit him, I didn't know if I'd be able to stop, sir."

"I didn't doubt it for a second," Axel said.

Bayden glanced up at him. "You'd have stopped me if I couldn't have stopped myself."

"Yes." One word from him would have cut through Bayden's rage. Axel had known it. The fact that Bayden had realised it and trusted him to do it almost made it worth having to watch the fights. He pressed a kiss against Bayden's temple. "So good."

* * * * *

"You said you'd take the money," Bayden reminded Axel.

Bayden had undressed the moment they stepped into the flat that night. Now he was naked, the money was itching against his palm in his need to hand it over.

Axel held out his hand.

Bayden gave him the notes. "It's eight hundred. The money you lent me to start the bet is there too."

Axel put the notes in his pocket without checking them. Bayden hadn't been sure that humans were physically capable of doing that.

The notes hadn't weighed much, but Bayden felt like seven-hundred pounds in weight had been lifted off his shoulders. He smiled with relief, but all he could do then was wait.

A collar. A collared submissive. An alpha's mate by any other name. It was all Bayden could do not to tremble with expectation.

They'd taken one thing at a time, just like Axel wanted, and now, the time for this had come.

Axel ran his fingers over Bayden's neck.

A shiver caressed Bayden's spine. He smiled up at Axel.

"Not tonight, pup."

Bayden jerked back in surprise.

Axel didn't follow him. "When the marks from the fight have gone."

"But you said they don't matter!"

"They don't mean anyone else has a claim to you, but I still want them healed before I collar you."

Bayden looked down. Folding his arms, he tucked his bruised knuckles out of sight. There was no way to hide the rest of the scrapes and bruises. The breath caught in Bayden's throat. He looked to his clothes. He shouldn't have taken them off without an order. Stupid!

Axel was an alpha, and an alpha was always right, but Bayden couldn't stand there another second. He couldn't wait around to hear Axel dismiss him. Bayden turned his back on Axel and headed for the spare bedroom.

Axel caught up with him within a few paces. Bayden stopped as soon as Axel grabbed his arm, but he couldn't turn to face him.

"You're not in trouble."

Bayden kept his back to Axel, kept his arms folded and his knuckles tucked out of sight.

"I'm not saying I don't want you in my bed." He slid his arms around Bayden from behind.

"You want to leave your marks too?" Bayden asked, cautiously.

"No. No more marks tonight."

It took all of Bayden's self-control to stay where he was.

Axel slid his hand up to Bayden's throat and drew a line on it. He could have been thinking about a collar. He could just as easily be thinking about the bruises that guy had put around his neck when he'd choked him.

"Yes," Bayden whispered.

"Is that what you want?" Axel asked, without needing any further explanation.

Bayden nodded rapidly.

"Go into the bedroom. I want you on the bed, slicked up and ready for me by the time I join you."

The moment Axel released him, Bayden rushed to obey his orders. His fingers were clumsy with need, but he completed the orders as fast as he could. Then, he waited, trembling with hope.

Another minute passed before Axel strode into the room. He'd left his clothes outside. He was in one of those moods where words weren't important to him.

Bayden swallowed rapidly. There was no need for a knife this time—he didn't have any clothes to get in the way.

Axel caught hold of Bayden's shoulders and spun him around before pulling him back tight against his body. Balanced on the edge of the bed, Bayden had no choice but to rely on Axel to support him.

Axel put his right hand over Bayden's mouth, forcing his head roughly back and pinning it against Axel's shoulder.

Reaching down between them, Axel guided his cock to Bayden's hole and pushed into him, hard and rough. Bayden whimpered his pleasure against Axel's palm.

"Grab my right wrist."

Bayden obeyed, wrapping his fingers around the skin just below where Axel's tattoos started.

"That's your safe word. Let go of my wrist and I'll stop."

Bayden tried to nod, but Axel's hand against his mouth was unyielding.

"There won't be any marks tonight," Axel whispered in his ear. "But I don't have to get rough like that to show you how every breath you take will belong to me once you're wearing my collar."

Bayden murmured his approval, but little sound made it past Axel's hand. Axel wrapped his other arm around Bayden's torso, holding him in place as he altered his grip over his mouth so he pinched Bayden's nose.

"Every breath." Axel's words were more a growl than a whisper. He rocked his hips, pushing deeper into Bayden's arse.

Pleasure rolled through Bayden, but as the seconds passed and Axel's hand remained over his face, sealing his mouth and nose, Bayden's lungs began to burn.

Another thrust, more pleasure, but no air.

He'd felt that way before. But that had been different, hadn't it?

Axel lifted his hand, letting Bayden gasp.

"Good boy. I've got you." Axel put his hand back in place.

It hadn't been long enough for Bayden to properly catch his breath.

Axel pushed into him again. Each thrust hit his prostate and made Bayden want to whimper with bliss, but there was no sound and no oxygen.

"You're mine, pup."

Axel found a rhythm he liked and rode Bayden hard. Even if he'd been able to breathe normally, Bayden knew he'd have been out of breath within minutes. The occasional permission to force fresh air into his lungs wasn't enough. He tightened his grip on Axel's wrist, anchoring himself to his alpha as his mind spun and his body writhed.

Pleasure. Possession. Axel's control over him wasn't just about the way he had his cock buried in his arse. Axel had wormed his way into Bayden's brain months ago. He'd been lodged in his heart for what felt like a lifetime. Now his lungs belonged to his alpha, belonged to his master.

Bayden twisted against Axel and tugged at Axel's grip on him as his orgasm tore through him. Bayden's cum spilled across the bed sheet. The world turned grey and flickered into and out of existence. Bayden's only solid point of reference was Axel's wrist. He held onto it as if his life depended on it. In that moment, he had no doubt that his life really would end if his grip failed him.

Blackness closed in, but it wasn't frightening. He still had hold of Axel's wrist.

Bayden jerked as bright light suddenly exploded back into his world. Everything had moved around him. He tried to flail around in an effort to get his bearings, but someone was holding him tightly, refusing him any space or freedom.

"It's alright, pup. You're okay. I've got you."

As soon as he heard Axel's voice, Bayden's panic evaporated. He stopped trying to get free. His nose and mouth were uncovered now. He panted for breath, desperately forcing more and more air into his lungs.

Bayden blinked at his surroundings. They were both lying on the bed. The mattress was soft beneath him. Axel's body was hard against his back.

Their bodies weren't joined together any more, but there wasn't an inch between them. Any desire for space or freedom gone, Bayden pressed back against Axel, trying to get even closer to him.

Axel held him a little tighter in return. "That's right. Good boy."

Bayden remembered coming, but that was all he remembered. "I..."

"You passed out for a few seconds when you came, that's all."

"Did you come?"

Axel chuckled. "Yes, pup. You don't need to worry about that."

Bayden nodded. All was well. He looked down and realised that he still held Axel's wrist. His knuckles were white, so was the skin beneath his fingers. He snatched his hand away. "I—"

"You did exactly as you were told," Axel finished for him.

Bayden ran his fingers over Axel's wrist. He'd left a red mark there. It would be a bruise by the morning. He tugged Axel's hand up to his mouth and kissed the skin, as if that could help.

Axel pressed a kiss to the back of his head. "It's fine, pup. And if it leaves a mark, that's fine too."

"Humans heal really slowly."

Axel chuckled and guided Bayden to roll over and curl into his side. "It's only the marks from the fights that need to disappear before the collaring, not ones we put on each other."

Bayden looked down at his knuckles.

"It won't take long, a day or two at the most."

That still felt like forever, but Bayden nodded his acceptance of Axel's decision.

"You can use the time to think about what your new limits are going to be."

Bayden shook his head. "Mates don't have limits."

"Submissives do, including collared submissives."

Bayden tried to shake his head again, but Axel stopped him short. "Do as you're told, pup. Think about it for me."

It was impossible to disobey an order put like that. Bayden nodded and pressed another kiss against Axel's wrist.

Chapter Thirty Seven

"You're perfect."

Bayden turned away from the mirror on the wardrobe door. The hour he'd just spent in his wolf form had finished the process. The marks from the fight were all gone. If that was the only thing Axel was waiting for, there was no reason to put off the collaring for another second. Bayden held his breath and hoped.

Axel beckoned Bayden out of the bedroom to sit next to him on the sofa. "Have you been thinking about your limits?"

"Mates don't have limits," Bayden reminded him, very politely.

"Limits are the sub's version of rules. If you can't have limits, does that mean I can't have rules?"

Bayden shook his head rapidly. "Wolves don't have limits," he corrected. That was a much better statement. "Humans can have rules."

Axel stroked his cheek.

"I like it when you set rules," Bayden offered.

"I like it when you set limits," Axel shot back at him.

Bayden frowned. Things that Axel liked were important, but... "A list of things you're not allowed to do with me would be..." He shook his head.

"There's nothing you can think of that you wouldn't ever want me to do?" Axel asked.

Bayden shook his head. "Whatever you want."

Axel stroked his fingers through Bayden's hair. He thought for a long time. Bayden sat in silence, unable to come up with a single helpful thing to utter.

"What's the worst thing I could do to you?" Axel asked.

Bayden glanced at him from the corner of his eye.

"I'm not asking you to set a limit, I'm ordering you to answer my question."

Bayden looked down. "Tell me to leave, sir, that you don't want me to be part of your pack or your mate anymore."

Axel slid his arm around him and tugged him closer. "That's not going to happen. I mean while we're together—what's the worst thing."

Bayden stared down at his hands, where he'd wrapped his fingers into a complicated knot. The answer was obvious but it was several minutes before he could force it past his lips. "My bike, sir."

"Take your bike away and leave you riding pillion behind me?" Axel asked.

Bayden nodded. The air had lodged in his throat. Speaking was out of the question. All he could do was repeat over and over again that Axel wasn't like other humans. Axel wouldn't use that information to hurt him.

"I'll give you a choice," Axel announced. "You can set that as a limit." Bayden shook his head, but Axel ignored that and carried on. "Or, you can set it as part of the punishment you'll receive if you ever break my most important rule for you."

Bayden looked up at him.

"If you break that rule, you'd lose your bike, but that would be the only reason you could ever lose it. I'd never take it away from you for any other reason, or because you broke any other rule. Your bike would be completely safe as long as you obeyed that rule."

"What's the most important rule, sir?"

"You're not allowed to let yourself get hurt if you have a choice."

Bayden met his gaze.

"You don't take bets that involve letting someone hurt you—whether it's a whipping, a beating or anything else. If you take a bet on a fight, you fight back. If someone tries to start a fight with you outside a bet, you either walk away or you finish the fight without letting them hurt you. You don't just let anyone hurt you."

Bayden stared into Axel's eyes. He'd seldom seen him look so serious about anything. Memories flashed through Bayden's mind. "I..." He closed his eyes. "I don't want trouble."

"Tell me what the end of the rule is," Axel ordered.

Bayden thought back. "When I have a choice, sir."

Axel nodded. "I know there have been lots of times in the past when you didn't have a choice."

Bayden shook his head. "Free wolves always have a choice. It's—"

"Not what a human would call a choice," Axel cut in. "With a cop like Granger, there was nothing you could do to stop him abusing his position."

Bayden shifted uncomfortably in his seat, his heart beating faster and faster.

"With Ford and Richards, you had a different sort of choice. You could have chosen not to let them hurt you. There wouldn't have been trouble if you did that, would there?"

Bayden took a deep breath. Memories rolled through his mind, all the different choices he'd made over the years. He studied where Axel's hand rested against him, holding him close for no other reason than because Axel liked doing that, except maybe because Axel knew Bayden liked him doing that.

"You're not allowed to let yourself get hurt if there's a choice which allows you to avoid both getting hurt and getting in trouble," Axel said. His voice was expressionless. His lips curved into a smile. His scent was sad.

"I can do that. I won't break the rule, sir."

"And you'll know that your bike is safe."

Bayden nodded. Axel's sadness didn't disappear. Bayden's willingness to follow the rephrased rule hadn't really fixed anything. Pulling his feet up onto the sofa in front of him, he wrapped his arms loosely around his knees.

"What do you feel most guilty about—your old pack still being important to you, or me being more important to you?"

Bayden closed his eyes. "Both, sir." Thinking his bike was important just because it had been important to his last alpha was wrong. Ignoring what his father had wanted just because he was with Axel now was wrong too. Everything he did was wrong.

Axel stroked his hand up and down Bayden's arm. "When I came out, a lot of things changed. I lost a lot of things that were important to me."

Bayden opened his eyes. Axel rarely spoke about that time in his life, but when he did pain still touched every syllable, no matter how hard he tried to hide it. Bayden stroked his arm, instinctively copying the method Axel used when trying to make him feel better.

"Most of my family and friends stepped back. My community, my church, it all disappeared from under my feet. When I realised there was no way to fix what I'd had with them, I built a new family, and new community. There's not one man who rides with me who I wouldn't take a bullet for. Losing them would kill something inside me." Axel tucked a knuckle under Bayden's chin, keeping him looking him in the eye. "If it was a choice between you and them, it would be the easiest decision I ever made. It would be you. Every time. No hesitation."

Bayden swallowed.

"That's not about betraying your pack, pup. It's about putting your mate first. It's the difference between people you love and the person you're in love with. It's nothing to feel guilty about, nothing to be ashamed of."

"I do love you, sir, so much," Bayden whispered.

"I love you too, pup."

When he smiled, he made it impossible for Bayden not to smile back. Axel's sadness gradually faded away. Everything was fine. Relief rushed through him, making him almost as dizzy as he'd felt when Axel stole the oxygen from him the previous night. Bayden dipped his head and rested it on Axel's shoulder. From there, it was impossible not to move on to nuzzling against his neck.

"Not so fast, pup."

Bayden looked up.

"One more. I want one more thing from you. If you don't want to call it a limit, you can call it something that would work as a punishment."

Bayden rested his head on Axel's shoulder.

"It can be big or little. Something we've done that you don't like, or…" Axel coaxed Bayden into looking up. "There is something we've done that you don't like." His ability to read people like a wolf was getting better all the time. He spoke with complete confidence.

Bayden swallowed. "It's not important, sir."

"I've decided it's important," Axel corrected. "That means it is."

"It's not a limit, sir."

"But it is something that would make an effective punishment?"

Bayden said nothing.

"If you knew doing a particular thing would lead to it, you'd avoid doing that thing?" Axel pushed.

Bayden nodded.

Axel looked more serious than ever. "Tell me."

Bayden stared at Axel's shoulder.

"You can take whatever time you need, pup, but you are going to tell me."

"It's not…" Bayden sighed. "You only do it when I screw up anyway, sir, so…"

Axel stroked his hair and whispered in his ear. "Tell me. You won't be in trouble."

Bayden squirmed. Axel ignored that.

"I don't like it when you change your mind, but you wouldn't change it unless I did something you don't like, so it's—"

Axel stroked his thumb back and forth over Bayden's lips to silence him. "Slow down." He frowned as if he didn't understand. "You don't like it when I change my mind about what?"

"Screwing me," Bayden whispered.

A few seconds passed and Axel's frown cleared. "You don't like being prepared but not topped?"

"It's my fault for—"

"I've never changed my mind about screwing you," Axel cut in.

Bayden glanced up at him.

"Every time I stopped it was because I never intended to top you to begin with. It wasn't about getting you ready, it was about teasing and making you frustrated."

Bayden frowned.

"But I think it did more than that. It made you feel rejected."

Bayden shrugged.

Axel pressed a kiss to his temple. "You're good for telling me." He tipped Bayden's head back to press another kiss against his lips. "Do you think you can keep telling me things like that?"

Bayden hesitated.

"If you can give me information on what would work as a punishment, I'll stop nagging you about setting limits," Axel whispered in his ear.

"Yes, sir."

Axel smiled at his enthusiasm and tugged him closer.

Bayden nuzzled his neck and pressed a kiss against the tip of a tattoo.

"Wait, pup. There's something important we have to do first," Axel corrected.

Bayden pulled back, all tense again.

Axel couldn't hold himself in check for another second. He reached into his pocket and pulled out a length of silver chain.

Bayden relaxed the moment he saw it. He slipped out of Axel's embrace to kneel on the floor at his feet. His hand rested on Axel's leg, and he soon had a tight grip on his jeans.

Axel turned the tag so Bayden could see the inscription. *Bayden Wolf*. And, on the other side, *Axel Carmichael's Mate*.

For several seconds, Bayden just stared at it. He didn't reach out to touch, but his longing was palpable. The lupine wording had obviously been a good choice. Bayden looked up at him. "Please, sir?"

"I'll be the only one with a key." Axel showed him the padlock that would link the ends of the chain together. "If you ever want to take it off, you'll have to ask me to remove it for you. I might not say yes."

Bayden shook his head. "I'd never ask, sir." He squirmed on his knees. "Please?"

Axel smiled at his earnest expression. He undid the padlock, looped the chain around Bayden's neck and locked it in place. The actual collaring only took seconds.

That was it. Bayden was his. Axel stared down at him, taking in every detail.

Bayden naked was always hot as hell. Bayden naked and collared was a whole new layer of perfection.

For a full minute, Bayden knelt still and silent. Finally, he spoke. "Can I?" He waved his hand toward the bedroom. "Just for a minute."

Caught off guard by the request, Axel found himself nodding permission that he'd had no intention of granting.

Bayden was back just as quickly as he'd promised. "I know you said the more dominant mate doesn't get anything, but..." He handed Axel a small paper bag.

Something rattled within the wrapping.

Axel peeked inside. At the bottom of the bag was another length of silver coloured chain, and a loop of leather. Axel took it out of the packaging. A lead. The quality of the workmanship implied that it had been bought in a leather shop rather than a pet shop, but it was still undeniably a dog's lead.

"It's what you talk about with the other Dragons, sir," Bayden whispered. "Not just about putting a collar on me. A collar and lead."

Axel looked up.

"You don't say it when you talk to me, because you're worried that I'll think it means you want to treat me like a dog."

"And what do you think?"

"I think it's something you want, sir. And I think you'd want the same if I was human."

"Yes, I would."

Bayden nodded. It was obviously an idea that he was still uncomfortable with, but the determination in his eyes was stunning. Axel was Bayden's mate now, and Bayden's mate was going to have exactly what he wanted.

"This is why you wanted permission to go out," Axel realised. "That's where you went with Evan — to buy this for me."

Bayden nodded.

"Thank you."

Bayden hesitated for a few moments before he spoke again. "There used to be a tradition. When a wolf joined a new pack, he took the new pack's name. We can't do that anymore."

"If the campaign to overturn the anti-pack laws succeeds, you'll have a few extra options."

Bayden nodded, but the idea didn't seem to make him feel better about anything.

Axel stroked Bayden's hair back from his face as he realised why. "I'm sorry the names were lost, pup."

Bayden "They weren't lost, sir. They were outlawed, to stop wolves from thinking of themselves as part of a pack."

"Yes, I know."

Bayden closed his eyes. He took a deep breath. "Brynmawr or Penllwyd." They were mere inches away from each other, but the words were still barely on the edge of hearing.

"Pup?"

"Just because we can't tell most humans something, doesn't mean we forget, sir. My mother would have been born into the Brynmawr pack. My father would have been a Penllwyd, unless he started a new pack from scratch — alphas do that sometimes." Each time he said one of the pack names, his voice dipped to a murmur.

Axel pressed a kiss against the top of his head. He could imagine the words being whispered that softly from one generation of wolves to the next all the way down through the years. Axel tugged Bayden up onto the sofa with him.

I'll put your full name on your collar. He bit the words back just in time. That wasn't the kind of promise Bayden would want from him. "I won't tell anyone."

Bayden nodded and curled in closer to him. It was obvious how much sharing the information had cost him. Axel looked heavenward, but there was no getting away from it under the circumstances.

"Gabriel."

Bayden tilted his head to the side.

"Gabriel Axel Carmichael. Gabriel was one of the Archangels in the Bible. When I was seventeen, me and my father had a huge row about me being out. He said he and my mother should never have called me that. I was a disgrace to the name of one of God's chosen messengers. I told him where he could shove the damn name and..." He shrugged. "I've stuck to my middle name ever since, and made the change legal a few years ago. Axel sounds a damn sight more sensible for a biker anyway."

Bayden stroked his cheek. "I like Axel, sir. It's a good name. Strong."

Axel pressed a kiss to Bayden's forehead, but there was something very wrong about his sub being the one who comforted him. Axel looked down at the collar—his sub. "You know everyone's going to notice your collar the moment they step into the pub tonight."

Bayden met Axel's gaze and held it. "Good."

Chapter Thirty Eight

It was disconcerting, being in a room full of humans who were all staring at his neck. Bayden ignored them as best he could and concentrated on his job. It was one of the Saturday nights when the back rooms would open to everyone at ten o'clock. A lot of guys had got there early and were now milling about, assessing which dom might want to play with which sub later on.

Bayden pushed the sleeves on his hoodie up past his elbows and started collecting the empties from the various tables in the main bar room. He'd assumed that everyone would have lost interest in his neck after an hour or so, but no. Apparently, people were going to stare at his jugular all night. The fact that plenty of humans had turned up to play wearing collars wasn't denting anyone's fascination with seeing a werewolf in a collar at all.

Weaving his way between leather clad figures, Bayden soon found himself at the table where Axel and most of the Dragons had congregated to sort out who would be in charge of which bits of the pub once the games started.

Bayden already knew his job. He spotted a couple of empty bottles in front of various Dragons and picked them up.

He turned around and almost collided with Evan coming in the other way carrying a tray of full bottles.

"Congratulations on the collar." He dipped his voice then. "Did he like what you bought him?"

Bayden nodded. Axel hadn't said much, but he'd put the lead into his pocket before they come down to open the pub. He wouldn't have done that if he hadn't been pleased with it.

Griz stood up. He took the tray of drinks off Evan and set them on the table before turning to Bayden. "It looks good on you."

Bayden dipped his head once in acknowledgement of that fact.

"Can I check the tag?"

Bayden glanced across to Axel and received a nod.

Griz caught the gesture too. His fingers were thick and looked clumsy, but he took hold of the tag gently. He didn't tug at it when he turned it over so he could read each side. He smiled and nodded his approval. "It's looser than most collars." There was no criticism in his tone.

"So I can shift," Bayden explained. He stepped away from Griz, instinctively putting himself closer to Axel.

"Did Axel get you that hoodie too?" Hale asked, from his seat on the other side of the table. He was leaning back on the rear legs of his chair, his expression unreadable.

Bayden frowned. "Yes." He'd bought the jeans Bayden was wearing that night too. Axel liked getting him things to wear — liked to see him wearing things that he'd bought him. It wasn't about money, it was about marking his territory.

"The collar's just right, but I think we can improve on the hoodie," Hale said.

Bayden opened his mouth to tell Hale what he could do with his opinions, but Axel put his hand on the small of Bayden's back and shook his head.

Bayden hesitated, wondering if he'd understood the rules about standing up for himself as thoroughly as he'd thought he had.

Axel looked up at him from his seat. "Not because he's a cop, because he's trying to be nice. It doesn't come naturally to him, so you have to be patient."

Bayden turned back to Hale. But Hale's attention was all on the carrier bag Drac was handing him.

"Lose the hoodie."

Bayden checked with Axel. Another nod. Bayden set the empties on the table and shrugged off the hoodie. Axel took it from him as Hale came around the table.

Hale reached into the bag and took out a leather jacket. It had The Black Dragons' insignia on the back. The club's name curved over the top of the dragon logo. Underneath were two name patches. On the left, Bayden. On the right, Axel's Pup. Bayden's palms turned slick with nerves.

Hale held the jacket out. Bayden just stared at him, frozen in place, not quite able to believe it was happening.

"Go on, pup." Axel nudged him forward. Everyone was watching. Bayden's heart raced faster than it ever had when they were watching him fight.

For the first time in his life, Bayden willingly dropped his guard and turned his back on a cop. He slipped his arms into the jacket, and Hale lifted it into place. It settled comfortably around his shoulders, fitting perfectly along every seam, as if it had been made for him.

Axel stood up. As Bayden looked up at him, Axel dipped his head and whispered in his ear. "Welcome to the pack, pup."

Bayden closed his eyes, relishing the relief that flooded through him. When he opened his eyes, he looked down at the hoodie Axel still held. "You bought me that, sir."

"I bought the jacket months ago. The other guys are just playing delivery boys."

Bayden stroked his fingers over the surprisingly soft leather.

"They took a vote last night. It's official," Axel murmured to him. "Once a Dragon, always a Dragon, no matter what."

Bayden nodded. His other hand went to his collar.

"That is forever too," Axel reminded him.

"Yes, sir."

The jacket was addictive. Even when Bayden went back to work, he found himself running his fingers over it every time he had a few seconds to spare. When his shift ended and another bartender arrived to replace him, Bayden stepped out from behind the bar, but he didn't leave the jacket hanging on a hook back there, the way Axel usually did. He kept it on despite the heat.

Axel wasn't immediately within sight.

"Congratulations again."

Bayden turned to find Evan standing behind him. Not sure what to say, Bayden just nodded.

Even shuffled his feet. "Griz said I can start tagging along on your next ride. He asked Axel, and he said it's fine."

"You'll like it," Bayden said. "It's—"

"You're the wolf, aren't you?"

A guy stepped way into Bayden's personal space. He grabbed hold of Bayden's wrist. He was drunk—not the happy kind of drunk a lot of the men who'd finished playing would become as the night went on—the kind of drunk that meant he no longer had any sense of self preservation.

"Back off." Polite. Calm. Even if he was on his break, Bayden was still at work and—

The guy yelped. He dropped to his knees and snatched his hand away from Bayden's wrist. Bayden blinked at him. Then he noticed that the guy's other wrist was twisted painfully up behind him. He wasn't on his knees through choice, but because that was the only way to prevent his shoulder being dislocated.

Bayden looked up at Axel, but Axel's attention remained fixed on the guy whose wrist he held.

A ring of men formed around them as people both backed off and crowded in to get a better view.

"It takes a special kind of stupid to push your luck with a collared submissive," Axel bit out.

The guy muttered something.

"You want to drink in a pub like this, learn the difference between a necklace and a collar—fast."

He shoved the guy aside. The man fell, but was soon up again and scrambling into the safety of the crowd.

Axel turned and raised an eyebrow at Bayden. "What?"

"I could have dealt with him, sir — without killing him, or getting hurt."

"I know."

Bayden frowned, not sure what he was missing.

Axel stepped closer. "I watched the fights, pup. I watched the bets that made a complete mockery of a scene. I stood there and watched men screw you and order you around. And I didn't do anything about it, because I didn't have the right. You hadn't given me the right. But this," Axel caught hold of the lock on Bayden's collar. "This gives me the right. I never have to stand back and let another man lay a hand on you ever again."

Bayden swallowed.

"I know you can take care of yourself. I know you can drop any man in here, me included. But I have the right to step in now." And it was obvious just how much he loved that right. "Any questions?"

Bayden shook his head.

Axel smiled down at him, but something over Bayden's shoulder soon caught his attention. His smile disappeared. "Speaking of unsettled scores…"

Bayden turned around. Richards stood just inside the door. He was flanked by his friends.

Axel stepped forward, but when Bayden put his hand on Axel's arm, Axel stopped and waited to see what he had to say.

Bayden cleared his throat. "What are you going to do, sir?"

"Don't worry, pup. I won't hurt him. I'm just going to get rid of him."

Bayden looked from Axel to Richards and back again. He tightened his grip on Axel's arm. "Let him stay, sir."

"What?"

Bayden looked down, fighting against instincts that would always tell him to let his alpha do whatever he wanted. "You said before, that a collared submissive was allowed to ask his...his master for things. That I should always say if there was something important that I..."

Axel turned back to him as he faltered. "Richards staying is important to you?"

Bayden nodded. He let go of Axel's arm and moved his hand to rest it against Axel's chest as Axel encouraged him closer.

"Why?"

"Because something you said about him before was wrong, sir."

Axel made him meet his gaze.

"You said he wouldn't know real submission if he saw it, but I think he would. I think if he saw the real thing, he'd know that what he gets off men is nothing like that." Bayden took a shaky breath, not quite able to believe he'd been brave enough to say all that out loud.

"You want him to see you submit to me?" Axel asked.

Bayden swallowed. "I want everyone to see."

"You know the rules. I don't perform for an audience, you won't be allowed to either."

"Five seconds or five hours," Bayden quoted. "Whatever you want, sir. Once the scene starts, I won't be thinking about anyone other than you—no matter how many people are watching us."

Axel stroked his fingers through Bayden's hair. He seemed to think about it for a long time.

"I'm not ashamed of submitting to you, sir. There's no shame in following a more dominant wolf's lead, or in pleasing my mate." He was helpless to stop his hand tightening into a fist around Axel's T-shirt. "I won't embarrass you in front of them, sir. I swear, I'll—"

"That's never been an issue."

Bayden nodded. And that was it; there was nothing left for him to say. He'd made his request. It was all up to Axel now.

* * * * *

Axel stared down at Bayden. It was what Axel had wanted from the start — for his pup to trust him enough to tell him what was important to him.

"Be sure, pup. If I feel your attention wander, I'll bring it back to me, and I won't care who sees me do it."

Bayden nodded.

"You know what I expect you to do."

Bayden's grip on his T-shirt didn't lessen in the slightest. "I won't hide anything from you, sir. I won't lie to you." His fingers twitched. "I'll say my safe word if I need to."

And that was the one thing he'd never been able to bring himself to offer him before.

Success rushed through Axel, raw and primitive. He caught hold of Bayden's wrist and dragged Bayden's hand away from his T-shirt. He headed toward the bar, pulling Bayden through the crowd in his wake, but he bit back the instinct to lead Bayden straight to that room. He stopped at the Dragons' table. "Change of plans. One of you needs to take my shifts keeping an eye on the back rooms. Sort it out between yourselves."

He saw Griz and Hale look past him to Bayden and knew that they both realised he intended to be distracted for the rest of the evening while he and Bayden celebrated.

"Fair enough."

"And I'm opening room one early," Axel added.

"Okay."

"And Richards is here. Don't throw him out."

All necessary items ticked off his list, Axel headed for back room one. Bayden had little choice but to remain less than half a step behind him — it was that or lose his wrist, but the rest of the guys who followed did so because they'd been waiting to see him do a scene with Bayden for months and had more sense than to miss this opportunity.

Axel unlocked the room and led Bayden straight to the Saint Andrew's Cross where Bayden had done his original bet with Richards. "You know what happens next?"

"Whatever you want, sir." There was a calm note in his voice — one that only ever existed in a scene.

Axel heard men moving around behind them, crowding into the room and vying for a good view-point, but Bayden didn't even glance in their direction.

"Forty with a whip."

"Yes, sir."

"No bet. No forfeit. Nothing to prove." He stroked his cheek. "You can't do battle with someone on the same side as you, can you, pup?"

Bayden smiled. He glanced up at Axel, shy in the way Axel had only ever seen him look when they were alone or unobserved. "On bare skin, sir?"

"A bare back. Keep the jeans on."

Bayden removed his jacket. Axel took it off him, and his vest. He glanced at the front row of the crowd. The Dragons were all there. So was Evan. Axel pulled off his own T-shirt and left all the clothes with Evan and Griz.

The cupboard in the corner where the Dragons kept their personal toys yielded a cat of nine tails. Axel checked each strand. Dozens of men watched him. The only gaze he was truly aware of was Bayden's.

Satisfied the implement was in perfect condition, Axel turned to Bayden. A nod to the cross was all it took.

Bayden arranged himself against the dark lengths of wood, reaching up to grip the loops where bondage could have been attached if Axel had been inclined to use it. He stepped up behind Bayden and placed his hand on the small of his back.

"Forty."

"Do you want me to count them, sir?"

"No, that's still my job."

"Yes, sir." Bayden smiled at the memory. So did Axel. In some ways, Bayden really had trusted him right from the start. Now, it was time to take that trust up a notch.

Axel pressed a kiss to Bayden's temple and stepped back. He ran the tails of the cat through his fingers several times, making Bayden wait. Tension built up in Bayden's muscles. His shoulders rose and fell as he took a deep breath and let it out slowly. His tension began to ease as he found a quiet place inside his head.

He would love to be whipped hard. Axel had no doubt that Bayden would love both the sensation and the show it would put on for the other guys. Maybe if he'd asked to display his skills in masochism or sheer bloody mindedness, he'd have got what he wanted.

Axel brought the cat down against Bayden's back, hard enough to sting, but nowhere near hard enough to hurt. Any man in the pub could have withstood that kind of blow.

Bayden dipped his head forward. Submission — accepting that he wouldn't necessarily get something that would impress anyone but his master.

Another lash, not much harder than the first.

Axel heard some muttering in the crowd, from the men who didn't have a clue.

Forty. Axel had plenty of strokes to play with. By the end of the first ten, the mumbling was starting to take on a different tone. Axel brought the cat down harder, but that wasn't what had caught people's attention.

Bayden was doing exactly what Axel had trained him to do, what Axel had insisted he do from the very first time he spanked him. Bayden was looking for more. He leaned back as far as his grip on the bondage would allow, offering his skin to the cat, welcoming each blow. Axel's cock stiffened beneath his jeans.

A pleased little whimper hit the air in the wake of a harsher blow. Bayden was starting to enjoy his whipping. Axel let him feel a little more, let the marks build up and flourish in the cat's wake. Lines spread across Bayden's back. It wasn't like the cane, Axel couldn't spread the lines out in neat little rows, but they had a beauty all of their own. Bayden's response to them made every mark stunning enough to make Axel's heart race.

Bayden arched. Axel forgot how to breathe, but he didn't forget to keep count.

Twenty.

Axel stepped forward. Bayden's breaths were ragged. He looked over his shoulder. His eyes were unfocused.

"Sir?"

Axel ran his fingertips up Bayden's spine from the waistband of his jeans, all the way up to his hairline. Bayden moaned, arching into the contact like a kitten. Axel smiled down at him. As Bayden pulled away from the cross, Axel saw how hard he was.

He stroked down Bayden's back and onto the seat of his jeans. Bayden rocked his hips, damn near wiggling his arse in invitation.

"Later," Axel said, taking his hand away.

Bayden blinked at him.

Axel moved the cat from one hand to the other, and Bayden murmured his approval. He tugged at the restraints he held and nodded enthusiastically. "Please?"

The word wasn't said for an audience, but it was still loud enough for the closest men to hear.

Axel stepped back. No need for a warm up this time. Bayden was ready to enjoy the real thing.

Axel brought the cat down hard against Bayden's back. Bayden tossed his head. His grip on his bondage turned white knuckled. No time to recover. Axel kept going.

Bayden twisted and bucked, overloaded with pain he'd turned into pleasure as he opened himself up and made it part of him. He thrust his hips back, as if he thought that leaning far enough would let him find his master's cock behind him.

Axel flicked the tails harder, snapping his wrist to make the whip dance against Bayden's back. There was no one but Axel in Bayden's world then. Axel would have bet his life that Bayden had no idea there was anyone else in the room. It was just him, his master and his submission.

It was the hottest thing Axel had ever seen. Thirty-eight and Bayden was right on the edge. The way Bayden rubbed himself against the cross with each blow, it was just possible, as long as Bayden didn't hold back…

Thirty-nine—hard and hot on the heels of the last one.

Bayden tossed his head back again. His howl cut through the air. He writhed against the cross as he came in his jeans.

Axel brought the fortieth lash down while the howl still hung in the air. Bayden slumped against the cross.

Axel dropped the cat. He sprang forward, caught hold of Bayden's waist and steadied him. He'd barely been able to stand last time, and that had been when he'd been blocking everything out. This time had been far more intense for him.

"You can let go of the cross. I've got you."

Bayden lowered his arms. He turned within Axel's grip. He barely managed to face him before his knees gave way. Axel pulled Bayden against his body, keeping him upright.

Bayden looked up at him. "Please?"

Axel eased his grip as he realised that it wasn't dizziness taking Bayden down to his knees, it was submission.

There was no sarcasm, no cracks about working harder in the gym. There was no performance for the crowd. As Bayden knelt at Axel's feet, there were no words either.

Bayden rubbed his face against Axel's fly, kissing the line of his erection through the worn denim. Submission and a desperate need to please—to be accepted. Axel slid his fingers through Bayden's hair and welcomed him close.

Bayden whimpered and lapped at Axel's jeans, begging for access.

Axel undid his fly and freed his erection in a few brisk motions.

He'd seen Bayden go down on other men in that room, when the bet demanded it. It was quick — skillful, but rapid. They were blow jobs he'd taken no pleasure from, ones he finished as quickly as he could.

Now, Bayden's tongue darted out in flashes of pink as he delicately lapped at Axel's shaft, exploring every inch of him with his tongue. Nuzzling against him with kisses that bordered on worshipful, he worked his way over Axel's balls and back up to his cock.

Moans and gasps of pleasure filled the air, as if Bayden were the one being granted a treat. Axel slid his fingers through Bayden's hair and kept his other hand on Bayden's shoulder, supporting him.

Bayden wasn't the only one who'd loved each second of the whipping. Every lash had gone straight to Axel's cock. As delicate as Bayden's attentions were, Axel wasn't interested in being teased tonight. The tiniest pressure against the back of Bayden's head and Bayden changed tactics. The moment he knew Axel wanted to come, he deep throated him and took him to the root.

* * * * *

Bayden peered up at Axel, watching pleasure flash across his face as he came. Missing a single drop would have been sacrilege. Bayden kept his lips sealed tight around Axel's cock until he was sure he had taken everything his mate was willing to give him.

He didn't pull back until Axel gently nudged him away so he could do up his fly. Bayden didn't try to help. There was little point when his hands were still shaking with an overload of adrenaline and pleasure. Bayden didn't move at all until

Axel guided him up onto his feet to walk the few steps to the nearest chair. Axel sat down and Bayden dropped to his knees in front of him once more.

His back burned. His mind spun. His cum was turning sticky in his jeans. But, Axel welcomed him close with a hand on the back of his head, and the world was perfect.

Bayden leaned against him, unable to stop himself from trembling. Axel murmured half words to him, his tone all praise and reassurance. Safety and acceptance wrapped around Bayden. He grabbed the waist band of Axel's jeans, desperate to keep hold of every wonderful thing that suddenly filled his life.

"Good pup. That's right. You're fine. Good wolf."

Axel kept whispering to him, but Bayden's grip on his jeans remained white knuckled. After a little while, Axel leaned to one side in his seat and took something out of his pocket.

"You can hold on as tight as you want, pup, but you don't need to. It's not your job. I've got you now, and I won't let go." He clicked the lead Bayden had given him onto the collar. Other people were still there. It was hardly silent. The click still sounded very loud.

"You've got your pack, and your mate, and your alpha. You're the safest wolf in the whole world, pup." He slid his hand through the leather loop on the lead, and gathered the chain in his fist until all the slack disappeared.

Bayden sighed his relief. Releasing his hold on Axel's jeans, he slid his arms around Axel and rested more comfortably against his alpha. "Yours."

"That's right, pup. Mine — always."

About the Author

Kim is a bisexual submissive from Wales (UK). First published in 2008, she has since released 100 BDSM erotic romance titles ranging from short stories to full-length novels. Having worked with a host of fantastic e-publishers, she has just moved into self-publishing.

While she has occasionally ventured towards other pairings, Kim's first love is still, and probably always will be, Male/Male stories. But, no matter what the pairing, from paranormal to contemporary, and from the sweet to the intense, everything she writes will always feature three things - Kink, Love and a Happy Ending.

You can find out more about Kim's books on her website kimdare.com.

Also by Kim Dare

Series

Werewolves & Dragons
The Avian Shifters
Kinky Cupid
FIT Guys
Hearts and Handcuffs
Thrown to the Lions
Rawlings Men
Sex Sells
Sun, Sea and Submission
The Whole A-Z
Pack Discipline
G-A-Y Lust Bites
Perfect Timing
Collared
Pushing the Envelope

Kim has also written several free short stories.
You can find links to them on her website.